Obsessed

Also by Devon Scott

Unfaithful

Obsessed

DEVON SCOTT

Kensington Publishing Corp.
http://www.kensingtonbooks.com

DAFINA BOOKS are published by

Kensington Publishing Corp.
119 West 40th Street
New York, NY 10018

All Kensington titles, imprints, and distributed lines are
available at special quantity discounts for bulk purchases
for sales promotions, premiums, fund-raising, and edu-
cational or institutional use. Special book excerpts or
customized printings can also be created to fit specific
needs. For details, write or phone the office of the Kensington Special Sales Manager: Kensington Publishing
Corp., 119 West 40th Street, New York, NY 10018. Attn:
Special Sales Department. Phone: 1-800-221-2647.

Dafina and the Dafina logo Reg. U.S. Pat. & TM Off.

ISBN-13: 978-0-7582-5161-9
ISBN-10: 0-7582-5161-0

First trade paperback printing: May 2009
First mass market printing: March 2010

10 9 8 7 6 5 4 3 2 1

Printed in the United States of America

For my father

Acknowledgments

Relationships fascinate me. It's the drama, especially what goes on behind closed doors, that I like to explore. I hope you will enjoy the ride I take you on while giving you something to consider.

I would like to thank the many book club members and readers who have reached out to me regarding my debut novel, *Unfaithful*. Thank you for your support and feedback. I very much appreciate it.

To Shantel: Thank you for your love, support, and assistance in the writing of this book. You continue to inspire me, and I am blessed to have you in my life.

Until next time . . .

Prologue

The man leans in toward the gleaming widescreen display. His eyes burn and head throbs. Fingers to his temples, he attempts to quell the pain. He reaches for the Tylenol, pops the childproof top, and sprays his palm with pills, spilling a few onto the floor. Ignoring those, he swallows eight, chasing them with bottled water before returning his attention to the screen before him.

The image should soothe. But it does not.

He sits in his office, surrounded by expensive equipment, an array of whirling hard drives, silicon, and brushed aluminum. The only light emanates from three high-definition monitors connected to an encrypted network of desktops and servers, and more importantly, to the world beyond via high-speed broadband.

Fingers on the chattering keyboard as he types, enlarging the view.

A nude woman, splayed before the camera. Hands on the bed, pushing her hips upward. Her sex in plain view, ripened, and moist, he can tell even from here. The man leans closer until his eyelashes touch the warm LCD, the pounding in his head a staccato rhythm.

What a piece.

Legs the color of mocha chocolate.

Smooth, like only he can imagine.

Full breasts, dark, erect inviting nipples.

A smile that dazzles with its brilliance.

That's what gets him the most.

Her smile. The way she plays to the camera. Teases it with her seductive ways.

Fucking *bitch*. Kennedy. The wife. Just speaking her name makes him seethe with anger.

Click. Next photo.

Same gorgeous woman. This time with a companion.

Thin framed, killer bod. Butterscotch complexion. He feels himself stiffen. Weave halfway down her back. Remembering the way he used to pull it as he thrust behind her.

Next photo.

Bodies pressed against each other as their lips make contact. Eyes shut and expression say it all— *this* is rapture. He's dizzy with fury. It's like bile that drips painfully within his chest, destroying everything in its acidic path.

He's sitting in one of those expensive leather chairs executives own. He leans back now, hide creaking as he releases himself from the confines of his jeans and boxers. Sitting back down, he experiences a sliver of freedom. The roar in his head has yet to subside. It's like a raging river that rushes along, the whoosh from waters sluicing against rocky outcrops. His member hardens, eyes scanning the pixels as if he can hear their breathing. Their heartbeats.

Click.

Butterscotch atop sexy Mocha. Her legs are almost closed. But not quite. He can see her labia peeking out from between her legs, and he can't help but stare breathlessly. He begins to stroke himself, fighting the rush in his head that threatens to blind him. Skin dry, almost chafed, he pumps himself slowly, feeling the blood engorging, like a balloon inflating.

Click.

Mocha and Butterscotch's stares are captured by the camera. Their dual smiles radiating outward, sickening him with their fucking glee. He spits in his hand, then clasps it around his dick, stroking purposefully. The rage is a river. He can feel it taking over. Building . . . expanding, a turbulent vortex. The thump in his head is like house music. Only one thing can stop it.

Click.

Dude comes into view. Fucking Michael. The husband.

Atop Butterscotch, sinewy brown back muscles shine. Dude reaches for her ankles. The tat on her ankle, the spot of red ink visible between fingers— the spider, clearly seen.

Black widow.

Ass to the camera, the man can't tell if he's inside of her yet. Mocha kissing Butterscotch's nipples while rubbing her own clit. Next shot leaves no doubt.

The pain is blinding. *Dude's* buried to the hilt. He's entombed. Their eyes are locked, and her expression says it all—*this* is rapture.

The rage wells up at the couple whose sexual zeal is on display before him. This man and woman, whom he has never met, but promises to get to know like that back of his fucking hand.

Michael and Kennedy. Husband and wife.

The perfect couple. Not a care in the world. At least not yet.

They think they can swoop in and fuck with someone's life? Pluck the very thing that is most precious from his fingertips?

No. He will *not* let that happen.

The migraine pulses at his temples and his engorged member. He increases his stroking and his pumping, fingers working the mouse as he flicks back and forth between photos, feeling the pressure build.

Legs the color of mocha chocolate.

Smooth, like only he can imagine.

Full breasts, dark, erect inviting nipples.

Dude's cock deep within black widow.

Entombed, rapturously.

He explodes, a blend of pain and pleasure rippling outward.

Warm semen on cool dry skin.

In an instant the rush subsides. The rage ebbs.

The pounding is still there, but it's sinking like wet quicksand. His breathing slows, and soon all he can hear is the silence of his house.

Sap dripping between fingers, the man experiences intense sadness.

Then a stab of extreme pain.

Michael and Kennedy robbed him of his most precious jewel.

Staring at Black Widow's eyes that are locked onto Dude's as he filled her, the man's fury returns.

Fucking *robbers*.

Michael and Kennedy will pay.

They won't know what hit 'em.

That's for sure.

Chapter 1

Zack comes into the bedroom holding a stack of Xbox 360 games. Kennedy stands in front of the bed, packing. She's got one suitcase already full, and is placing a pair of boots into a designer bag. She glances down at him with a smirk.

"What are you doing with those?" she asks, noting that the stack is almost to his nose.

"You said I could bring my games to Jeremy's," her son replies, obsidian eyes wide.

Kennedy has to smile as she remembers that a seven-year-old takes everything you say *literally*.

"I didn't say *all* of them, Zack!"

"These aren't all of them! I left four downstairs, Mommy." Zack pouts, as he's fond of doing. Kennedy goes over to him and kisses his cheek, stroking his hair. Sometimes the maturity level of her son makes her pause.

"How about you pick five of your favorites? Don't forget Jeremy has plenty of Xbox games, too."

"Ahhhh, Mom!"

Zack storms out, passing his father, who's standing in the doorway, watching the exchange with amusement.

"Mom never lets me do what I want!" he exclaims to his dad, who just nods wretchedly.

Kennedy turns to Michael, whose arms are folded across his chest. He watches his son go down the stairs before returning his attention to the bedroom.

"He's your son, that's for sure," she remarks. Michael grins.

Kennedy returns to her packing. She is tall—close to 5' 9" and weight proportionate to her height. She wears her hair in a ponytail, slightly below her shoulders. A pair of tight-fitting Levi's, Michael's favorite, hugs her curves like a winding country road. Her jeans are tucked into caramel colored knee-high boots, and a light sweater tops her ensemble. Kennedy reaches for her toiletry bag and another pair of boots, these tall and black, fitting them into the designer bag. Michael shakes his head.

"You know we're only going for away for a weekend."

"A girl can never bring enough clothes."

"If you say so." Michael moves behind his wife, placing his hands on her hips. He moves in until no space separates them, wrapping an arm around her chest, feeling the flesh as he nuzzles against her neck.

"Sexy-ass," he whispers in her ear.

Kennedy grins while pushing against him. "Don't start nothing you can't finish," she says.

Michael cups her breasts in both hands, feeling their weight. He kisses her neck and chin. "Think I won't?"

Kennedy turns and kisses him once on the lips. Then again, opening her mouth, tasting him this time. "I know you will, big daddy. Now let me finish."

Kennedy pushes him away, grinning as she witnesses him pouting. "You are your son's father, that's for sure."

"You're lucky *our* son is downstairs, that's all I can say."

"I know, baby."

"We're gonna finish this later. Wait until we get to the hotel."

"I can't wait."

"Gonna tear it up."

"I know you will, big daddy."

"Gonna eat it good, too."

"I'll feed you myself!"

Michael grins. Kennedy stares at her husband for a moment: tall, good-looking, in shape, short hair, trimmed mustache and goatee. Dark jeans, button-down striped shirt, sleeves halfway rolled up his forearms. She resists the urge to kiss him again. *Don't start*, she tells herself silently.

Michael retreats to the main level. Ten minutes go by before she comes downstairs, lugging her bags. Michael meets her at the bottom of the landing and takes them from her, placing the bags by the door. She peeks into the family room, spying Zack on the floor in front of the plasma, watching something on Nickelodeon. He's wearing his TMNT backpack, ready to go. She goes into the dining room, grabbing her laptop from the table as Michael glides behind her, shaking his head.

"Oh no you don't," he says, prying the computer from her fingers.

She follows him quickly into the den. "Baby, I just need to—"

"Stop," he says, spinning around, finger to his lips. "This weekend is a getaway. Get-a-way. No laptops. Those are the rules." He puts the laptop down on the desk and powers down the desktop computer and monitor.

"But I have to finish this brief—"

"Stop." Michael holds up his hand. "You are not the only attorney in this house. Nevertheless, there will be no briefs or work of any kind this weekend. Understand?"

"Are we ready to go yet?" Zack is behind them, glancing curiously at his digital watch before eyeing his parents.

Michael smirks. "As a matter of fact, we are. Go get in the car."

"Cool! I'm calling Jeremy." Zack digs into the lower pockets of his cargo pants and pulls out a cell phone. It's one of those designed especially for kids, featuring a Chaperone feature that lets adults see where their children are. He flips it open expertly, speed-dialing Jeremy as he saunters away. Michael shakes his head before returning his attention to his wife, who has managed to place the laptop behind her back.

"You are not slick," Michael says. "Don't make me kick your ass. Now, put the laptop down so no one gets hurt."

Kennedy sighs heavily while grabbing her leather jacket and heading for the door.

Chapter 2

"I call shotgun!" Zack squeals.

"Boy, if you don't get in your car seat," Kennedy exclaims.

They stand outside their stone, three-level, one-garage townhouse located on Taylor Street in Northeast D.C. The street is tree-lined and quiet. All of the rowhouses, as they're called in the District, are stone, some the color of dark mud, others the reddish brown hue of autumn or the dull gray of slate. All are well-kept, with small, manicured bushes and shrubs. Michael and Kennedy bought this home shortly after they were married seven years ago. They were looking for something they could stretch out in and raise a family. The location is decent, as far as the city goes—quiet, Metro-accessible, a short drive from the private school that Zack attends and the downtown association where Kennedy works as a lawyer. Michael, who is also an attorney but works instead for a government agency, can make the short drive downtown as well or take Metro.

Their luggage—Michael's garment bag, Kennedy's two suitcases, and Zack's gym bag and his backpack—is sequestered in the back of Michael's

Range Rover. Kennedy's BMW is tucked in the garage. Michael jumps in the front seat and starts the engine as Kennedy supervises Zack buckling in. Once everyone is set, they take off.

The drive to Jeremy's home, north of Children's Hospital and Catholic University, takes about ten minutes. Michael double-parks on the narrow street. Then Kennedy gets Zack to the sidewalk. He quickly hugs her and races up the steps to the door, ringing the bell as his father gets out, leaving the engine running.

"Hey, can I get a hug or something?" he yells to his seven-year-old son.

"Oh, yeah. Sure, Dad." Zack races down, backpack bobbing against his thin shoulders. Arms reach up around his father's neck and hug him. "Buy me something in New York, PLEASE?"

"Is that all I'm good for? Lord!" Michael grins as Zack heads back up the stairs.

Jeremy yanks open the door and the two boys high-five each other before dashing inside. Jeremy's mom, Lori, comes outside, a good-looking thirty-something woman of color, dressed comfortably in sweats and running shoes. She waves at Michael as Kennedy climbs the steps. They meet halfway.

"Hey, girl," Kennedy says, embracing Lori. "Thank you so much for taking Zack this weekend."

"You know it's not a problem," Lori says. "We're going to have a great time. I'm taking the boys to the movies tonight, and we've got plenty of things to keep them occupied all weekend."

"That's great. Zack's been talking about this sleep-over all week."

"Jeremy, too. You guys have fun. Don't worry about a thing—I've got your number if we need to reach you," Lori says before dropping her voice down a notch. "Wish I was going away with my husband. You need to have enough fun for both of us, you hear me?" She winks at Kennedy. Kennedy grins back.

The ride to Union Station takes less than fifteen minutes. Michael parks on the upper level, and together they lug their bags into the Amtrak station. They have a three PM reservation on the Acela Express and a half hour to spare before the train departs. Check-in is a breeze. They retrieve their boarding passes from an automated kiosk and grab a Caramel Frappuccino and a Danish from the Starbucks across from the waiting area. They take adjoining seats close to their gate and collectively breathe a sigh of relief.

"The vacation begins," Kennedy says, placing a hand on Michael's lap and leaning in until their foreheads touch.

"Love you, baby," Michael responds, taking her head in his hands as he kisses her lips gingerly. Kennedy, for a moment, loses herself in the closeness of her husband, loving the feeling as she always does of her tongue on his. She opens her mouth wider, inviting him in, then pulls back, suddenly aware of her surroundings.

"Love you more," Kennedy remarks back in breathless anticipation of things to come.

Chapter 3

Their train rushes along, past buildings, warehouses, and backyards. Trees fly by as Michael glances out the window. Kennedy sits across from him, Amtrak-issued blue blanket draped over her lap, no one beside either of them. The ride is comforting, the train rocking slightly back and forth as it hurtles north toward Wilmington, Philly, Newark, and their destination, New York City.

The car is not at all crowded. Michael thought every seat would've been taken, seeing how today is Friday afternoon. But the travel gods are watching over them. Kennedy sits with her legs crossed, foot tapping to a beat on her iPod that only she can hear. In her hand is her trusted BlackBerry Pearl, which she is never far from. Head down, her fingers peck incessantly over the tiny keyboard—type, pause, type, repeat.

Michael has brought several magazines to read. They lie untouched on the seat beside him. The motion of the train is therapeutic, making him groggy. He's got the rest of the trip and weekend to flip through the pages, so he lays his head back on the cushion and closes his eyes. He drifts off only to be awakened by a vibration on his hip from his cell phone. Opening his eyes, he observes the expanse of water as the train passes over a low bridge. The effect is that they are gliding over the water, traveling via hovercraft or low-flying helicopter. Michael reaches for his own BlackBerry as he stares at the scene before him for a moment more. It is peaceful and serene.

Back to the vibrating BlackBerry . . .

He owns a silver Curve.

His wife, a black Pearl.

Michael checks the oversized screen. An IM message. He opens it and has to smile. It's from a woman.

The woman sitting across from him.

HEY HANDSOME

He glances up. Kennedy's head is down, but she raises it momentarily. Their eyes meet; she smiles seductively, then lowers her head, fingers never leaving the keyboard. He responds.

HEY MS. SEXY THANG. WHATS ON UR MIND?

This time Kennedy doesn't look up. She's busy replying, foot continuing to tap as her iPod whirls away.

YOU

Michael makes eye contact with Kennedy. He raises his eyebrow as if to say, "Yeah? Go on. . . ."

Head drops back down, and she types and sends.

THINKING ABOUT U MAKING LOVE TO ME

Michael grins. His fingers go to the keys, composing a response.

REALLY? DO TELL

When Kennedy is concentrating on something, she inadvertently taps her tongue against her teeth. Michael observes her doing this now, and he finds it incredibly sexy.

IM WET

Michael looks up into the eyes of his wife. She's staring at him, eyes unblinking, her smile driving him wild. Michael cocks his head to the side and opens his mouth to speak.

"Right now?" he asks, his voice low.

Kennedy slowly removes the earbuds and shuts off the iPod. She leans forward.

"Find out."

Michael leans back and sighs. "Damn," he whispers. He fingers the Curve, typing a response.

UR MAKING ME HARD

Their stares lock once again.

Kennedy uncrosses her legs and stands, moving Michael's pile of magazines in order to sit beside him. She re-drapes the blanket over both of them. She nuzzles close to him, her hand slowly gliding up his thigh. Her head is facing him and the window, lips dangerously close to his ear.

She whispers, "Will you fuck me later?"

Michael's breathing spikes. His eyes scan over the other passengers, but they are lost in their own reveries.

"Yes, baby."

Her hand creeps upward, dropping to his inner thigh. Fingers splayed, feeling the rise as he hardens.

"And eat me?" The words are puffs of air against his ear.

"You know I will. Love tasting you . . ."

Her fingers are on him, finding the outline of his manhood and massaging it. She squeezes his dick, feeling it grow between her fingers. Michael licks his lips and leans back farther as Kennedy unzips his jeans. She catches his stare and smiles—that seductive smile that drives him insane.

A moment later Kennedy's hand is massaging his cock through his boxer shorts. He's fully hard now, and Kennedy clutches him in her hand, the fabric and her fingers constraining him. She slips her fingers beneath the boxer shorts and is rewarded with the fullness of him. Fully engorged. Her fingers wrap around his girth and squeeze as she nibbles on his neck. Her lips graze his earlobe, tugging on it playfully.

"I love that you're so big. . . ."

Michael turns his head to her.

"You make it that way, Ken."

Kennedy begins a slow stroke, taking her time but maintaining pressure as she jerks him.

"I want you in me."

"Does Amtrak have the equivalent of a mile-high club?" Michael asks playfully.

"I wish."

Kennedy glances around at the other passengers. There is no one occupying the seats directly across the aisle from them. She glances back at her husband momentarily before lowering her head, pushing the blanket down in the process. Michael's eyes grow wide. Her mouth consumes him in an instant. Kennedy takes him deep and fast into her throat. Several up and down strokes of his hard dick in her hot mouth, her hand providing the friction, before she sits up, covering him quickly with the blanket.

Michael is speechless.

Kennedy kisses him on the mouth passionately while giving his cock a final tug. Then she places it back inside the confines of his underwear. The entire deed lasted less than five seconds, but it was exquisite in its approach and execution.

"Always wanted to do that," she says with a gleam of longing in her eyes.

Chapter 4

The bellman finishes depositing Michael and Kennedy's bags in their hotel room and gives them a quick tour. King-size bed, room done up in shades of purple and red, eclectic photographs on the wall, an oversized chaise lounge made of comfortable upholstery. In the bathroom, an enclosed-glass shower stall for two and a separate Jacuzzi spa that's big enough for the both of them. Michael palms the bellman a ten-spot and closes the door. Kennedy rushes to him and wraps her arms around his neck, pulling him close and offering up her tongue, which he readily takes.

"I LOVE it!"

"Me, too," Michael responds.

"This view . . . ," she says, going to the window. They are on the fifty-first floor, facing west. The Hudson River shimmers in the distance. It is dusk, and lights in the neighboring skyscrapers are beginning to blink on. They linger at the window for a moment admiring the picturesque view as Michael stands behind his wife, holding her waist. They remain that way for a moment before Kennedy turns to Michael and says with a grin, "I'm starving."

They find a restaurant within walking distance of their hotel in the Theater District, an Italian spot with plenty of atmosphere that serves generous portions, family style. Their entrées: veal parmigiana and clams in red linguine sauce. They share a very good bottle of Pinot Grigio between them while waiting for the food.

Michael, much to Kennedy's contentment, sits not across but beside her in a cozy booth. While sipping their Pinot, Kennedy and Michael recount the ups and downs of their week. Their rule—they are allowed to spend no more than an hour bitching about their respective jobs. The rest of the time is to be spent on positive rhetoric. Not that either of them focuses on the negative. Their jobs are fulfilling, and for the most part they have bosses who are supportive and coworkers who are pleasant to be around. They chat about Zack and his school and friends, their family, and each other.

Once the veal and clams arrive, Michael has Kennedy laughing about one of his friends/coworkers. Marc is a senior attorney at Michael's agency. He's white and a few years shy of retirement. The Sean Connery look-alike is comical—he's constantly hitting on the young interns and associates. He likes them young, fresh out of college. Anything older than twenty-two or twenty-three won't do.

"The guy is slick," Michael exclaims while forking a sliver of veal into Kennedy's mouth. "He knows the boundaries with respect to his job. So as to not seem like he's harassing these women, he attempts to hire them as his personal dog walkers for his two German shepherds."

"I don't like him," Kennedy says.

"I know you don't," Michael replies, laughing. "But you have to give him credit—he is relentless—

and it seems like every other week he's getting one of the nubile young things over to his Georgetown condo under the guise of getting to know his dogs."

"Nubile young things? Michael, if I didn't know any better I would think you actually admire him," Kennedy says.

"Ken, I admire his perseverance. The guy doesn't give up, even though he's not getting any!"

Kennedy's turn.

She has a coworker, a paralegal named Jacqueline. Jackie, as she's called, is dating this uptight dentist named Freddy. Michael remembers meeting them at an office function earlier this year. The dentist said all of two words the entire evening.

"Jackie went down south with him for his homecoming last weekend," Kennedy explains. "While there she happened to check his phone and saw all of these text messages from other women."

"She just happened to check his phone?" Michael asked.

"I didn't get into all that."

"Okay . . ."

"Anyway, she finds these messages, and they were definitely inappropriate for him to be having with anyone who was not his girlfriend."

"Like?"

"Like 'I made it safely, baby' and 'Missing you and what you did to me last week.' "

"Ouch." Michael takes a sip of the Pinot and forks some of Kennedy's clams into his mouth.

"So, get this. Freddy is sleeping when she's doing all this. She goes into the hallway and calls these women on his phone. Two answer. She asks who the fuck these bitches are and what they have to do with Freddy."

"Oh boy. Shit hits the fan," Michael says.

"Sure does. One woman tells her outright, 'I was dating him, but he tried to fuck me without a condom, and I wasn't having that!' "

"You're kidding? He should know better," Michael exclaims.

"I know. The other woman says that she is Freddy's cousin."

"What? Just how gullible is your friend?"

Kennedy laughs. "Jackie confronts Freddy—she wakes his black ass up, and guess what he says?"

"I can't even imagine how the good dentist handles this one."

"He says, 'I can't believe you went through my phone without asking!' " Kennedy laughs some more as she pauses to enjoy her food. She has a touch of red sauce on her bottom lip, so Michael takes his napkin and dabs at the spot.

"Typical male response," Michael says. "Deflect the conversation away from the real issue."

"Exactly. What's truly sad is that she started to doubt herself."

"Hold up. I'm sure she pressed him about what the woman had said regarding not using a condom. I mean, how can he *not* address that?" Michael asks.

"Well, Freddy managed to do exactly that. He refused to speak to her, and the next day went to a football game without her."

"She's an idiot," Michael exclaims. "Freddy treats her like shit because he can. Because she lets him."

"True. The whole thing sickened me to hear. It made me realize how lucky I am to have what we have." Kennedy leans in and kisses Michael on the cheek. "I'm blessed to have you in my life, Michael," she says.

Michael glances her way and smiles.

"Does this mean I'm getting some tonight?"
Kennedy groans while rolling her eyes.
"You could fuck up a wet dream, you know that?"

After coffee, no dessert, they walk back to the
hotel hand in hand. When they are inside their
room, Michael throws off his running shoes and
opens the drapes wide so that the splendor of Manhattan at night invades their window. He climbs
onto the bed as Kennedy begins to undress.

"I guess we should start getting ready," Kennedy
says.

"Good idea. Ladies first."

Kennedy retreats to the bathroom and closes the
door. Michael reaches for his BlackBerry Curve and
checks e-mails and voice mails. Afterward he presses
a few keys, enabling the Chaperone feature on his
phone to locate his son.

A few moments later an address displays on the
screen.

A District of Columbia address.

Jeremy's house.

Technology is a godsend.

He wonders what Zack is doing right now. Undoubtedly huddled in front of Jeremy's Xbox 360
playing *Test Drive Unlimited, Top Spin 2, Amped 3,* or
Call of Duty 2 (his favorite).

Michael lays his head back and naps.

Kennedy makes a grand entrance close to an
hour later. What Michael sees takes his breath away.

"My goodness . . ."

She stands before him, her hourglass-shaped
body clad in a formfitting little black minidress
that stops at the tops of her thighs. A plunging V
neckline is open to right above her navel. Less

than half of each breast is confined by fabric; the rest of her smooth, lovely flesh is on display. Black, shiny, needle-heeled boots end slightly above her knees. Her hair, flat-ironed straight down her back, is flawless. A pair of diamond-drop earrings in 14K white gold is her only jewelry. Her makeup looks professionally applied. Michael is speechless. He goes to her slowly, marveling at her as if she's an apparition, reaching out to touch her, inhaling a scent of heavenly perfume.

An hour ago his wife was standing before him. Now this creature has emerged, something else. Something brand new to consider. A vixen. A siren. A dream.

Michael is inches from her face. His heart is pounding, and he is growing hard. He focuses in on the raisin-and-champagne–blended eye shadow. The red Bordeaux lip gloss. He resists the urge to lick her lips and taste her. Consume her right here and now. He is that hungry.

"Who are you?" he asks dubiously, in breathless anticipation.

And she responds, "My name is Celestial, and I'm your deepest, darkest fantasy come true."

Chapter 5

The taxi drops them off on a quiet street on the Upper East Side of Manhattan, East Seventy-fifth Street, to be exact, a block away from Fifth Avenue, which lines Central Park, and a half-dozen blocks from the Metropolitan Museum of Art. Michael pays the mahogany-hued driver, who has been staring incessantly at Kennedy through his rearview mirror ever since they got in. She nudges Michael and whispers to give the man a nice tip. Michael rolls his eyes while breaking off a twenty, telling the West African to keep the change.

The night air has chilled slightly, and Michael puts his arms about Kennedy's shoulders; a beefy male greeter/doorman is standing in front of a narrow, reddish brown building, five stories tall, with beautiful oval windows. The man is dressed in designer black—yet he's white, bald, and reminds Kennedy of that guy on Jerry Springer who's always breaking up fights. Michael, wearing a well-tailored charcoal multistriped three-button suit with a collared button-down blue shirt, walks up and hands him their invitation—a black-on-black card with the word *BLISS* in large embossed letters. Underneath,

the address, date, and time. The greeter beams at
Kennedy, and, as an afterthought, at Michael, too,
takes the invitation and fingers it, as if checking
for its authenticity, before consulting a PDA. Michael
gives him their names, the Jerry Springer guy uses
a steel stylus to check them off a list, and he goes
to the door, holding it open for them.

Years ago, Michael and Kennedy were vacationing in the Bahamas. There they met a well-traveled,
engaging, hip-hop Generation Y philanthropist
who became quite fond of them. They spent much
time together, getting drunk and high, gambling
and partying until the sun came up. RESPECT, as
he's called, is well known in the African-American
community for being a poet, a contributor to many
start-up Harlem businesses, and, mostly, a party-
goer and thrower. Many actors, musicians, artists,
and even politicians have coveted his invitations,
for they know that there ain't no party like a RE-
SPECT party, and a RESPECT party . . . Well, you
get the idea.

They enter on the first level and move toward
the back of the building. The home is deep and
surprisingly large. There are a fair amount of people milling about. A brushed aluminum bar in the
back room overlooks the patio. Dark walls, African
art hanging and spotlit from above, smooth jazz
emanating around them like fog, a few couches
and love seats where folks can chill. Everyone is
well dressed. A mix of black and white, some Asians,
some Latinos, a few Europeans. Mostly a mid- to-
upper-twenties-and-into-their-thirties crowd. Michael
spots a well-known rapper on one couch with his
entourage of females. They make for the bar,
Kennedy's hand in Michael's, as all eyes clock them.
Michael nods to those who stop in midsentence to

check out his wife. Behind the bar is a tall, good-looking brutha who is shirtless and wearing his hair in cornrows. He's got a bunch of tattoos across his chest and down his arms.

"What can I get for you two?" the bartender asks. Michael appraises him. His words and demeanor belie his thuggish looks.

"What do you feel like having?" Michael asks his wife. The bartender flashes a smile at Kennedy. She replies, "I'm not sure yet."

"I'll have a mojito if you're making them fresh," Michael says.

"Of course. I've got fresh mint right here," the bartender says, holding up a few sprigs between dark fingers, "and I use cane sugar."

"Sweet."

"And for the lady?"

Kennedy purses her lips with indecision. "Not sure what I'm feeling right now. Can you suggest something or just surprise me?"

The bartender considers her for a moment and then nods. "Not a problem." He begins on Michael's drink, mashing the mint sprigs in a tall glass. Moments later he is presenting Michael with his drink and then proceeds to make Kennedy's. She watches him as Michael tests his and gives the bartender dap.

"Much respect," he says.

"Yeah, mon!"

A half minute later the bartender slides a glass in front of Kennedy. She glances at it, then eyes him.

"What is it?" she asks.

"Taste it first," the bartender tells her.

She does.

"Mmm, that's good. Baby, taste this."

"You like?" the bartender asks.

"Yes, thank you. What is it?"

The bartender leans in, chiseled forearms on the bar top. "It's called a Piece of Ass. No disrespect. Amaretto, Southern Comfort, and sweet and sour mix."

"None taken," Michael says. "Besides, you got it right."

He smirks while putting his arm around Kennedy's waist. The bartender's eyes drop to Kennedy's near-perfect breasts. He licks his lips unconsciously.

Michael tips him, and he and Kennedy clink their glasses together. Michael's mouth goes to Kennedy's ear. He whispers, "You are, without a doubt, the most beautiful woman in here."

"Let's see if that is true," she replies. And together they set off to investigate the rest of RE-SPECT's party.

Chapter 6

Second floor.

Dark walls, low lighting, up-tempo music, a denser crowd milling about various rooms that are devoid of furniture save for colorful low couches and love seats in shades of navy, pink, and emerald. A number of couples are dancing, working it out in the back room overlooking the patio. Kennedy and Michael meander their way through the crowd, recognizing a few people. Mostly television and film stars whose names they can't place.

From behind them, a voice booms above the din of music. "Stop the damn press! Who is this vision before me?"

Kennedy turns. Michael follows a moment later.

The man facing them is light-skinned, bald, with a neatly trimmed goatee, dressed in a pair of baggy jeans and a white V-neck tee covered by a burgundy velvet smoking jacket. His features resemble those of the artist Common. Around his neck is a thick chain attached to an enormous R. It could be silver, but it's more likely platinum.

"RESPECT!" Kennedy exclaims.

"Hold up? Who is this fine specimen standing

before me? I know that brutha behind her. . . .
Michael, my man!"

RESPECT and Michael hug each other. RESPECT
stands back, admiring Kennedy at arm's length before he pulls her close.

"Goodness gracious, you are looking foine!" he
says.

"Good to see you, too!"

"I was hoping y'all would show. How are you?"

Michael says, "We're good. Look at you! Dapper,
as usual."

RESPECT grins. "Someone's gotta do it. Come
on, let me introduce you to some of my peoples."

He takes them along, introducing them to his
guests. RESPECT knows everyone, and once introductions are made, he is hard pressed to forget a
name. He introduces Michael and Kennedy to a
bunch of folks sitting around a cube made of
brushed steel and glass. RESPECT states not only
their names but also what they do for a living. One
thing about RESPECT, he loves to be around powerful people—the movers and shakers.

Hand around Kennedy's waist, he shushes everyone around the cube with his free hand and then
begins the introductions. "Listen up, cause there
will be a test afterward! Let's see—that's Keenya;
she's with the mayor's office—you wouldn't know
it, with her fine self. Next to her is Jill—singer/
songwriter. Beside her is Jake—music-video director. I KNOW you've seen his stuff—Beyoncé, Jay-Z,
Lil Wayne, who else? Don't matter—anyone who's
anyone, right, Jake? Next to him is his main squeeze,
Trinity. What? Girl, stop trippin', you know it's true."
RESPECT pauses to give dap to Jake as Trinity sits
with her arms folded across her chest like she's mad
at somebody. "Next to Trinity is Paul, investment

banker extraordinaire. And last and definitely least, just playin', that's Doug, A&R rep for Sony BMG Music. Everyone, may I present Michael and his wife, Kennedy, with her fine self!"

Michael and Kennedy say hello. RESPECT doesn't give them but three seconds before pulling them past the dance area to the staircase that leads to the third floor. As they ascend, he says, "I'm really glad you two made it."

"We appreciate the invite, as always."

"You know it!"

The third level is red-velvet wallpaper and Brazilian cherry hardwood floors, Polk Audio speakers spitting old school: Cherrelle, Alexander O'Neil, Dazz Band, the Time. A bunch of folks congregate around a piece of Australian Outback art, a dozen nude black-and-white photographs, low couches, and a polished bar in the back, the bartender commanding a brisk business. RESPECT introduces Michael and Kennedy to a well-dressed couple off by themselves near a window overlooking Seventy-fifth Street.

"Hey, let me introduce you to some good friends of mine," RESPECT says, touching the elbow of the gentleman. "This is Michael and his wife, Kennedy. James and Lauren." The four shake hands as RESPECT bounces off to say hello to someone else.

James is dressed in dark slacks and an oversized sweater. Thin-frame glasses adorn his clean-shaven face. Lauren is wearing a black dress with sequins and pearls.

"So, what do you do?" James asks, a bit formally.

Michael and Kennedy have this game that they play. When they're out, especially away from home, they like to take on a different persona, a new identity, if you will. Kennedy answers first.

"Well, I'm in the adult-movie business," Kennedy says, almost sheepishly. "Actually, I'm an adult-film actress." James's eyes almost bug out. Lauren, whose hand was rather loosely draped in the crook of James's arm, suddenly pulls him closer.

"Really?" James responds. "Are you . . . serious?"

Kennedy nods without blinking. She notices that James is now allowing his eyes to roam over her dress, stopping several times at her full breasts.

"Totally. Most of my films are distributed overseas. My stage name is Celestial. You can Google me if you'd like."

"Wow," James says, trying to recover without looking stupid. "That's . . . amazing. I'm impressed. And you?" he says, tearing his eyes away to glance at Michael, who is standing casually, sipping his mojito with one hand in his pocket.

"Me? I'm a director and producer. *Her* director and producer." Michael is eyeing Lauren, who has said nothing and looks scared.

"That's . . . Wow, that's pretty cool. Nothing like working with your spouse," James retorts.

"Wouldn't have it any other way," Kennedy says. She sips at her drink, savoring the taste.

"What is that you're drinking?" Lauren asks, attempting to steer the conversation to higher ground.

"It's called a Piece of Ass. Would you like a taste?"

Lauren almost chokes on her tongue as Kennedy shrugs innocently.

Chapter 7

An hour later.

Michael and Kennedy have danced a few songs, made their way to the fourth floor, where they've chatted with some more folks, and taken a seat by the window to enjoy the sights. The party is nice— not so crowded that you can't move, a nice mix of intellectuals and creative types, and the music not so loud that you can't hear your own conversations. Michael gets up to refresh their drinks. He stands several-people deep by the bar, awaiting his turn behind a tall, honey-complexioned woman wearing a red halter cocktail dress. Her hair is wavy and travels halfway down her back. She gets her drink and turns, finding herself eye to eye with Michael. He scans her up and down quickly, noting her curves and straight white teeth. She is, in a word, gorgeous.

"That looks dee-lish," he says.

"You referring to my Cosmo?" she asks, beaming a dazzling smile.

"Of course." Michael laughs.

"Let me check." She takes a quick sip, swallows, and nods her head. "I highly recommend it."

"I'm usually a mojito kind of guy, but I'm tempted to try something new tonight."

"You should. You won't be disappointed."

Michael sticks out his hand. "I'm Michael."

"Makayla." She places her hand in his. Her flesh is warm, and Michael takes several seconds to squeeze it. "How does it feel to be the topic of conversation?" she asks.

"Excuse me?"

"You're with the stunning black woman over there. Everyone's talking about the two of you."

Michael replies, "You don't say?"

"Yep. Word is she's an adult-film star and you're her director."

"All true," Michael says.

"Interesting," Makayla says, eyeing him up and down in a flirty kind of way. "Some of us were wondering what kind of films she does?"

Michael gives the bartender his order before turning his attention back to Makayla. "Celestial is known for her girl-on-girl movies. You can say that's her specialty."

"Really? No *guy*-on-girl action?" she asks.

Michael shakes his head. "Nope, I'm old-fashioned. The only man I want inside of her is me."

Makayla laughs. "I see. But it's okay with you if another female taps that—excuse my French—ass?"

Michael doesn't blink. "Most definitely. It's something that gets us both off." He lets that sink in for a moment before continuing. "It's a win-win, you feel me?" Makayla nods. "So, wha'd'ya say I introduce you to a real-life porn star?"

*   *   *

"Girl, you are working that dress!"

Makayla and Michael have rejoined Kennedy, who is perched on a plush, forest green love seat.

"Thank you."

"No, I mean it. That thing is fierce, and you've got the body to go along with it."

Kennedy smiles while making eye contact with Makayla.

"You're doing some damage in that little thing of yours, too."

Makayla feigns surprise.

"This li'l thing?"

Michael shakes his head. Prince segues into Pebbles.

"Dance with me?" Kennedy says to Makayla while handing her drink to Michael.

"Sure."

"That is, if you don't mind being seen with a porno star."

"Oh, I don't mind one bit," Makayla says with a sparkle in her eyes.

The two women walk to the dance area and begin to move. At first they dance around one another, keeping their distance, not invading each other's space. But as the song progresses, the rhythm and beat take over, and Kennedy finds herself shifting closer. Makayla is watching Kennedy as she swings her hips, zeroing in on her smile as she grooves to the song. She leans in, stroking Kennedy's forearms upward until her hands are on her shoulders, then her neck. Kennedy closes her eyes and shudders from Makayla's touch, commanding her body forward; Michael and the rest of the throng have quieted their conversation to watch the unfolding action.

Kennedy and Makayla are eye to eye now, heads
and necks moving to the beat as the two women re-
volve around one another. Six inches separate them
as Kennedy parts her lips while inhaling a breath.
Makayla does the same, using the tip of her tongue
to wipe at the flesh of her lip. Kennedy is watching
Makayla closely, observing the movement of pink
tongue as it flickers against moist brown lips.
Makayla directs her stare down, taking in the fullness of Kennedy's breasts, her nipples that have
sprouted like a flower in the springtime and are
struggling against the material of her minidress.
Pebbles and Babyface take it to the bridge, and
Makayla grasps Kennedy around the waist, pulling
her close. Their bosoms touch, and it seems to
Kennedy that all activity on the horizon has ceased.
The ebony woman with her hair cut dangerously
close to her skull and the heavily painted-on gold
lip gloss has evaporated. The twin, coked-up white
models, poster children for the Dolce & Gabbana
Women's Collection—their chatter ceases, as does
their motion. And even Michael, caught leaning
forward, mojito poised at his lips, glass tilted, ice
cubes twinkling, seems to have faded into darkness. Now it's just Kennedy and this lovely creature, Makayla, and the feel of her breasts, soft and
warm, on her own. And Kennedy experiences a
quickening desire to close the gap farther still and
feel this delightful thing's hot breath on her own
mouth and tongue. But instead she smiles, gliding
back to a safe, respectable distance, Pebbles mor-
phing into Earth, Wind & Fire, and now her horizon is in motion once again.

Kennedy makes eye contact with her husband,

and in that unspoken language they've shared and perfected over the years, she lets him know that it's time to leave.

Michael understands perfectly.

Chapter 8

The room key slides into the card reader and the LED blinks green. Michael pushes open the door and stands aside. Kennedy enters, followed by Makayla.

The drapes are open, providing an unobstructed view of the city. Makayla utters "Wow" while going to the window. The Hudson is dark, almost black, and moving slowly, giving the illusion of molten lava. A large cruise ship, its lights ablaze, has docked at the Manhattan Terminal adjacent to the West Side Highway. Michael excuses himself to grab some ice. He returns a moment later as Kennedy is pulling off her boots and getting comfortable on the bed.

"What can I get you to drink?" Michael asks of Makayla, opening the walnut minibar near the television and dresser.

"I'm in the mood for a Piece of Ass!" She flicks a glance over at Kennedy as she laughs.

"Oh, BEHAVE!" Michael replies in his best Austin Powers voice. He bends down and checks out the minibar.

"A beer is fine," she says, taking off her pumps

and reclining on the chaise lounge, crossing her legs at the ankles.

"Ken?" Michael asks his wife.

"Mind whipping up a rum and coke?"

"Sure, baby." Michael fixes her drink. He hands it over and takes a beer for himself.

"A toast," he says, holding his bottle in the air. "To new friends . . . and swimming with bowlegged women!"

"Ignore him!" Kennedy shouts. Makayla takes a swig from her beer and tips her head back, closing her eyes.

"Mmm, this hit the spot!" she says. Kennedy sips her drink as Michael goes to the clock radio and flips it on, searching for an appropriate station. He finds one—smooth jazz—and turns it up as Kennedy raises her glass overhead and moves it along to the slow jam.

"Can you dim the lights?" Makayla asks, opening her eyes to look at Michael. "That is, if you don't mind."

"Good idea," Kennedy seconds.

Michael switches on a lamp by the bed and cuts off the overhead light. He takes off his jacket, draping it on the edge of the bed by his wife's feet. He leans against the wall, dividing his stare between Makayla, who is watching him, and Kennedy, who is observing Makayla.

"This is . . . nice," Makayla says.

Kennedy considers her for a moment more before rising from the bed and going to the chaise lounge. Makayla tracks her silently. She sits on the edge of the lounger, draping an arm over Makayla's legs. Makayla tips her beer up to her lips and takes a swig. She swallows hard, staring into Kennedy's soft eyes. Makayla puts the bottle down as Kennedy scoots up, positioning herself near Makayla's thighs. Kennedy uses her fingernail to trace figure eights on Makayla's honey-colored skin. She focuses on the action for a moment, no one saying a word, the music soft, hypnotic, and soothing. Makayla emits a mellifluous moan.

Kennedy finds the hem of Makayla's dress. Her fingers glide lightly over the fabric, meandering around in no confident path, following the inside edge to her silky thigh but then moving upward toward that space where thighs converge. Makayla reaches for Kennedy's free hand. For a moment her fingers are poised just above the wrist, not touching skin. But then she does make contact, ever so softly, tracing the lines that Kennedy's raised veins compose.

Makayla's other hand goes to Kennedy's shoulder. She draws a line down along her forearm, going unhurriedly, and then back up, head cocked to the side comfortably, observing Kennedy, and Michael, who continues to stand by the wall. They make eye contact—Michael and Makayla—and she gives him an affectionate smile that he returns.

Kennedy's hand is in Makayla's lap. It is warm, soft, and she rakes several fingers along Makayla's abdomen, feeling her navel. She moves her fingers upward, leisurely, not in any rush, listening to the sound of Makayla's breathing, which has its own tempo and rhythm. Makayla's fingers have moved laterally—she holds her hand flat as she touches the side of Kennedy's breast. Her digits glide from smooth, mocha skin to black fabric and back to smooth, mocha flesh again, experiencing the rise of Kennedy's nipple as she makes contact.

Kennedy's stare goes to Makayla's. She leans forward, and Makayla comes off the chaise lounge, meeting her in the space between. Their mouths touch, and they kiss, softly at first, as Kennedy's hand comes up to stroke Makayla's face—soft, moist lips pressing against one another. Makayla opens her mouth, and Kennedy slips her tongue inside.

The feeling is extraordinary. Her warm breath is in Kennedy's face. Their cheeks are touching. Makayla's tongue unites with Kennedy's as they press against one another. Their tongues are accommodating; they glide along each other, slowly flicking against the fleshy surfaces as their bodies drive together. They continue the dance with their mouths, their lips, their tongues, exploring one another as Kennedy takes Makayla's upper lip into her mouth, tugging lightly on the flesh between her teeth. Makayla responds: a quick guttural moan as her bottom lip is devoured. Lips are consumed like flavorsome meat, cooked to perfection, a savory filet.

Makayla's hands go to Kennedy, wrapping around her neck as the two women continue to kiss. They are hungry, Michael can see. Their moans become louder, their movements more frantic. Kennedy reaches for the top of Makayla's dress and pulls it down her chest. Her breasts come into view, dark emergent nipples that Kennedy rushes to. Makayla is pushed back into the precincts of the chaise lounge as Kennedy licks at Makayla's flesh, long full strokes of her tongue around dark patches of areola, twirling each nipple between her fingers, pulling them taut. Kennedy puts one breast in her mouth, then another, sucking on them madly as Makayla grabs her head in her hands. Her legs come off the chaise and wrap themselves around Kennedy's waist as Makayla bares Kennedy's breasts.

Then it's Makayla's turn to feast, and she does so with a vigor that causes Kennedy to cry out in a way that makes Michael ache with desire.

Michael watches intently, hand snaking down to feel himself growing hard under his suit pants. He moves to the bed and sits down, removes his shoes and gets comfortable, observing Kennedy reach under Makayla's short dress. Her legs part as Kennedy's fingers find their mark, feeling her moist sex beneath her panties. Makayla emits a low groan of satisfaction.

"Oh my God," she utters as Kennedy massages the wet spot, slithering down until her knees are on the carpet, her near-perfect ass cheeks rising from her minidress. She grasps Makayla's panties and slips them down her legs. When they are off, she tosses them in the direction of Michael, who catches them easily, staring absorbedly at the scene before him. Kennedy next grasps Makayla's ankles and parts her legs. Michael spies a narrow patch of pubic hair, but then his wife's face is lowered as Makayla grabs Kennedy's head with intention.

"Oh my God!" she utters again, head thrust back, eyes rolling back into their sockets as Kennedy tastes her, licking at her clit before slipping her tongue down and between the slippery folds. Michael removes his shirt and slips off his pants and boxer shorts, before lying back down. He wraps his fingers around the girth of his rock-hard cock and begins to stroke himself, his stare riveted to the activity. Kennedy feeds on Makayla as she groans incessantly, sucking on her flesh as if this were her final meal. Her head is relentlessly in motion as Makayla, legs splayed wide, ass and pelvis bucking to Kennedy's thrusts of her wonderful tongue, holds her head as she feasts voraciously. After a time,

Kennedy rises; she turns to Michael, her chest heaving, lips and chin glistening with Makayla's juice, and says to her husband, "You need to taste this."

Michael meets Makayla's stare. Her gaze flickers for an instant, roaming over his taut upper body and down to his hardened dick with its bulbous head. Makayla exhales a breath and licks her lips, contemplating all that he has to offer.

"May I?" Michael asks, his voice just above a near whisper.

Makayla answers simply. "Hurry, please. . . ."

Kennedy rises as Michael comes off the bed. She takes him in her palm and gives him a quick squeeze. He kneels, hands roaming over Makayla's thighs, abs, and breasts. He kisses her softly, their lips and tongues becoming acquainted before his head dips down. Michael kisses her clit, flicks his tongue against her hot flesh, tasting her sweetness as Makayla opens her thighs wide, reaching for his head and pushing it down, commanding him to consume her.

Michael does.

He sucks on her, first slurping in one side of her labia before feasting on the other, opening his mouth wide to feed on her entire sex, consuming her whole. Makayla is beyond heaven. Her head is thrashing about, her hips bucking as she grits her teeth.

"You are gonna make me come!" she squeals, eyes roaming over to Kennedy, who has gotten naked and lies splayed on the bed, fingers embedded within her own slippery folds. Michael increases his licking, using his fingers to spread Makayla's pussy wide as he fucks her opening with his tongue, digging deep inside of her, lapping at her with all the fury he can muster. Makayla rises off the chaise lounge as she unleashes, her pelvis bucking in a frenzy of passion. She cries out as Michael laps up her juice. Her sap glazes his chin and mouth, and Makayla collapses back into the lounger, clamping her legs shut as she turns on her side, shivering as the last of the delicious pleasure bombs go off inside of her, rippling outward to far-flung nerve endings that register the molten fire.

Michael reaches for his wife, and they kiss, mouths ajar as they savor Makayla on their tongues and lips, her scent hanging thick in the air. The music envelops them like an old, comfortable blanket. It is a slow, steady groove, a chill-out rhythm that is ideal for what's to come next.

Chapter 9

Michael unwraps the condom. He glances down as he sheathes himself before looking up, observing Makayla and Kennedy in all of their glory.

It is a sight to behold.

Kennedy is splayed on the chaise lounge. Her legs are spread wide, knees bent, feet up on the arms of the lounger. Makayla is on her knees before her, hands stroking Kennedy's inner thighs as Michael zeroes in on her honey ass. The light from outside paints that ass perfectly. Michael marvels at its form as he stands not far from her, noting the smooth lines and contours. Makayla leans forward, pressing her face into Kennedy's crotch, her mouth on her clit and lips, inhaling her heavenly scent as she tastes her. Kennedy begins an incessant moaning, and Michael is stroking Makayla's ass with his palm. Her skin is warm and flushed, almost hot to the touch—and there is a glow to her hide. But what Michael ponders is the tactile sensations that seem to course from his fingertips to the pounding in his chest and the seeming expansion of his cock, which bobs dangerously close to her opening. The feeling is indescribable; and

Makayla is reacting and responding. She glances back for a moment, making eye contact with Michael, a gleam in her eye, a sparkle that conveys she's enjoying his touch.

Makayla goes back to her feeding, head down, lifting Kennedy's legs up until her feet are pointing to the ceiling. She applies pressure forward, pushing Kennedy's knees to her chest as she attacks her pussy with a vengeance. Makayla takes Kennedy's sex into her mouth, rubbing her lips, nose, cheek, and chin around, her entire face glazed as she feasts ravenously.

Michael takes both hands and lays them on Makayla's ass. She bends forward, presenting herself to him, and Michael uses the back of his hand to feel her wetness. He can see it glistening, and a spike of pleasure courses through him. He wants to impale himself in this woman so fucking badly he can taste it.

So he does.

Michael enters her slowly. She gasps as his hard dick breaches her opening, not from any pain, but from the sheer pleasure of feeling him fill her up, brown inch by brown inch.

Michael glances downward, watching himself slide inside, disappearing amid the honey flesh of her plump ass. And when he is all the way in, Michael pulls out painfully slow, allowing himself and Makayla to feel the fullness of his member and her flower, which fights to keep him entombed.

Makayla has ceased eating Kennedy. Her head is down and between Kennedy's legs, eyes shut as Michael begins to pump her, long, full strokes of his wonderful cock as she rocks against his pelvis. Kennedy takes Makayla's face in her hands and kisses her, slipping a tongue inside as the lounger begins to shudder from Michael's thrusts.

"You like that?" he asks, one hand on the curve of her back as his other hand reaches for her hair.

Makayla turns back and beams, eyes closing momentarily before reopening. A seductive stare that spikes his heart.

"God. Please don't stop," she says, and it sounds like pleading.

Michael reaches for Makayla's waist and pulls her into him, the two of them melding into one as he slams against her. Her yoni is a glove; it wraps around him, impeccable leather—formfitting, smooth, and silky as he buries himself to the hilt. Reaching for her shoulders, he pulls her up until she is almost upright, her torso parallel to his. Then he reaches for her pert breasts, palming the flesh as he pummels her from behind. Makayla cries out.

"My God, I feel you in my stomach!"

Michael and Kennedy grin.

Kennedy leans forward, placing her hands atop Michael's and squeezing his fingers as they clutch those twin honey mounds, then shifting to caress her own wet clit before feeling Michael's cock that jackhammers Makayla's pussy. Makayla's fingers are a blur, stroking her clit furiously from side to side as she's pounded in and out, and Makayla feels her orgasm well up and take control. She cries out as she comes, Michael a fury behind her as he grasps her arms, whaling away with his member as the pleasure lets loose.

Soon Makayla is collapsing to the rug as Michael pulls out, tearing off the condom and plunging himself into the waiting cavern of his wife. He fucks her with reckless abandon, picking up where he left off with Makayla, mashing Kennedy's breasts together with his hands as he pounds her, Kennedy crying out all the while. Michael joins her, their dual screams mixing with the slow-jam music to create a symphony. And then husband and wife are coming together, Kennedy grabbing Michael's ass and her fingers raking savage rows of crimson across the flesh there as Michael tilts his head back, eyes scrunched shut, grimacing from the pain of her fingernail digs and the pleasure of being set free.

Chests heaving, pulses racing, faces contorted in pleasure. His cock turns to steel as he discharges into Kennedy. Michael collapses on top of his wife as he struggles to find his breath. And then he feels Makayla on him from behind, her warm, smooth breasts brushing across his back. Pressing into him, her slender arms wrapping themselves around their bodies like a vine as the three of them, Makayla, Kennedy, and Michael, surrender to the feeling that has just consumed them.

Pulses return slowly to normal.

Breathing becomes less harried and stressed.

Eyes close, and they dream.

The room is soon quiet. There is no longer any movement.

Nothing . . . save for the pulsing fervor that, like the soft, smooth jazz from the clock radio, surrounds, invades, and completely fulfills. . . .

Chapter 10

"MOM-MEEEEEEEE!" Zack cries out.

Michael and Kennedy are clad in white terry-cloth robes with the hotel crest on the front, hair still wet from the shower. Kennedy is on the bed, BlackBerry Pearl to her ear as Michael deals with the room-service staff that has just arrived.

"Over here is fine," Michael says to the young Middle Eastern man who pushes a white cloth-covered table with their breakfast into the room.

It is close to ten AM.

Makayla is gone.

Gone during the night—around four-thirty AM.

"I miss you!" Kennedy exclaims into the phone as Michael palms a fiver into the departing staffer's hand, shutting the door behind him.

"I miss you too, Mommy. What did you buy me?" Zack asks, through with pleasantries.

"Well, Daddy and I are going out today to find you something nice, I promise."

"Jeremy has *Halo 4,* Mom. It is SO cool!"

Kennedy frowns.

"That's nice, Zack, but I don't think that game is

appropriate for your age." She glances at Michael and rolls her eyes.

"Miss Lori says that Jeremy and I can play it as long as we're good. And I'm being real good, Mommy."

"I'm very glad to hear—"

"We went to the movies yesterday. Miss Lori bought Jeremy and me our own popcorn!" Zack giggles. "And Miss Lori let us stay up until eleven-thirty! She is so cool. How come you never let me stay up that late?"

"Well, honey—"

"Jeremy's dad is taking us to Costco later. He said that if Jeremy and me help rake up all the leaves in the backyard, he'll buy us a toy. EACH . . . But, Mommy, there are so many leaves!"

"I'm sure there are. That's nice of—"

"He said a curse word last night."

"Who?" Kennedy gets up and heads over to the table, uncovering the entrée plates. Michael smacks her hand away, but she grabs a piece of crispy bacon anyway, stuffing it into her mouth. Michael shakes his head.

"Jeremy's dad. What are you doing?"

Kennedy chews, then swallows, grinning.

"I'm eating, honey. A piece of bacon."

"Miss Lori made us a big breakfast today with pancakes and sausage. But there were blueberries in the pancakes, and I don't like blueberries!"

"I know, Zack. I hope you ate them anyway."

"I did, Mommy. After I cut them out."

Kennedy removes her BlackBerry from her ear and stares at it for a moment, shaking her head.

"I'll let you speak to your daddy. Love you!" She hands the phone over to Michael, who takes it and begins talking. Kennedy makes her way back over to the table and removes the plate covers, staring at their breakfast.

Western omelet, honey-glazed pecan French toast, an order of thick, well-cooked bacon, a side order of pancakes, and two coffees. Kennedy seats herself, pouring a cup of java for herself and for Michael. Grabbing a plate, she forks some of the omelet onto it before adding two pieces of French toast, three pieces of bacon, and a pancake. Satisfied, she begins to eat as Michael says his good-byes and hangs up.

"Thanks for waiting," he says with a smirk.

"You know I'm hungry, baby," she retorts.

"Yeah. That was some workout last night."

"I'll say."

They eat for a moment in silence. Michael revisits the evening in his mind. He sees Makayla and Kennedy, their nude forms pressed together on the chaise lounge as the light from the window illuminates their bodies. As they lay there, eyes closed, breasts rising and falling evenly, soft jazz enveloping the room, Michael had reached for his Black-Berry Curve and framed the two women within the tiny screen. Makayla, her foot resting atop Kennedy's, her honey-colored sculpted legs and curved ass against Kennedy's mocha-complexion loveliness, a sight to behold. Michael snapped a few pictures before Makayla stirred and got up.

Kennedy felt her lover rouse and did the same.

Michael asked if it was all right to take some photos.

Makayla nodded her head yes.

While Kennedy forks a bite of French toast into his mouth, Michael reaches for his Curve and flips it on. The screen comes to life. Michael chews as he glances at the pictures before him.

"Let me see," Kennedy says.

He scoots over, and together they go through the photos. There are five.

Three of Makayla and Kennedy. Naked on the chaise lounge, lying together cheek to cheek, arms lazily across each other, breasts touching; on the bed, both on their stomachs, Makayla's legs slightly spread, while Kennedy's leg drapes across Makayla's thigh—both staring back into the camera; and one by the window, a close-up of the two women embracing, eyes closed, mouths opened, tongues intertwined.

Two photos of Michael and Makayla. Michael standing behind Makayla, his hands cupping each breast as they stare into the camera and smile; and the two of them on the bed, her head in his lap, her mouth on him as he grasps her hair.

Kennedy takes his Curve and studies the photos. Michael eats, watching her.

"Last night was wonderful," he says, breaking the silence.

"Indeed." Kennedy examines the photos some more. She fills her plate with the remains of the omelet, a few pancakes, and a slice of bacon. Michael takes what is left.

"Makayla is a very sensual woman. I really enjoyed her," Kennedy declares.

"I could tell you did," Michael replies.

"Yeah, looks like you did, too."

She eyes Michael for a moment. He nods while chewing.

"Most definitely. We'll have to hook up with her again. Hopefully soon."

Kennedy gets up from the table and crosses the carpet to the nightstand. She picks up a business card and fingers the edges while glancing at it.

Michael, meanwhile, has reached for his Black-Berry Curve again, and is flipping quickly through the pics captured by the camera phone. He presses a few buttons, e-mailing the photos to his AOL account.

"We've got her contact info, and she said she's game for another go-round," Kennedy says.

"Perhaps she'll meet us in Baltimore," Michael says.

Kennedy returns to the table with the card. She places it on the table; Michael picks it up.

"We're just a short train ride away from there."

Kennedy refreshes her coffee and goes to the window, staring out at the new day. Michael wipes his mouth with a napkin and pushes back from the table, sipping his coffee. He watches his wife silently.

"I love what we have," Kennedy says, her stare still trained outside the window.

Michael rises and goes to her, standing behind her. He wraps his arms around her torso and holds her tight, the two of them rocking gently on their heels.

"Me, too, baby."

"I've never felt this safe," Kennedy continues, holding on to Michael's arms and nuzzling against his neck. "Never felt this honest . . . never felt that I could express myself sexually the way I do with you."

"Even with your ex-husband, Joe?" Michael asks.

"Jesus, Michael, you really know how to ruin the moment." Kennedy attempts to pull away, but Michael tightens his grip, restraining her.

"You know I was just joshing, baby. My apologies for being stupid."

"It's okay. I'm used to it."

Michael makes a face and pulls her to the bed.

Kennedy yelps while putting down her coffee. Michael gets on top of her and parts the terry-cloth robe as one hand feels her breast.

"Well," he says, "you can't be all that smart, since *you* married me!"

Michael bends forward, kissing his wife on the lips. Kennedy wrestles against him for a moment, but then her arms go to his neck, pulling him down on top of her.

"I married you, Michael, because of your big dick. 'To have and to hold, and to *fuck* in sickness or in health.' "

In the brief tussle, Michael's robe parts. He rubs his already hardened manhood against Kennedy's moist opening as she moves her hips sensuously against him.

"So fulfill your wedding vows, Husband. Fuck me like you vowed to do . . . like you fucked *her* last night. . . ."

Chapter 11

The man walks briskly from his parking space and into the cool morning air. The sun is out, and it's blue sky to the horizon. An otherwise perfect day, save for the migraine that threatens to debilitate his entire day.

He wears dark jeans, a blue blazer with pinstripes, and an open-collared yellow shirt. He smiles at the guard in the bright lobby, feeling sorry for the guy since he needs to be here working on a Sunday. While standing at the gleaming elevator, he stares at his reflection in the polished metal doors. On the outside, he's a picture of health, good fortune, and success. Inside—he's dying a slow death.

Fingers to his temple, he massages the skin as the elevator door opens. He steps inside. A young woman he hadn't noticed until now enters behind him.

"Good morning," he says cheerfully, although he feels anything but cheerful.

"Good morning," she replies back in a demure voice, her eyes down, as if afraid of conversing with him. She stares straight ahead, and he uses the opportunity to sneak a quickened glance her way:

shoulder-length brown hair, thin-framed, jeans-clad, taut cotton top, C-cup breasts, and nice, full ass. What is it about these young things nowadays with their big titties and plump asses? God knows they didn't make girls with racks and trunks like this when he was growing up. Must be something in the water.

The man steals another glimpse. She's a bit too skinny for his taste, but she's young, and afraid of him, he can tell—and he likes that. He feels himself begin to harden beneath his dress pants. Staring down, taking in the curve of her denim-covered round ass, he fights the escalating desire to punch the stop button, throw her back into the wood-paneled corner as she stares at him with an un-fathomable look, and peel down those jeans to impale her. Oh, she wouldn't know what to do with his cock, he muses. No, sir. She's never been ridden, this much he can tell.

But instead of palming the stop button and get-ting dirty, he just sighs heavily, as if deep breathing will somehow purge him of these negative thoughts.

It does not.

The headache is still there—a dull, ever-present entity that he's learned to live with. Maybe it's a tumor in the brain. Maybe his doctor will tell him he has less than six months to live. Wouldn't that be something? Wouldn't it? Then he could go out with a bang, the way he dreams of leaving this dread-ful place, not giving a fuck whom he takes down in the process.

The elevator door opens. The man waits for the young woman to exit. He follows suit, stepping quickly in the opposite direction, down the hallway that leads to his suite. He opens the door and winds past several offices and his assistant's cube. He unlocks the door to his office and goes inside, shutting the door, as is his habit, even though it is the end of the weekend and no one else will be here.

The man sits at his desk—sleek glass and shiny aluminum. His computer, an 8-core Apple Mac Pro with dual 30-inch Cinema HD displays, is in sleep mode. A laptop connected to a separate LCD is powered down. He touches the mouse, and it comes to life almost immediately. Logs in with his ID and password. Then checks his in-box, which has about forty unread messages. Ignoring those, he opens a new message window and hovers his fingers above the keyboard.

Cracking each knuckle, the man focuses on the sound for a moment before reaching into his desk drawer and pulling out a Tylenol bottle. He pops a handful of capsules into his palm—six, eight, he's not sure—and swallows them down with bottled water left over from yesterday.

Fingers rest on the keyboard again.

He grimaces as the pain thunders. He feels the ache in the back of his neck—the steady drone like rain. His forehead. His sinuses. They all hurt . . . like hell.

He closes his eyes. Reopens them.

Fucking pain.

Will it ever stop?

Ignoring the searing ache and pounding inside his skull, the man calls up the images.

They bring him absolutely no relief.

Unhurriedly, the man begins to type.

Chapter 12

Michael walks into the house, followed closely by Kennedy and Zack. It is Sunday evening and dark outside. Michael tosses his keys on the hallway table as he drops his bag by the stairs. Kennedy does the same.

"Zack, be a good boy and bring your stuff up to your room," Kennedy says.

"Okay, Mommy." He scoots up the stairs, quickly out of sight. Michael walks the first floor of their home, flicking on lights as Kennedy fingers the mail from the weekend. Michael walks into the den and powers up the desktop computer, dropping his BlackBerry on the desk. As he waits for the machine to boot up, he returns to the kitchen, where he pours himself a glass of orange juice and scans the letters. Disinterested, he throws the pile of mostly junk mail back onto the table.

Back in the den, he sits down and pulls up a Web browser. Like most people, Michael has multiple e-mail accounts. The main ones, his personal Yahoo! and his work e-mail, are synched to his BlackBerry. The others, the Gmail and AOL accounts, are not.

On the quiet train ride home, Michael had spent

some time checking his e-mail. So he's already up to date on his Yahoo! and work e-mail. Now he does a quick scan of his Gmail mail. As usual, it's mostly spam. A few "real" messages that he reads but doesn't respond to right away.

Michael knows that after Zack is put to bed, Kennedy will spend the rest of the evening working on her laptop. That's to be expected, since she went an entire weekend without it, which is a pretty big feat. He'll be cool with her working—Michael will take a shower and then retire to the couch in the family room, remote in hand. He's thinking about the stuff that is on his DVR and what, if anything, of interest is on television tonight.

He logs in to AOL next. He's greeted with the familiar "You've got mail" voice and scans his inbox. He zeroes in on the messages he sent himself from his BlackBerry earlier today. The photos of their tryst with the lovely Makayla are there, and Michael resists the urge to open them now. Better to wait until Zack is fast asleep before pulling up the images in their entire splendor on the large computer screen. He can hear Zack on the steps, taking them quick, as he's prone to do.

"Zack, slow down!" Michael yells, his eyes going to a message with a blank subject heading. He scans the address field: hate620@fastmail.com. One he doesn't recognize. He clicks on the message, and a new window pops open.

FUCKERS. YOU AND THAT BITCH WILL RE-GRET FUCKING ME OVER.

Michael does a double take. He rereads it. Checks the header to see if it was addressed to him explicitly. It was.

Michael crinkles his forehead. WTF? His first thought is to hit Reply and bang out "Who is this and what are you talking about?" But the lawyer in him knows that it's better to take a step back before doing anything rash.

Zack rushes into the den, eyes wide.

"DADDY, you said I could open my present from New York as soon as we got home!"

Michael quickly closes the message window and smiles at his son. He minimizes the main AOL window and gets up as Michael drags him into the hallway.

"Okay, okay," Michael exclaims. He bends down and unzips the outer pocket of his garment bag, reaching in up to his elbow. "Now, where did I put that present?" he says. "Hmm, I don't see it here."

"DADDY!"

"Okay, okay! Can you NOT wake up the entire neighborhood?"

Kennedy has joined them, arms folded across her chest as she observes amusedly.

Michael pulls out a plastic bag and hands it to Zack. He tears through it, pulling out a white T-shirt with I ♥ NY! emblazed in black letters with a red heart on the front. Zack looks up at them with a sour look on his face.

"Thanks. Is this it?" he asks disbelievingly. Kennedy rolls her eyes.

"You can be so ungrateful, Zack. Give it, I'll wear it," Michael says, snatching the tee out of his son's hand.

"Daddy, be serious!"

"Okay." Michael reaches deeper and pulls out another plastic bag, this time encasing something heftier. He passes it to Zack, who glances quickly at his mom while reaching inside. He pulls out a Transformers Optimus Prime action figure. Zack's eyes grow to saucers.

"Oh my God!" he exclaims.

"Zackary Christopher Handley!" Kennedy scolds.

"Sorry, Mommy, but this is WAY cool! Wait until Jeremy sees this. He's gonna be so jealous. Thanks, Mommy! Thanks, Daddy!" Zack yanks away the plastic and paper backing, pulls out the figure, and skips away to the family room.

"Do you mind getting him ready for bed?" Kennedy asks. "I need to spend a couple of hours on the laptop and don't want to be up all night."

Michael eyes her. "What do I get out of the deal?" he asks with a smirk.

"My undying gratitude," she retorts but gives him a playful squeeze.

Michael grins as he says, "Zack, you can play for ten more minutes, and then it's bath time."

"Ahh, Daddy!"

Michael shakes his head as Kennedy disappears. He heads back to the den. He sits back down and calls up his mail again, reopening the offending message from hate620@fastmail.com.

FUCKERS. YOU AND THAT BITCH WILL RE-GRET FUCKING ME OVER.

Michael stares at the screen for a moment. He contemplates calling his wife over to see it, but quickly decides against it. Kennedy will worry and overanalyze things. Better to leave this alone, seeing as how it's probably a mistake.

Michael stares at the message for a moment more before unceremoniously hitting Delete.

* * *

I haven't fucked anyone over, Michael tells himself as he signs off from his desktop.

Neither has Kennedy.

We are good people. We are law-abiding, tax-paying citizens. We try to raise our son right, leading by example. We both come from good families. We have kind friends and good coworkers. We've never hurt anybody.

We have nothing to worry about, he muses.

Michael hopes this last part is true.

Chapter 13

Life, which for Michael and Kennedy had been stimulating and rejuvenating on the weekend, goes back to normal on Monday.

And normal for Michael, Kennedy, and Zack is pedal to the metal.

They awake at six.

Michael is in charge of breakfast most days, unless he has an early meeting. Kennedy has the task of getting Zack dressed and situated before she gets herself ready. Michael will then feed him. Rare is the day that the three of them have breakfast together. Kennedy normally takes her breakfast to go.

Usually Kennedy drops Zack at school, but today she has to be in the office extra early, so Michael has that duty.

Kennedy, dressed in a sharp pinstripe pantsuit, kisses her men good-bye in the kitchen, wishes them both a good day, and heads downstairs to her BMW. After cleaning up and wiping Zack's face and fingers clean of syrup, Michael follows Kennedy out the door, strapping his son into the Range Rover and heading to school.

Traffic is as to be expected. Michael drops Zack off about fifteen minutes later. He is unbuckling his seat belt to get out and give his son a hug, but Zack swiftly extricates himself and jumps out of the SUV, spying Jeremy on the sidewalk. The two, once they see one another, are lost in their own world. Michael wishes them a good day and drives away.

He gets on North Capitol Street heading south, and surprisingly traffic is light and moving. Past Union Station he bears right onto Louisiana Avenue, then a series of right turns onto Constitution and Pennsylvania Avenues. His commute ends at the Department of Commerce on Fourteenth and Constitution, where he works. Michael parks in the underground garage. He is in his office and logged in to his computer, ready to start his day a few minutes shy of eight AM.

Less than two miles away as the crow flies, Kennedy is in a conference room in an unassuming brownstone off New Hampshire Avenue, that houses the National Association of Urban Development. Jacket off, fingers poised over her laptop, she reworks a brief with her paralegal, a bright young man named Daniel. The two make small talk; Daniel asks about Kennedy's weekend, and she gives him scant details before inquiring about his. Daniel is single, good looking, and gay, so he's always getting into something. Kennedy can count on him for a good laugh or two.

Both Michael and Kennedy are hard workers. They are focused and stay busy at work, very rarely taking time for themselves. Most days they talk only once on the phone, preferring to text each other. Today is no different. There are back-to-back meetings for Michael until lunchtime, then a quick walk down the street to buy a sandwich and stretch his legs. Kennedy and Daniel are hunkered down in the conference room until after lunch—a Caesar salad with grilled salmon—then it's back to her office, where she returns phone calls and e-mails, followed by several meetings with senior staff.

It's amazing to both Michael and Kennedy how quickly the feelings they had over the weekend dissipate by Monday afternoon. Life always pulls one back to the here and now, and regardless of how much they enjoyed their encounter with Makayla, now, several days later, it's as if their dalliance were a dream.

Several times during the day, Kennedy pauses in her work to consider their weekend. She smiles to herself as she remembers the scent and taste of Makayla.

Less than two miles away, Michael, in the privacy of his office, is doing the same. Face to the glass of one window, he takes a moment to remember Saturday night in all of its splendor—the way he felt at that exquisite moment he entered Makayla, glancing downward as he disappeared amid the honey flesh of her heart-shaped ass.

A beautiful wife. A wonderful son. A great job. Health, success, and a lifestyle that 99 percent of the male population would die for.

Michael knows he has it good.

He counts himself lucky.

He smiles at his reflection in the window.

Several miles away, Kennedy pauses to do the same.

Neither realizes this is the calm before the storm. . . .

Chapter 14

Later on that night, the three of them—Michael, Kennedy, and Zack—have just finished dinner and are cleaning up. Michael places the dishes in the dishwasher, Kennedy puts their leftovers away in Tupperware, while Zack washes off the table as best as a seven-year-old can. He quickly retires to the family room to sit cross-legged in front of the plasma. Michael goes to the den, where he finds a message waiting on the computer.

It's from Makayla.

He scans it quickly and grins.

"Sweetie," he yells, "we got an e-mail from Makayla." Kennedy has her laptop on the coffee table booting up. Her head comes up, and she stops what she's doing.

"Oh, really?" She glances at Zack, who is deep into the Disney Channel, and walks into the den to find her husband at the computer. She comes up behind him and reads over his shoulder.

K & M—Just a quick note to say just how much I enjoyed meeting the two of you this weekend.

I must admit I thoroughly enjoyed our encounter and spent the rest of the weekend recalling one delicious detail after another. I hope our paths will cross soon, as you've whetted my appetite for more. ☺ If you don't mind, I'd love a copy of the photos we took. Thanks.
All the best,
M.

Michael glances at his wife to read her reaction.

"That was nice of her. I had planned on e-mailing her later on this evening."

"Do you want to respond?" he asks. Kennedy gestures for him to give up the chair. She sits, clicks Reply, and begins to type:

M—We, too, were delighted to meet you. We enjoyed ourselves immensely and are anxious to get together again. Perhaps Philly or B-More will work. Let's check our schedules and figure something out!
Ciao,
K.

She glances back at Michael, who has been reading over her shoulder. He nods his head in agreement. "Let me attach the pics."

"Wait until I'm back in the family room so I can ensure our son isn't going to pop in here."

She kisses his forehead before exiting. Michael stares at the screen and smiles. His grin is erased as he recalls the message from last night.

FUCKERS. YOU AND THAT BITCH WILL REGRET FUCKING ME OVER.

For the tenth time, Michael ponders who could have sent the message to him, and why. A full day has gone by, and he's heard nothing further from the sender. That brings him some level of comfort.

Michael turns his attention back to Makayla's e-mail. The thought of the three of them getting together again stirs his loins.

You've whetted my appetite for more.

Us, too, Makayla. Us, too. . . .

Michael attaches the photos to the e-mail.

He's smiling as he clicks Send.

Chapter 15

Tuesday, midmorning.

Kennedy sits with her paralegal, Daniel, in the conference room at the National Association of Urban Development. Papers and law books are strewn across the expanse of table space as they confer, their legal pads filling with blue ink. Sunlight blazes in, warming the room. For a moment it's just the back and forth between Kennedy and Daniel—relaxed and spirited. But then Kimberlyn, the association's lone receptionist, scampers in breathlessly. There is a look of dread on her normally calm face. Without preamble she states, "Kennedy, come quick." She tries to add some words but falters, so she closes her mouth. Kennedy's entire body tenses, and her first thought is Zack, followed a millisecond later by Michael. Are they all right?

"What is it?" she asks, almost frantic, rising from the table and scooping up her BlackBerry. Kimberlyn's eyes keep roving to Daniel, who has stopped writing and is sitting in stunned silence, waiting for further details.

"An e-mail. You need to see it."

Kimberlyn holds the door open as Kennedy rushes out, telling Daniel to stay put. Out of earshot, she asks, "An e-mail? Concerning what?"

"You." Kimberlyn's eyes are downcast. Suddenly Kennedy is acutely aware of the stillness in the office. It's as if work has ground to a halt. As she marches behind Kimberlyn to her office, she notices with a rising sense of dread that the staff is staring at her. Kennedy's stomach knots around itself. Just what the hell is going on?

Kennedy's office is in the corner of the building, a fifteen-second walk from the conference room. In that time Kimberlyn has maintained silence; the staff of about ten people is clocking her position the way an owl does its prey. She feels sick and has no idea why.

Kennedy reaches her office and stares at the computer screen. Kimberlyn closes the door and presses her back into the wood quietly. Her lips are mashed tightly together. Kennedy sits and calls up her e-mail, willing her hands to stop shaking. At the top of her in-box is a new message in red from a sender she does not recognize:

egnever620@yahoo.com. Subject: *Interesting.*

Kennedy glances over at Kimberlyn, who in a whispery voice says, "Most of us at the association received it." She pauses while Kennedy opens the e-mail and a gasp escapes from her lips. In the half second it takes for her eyes to lock on to the image that stops her heart cold, she knows she's finished. Kennedy's face goes white. She stabs at the mouse, shutting the offending window as she mouths to herself, "Oh my God!" Her hand is at her breasts as Kimberlyn clears her throat.

"I'm trying to track Reginald down. Perhaps he can delete it from the mail server, but . . . it may be too late. *Everyone's* seen it."

Kennedy is deteriorating; she witnesses it in her own reflection from the computer screen. The face staring back at her registers severe horror. An image is burned into her retinas: Kennedy's nude form in the throes of heated lovemaking. The lover in the photo: another woman.

"I'm so sorry, Kennedy. I'll do what I can to reach the IT guy."

Kennedy doesn't turn when Kimberlyn leaves, closing the door quickly behind her. She remains still in front of her computer, not breathing, as if catching the breath in her throat will somehow erase this obscene incident that has her doubled over in pain. A moment passes before she exhales. Then she calls up the offending e-mail.

There it is.

No text. Just three images, one atop another, all of her and the woman in vibrant color and crystal clear, completely nude and sexually explicit.

Nothing left to the imagination.

Old photos, close to four years ago, from an encounter she and Michael had with a woman in Belize. Kennedy hastily deletes the e-mail and turns to reach for her phone. A knock at the door breaks the cacophony inside her mind. She ignores the noise and instead speed-dials Michael. Her door opens and Jackson Blair, executive director of the association, walks in. His face is grave as he shuts the door behind him, taking a seat across from her.

He shakes his head morosely before speaking.

"This is bad." Jackson lets the weight of his statement sink in before continuing. "As far as we can tell, the pictures have been mailed to a number of colleagues outside NAUD."

"WHAT? HOW?" Kennedy is numb. Her entire body vibrates with fear.

"Unknown." Jackson's voice is steady. "We're looking into that as we speak. The first order of business is damage control. Right now it's got us shut down."

"Oh God." Her head is in her hands. Jackson stands.

"I'm sorry, Kennedy. Your personal business should be of no concern to us. But this"—he holds his hands wide and gestures toward the ceiling—"this . . . is *tricky*. As an attorney, you know better than most how these things can be misconstrued. So let us deal with it. Right now I need you to go home and wait to hear from me before doing anything rash. Okay?"

Kennedy is rising now, grabbing her purse, her BlackBerry, and her coat from the rack in the corner. She moves past Jackson, who pats her shoulder lightly, but the action does nothing to console her. He says nothing further. Words cannot comfort her now.

In an instant, Kennedy's world has shattered.

She heads toward the stairs. It takes every ounce of strength she can muster to will her legs to move. All eyes are upon her. *It's a dream,* Kennedy tells herself as she shuffles along the low gray carpet, eyes downcast, feeling the stares bore into her like deep puncture wounds.

It's a nightmare, and the silence is deafening.

Chapter 16

The call goes immediately to voice mail. So Kennedy dials Michael's work number instead. A receptionist picks up.

"Is he in?" Kennedy pants, seemingly out of breath.

"I'm sorry. Mr. Handley is in a meeting," she says with a hint of attitude.

Kennedy is in no mood.

"This is his wife, and it's an emergency. I need you to go get him out of the meeting. Now. I'll hold."

Kennedy drops her BlackBerry onto the passenger seat as she steers around a taxicab. It's double-parked, most likely to pick up a fare. Amazingly, the taxi driver honks his horn, but Kennedy isn't focused on that. She's tapping her left hand on the steering wheel, counting the seconds until her husband comes on.

He gets on about three minutes later.

"Kennedy? What's wrong?"

Michael hears his wife crying. "Baby? Talk to me!"

Kennedy blurts out, "My job received an e-mail

with nude photos of me and that woman from Belize. Oh, Michael!"

"WHAT?" he yells in amazement. "An e-mail? From whom?" Michael closes the door to his office and takes a seat, calling up his work e-mail.

"I don't know from whom. All I know is that it went to the entire fucking association!"

Michael's e-mail is clean, as far as he can tell. No new messages. He breathes a sigh of relief.

"The pictures are of you and which girl?" he asks.

"The woman we met in Belize four years ago."

"Jesus." Michael's mind is racing. He's wondering who sent the photos. They've had zero contact with the woman. At least, he hasn't had any contact with her.

"And you haven't contacted her or her you?" he asks, immediately regretting the question.

"NO, Michael. I would have told you if there had been contact. *You* know that."

"Okay. Let me think."

He can't even recall *her* name. Why would anyone send nude pictures to his wife's job? Suddenly Michael remembers the e-mail that was waiting for him when they returned Sunday night. He feels his veins go ice cold.

"Where are you?" he asks.

"Heading home. Jackson told me to leave. . . ."

"Oh fuck."

Kennedy is suddenly racked with sobs. Her wailing comes through the phone loud and clear.

"Baby, I'm sorry. Please don't cry. We'll figure this out."

"Figure this out?" Kennedy retorts, wiping her face with the back of her hand, her makeup cascading down in rivers. It's the least of her worries right now. "My fucking *career* is over, you get that?"

Michael swallows hard and shakes his head. Before he can respond, his wife's voice is loud and cold. "I need you to meet me at home." A second later she adds, "Now, Michael."

Michael knows this is not a request.

He powers off his computer and heads for the door.

When Michael walks in the front door, Kennedy is waiting for him in the kitchen. She appears regal, standing in her pinstripe brown suit with her back to the island, a mug of hot tea in her hand, its wispy curling steam wafting upward. Michael kisses her perfunctorily, observes her unfocused, blank stare.

"We're going to figure this out," he says, rubbing her shoulder.

For a few seconds she is silent, as if she hasn't heard him. Then her gaze rises to his as she asks, "Have you checked your e-mail?"

"Yeah. Nothing in mine. I was going to check AOL now." Michael swallows hard and downshifts his gaze. The action does not go unnoticed.

"But?" Kennedy is staring at him.

"Nothing."

"Michael. What?"

Should he have said something on Sunday about the hateful e-mail?

In retrospect, yes. But at the time, not saying anything seemed like the prudent thing to do.

He raises his stare to meet her own.

"I got an e-mail on Sunday from someone I

don't know. Something about 'You and that bitch fucked me over.' I deleted it."

Kennedy takes a moment to process what has been said.

"It said what?"

"I don't recall the exact words. Here—let's see if it's still in the trash."

Michael walks into the den, followed closely by Kennedy. He sits, logs in to the desktop and clicks on the AOL icon. Moments later he's staring at his in-box. No new messages other than spam. Michael opens the trash folder and finds the offending message.

No subject header. Sender: hate620@fastmail.com.

FUCKERS. YOU AND THAT BITCH WILL REGRET FUCKING ME OVER.

Kennedy leans toward the screen for a moment before straightening up.

"And you didn't feel the need to share this with me . . . why?"

She is seething.

"Ken, I didn't see the need to worry you. I thought it was a mistake. Meant for someone else."

"And now? You still think it's a mistake?"

Michael purses his lips, contemplating the question.

"Now I don't know. We need to figure out who sent those pics."

"You should have told me about the message, Michael."

"Okay, Kennedy."

"Where are our photos?" Her arms are folded tightly across her chest.

"Where they've always been," he replies.

"Show me."

Michael points to the external drive sitting alongside the monitor. "They're all on this drive here. Buried underneath a bunch of subdirectories."

"And the external drive is connected to the computer all the time?"

"Yeah. I didn't think there was a problem with keeping it connected all the time."

"Can someone access the drive from outside our home?" she asks.

He turns to look at her.

"I don't see how. We've got a firewall, and the machine is password protected. And our wireless is protected by password as well."

"Yet someone got those photos. And sent them to my job."

"Yes."

Kennedy reaches over and yanks out the USB cable from the external drive. Then she pulls the power cord from the back. The drive goes silent.

"You think that's really necessary?" Michael asks.

Kennedy's eyes narrow.

"Damn straight."

She rubs at her temples as she leaves the room.

Chapter 17

The rest of the day is trying for both of them.

Michael finishes out the day attempting to work from home but gets very little done.

Kennedy can do nothing but worry. She sees her entire career imploding before her face. She has no one to call—Kennedy has plenty of friends, coworkers whom she confides in and, of course, family members, but none of them can know what has happened. How do you tell your best friend or your mother that nude photos of you and another woman are making the rounds?

Michael suggests she lie down for a few hours. But Kennedy, being the motivated, high-metabolism woman she is, can't stomach taking a nap in the middle of the day. She tries to work, but her mind won't concentrate on anything.

Why on earth would someone do what they had done to her, humiliate her, practically ruin what was, up until today, a stellar career?

She can't fathom it.

As she sits on the couch in the family room, the stereo set on low to a smooth-jazz station, she reflects on the woman in the photo.

What transpired between them occurred almost four years ago. She and Michael had gone down to Belize for a winter vacation. Zack had stayed with Kennedy's parents in Atlanta. They had hooked up with this woman—whose name escapes her now. They had met at the resort, shared lunch and a good number of drinks, then frolicked in the pool together before retiring to their hotel room later on that evening. The encounter had been a wonderful one. Unrushed, plenty of foreplay, and enough interaction and attention to satisfy both Michael and Kennedy. The next day they had gone back for seconds and thirds, as Kennedy recalls without the usual grin. What had happened to the woman? They had exchanged contact info, as they sometimes do with partners, but had never heard from the woman again. Not too surprising given their circumstances.

What happens in Belize stays in Belize. . . .

Could these photos have been sent from the woman?

Not likely.

They never shared the pics with her or anyone else, for that matter. As far as Kennedy knows, the photos have been on their external drive all this time. . . . Only Michael would know for sure, but he doesn't share the intimate details of their sex life with anyone without her permission. Those are the rules, and up to this point, she's never had any reason to think Michael could be up to something behind her back.

More likely, someone had gotten into the computer. But how? And more importantly, why?

Those questions would keep her up tonight, sleepless and frenetic, craving answers. . . .

* * *

Michael offers to pick up Zack and grab some dinner. Kennedy is grateful for the quiet. Her husband has been really wonderful, attending to her every need this afternoon, but his actions are beginning to grate on her nerves. She hasn't been able to do much—and talking about it just makes her angrier than she already is.

They return around seven o'clock. Zack runs in, backpack clad and full of energy, with Michael behind him, pizza and breadsticks in tow.

To Kennedy's surprise (and that of Michael), she actually dozed off while Michael was gone. She had been on the couch with her laptop when she fell asleep. Michael notes that she still looks depressed, but at least she's putting on a happy face for their son.

They eat their pizza while hearing about Zack's day. Afterward, he retires to the family room and the Xbox 360. While cleaning up, Michael notices the message light on their cordless phone blinking. He reaches for it to retrieve the message.

It's from a woman. No one he recognizes.

"Hey, you. I just wanted to say that I'm running late, but I'm on my way. I can't wait to see you. To be honest, I've been thinking about you all day. Thinking about the wonderful things you always do to me when we're alone. Well, guess what? I can't wait to be alone with you tonight. I'm wet just thinking about it and of you. See you soon . . . Ciao bella."

Michael stares at the phone. He hits a key to replay the message. Listening to it, he eyes Kennedy curiously. She catches his gaze and raises an eyebrow. Finally she asks, "What is it?"

Michael hands the phone to her. "A voice mail from some woman—no name."

Kennedy puts the receiver to her ear and listens.

Her eyebrows crinkle. She presses a button and frowns.

"From an unknown number," she says, checking her watch, "left about a half hour ago."

"You didn't hear the phone ring?" Michael asks.

Kennedy shakes her head.

"Nope. I told you, I dozed off. I'm surprised I didn't hear it, though." Kennedy saves the message and hangs up. Her brow is still furrowed. "It doesn't make any sense."

"Wrong number?" he offers, knowing it sounds lame.

"After everything that's happened? I don't think so." Kennedy struggles to keep her voice even, with Zack in the next room.

"I disagree. It probably comes down to nothing more than a wrong number. The message isn't threatening—it doesn't reference you or me by name. It contains nothing that points to us or to something we've done. I think it's simply someone misdialing and not realizing it."

"Okay. But to be safe, I'm thinking we should call Joe."

It takes a few seconds for Michael to process what his wife has just said. He turns and faces her, his cheeks suddenly flushed.

"Absolutely not!" Michael does nothing to hide his anger.

"Keep your voice down!" Kennedy grabs his arm and leads him into the den, out of the earshot of their seven-year-old.

Voice low, her stare locked onto his, she says, "Joe is a police officer and—"

"And your ex-husband. No fucking way I'm getting him involved in this. I don't want him seeing naked pictures of my wife with another woman."

"Michael—I don't want that, either. But things are happening that neither of us can explain. First that hateful e-mail on AOL. Then compromising pictures of me with a woman e-mailed to my job. Now some chick leaving messages on our answering machine. It may not affect you that much, but this shit has blown me away. And I'm not about to sit back and let nature take its course. We need to do something."

"Yeah. We do. But Joe isn't an option. End of story."

Michael glares at his wife before marching away.

Chapter 18

Ten-eighteen PM.

Michael presses the button on the remote, powering down the wall-mounted plasma. They're in bed, a king-sized espresso-stained oak bed of minimalist design. Matching nightstands against a soothing blue wall, blue/purple/black bedspread, and blue and black pillows create a calming setting. It is what is needed right about now. He glances over at Kennedy, who is struggling to get comfortable under the weight of the covers.

"You okay?" he asks carefully.

Kennedy settles toward the edge, away from him.

"I guess."

"Heard from Jackson yet?"

"Nope." Her voice is matter-of-fact, with a trace of sarcasm.

Michael nods to himself. "I'm sure you will. It's a bit premature for him to call you without any facts."

"You sound just like a lawyer."

"What does that mean?"

"Nothing. I just wish he had called. It's driving

me crazy, not knowing if I have a job to come back to."

"Ken—you're the general counsel to the association. They have no grounds for firing you."

"Of course they do. Whether or not I had anything to do with willfully sending those photos, my conduct outside of work does not bode well for me."

Michael knows this to be true but stays silent on the issue.

"You need to stay positive. There are a number of likely outcomes. Don't focus on the negative ones."

"Easy for you to say."

Michael is quiet for a moment.

"Have you tried calling Daniel?"

Kennedy glares at him.

"And say what?"

"Sweetheart, you and he are close. He doesn't bullshit you, and he won't now."

"I'm his boss."

"So what? Who else in that office can you really trust? He's the one. So call him—if for no other reason than to check in and see what's going on."

Kennedy plays with her hair for a moment, twisting the ends around her finger. Michael watches her closely.

"Maybe."

"It'll make you feel better."

"Okay."

Kennedy slips out of bed and reaches for her BlackBerry. Michael watches her speed-dial her assistant as she crosses the room toward the window. She parts the curtain, glancing down to the deck and small backyard that abuts a narrow alleyway. A six-foot-high wooden fence separates their back-yard from the alley.

Daniel comes on the line after several rings.

"It's Kennedy."

"I know," he says, voice animated. "How *are* you?"

"I'm okay. Actually, that's a lie. I'm frustrated, angry, and scared. Other than that, I'm fine." She tries to smile, but it comes out flat.

"I am *so* sorry, Kennedy. Is there anything I can do to help?"

Kennedy is appreciative of his concern.

"What's the word around the watercooler?" she asks.

"People aren't saying much. They know what happened, but Jackson did a good job of squelching further dialogue."

She asks, "How so?"

Daniel snorts. "You know Jackson. He pulled us all together as soon as you walked out the door. Told us to not discuss this situation with anyone and to immediately delete the e-mail. He said in no uncertain words that anyone found to have forwarded the photos to anyone, either internally or externally, would be summarily fired, no questions asked."

"Wow."

"Yeah. I think he's been personally calling any-one outside the association who may have been on the distribution list."

"Okay. I'm glad to see that he went to general quarters on this." Kennedy looks encouragingly at Michael. He nods imperceptibly. "Does Jackson know the extent of the . . ." Kennedy searches for the right word. "Extent of the e-mail distribution?"

"I don't know, but I doubt it. I do know that Reg-gie came in a little after lunch and began working on the problem from the technical end. He went around to each one of our machines and did some techie stuff—I assume he made sure we deleted the message and didn't forward it on. He checked your computer, too."

"Okay." Kennedy's mind is racing.

Daniel pauses, anxious to ask the question that burns in his mind.

"So, do you know who sent the e-mail?" he asks.

"No, I don't. Either someone gained access to my home computer, or . . ." Kennedy stops; she decides Daniel does not have a need to know anything further. "Anyway, I would appreciate it if you'd keep me informed. Call my cell anytime, if you hear anything. . . ."

"I will, Kennedy. Anything else you need for me to do in the meantime?"

Kennedy slides back into bed, pulling the covers up to her neck. "No, that's all for now. I need to speak with Jackson and find out what his next steps are. Thank you, Daniel."

She ends the call, places the BlackBerry on the nightstand, and lies flat. Michael extinguishes the light, and their room plunges into darkness.

"Sounds like that went well," he says.

"It did." Kennedy fills him in on the details.

"I'm glad Jackson acted promptly. Now your office mates can't sit around gossiping about you. They'll forget about this incident very quickly. Something else will take its place shortly. Life will go back to normal."

Kennedy doesn't respond. She turns onto her side, facing Michael. He can't see her but faces her nonetheless.

"What was her name?" she whispers.

Michael moves closer.

"Who?"

"The woman we slept with in Belize."

Michael thinks for a moment.

"Ana."

"That's right. I had forgotten."

"Really? I thought she was quite memorable."

Kennedy smiles for perhaps the first time this evening.

"Yes, she was. I meant her name, not what we *did*."

Michael places his hand on Kennedy's shoulder and strokes it softly.

"We never heard from her after our trip."

"No, we didn't. She didn't give us her information. As I recall, you gave her our e-mail."

"Yes, but she never wrote to us."

"Right."

"And you never sent the photos to anyone else." Kennedy hasn't phrased this as a question, but Michael knows it is.

"No, sweetie, I didn't."

Kennedy processes that.

"I'm scared," she says after a momentary pause.

Michael moves closer, until their bodies are touching.

"I know you are. But we'll get through this, I promise."

"It doesn't make sense. It feels like someone is trying to get back at me or at us for something. But what? I haven't done anything wrong."

"I know. It doesn't add up."

"And yet, those pictures are definitely of me. And of her."

Now it's Michael's turn to process her words. Husband and wife are silent, alone with their thoughts for a moment more. Kennedy breaks the hush first.

"Can I ask you a question?" she asks.

"You know you can."

"Is there someone on the side?"

"Where did that come from? Of course not."

"Someone is angry with me. With us. This feels to me like the actions of some scorned lover."

"No, Kennedy, there has never been anyone on the side. I think you know that."

"Then how do you explain what is happening?"

"I can't, Ken. I've been pondering that very question ever since you first called me this morning. We haven't fucked anyone over. We haven't messed with anyone's spouse or partner—"

"As far as we know," Kennedy interjects.

"I guess anything's possible. But we've been upfront with those we've hooked up with. We've been careful about providing too much personal information. We don't do this close to home, so that we aren't running into folks we know. So I'm not sure what it could be."

"And yet, today my entire job found out that I'm bisexual."

Michael pulls Kennedy to him, wrapping his arm around her. Her head goes to his chest.

"You've done nothing wrong. You're a damn good person, Kennedy. You're a loving wife, a devoted mother, and an excellent attorney. You work hard, juggle your family responsibilities like a pro, and yes, you play hard, too. That's not a crime."

Michael feels the tears on his chest. He strokes his wife's hair.

"Then why, Michael, do I feel like a criminal?"

Chapter 19

Sometime after eleven.

The man sits on the leather recliner in his living room, the house dark save for the light coming from his laptop screen. It is quiet, too. No one is here, save for him.

It wasn't always this way.

This once was a home full of life, full of hope.

But no more.

Now he tries not to focus on the sounds the house makes when he's alone—groans, beams creaking, the wind rustling against the aluminum siding. He doesn't consider the fact that most of the rooms are bare, the furniture gone. It's not that he can't afford to replace things. It's never been a money issue. It's just—what? Buying furniture and decorating—breathing life back into a cold, gray house—well, those are a female's domain. What is needed here is a woman's touch.

A woman—he pushes those thoughts out of his mind.

Instead, the man considers what he's accomplished to date. And he is pleased.

He wonders what *they* are thinking about right now. LOL—Laughing out loud.

That's what he does now. He laughs out loud, knowing that the rug has been pulled out from under them. And with a satisfied grin, he considers that this is only the beginning.

Staring at the laptop screen, he pulls up a travel site. Moments later he is checking flights. Hotels—there are so many to choose from. Grinning and humming, he clicks along, confirming this and that. Rental car? *Why, yes! I'll definitely need one of those,* he muses.

Thirty minutes later, after completing his task, the man is feeling good.

He's temporarily forgotten the groans and beam creaks. He's, for the moment, not focused on the lack of furniture or the coldness of the house. Instead, he's pumped. Fired up.

Opening a new browser window, he calls up e-mail. Logs in. New message. His fingers are nimble tonight. They seem to fly over the keys, rattling as he types, humming along to one of those tunes he can't quite place. He sits back, satisfied, and clicks Send. Grins, the e-mail is on its way.

The man gets up and stretches.

He feels alive, more in control than he has in the past six months. Yes, this is what it's all about, getting back in the saddle, getting back in control, hands on the steering wheel, and *driving*.

The man snaps the laptop shut and stops suddenly. There is no sound, no disturbance, yet his body remains still, as if he's aware of someone in his house. He considers a new train of thought as his eyes dart around.

His head is not pounding.

There is no migraine.

For this the man gives a silent prayer of thanks as he makes his way silently upstairs to his bedroom.

It is after one AM when Michael slips stealthily out of bed. He does so not because he's attempting to hide his actions but because he does not want to wake his wife. Today has been trying for her. Kennedy needs her sleep, and Michael doesn't want to do anything to upset that.

He's been awake for the past twenty minutes, just staring up into the darkness. He can hear Kennedy's steady breathing, and he should be deep into REM sleep as well. Yet he can't sleep. Too much has happened today. He feels helpless, and he hates the fact that he can do nothing to ease his wife's pain.

Michael eases out of the bedroom. His first stop is Zack's room. Their son is fast asleep on his side, the Transformers Optimus Prime action figure in his clutches. Michael smiles as he pets his son's head.

Downstairs to the first floor and into the den.

The desktop is in sleep mode, but it comes to life with a quick touch of the mouse. He sits down, calling up a browser to scan his mail.

It's as if he's had a premonition that something bad is about to happen. And that is the reason why he can't sleep. He knows it's related to what has transpired today. He senses that this thing that has happened to them is not done.

Calling up AOL, scanning the in-box for fresh messages, he sees one that catches his heart.

When he opens it, his blood turns cold.

Reading the message, there is no longer a shred of doubt.

Chapter 20

The BMW roars to life. Ninety seconds later, Kennedy puts the automobile into gear and pulls into the street, Zack watching her in the rearview mirror.

"What's wrong, Mommy?" he asks inquisitively.

She glances back at him and proffers a weak smile. Even a seven-year-old can sense its lack of authenticity. "Mommy's fine. I just don't want to make you late for school."

Kennedy has the duty of dropping off Zack. She's not heading into work today. Michael left an hour ago.

She heard from Jackson Blair first thing this morning. He asked how she was doing then got straight to the point.

"Kennedy, I'd like for you to take some time off."

Kennedy gulped and silently counted to four.

"How much time?"

"A couple of weeks. Until this thing blows over."

Kennedy was livid and did nothing to hide her resentment.

"Two weeks? You've got to be kidding. We're a

small association. No way your legal counsel can be gone that long."

"Kennedy—let me worry about that. Besides, I think it would be best if you were not here. I don't want any further distractions, and that's exactly what you'll be if you're in the office. A distraction to those here."

"You're serious?"

"Kennedy, I'm not firing you. If I were, I would tell you and be done with it. I just want to give our office a breather from yesterday's incident. Take a couple of weeks and then come back. This thing will have blown over by then—our people will be focused on other issues. Trust me."

Kennedy's exhale is audible.

"Jackson, can I at least continue working? I can't sit on my butt for two weeks and do nothing, you know that!"

"I do not want you communicating with the staff."

"Jesus, Jackson—throw me a bone, please. At least give me Daniel. I'll funnel stuff through him. That way no one except you is communicating with me directly."

Jackson pondered her request. Kennedy held her breath. It seemed like forever, but finally he spoke.

"You work from home. You only communicate with Daniel or me. And you do nothing—no work—for another forty-eight hours."

"Jesus, Jackson."

"That's my final offer. Take it, Kennedy."

Kennedy plays the conversation over in her head as she steers onto South Dakota Avenue. Traffic is light, and for that she is grateful. Through the rear-view she spies Zack sitting peacefully in his car seat, his attention directed to the DVD player situated in the headrest. Kennedy is appreciative of the momentary quiet.

She doesn't agree with Jackson's decision to keep her out of the office, but then again, she knows she's lucky. It could have been a whole lot worse.

Worse.

That gets her thinking about the new e-mail.

Michael had shared it with her this morning.

YOUR WIFE'S A SLUT AND NOW EVERYONE IN HER OFFICE KNOWS IT. HOW'S IT FEEL WHEN SOMEONE FUCKS YOU OVER? I SAID YOU AND THAT BITCH WOULD REGRET IT AND YOU WILL. I PROMISE.

Sent from egnever620@yahoo.com.

The pain was instantaneous. It was as if every muscle conspired against her—they all constricted, and suddenly Kennedy felt faint. She had to reach out to her husband for support. Michael was speaking, but the words were hollow and didn't make sense.

Then she could no longer hear him.

All sounds had vanished.

The only words that had clarity were those in front of her.

Words that cut straight to the bone.

It was Michael who spotted it first.

egnever620@yahoo.com.

The same e-mail address from the sender of the offending photos that went to her job.

egnever.

Revenge spelled backward.

Chapter 21

Joe Goodman glances at the cell phone ringing and vibrating on the marble counter. He had been reaching for the electric coffeemaker when his cell went off. He frowns; the number appears familiar, yet he can't quite place it. Joe flips open the cell and presses the phone to his ear.

"Detective Goodman," he answers in his baritone voice. Joe is a big man: six feet two inches tall, two hundred and twenty-five pounds, dark-skinned, with short hair and a manicured beard. His rugged good looks are marred by a three-inch curved scar on his right cheek—courtesy of a seventeen-year-old drug dealer from D.C. whom he shot in the head after the teenager knifed him. Joe played football at Virginia Tech and still works out on the regular. He's dressed casually this morning: jeans, dark sweater, and black work boots. A .40-caliber Glock 22 is strapped to his right hip, next to his Metropolitan Police Department badge.

"Joe? It's Kennedy."

For a moment, Joe is quiet.

"Kennedy? As in ex-wife Kennedy?" He pours

the freshly made coffee into a ceramic mug and tears open two packets of Sweet'n Low.

"Yes, Joe. This is your ex-wife," Kennedy says, more subdued than she had intended. Joe is digging in the refrigerator for the milk, which is in the back, behind the OJ, soda, and water.

"You all right?" he asks, noting her submissive tone.

"Can we meet?" Kennedy asks. "I need to talk to you."

Joe checks his watch. It's just past nine-thirty; he's not on duty until noon. "Okay," he says. "Where do you want to meet?"

"You still in the same place?"

"Yup."

"Good. I'm in the neighborhood. I can be there in five."

The call goes dead, and Joe frowns, touching his scar, a habit when something troubles him.

They sit across from one another, a plate of muffins between them. Kennedy sips at her coffee while breaking apart a cranberry-orange muffin. Joe works on a bran muffin, slathering the halves with butter.

"I see you're still eating healthy," she says.

Joe stares at her uncomprehendingly.

"What are you talking about?"

Kennedy nudges her chin in the direction of his plate. "You've used like five pats of butter on that poor little muffin, and I've lost track of how many sugars are in your coffee."

"I'll have you know my cholesterol is under two hundred—"

"Due to medication, no doubt!"

Joe considers his ex for a moment with deadpan eyes.

"It's great to see you, too, Kennedy. We should do this more often."

Kennedy grunts while Joe stirs his coffee and takes a satisfied swig. "So, what's new? I know this isn't a social call," he says, giving her his attention.

"I need your help, Joe. If it wasn't serious, I wouldn't be here."

"Go on."

Kennedy eats a few bites of her muffin before wiping her hands on a paper napkin.

"Last Sunday night, Michael and I received an e-mail from an unknown person. It was threatening, but we thought it was probably addressed to the wrong person. Then on Tuesday, while I was at work, my job received an e-mail. It went to most of my coworkers—again, it was from an unknown person, but this time the e-mail contained . . . it contained revealing photos."

Joe is watching her closely. He can sense her discomfort. She lowers her gaze and swallows hard. Joe waits for her to continue. When she does not, he asks calmly, "Revealing photos of whom?"

Her gaze rises to meet his.

"Me."

"Okay." Joe processes what he's heard so far. He pulls out a wirebound memo pad and makes a few notes. "Any idea who sent the messages?" he asks.

"None."

"Did you happen to notice if the two e-mails were from the same sender?"

"They are not."

Joe nods.

"Any enemies or someone who has reason to harm you?"

Kennedy shakes her head. "None that I know of."

"How about your husband?"

"No."

"Okay."

"Are you seeing anyone?" he asks.

"You don't sugarcoat it, do you?" Kennedy replies.

"Just doing my job," Joe says. "I assume that's why you're here."

Kennedy glares at him.

"No, I'm not involved with anyone, Joe. And neither is my husband. We have a very good marriage."

Joe accepts what she says at face value. He switches gears. "Who has copies of the photos that were e-mailed to your job?"

"No one." Kennedy adds, "As far as we know."

Joe leans back, sipping his coffee. "So, I assume they are your photos. You took them or Michael did." He glances at Kennedy, who nods. "And you're telling me that neither you nor he shared the photos with anyone else?"

"That's correct."

"And yet they made their way to your job. How did that happen?"

"You tell me. We assume our PC at home was compromised in some way."

"Has your home been broken into?"

"No."

"Who has a key to your place?"

"Besides Michael and I, my parents and his."

"Any workers having access to the house? Recent repairs, housecleaning, babysitters, et cetera?" Joe has demolished his muffin and is eyeing Kennedy's. She pushes the plate with her half-eaten one over to him. Joe grunts happily.

"We have a cleaning service that comes biweekly. And yeah, occasionally we get a sitter for Zack."

"So one of the cleaning crew or your sitter could have easily seen the pics on your computer and made copies."

"That's not possible. The computer in the den is password protected. And the photos are on a password-protected external drive and hidden deep in a subdirectory."

"And you've never gotten up from the computer, leaving it unattended? In other words, isn't it possible that you or your husband forgot to set the password when leaving for work or when you went out?"

"Michael says no. But I don't know, Joe. Honestly, I don't know."

Joe scribbles a few more notes.

"Your husband has not received any e-mails containing incriminating photos, right?"

"Correct."

Joe nods. "And these photos. They're just of you, the two of you, or what?"

Kennedy takes a gulp of her coffee. She grits her teeth as she sets the mug down. Joe looks up from his memo pad. Kennedy is taking several seconds too long to answer. He contemplates what her answer might be, and feels sorry for his ex. She may be many things, he muses, but none warrant this.

Joe is unprepared when after a prolonged sigh the words escape from Kennedy's lips.

"Nude photos. Of me and another woman."

Chapter 22

"Let me get this straight," Joe Goodman, Metropolitan Police Department detective and ex-husband of Kennedy, says with a touch of mockery. "You were with a woman? As in sexually?"

"Yes, Joe." Kennedy has lowered her voice. She takes a sip of coffee, hoping it will calm her nerves. Regrettably, it does not.

"And your husband is aware of this?" he asks disbelievingly. His voice has risen in volume, causing Kennedy further grief.

"Yes, Joe. He took the pictures." She adds hesitantly, "Can you keep your voice down?"

Joe glances around the coffee shop. The nearest patron is several tables away, and her attention is on the laptop computer in front of her.

"I can't believe this," Joe hisses. Suddenly Kennedy is afraid. She reaches for her purse and rises.

"Forget it, this was a bad idea."

Joe looks up and reaches for her arm.

"Sit down."

She glares at him, but her eyes soften when he adds, "Please."

She does. Joe consults his memo pad. For a few seconds neither speaks.

"So you're with women now?"

"Jesus Christ, Joe. What do you want me to say? Are you going to help me or not?"

"Hey, just trying to understand what we've got here. I mean, wow—look at you. Who would have thunk it? Little Miss Goody Two-Shoes getting her groove on with chicks."

"You are such an asshole, you know that?" Kennedy does nothing to hide her disdain. "What is so hard for you to comprehend? Yeah, I get my groove on with women. So fucking what? There's plenty of more important shit in the world for you to be worrying about. Plenty of bad people out there, in case you haven't noticed. And I know you are not sitting there judging me."

"What's that supposed to mean?" Joe asks with raised eyebrows.

"Please, Joe. I DIVORCED your ass because you were out all hours of the night in those skanky titty bars on Georgia Avenue doing Lord knows what while I sat at home waiting for you. Wondering if you were coming home, wondering if today would be the day you got shot by some lowlife."

Kennedy is visibly upset. She lowers her voice until it's a near whisper.

"Don't you dare criticize me or my actions. I did nothing wrong. I don't deserve this. My life has been turned upside down. Someone is stalking me, and I'm terrified. So do something about it. Help me, Joe. Do your job."

Joe takes a moment to consider the woman sitting across from him. He sips his coffee, eyeing her as he contemplates her words. He reaches for his cheek and follows the scar as it curves upward. Finally, after another minute, he shakes his head.

Joe smiles briefly.

"When you and I were married, I wanted for us to have a threesome. Remember, I asked you numerous times? Was hoping it would spice things up."

Kennedy makes eye contact with him.

"Our marriage didn't need spicing up. It needed for you to act like a husband. Not a free agent."

Joe winces from the harsh words.

"Wow. Who's sugarcoating things now?"

"What am I supposed to say, Joe? It didn't feel right at the time. You and I had serious marital issues. I couldn't even think beyond what was happening then. Now, things are different. I'm in a different place. I'm sorry, but that is where I am."

"Okay. But still, I can't believe you and your man are swingers. That's just wonderful!"

"Joe, I loathe that term. I don't even know what that means. It sounds so, I don't know, filthy."

Joe holds his hands up in surrender.

"Okay. Let's move on. Yes, Kennedy, I will help you. As you know, it's not my jurisdiction, but I will do what I can."

"Thank you, Joe. That's all I can ask."

"Right." Joe consults his memo pad. He closes it and drains the last of his coffee. "One more thing. Was this"—he searches for the right word—"this encounter with the woman in the photo, was she the only one? I guess I'm asking, have there been other sexual encounters or was this a one-time deal?"

Kennedy tips the coffee cup to her lips. She swallows hard.

"There have been others."

Joe nods somberly.

"I'm going to need contact information for . . . all of them. Whatever you've got, Kennedy. We'll start there."

Kennedy gets up as Joe stands. She reaches across the table and hugs him briefly.

"Thank you, Joe. I really mean it."

Joe scratches his scar while flashing a brief smile.

"Yeah, sure. I mean, what are exes good for?"

Chapter 23

Michael and Kennedy are lying in bed.

Michael's attention is on a leafy novel—the latest James Patterson book. He loves to read and is fond of letting anyone who will listen know that he is not one of those black men who is averse to reading. Quite the contrary, Michael loves to stretch out on the couch with a good book, preferring it to typically mindless male activities such as *Monday Night Football* or playing pool.

Kennedy, against the orders of her boss, is glancing over a legal pad full of notes. She and Daniel were on the phone for an hour—she gave him his marching orders and told him to get it done clandestinely.

Zack's been asleep for several hours now. Things are still tense, but with Joe on the case, at least they aren't sitting around being passive.

Speaking of Joe.

Kennedy needs to tell her husband about her ex's involvement.

Michael puts his book down and takes off his reading glasses. He glances over at Kennedy, who is eyeing him as if she is readying herself to tell him something.

"You okay?" he asks.

Kennedy blinks.

"I'm making it."

"I know you are, baby. I admire the way you're handling all of this. Most people would have crawled into a hole and stayed there until the coast is clear."

Kennedy smiles.

"I want to do that. I *think* about doing that."

"I know. But you won't. Not my wife."

They are silent for a moment, each alone with their thoughts. Michael shatters the peace first.

"I spoke to Makayla today."

Kennedy looks at him interestedly.

"You did?"

"Yup. Called her."

Kennedy waits for more.

"I wanted to check in, say hello and all. But the main reason for me calling was to ask her not to share the photos of us with anyone else."

Kennedy looks at his face.

"You didn't tell her what was happening, did you?"

"No, I didn't. But I wanted to make sure she's not e-mailing that stuff around."

"And? Is she?"

"No. I think she was offended that I asked. She said she likes to keep her personal life personal. And she hoped we'd do the same."

"Okay. What else?"

"Nothing much. . . . She reiterated just how much she enjoyed meeting us. I told her we felt the same."

"Cool."

"Is that it?"

"That's it. Why?"

Kennedy shakes her head.

"No reason."

Kennedy's face has taken on a look of impending dread. Michael recognizes it and asks, "What's wrong, baby?"

Kennedy sighs.

"I went to see Joe today."

"You WHAT?"

"Keep your voice down, Michael. Our son is sleeping!"

Michael ignores her.

"What part of 'keep your ex out of this' did you *not* understand?"

"Do not speak to me that way. Let me remind you that I'm your wife," she says.

"And let me remind you that I am your husband. This is not, contrary to what you may believe, only your problem. This is our problem—it affects both of us. You had no right to go and discuss this with Joe after I expressly forbade it."

Michael throws off the covers and jumps out of bed. He paces the room, eyes glaring at Kennedy as he struggles to control his breathing.

"What would you have me do, Michael? Sit on my ass and wait for the next e-mail to come in? What will it be next time? My job again? Yours? Our parents? No, I can't sit idly by. We need to be proactive. And Joe's our best bet."

"Your ex?" Michael hisses, before spitting out a laugh. "You've got to be kidding me. He's gotta be the most unobjective person on the face of the earth. Jesus." Michael heads into the bathroom to run the water. He splashes some on his face, grabbing a hand-towel to dry. He returns looking and feeling the same as before.

"You have a better suggestion?" Kennedy asks.

"Yeah. Contact the police."

"Joe is the police."

"Excuse me. Contact the police and get them to assign someone to this case who'll remain objective and work diligently to resolve this as quickly as possible."

"And Joe won't?" she asks.

Michael glares at her as if she's insane.

"What Joe will do is have the time of his life poring over our collection of pictures!"

Michael gets back into bed, this time as far away from Kennedy as is physically possible.

Kennedy leans in as he puts his back to her. She reaches gingerly for his shoulder.

"Baby, I did what I thought was the right thing to do. I'm scared. I know you are, too. We cannot sit around and hope things will work themselves out. There is someone out there who wants to hurt us. God knows why. Now, Joe has his faults. But he's a damn good detective. He's a good policeman. He can help." Kennedy pauses a moment before continuing, her voice down a notch. "He came through last time. . . ."

Michael spins in their bed and glares at his wife.

"Oh, so is that what this is about?" he asks with a snicker. "Payback time? You throwing Joe a bone? Give me a fucking break."

Kennedy sighs forcefully.

"Michael, please. Stop it. Stop acting like this. I need your support. We need to work together. We need to get Joe a complete list of everyone we've been with—contact info, whatever we've got—so he can jump on this case. I told him we'd get back to him ASAP."

"Great. Now I've got to assemble a list of our sex partners for a man you used to share your bed with. I'm sure he's waiting with bated breath for that shit."

Kennedy moves closer until her body is pressing against his. She lets her breasts nuzzle his back, feeling the warmth that spreads between them. She feels Michael's breathing slow; she knows her husband, so she presses even farther, increasing the pressure of her pelvis against his boxer-clad ass. She grinds ever so slightly and smiles as he drives back, ever so slightly.

"Do it for me, baby," she says in a whisper, her hand snaking down his arm and over his hip to the bulge that, like a stretching cat, is awakening.

Chapter 24

Flashback. Nine years ago.

Michael had just made the switch from working for a law firm to a government agency, realizing that in the end having a life was more important than having a career. Sure, he was offered a ninety-two-thousand-dollar salary fresh out of law school at Howard University. But it soon became apparent that the hours worked (on average eighty per week) meant that his hourly rate was a tad over twenty-two bucks an hour. Not bad for a twenty-five-year-old, but it was the hours that took their toll. He was working ten- to twelve-hour days, six days a week, and then putting in a "normal" workday on Sunday. No vacation, no time spent with his family. His social life shriveled up. Occasional meaningless sex with another overworked associate—she bent over a desk or in an unlocked telecom closet after midnight when the partners were gone.

Michael tolerated it for close to four years. It was amazing he held out as long as he did. In the end, he walked away, student loans be damned, because he was going insane. No amount of money was worth not having a life.

Kennedy came to the same conclusion as well.

She had graduated from the University of Georgia School of Law, passed the D.C. bar on the first try, and accepted an offer at the U.S. Attorney's Office in D.C., working in its civil division. It was exciting, important work—affirmative civil enforcement, aggressively pursuing fraud in the housing industry, dealing with HUD-related programs and their shady contractors.

She had met Joe while in Atlanta. He had spent a couple of years attending Clark Atlanta University pursuing a degree in criminal justice. They became friends though never dated, and after his grades slipped and financial-aid problems forced him to return home, she lost track of him. Then, two years later, she ran into him while in the D.A.'s office. He had joined the police department and was doing well there. One of their rising stars.

They began dating in the summer. Six months later, they were engaged.

The marriage lasted not quite two years. During that time, Kennedy got a new boss. She was a charming woman who morphed into a maniac after the first month on the job. Never pleased with anything anyone did, she received sheer joy from watching Kennedy and the other attorneys under her squirm. Her reign lasted two and a half years; thirty months of Kennedy hating life, dreading getting up every morning, going to the place that had become hell on earth.

In the end it was Kennedy's boss who broke the camel's back. It didn't matter that the work itself was satisfying. If the person who pulled the strings was evil, then it tainted everything around her.

Kennedy called it quits after four years with the U.S. Attorney's Office, opting for a kinder, gentler way of practicing law. The not-for-profit work was steady, interesting, and paid the bills. No, she wouldn't be a D.A. or a partner in a law firm, but she could have a family and a life.

And that was important.

Michael had appeared at just the right time.

The two met at a jazz concert. One of those weekend all-day affairs—eight to ten acts per day, lawn seating. Michael was with a couple of his law-school friends, Kennedy along with her sorors/friends.

Michael and his boys laid their blanket next to Kennedy and her girls. Everyone got to know one another over the next twelve hours. Michael and Kennedy had much in common—Juris Doctor, recently free from their hell jobs, and single.

Kennedy was still smarting from her divorce and had sworn off men. Michael found Kennedy beautiful but could see she was hurting inside. He took things slow—while most of the men who approached Kennedy were forward and very pretentious, Michael was laid-back, cool, as if biding his time. They exchanged numbers, but where Michael really shined was in the way he wrote to her over e-mail. Every day they communicated electronically, Michael at his new government job and Kennedy fresh with the association. They talked about everything under the sun, and Kennedy so appreciated the fact that he did not seem obsessed with the desire to get into her pants.

Joe had been controlling about everything—finances, where they ate out, the color of their wallpaper. She felt smothered being married to him. But with Michael, it was different. He was laid-back, confident in who he was. They rarely argued. They just went well together. Like they connected. Like they just fit.

After a year of dating, they got engaged. Marriage came shortly thereafter.

Zack arrived fourteen months later.

It began innocently enough.

A weekend getaway to Atlanta for the two of them.

Michael and Kennedy had been dating about six months. Things were going wonderfully between them. They decided to escape to Atlanta; the weather in D.C. had been cold and dreary. Michael had never been to Atlanta. Kennedy promised to show him around her alma mater.

While in Atlanta, they visited a strip club.

Actually, it was Kennedy's idea.

They had talked about her marriage to Joe on numerous occasions, and one thorn that kept cropping up was the fact that her husband had always spent his downtime in strip clubs rather than with her. Michael had listened patiently and without judgment. He had asked her one evening if she had ever considered going to one. Kennedy was silent for a moment. But then she answered yes, with the right guy.

They had had other conversations as well.

About sexuality—their fantasies and desires. One evening Kennedy shared hers with Michael. She admitted an attraction to women. She wasn't a lesbian—she still loved men. But the thought of being with a woman turned her on. It had been that way for a long time.

Michael asked if she wanted to be with another

woman. Kennedy had nodded silently. Michael knew he would make it happen one day.

And it did.

In Atlanta.

They were in a taxicab, heading back to their hotel after a day of outings when they passed a sign for one of ATL's gentlemen's clubs. Kennedy jokingly suggested that they go. So they went that evening.

The place was huge, one of those upscale joints where the women flowed like wine.

Beautiful women—nice cross-section. Black, white, Latino, European.

They found a table not far from one of the stages, where they could comfortably watch a few sets. Kennedy, at first, was reserved. But she opened up quickly. An hour after arriving, Kennedy was putting five-dollar bills into the dancers' G-strings while flirting shamelessly.

Michael had to smile.

He pulled one of the dancers aside and inquired about other services.

Soon they found themselves in the upstairs VIP lounge. It had cost him a pretty penny, but the privacy was worth it. Kennedy had been focused on a particular stripper who went by the name of Tunisia. She had pretty brown skin, an hourglass body, long jet-black hair, and a wonderful heart-shaped ass.

The room she led them to was semidark, thick curtains giving them seclusion and discretion.

They sat together on a small leather couch.

Tunisia shared a drink with them as Kennedy took in her features eagerly. Tunisia put down her glass and then proceeded to rub and kiss all over Kennedy. Michael watched as his girlfriend found heaven.

Tunisia stood and did a slow dance just for Kennedy. She reached for her breasts and played with her nipples underneath the cotton of her top. They kissed sensuously, and, after a lap dance, the stripper lay back and Kennedy got on her knees.

Michael will never forget that night.

The night he witnessed his girlfriend lower her head between the thighs of a dancer named Tunisia.

He witnessed Kennedy taste a woman for the very first time.

Witnessed the look of sheer joy on her face as she gave another woman pleasure.

Michael feasted on the dancer, too. But it was afterward, when Tunisia had gone, that Michael took Kennedy in his arms and kissed her hungrily, tasting the remnants of the stripper on his girlfriend's mouth.

That night, their tongues intertwined as Michael and Kennedy sucked impatiently at one another.

That night, Kennedy came harder than she had ever come before.

And she had Michael, and the memories of a stripper named Tunisia, to thank for it.

Chapter 25

Tara Reynolds, the fiancée of Detective Joe Goodman, walks in to the row house they share around seven-fifteen in the evening. She tosses her keys onto the kitchen counter and immediately notices Joe's shield and gun by a stack of mail. She frowns and turns, glancing up at the ceiling.

"Baby?" she calls out.

"Up here," Joe replies a moment later.

Tara is five feet five inches tall, a curvy black woman with shoulder-length dark hair. She's wearing a pair of brown slacks and a velvet tan jacket. She throws off her heels and begins to climb the carpeted stairs. When she reaches the top she rounds the corner, passing a guest room and bath. Their bedroom is directly in front of her, but she makes her way to the room on her right, which Joe has converted into an office.

He's hunched over his desk, which is by the window. A computer sits on the table, as does a docking station for an iPod. He glances up and smiles.

"Hey, you," he says, coming around the table to

greet her. His arms go to Tara's waist, and he pulls her into him, hugging her as their lips touch.

"Hey yourself," she retorts, enjoying the contact. Joe's hands slide down to her full backside as he massages the flesh. He grins as he hefts a cheek in each large hand. "What are you doing here?" she asks, looking up into his brown eyes.

Joe ignores the question as he kisses her on the mouth again, pulling her closer. She slips her tongue into his mouth as her hands snake around his neck. When he pulls back, she is eyeing him curiously.

"I see somebody missed me."

"Missed my baby girl something fierce," Joe says with a grin.

"So, answer my question. What are you doing here? Aren't you supposed to be working?"

Joe takes another step back as he nods his head.

"I put in a good six hours today, but had some stuff to look into, so I told the captain I'd be back later." Tara is leaning against the desk and Joe goes over to her, placing his hands on her waist again. "Besides, I wanted to spend some quality time with my baby!" His tongue goes to her ear as she pats him away playfully.

"Translation, you wanted some!"

"Same difference. But I'm here. So you should take advantage of the situation."

"I guess so. Let me go change."

She walks out of the office and into the bedroom. Joe follows behind her.

"Besides," he adds, "since you're going to be Mrs. Joe Goodman in less than a year, you might as well practice what the wedding vows preach. You know, 'To have and to hold, and to always obey . . .' "

Tara turns to him.

"I don't recall anything in the vows about having to obey."

"Oh, yeah. You have to obey your man. And right now your man is commanding you to take off all of them clothes."

Tara's jacket hits the bed. She unbuckles her belt and unbuttons her pants. "Is that so?"

Joe nods slowly.

Tara lets her slacks drop to the floor. Joe watches her as she steps out of them, her fit calves like those of a dancer's, enthralling. Her panties are black stretch lace boyshorts, and Joe squints as if in pain. Tara is unbuttoning her top, a silky white thing, exposing a black-laced bra. She unhooks it from the back and flings the bra to the bed, displaying her firm C-cup breasts. Joe is halfway undressed already, and almost trips when his ankle gets bunched up in his pant leg. Tara laughs.

"Don't kill yourself. At least not until I'm done with you." She winks and heads into the bathroom, where she runs the shower. Tara pops her head out and says to Joe, who is down to his boxers and socks, "Let me take a quick shower. I promise I won't be long."

Joe nods. He is preparing to lie on the bed, but decides to head to the bathroom instead. The door is open and he can see Tara through the translucent shower curtain. She is soaping up her body as he stares impatiently. He rests his hip on the doorframe as he watches her, feeling his manhood harden.

"Can I help you with that?" he asks.

"With what?" she replies, her back to him.

"Get clean."

Tara faces him and smiles. "Sure."

Joe is removing his boxers and socks, leaving

the pile at his feet. He is semihard now, gazing at his fiancée, watching the soap cascade down her body in rivulets. He takes a step toward her, one leg inside the shower as he says, "Kennedy came to see me today."

Tara has the washcloth to her neck when she stops and turns abruptly. "What did you say?" She turns the shower off, soap still covering her torso and midsection.

Joe backs up and repeats, "Kennedy came to see me today." He realizes too late that this was bad timing on his part.

Very bad timing.

Tara calmly opens the curtain as she stares in amazement at him. "Your ex came here?" Her eyes are laser beams.

"No, baby. She needed my help on a case. We met at a coffee shop." He almost uttered "the coffee shop down the street," which would have incited violence if Tara found out that Kennedy had indeed been to the house to pick him up.

"A case," Tara says, arms folded across her chest. Soap clings to her forearms and pubic hair, but she makes no move to wipe it away.

"Yeah. She's in trouble."

Tara nods, sucking her teeth. She ponders his words for a moment.

"And? She can't call the police like the rest of us normal folks?"

Joe grins sheepishly.

"Baby, come on. It's not like that."

An eyebrow is raised.

"Please tell me what it's like, then."

She stares at him for another few seconds before restarting the shower. "Let me finish my shower. I'll be right out."

Joe takes the hint, grabbing his boxers and socks, and retreats from the room. He closes the door quietly behind him, leaving Tara to stew in peace, alone.

Chapter 26

For a few seconds Joe considers lying naked on top of the bedspread as he waits for Tara to come out.

But it only takes a microsecond to see that this course of action will only make matters worse.

Tara is pissed.

And Joe is so damn stupid.

He was close—this close to having sex with his woman—and God knows why he chose that moment, that *exact* moment, to bring up his ex, Kennedy.

What the hell was he thinking?

He knows exactly what he was thinking. . . .

Joe grabs a pair of sweats and a faded DEA T-shirt and dons them. He exhales forcefully, angrily.

So stupid.

He could be inside her this very second. . . .

What he had to say could have waited.

But, of course, he's been unable to get Kennedy out of his head.

She was always so beautiful. And now, seeing her after all this time has caused him to remember what they once had.

Before things turned sour.

God, what a woman she was.

What a woman she is.

Stop it, he tells himself.

Kennedy is married. Besides, Joe is engaged—to a beautiful woman in her own right.

He can still hear the shower going, so Joe escapes to his office.

He glances at the legal pad on the desk.

Names, dates, locations. Other pertinent information that Kennedy has provided.

Names, dates, locations.

The list holds sixteen names.

Sixteen partners.

Sixteen sexual liaisons.

Joe lets the weight of that sink in.

Scanning the list, he notes the locations. His mind races as he conjures up images of these sensual trysts.

New York, Jamaica, Baltimore, Atlanta, Philadelphia, Miami, Paris, London, Aruba, the Dominican Republic, Belize.

Romantic getaways. Exotic locales. Sexual encounters.

He can't help but feel a rush of jealousy accompanying these thoughts.

Can't help wondering why it was Michael and not he.

Our marriage needed you to act like a husband, not a free agent.

A free agent . . .

Kennedy was right.

He was a fool back then. Joe had had something special, and he had fucked it up big-time.

His fingers go to the names on the page. He touches the dried ink and feels shame and regret.

It could have been him.

New York, Jamaica, Baltimore, Atlanta, Philadelphia, Miami, Paris, London, Aruba, the Dominican Republic, Belize.

It could have been him.

Joe turns. Tara, wrapped in a bathrobe, is standing in the doorway, watching him silently. Their eyes meet. Her arms are folded across her chest, as before. Joe traces the line of his scar absentmindedly.

"Spill it," she says after what seems like an eternity.

Joe sighs and begins.

"Kennedy and her husband are being stalked. E-mails have been sent to her home and her job, and she's been threatened. She asked me to look into it."

"And of course Joe Goodman just loves playing the black knight."

"What does that mean?" he retorts somewhat heatedly.

"Rescuing the damsel in distress. Said damsel being your ex-wife. How perfect." Tara turns on the balls of her feet and heads into the bedroom. Joe follows close behind her.

"It's not like that, Tara."

She has her back to him, but he reaches for her shoulder, gently applying pressure until she is facing him. "Look, baby, I love you," he says. "This is business. My ex-wife and her husband are in trouble. I am a police officer. This is what I do. There is nothing more to this than that."

"Are you sure?" Tara asks, her stare directed into his. "Because you were hurting when she left you."

Joe blinks.

"That was a long time ago. I'm over her. Been over her for a long, long time. You know this."

Joe reaches for her arms. His fingers interlock with hers. He kisses her gingerly on the forehead. Then, moving downward, to her nose, cheek, and finally her mouth.

Tara lets him kiss her. She holds nothing back. She responds by wrapping her arms around his back and moving closer.

"I just need to be sure," she says, voice barely above a whisper. "If we're to be married, I don't need anything getting in the way. Nothing from the past or the present. It's just me and you, Joe Goodman. No one else."

He kisses her again. She can feel him stirring against her. She can feel his strength and weakness all at once.

"I know," Joe says before kissing her lips sensuously, then the nape of her neck. "You have nothing to worry about. This I promise."

The robe opens. Joe steps back, marveling as he does each time he gazes upon Tara's loveliness. He touches her face, letting his fingers drop to her firm breasts and nipples, which seem to tighten at his touch. Her skin is smooth, silky, like a chocolate bar. Her hands are at his waist now. They slip under the fabric of the sweatpants and feel his taut flesh, descending until she finds what she is searching for. Tara wraps her fingers around his girth and begins to stroke him, feeling him harden to her touch. Joe pulls down the sweats as Tara holds on. The shirt comes off next, and suddenly Tara and Joe are falling onto the bed. His mouth is on hers, sucking her tongue into his mouth with an urgency that excites her. And then he is slipping inside her, not forcibly, but in a way that says I need you *now,* Tara sucking in a quick breath and moaning with pleasure as she opens her legs to accept him, his hands on her ass, massaging her in a way that drives Tara absolutely crazy.

"Do you love me?" she asks breathlessly.

Joe responds by pushing himself inside fully until there is nowhere left to go. They begin to move together, in a rhythm that is sweet and pure.

"Yes, baby," he responds, equally breathlessly. The feeling is one of sheer delight. Joe is home. Once again he has returned to the place where everything makes sense. He pulls, then pushes into her wetness and warmth slowly. "Baby, you know I do. . . ."

Chapter 27

The man walks into the 2020 Bistro & Lounge located in the Radisson Hotel in Crystal City, Virginia, smiles at the young female maître d', and gestures to the bar area. She steps aside with a smile, and he walks on. The place isn't very crowded this time of night. It's just after nine, and the dinner crowd is thinning. He takes a seat at the bar and orders a scotch on the rocks.

The flight in was uneventful. Security was a breeze. He'd checked two bags at the terminal, and he carried nothing suspicious in his carry-on—laptop, a paperback, a few magazines he bought in the airport newsstand, some gum, a half-empty bottle of extra-strength Tylenol, his MP3 player, and cell phone—innocuous stuff like that. He had to wait a long time at Reagan National's baggage claim—God knows why; how difficult is it to remove some person's luggage from the underbelly of a plane?—but these things can't be helped. Nonetheless, he's here now, perhaps a mile, no more, from the Fourteenth Street Bridge, which will take him into the nation's capital—tomorrow, when the time is right.

He can't wait. The excitement makes his brain spin.

But now he's in desperate need of a drink. His scotch on the rocks arrives; the man reaches into his jacket pocket, pulls out the Tylenol, pops the top, spreads six or seven Rapid Release gels in his palm, and downs them with two swigs of his drink.

His head is pounding.

The calm that had embraced him early in the week has gone, replaced with this incessant throbbing that threatens to drive him insane.

Or kill him.

His remedy?

Stay heavily medicated, and drink plenty of fluids.

Hence, the scotch on the rocks.

He orders another, shaking his head when the bartender asks if he'd like to see a dinner menu.

The liquor goes down hard, but the pain is fleeting. He can feel the Rapid Release gels spreading like spilled molasses. Soon, now, the pain will dissipate to a dull throb. The man is wired, on edge. He's close, he can taste it, and this has his adrenaline spiking. He's thinking about them—the couple he's come to see—and all he has in store for them. It's a mix of ravenous excitement and anxiety, as if he were having sex with someone in public. The idea of getting caught with one's pants down, literally—thrilling and yet terrifying at the very same time.

A well-dressed woman sashays up to the bar and takes a seat two stools down from him. She glances his way and smiles. And why shouldn't she? He's tall, over six feet two, good looking, in great shape, neatly dressed in jeans, a gray tight-fitting shirt, and a black microsuede sport coat. His bald head is freshly shaved and gleaming. But what will get her, he knows, is his killer smile.

A smile to die for.

He flashes it for her now. And she beams in return.

The bartender is in front of her, asking what she'd like to drink. She is indecisive, so the man clears his throat and leans in, politely asking, "Will you permit me to order for you? If you don't like it, you can send it back, no questions asked."

Flash the smile.

"All right. Thank you!"

He looks at the bartender. "French martini for the lady. Grey Goose, please."

"Excellent choice, sir."

The woman puts her purse on the stool between them. He observes her: middle-aged, blond, suit jacket and matching skirt, no nylons, very nice long legs. Her drink arrives; she sips it tentatively, then turns to him and grins, toasting him.

"Delicious, thank you again."

"Don't mention it," he replies.

She takes another sip, puts the glass down, and leans toward him. "So, do you come here often?" she asks with a smile. "I'm sorry, that sounded so clichéd."

He gets off his bar stool and moves until there is only one seat separating them. Signaling the bartender for another scotch, he answers, "First time for me. You?"

She waves her arm in the air in a dismissive way.

"Oh, no, I'm a frequent visitor here." She smiles again.

"Let me guess," he says. "Sales."

She stares at him uncomprehendingly. "Wow, you're good. How did you know?"

He shrugs his shoulders. "You've got that look—no, I mean that in a positive way. Speak well, very attractive, on your game. Yeah, definitely sales."

"Well, thank you. What else can you tell me about me?"

He smiles. "Let me see. We're here in Crystal City, so I'd say your clients are most likely federal government, and if I had to bet, I'd say you sell software, or some kind of technology."

She stares at him for a moment.

"Okay," she says. "This is scary."

He grins. "How'd I do?"

"Umm, dead on. I do technical sales for a software-development firm."

"Damn, I'm good!"

"I'll say. So, how about you? Business or pleasure?"

"Hopefully a bit of both. I'm Damian, by the way." He reaches out his hand. She takes it in hers, leaving it a millisecond longer than necessary.

"Lorie. And the pleasure's all mine. . . ."

Chapter 28

Damian opens his eyes.

He hasn't been sleeping, just resting after that intense workout.

His room is dim, the curtains drawn, the overhead lights off. Only the alcove light burns bright.

He glances around.

She is gone. He checks his watch. A little past eleven-thirty PM.

It didn't take long.

Lorie, the slut from the bar.

Some lighthearted conversation, another French martini, and it was she who suggested they go somewhere else. His head was a dull throb from the scotch, the Tylenol, and her laughter. But his dick was on high alert. He could use some relief; he needed to come hard and rid himself of this tension that he carried around like an ulcer.

She had shown up at the bar at exactly the right time.

They went back to his room after settling the tab. Once inside, she sat on his bed and crossed her nice long legs while he fetched two beers from the minibar. Lorie eyed the bulge in his jeans, and before long, she was sucking on him instead of her brew as he tweaked her nipples between his fingers. She had commented on how big he was. He just smiled and thrust himself deeper into her hungry mouth. Lorie was one of those middle-aged chicks that Damian just loved—a soccer mom who was dying to prove she still knew how to please a man. She sucked expertly on his cock, even made slurping sounds, and cupped his balls lightly as she kept the pressure around his shaft using her other hand. Damian was impressed. He actually had to stop himself, pull back and direct the slut to get undressed, lest he shoot himself all over her pretty little face. Once nude, he marveled at her body. It was quite nice—tight in all the right places, decent boob job, and a cute white-girl ass that he slapped with his hand, turning her flesh a bright red. He kept her on the edge of the bed, slid between her legs, spreading her thighs as he stuffed himself back inside her hot mouth, thrusting hard as he glanced down at the landing strip between her legs. He could see the lips peeking out from beneath the golden brown hair, and it turned him on to think that he was going to wear out that pussy very soon. Moments later, as Lorie glanced up doe-eyed at him, Damian unleashed into the back of her throat. It caught him off guard, to tell the truth, those few seconds, when out of nowhere he felt the pressure in the base of his balls rise, and suddenly he was on his toes, eyes scrunched shut and moaning as he flooded her mouth with his semen. Lorie was, for an instant, stunned, as if she hadn't expected him to come just yet, but then she began to suck like there was no tomorrow, jerking his cock as she swallowed his seed down in several large gulps.

What a good girl!

Damian was beside himself with glee. This slut deserved a prize.

So he laid her back on the bed and proceeded to lick her pussy. Lorie loved it, grasping at his bald head as he fed upon her, licking her this way and that, thrashing his head about until she raised her ass off the bed, breath raging as she practically screamed out his name. He tasted her juice as she beat and flogged his face with her dripping sex, squeezing his head between her thighs, nearly suffocating him with the intensity of her orgasm.

But that just made him hard again.

So he slid on a condom, flipped her over, and fucked her doggie style, grabbing her fake blond hair in his fist and yanking her head back as he pummeled her hard with long, full strokes of his cock in her pussy, full of pride as he slammed into her from behind, watching his dark meat glide effortlessly between her white butt-folds. The disparity between their hues fascinated him. He loved the contrast.

Then something inside of him soured.

It was as if the air had fouled.

His mind skipped to *them.*

Butterscotch atop Mocha.

Images that were permanently tattooed on his brain.

Labia peeking out from between her legs.

Mocha and Butterscotch's stares captured by the camera. Their dual smiles radiating outward, sickening him with their fucking glee.

The rage was a river. He could feel it taking over. Building . . . expanding into a turbulent vortex. The thump in his head was like house music. Only one thing could stop it.

He shook his head violently, attempting to free

himself of the pain. He tried to focus on the here and now, this cunt beneath him, legs splayed like the bitch she was, a dog in heat. He grabbed her ass as he rushed inside, then pulled out furiously.

He told himself to focus on the fuck. But it did no good.

Click.

Dude comes into view.

Atop Butterscotch, sinewy brown back muscles shine. Dude reaching for her ankles. The tat on her ankle, the spot of red ink visible between fingers—the spider, clearly seen.

Black widow.

Ass to the camera, he can't tell if he's inside her yet. Mocha kissing Butterscotch's nipples while rubbing her own clit. Next shot leaves no doubt.

Dude's buried to the hilt. He's entombed. Their eyes are locked, and her expression says it all—*this* is rapture.

Fucking bitches . . .

He uttered these words as a low growl. Lorie turned, in the throes of frenetic lovemaking, not sure she'd heard him correctly.

And it brought him back.

He blinked.

And just like that, the images disappeared.

It was just him and the blond bitch getting it on.

They were a machine of sexual activity, the intensity of her groans increasing until there was no doubt what came next. She exploded again, and Damian followed her moments later.

As he struggled to catch his breath, he had to admit the sex was sweet. She gave him exactly what he had needed. He kissed her hard on the mouth afterward, a move that surprised even him. But the feeling of euphoria didn't last long. She asked to use his shower and he grudgingly agreed. Thankfully, she was quick and was dressed and gone before long.

Now Damian glances over at the nightstand by the window. Lorie's business card is there where she left it. She had scribbled her cell number on the card before she amscrayed. Damian promised to call.

And who knows, he just might.
Another helping of dessert.
Something tasty, something sweet.
Something to keep the pain at bay. . . .

Chapter 29

Kennedy exits the townhouse just after eleven-thirty AM.

She has lunch plans.

Not Kennedy's idea, but Robin, her best friend, insisted.

So she relented.

They are to meet around noon. Mark and Orlando's on P Street, right off Dupont Circle.

She would drive, but parking would more than make up for the taxi fare. Instead, she has decided to walk to the corner and hail a cab.

The weather is cooperating today. She wears a pair of faded jeans, boots, and a light sweater under a thin leather jacket.

She's just gotten off the phone with Daniel. He's funneling stuff to her, and she's grateful to be working again. Her office mates are, according to Daniel, keeping their mouths shut regarding the e-mail incident. All praise to Jackson Blair.

Kennedy turns her attention to her lunch date.

She's anxious about seeing Robin. She's not sure what she'll say to her best friend. She knows she can't tell her the truth. Can't even contemplate her friends, even close ones, knowing the details of her lifestyle. Robin is good people—but she's conservative to a fault. She'd never understand Kennedy's insatiable want for another woman. So she'll keep those details to herself.

She'll be fine.

Besides, she needs to get out of the house. Even though she's back to working, albeit from home, she still feels restless. She misses the office. Misses the phone calls, the back-and-forth exchanges between her and Blair, her and Daniel. She's on the phone with him several times a day. Blair also. But it's not the same.

At least Joe Goodman has begun his investigation. She feels better about that. Michael's not too thrilled, but the alternative is worse. So, in the overall scheme of things, Kennedy can't really complain.

She reaches the bottom step of her stoop. Glances to the right down the street at the row of parked cars before heading left toward the corner and a cab.

Today is going to be a good day, she tells herself.

Now all she has to do is truly believe.

He watches her go.

Damian, head down for a moment, pretending to be reading from a clipboard or something.

He is in a white cargo van, courtesy of Enterprise. Parked on Taylor Street in the District, opposite side and down from Michael and Kennedy's home. Maybe three, four hundred yards away. Not too close. Doesn't want her or the neighbors becoming overly suspicious.

Back to the van.

Three 12 x 24–inch magnetic signs, vinyl lettering—signs he's purchased off the Internet. Signs that cover the Enterprise lettering.

Signs that say:

RANDALL & SONS, INC.
ELECTRICIANS
301-555-6453 1-800-843-6453

Company name made up. But the phone number underneath is valid—actually goes to a real electrician, should someone see the van and decide to place a call.

The signs are perfect—easy to roll up and carry in medium-sized luggage, and cheap enough to throw away when the need arises.

He's dressed appropriately today.

Jeans and Dickies work shirt. Randall & Sons, Inc. insignia on the left breast pocket. Shirt and patch Internet purchased. Navy blue baseball cap helping to conceal his facial features.

He picks up a cell from the passenger seat. It's a Virgin Mobile phone, pay as you go, purchased from a Best Buy back home. Paid cash for the phone, as well as the Top-Up card that he picked up from a 7-Eleven. Area code 678. Atlanta.

Not that he's from there.

He dials *67 to block Caller ID, then their number from memory. Waits until the answering machine picks up.

Satisfied, he hangs up. Glances around.

Nobody in sight, so he grabs his tools and exits the van.

Damian is whistling as he prepares to go to work.

* * *

Robin is sitting at a table by the window when Kennedy arrives at five minutes after twelve. They embrace and order a round of sweetened ice teas.

"Girl, it's good to finally see you!" Robin says once their waiter has retreated.

"I know, right?" Kennedy says, placing her leather jacket on the back of her chair and her BlackBerry Pearl on the table where she can get to it quickly.

"Miss I'm-too-busy-for-anybody."

"You know it's not like that."

Robin hmphs. "Whatever you say, Counselor."

"Anyways, how are you? It's been like forever, right? What's new?" Kennedy says, trying to steer the conversation away from her own misfortunes.

"Oh, no you don't!" Robin exclaims. "You need to spill it. What is up? You didn't say much on the phone—other than you're off from work for two weeks. What is up with that? You? Off from work? Hell, naw!"

Kennedy sighs. Luckily, their waiter reappears, and Kennedy is rewarded with a momentary reprieve.

They order. Kennedy selects the poached salmon served with asparagus salad, mâche, and lemon oil. For Robin it's the Maryland crab cakes with avocado and tomato.

"I'm waiting," Robin says once the waiter has gone.

Kennedy has been dreading this moment all morning. In the cab coming here she played various scenarios over in her mind, not coming to any conclusion. She stares at her best friend now, noting that there is sincere concern on her face. Kennedy sighs again.

"I'm in a bit of trouble," she begins. Robin waits

patiently for her to continue. "Someone, we're not sure who, is harassing us."

"Are you serious?" Robin asks.

"Unfortunately. We've gotten threatening e-mails and one went to my job."

"Shit!"

"My boss felt it would be best for me to stay away for a while."

"What did it say?"

Kennedy takes a sip of her ice tea. Her mouth has suddenly become very dry.

"I don't recall the details. Just disparaging remarks about me."

"My God. Who would send something like that?" Robin asks.

Kennedy shakes her head.

"I don't know. That's what we've been trying to figure out."

"Lord. What does Michael make of all of this?" Robin asks.

"He's as frustrated as I am," Kennedy answers.

"Has anything gone to his job?"

"No. Fortunately not."

Robin considers this. She stares at her friend across the table.

"What?"

"Nothing." Robin takes a sip from her glass and stares around the restaurant.

"What?" Kennedy asks again, a note of frustration in her voice.

"It's just. I don't know. Seems interesting that you're getting these e-mails and he's not. Makes me wonder, that's all."

"Makes you wonder what, Robin?" Kennedy inquires.

Robin's eyebrows rise as if that's all she needs to say.

"Say what's on your mind."

Robin wipes the hair from her eyes.

"I'm wondering what Michael's up to?" Robin says and stares at Kennedy.

"My husband's not up to anything, Robin." Kennedy sits back in her chair, getting pissed.

"Are you sure?"

"Yeah, Robin, I'm sure. Not everyone is like your husband. I mean, ex-husband."

Robin nods her head slowly.

"Nice. I see this is going nowhere. Forget I said it."

"No, what do you want me to say? I know Michael. He's not cheating on me, if that's what you're thinking. We have a great marriage—we trust each other. Michael wouldn't do that to me."

"Then how do you explain the e-mails to your job? Seems fishy to me," Robin says.

"See, this is why I didn't want to do lunch. Because I knew this was going to be the outcome."

Robin's eyes soften.

"Ken—you're my best friend. I'm just speaking from my heart. I apologize if I offended you. But best friends have to look out for one another. That's all I'm doing."

She reaches out and grasps Kennedy's hand. Robin squeezes it briefly.

"My husband is not cheating on me," Kennedy says, more firmly than before. "I'm sorry if you can no longer trust any man." She is about to say more but shuts down instead.

Thankfully, the waiter reappears. Salmon, asparagus salad, and Maryland crab cakes with avocado and tomato. Another round of sweetened ice teas for the two of them.

They eat their food and make small talk.

Both stay away from further discussion of Kennedy's problem.

But it is not far from either of their minds.

Chapter 30

Michael is enjoying a hot bath in the oversized Jacuzzi tub when there is a knock at the door. He has his head back against the tile, eyes closed, soap-suds filling the tub and caressing his brown skin. His iPod Touch is on the edge of the Jacuzzi, cranking out Herbie Hancock's *River: The Joni Letters*—the album that earned him a 2008 Grammy—as he unwinds from a long day.

A second knock, this one louder than the first. Michael opens his eyes, pulls out the earbuds as he asks, "Who is it?"

"Me."

"Come in."

Kennedy enters wearing a T-shirt and panties. "Hey," she says.

"Hey." Michael stretches, soapy limbs rising out of the water like a breaching whale. "What time is it? I must have dozed off."

"A little after eleven. Can I join you?"

"Sure."

Kennedy slips out of her clothes as Michael eyes her. She steps in cautiously and slides down beneath the bubbles, letting the hot water engulf her as Michael opens his legs so she can fit between them. They face each other as Kennedy leans back, closing her eyes.

"This feels good."

"Doesn't it?" Michael's foot rubs against Kennedy's waist. "Zack get to sleep okay?"

"Yep. I read him a story, and he was knocked out before I reached the end."

"Oh, good. He's such a trip," Michael exclaims.

"Yes, he is. That boy keeps me sane." She opens her eyes to glance at her husband. "You and him— my two favorite men."

Michael smiles.

They are silent for a while, enjoying each other's company without the need to communicate. It's enough to just be near one another. Sometimes a light touch can signal more than words ever could.

Kennedy breaks the stillness first.

"Robin said some things today that got me thinking."

Michael opens his eyes again and stares at Kennedy, waiting for her to continue.

"Just wondering why this person is targeting me. Why the photos didn't go to your job."

"I don't know," Michael responds quietly.

"Any theories?"

"None that we haven't discussed already."

Kennedy processes what's been said. She drips water onto her chest, playing with the bubbles while forming the next set of questions in her mind.

"You and I have always been truthful with one another. That's one thing that I feel separates us from other couples. The way we are honest and truthful with each other. I trust you. You trust me. That's why we can lead the lifestyle that we do. Because we are honest with each other."

"I agree," Michael answers, not sure where this is heading.

"When we first began talking about acting out our fantasies, I was hesitant because I wasn't sure I could totally trust you. It wasn't anything you did, but I just never had trusted a man so completely. You showed me that I could—and you took me to this place where our trust was absolute. And thus I felt, for the first time in my life, that I could be myself, completely free, with you. And so, we've done things that other people only dream of."

"I know, baby. Nothing's changed."

Kennedy nods.

"When we began this lifestyle, we agreed to certain rules. Such as, neither one of us would ever have a sexual liaison without the other's permission. We agreed that we would always tell each other if we've met someone we want to sleep with, before we slept with that person."

"Right."

"We made this promise to each other to be truthful. To let each other know if our feelings ever changed."

"Kennedy—what are you trying to say to me?" Michael asks, sitting up.

"I'm not trying to say anything to you. I guess I'm wondering if you've been truthful with me. What I'm asking is, have you kept your promise to me?"

Michael stares at her.

"Where is this coming from? You have lunch with your best friend and suddenly you question my commitment to you?"

"Michael, I'm just asking."

"If I've been faithful to you? You know the answer to that."

"I guess I need to know whether I can still trust you," she says.

Michael shakes his head.

"Unbelievable." Michael glares at her for a moment. "What did Robin say to you, exactly? Oh, let me guess. She doesn't trust me, because she can't trust any man after hers fucked her over so badly she thinks every last one of us is a dog. Right?"

Kennedy remains silent.

"Yeah, that's it. Her man was dogging her out for *years*, fucking anything with tits and an ass while Robin remained oblivious, thinking she had this charmed life. But then one day her whole world crashed and burned. She learned the truth, found out her entire universe was one big fat lie. Now she is a bitter woman, and every man is a dog. Every man, including the one you're married to.

"Let me tell you about my world," Michael continues, his stare drilling itself into Kennedy. "I have a beautiful wife who adores me. I am a father to an incredible little boy. My job is great. We've got this really nice home. My sex life is to die for. I consider myself one of the luckiest men in the world. Our lifestyle is incredible. So why would I go behind your back? There is no need. I've always been upfront about what I want. I've always been honest about my desires. Why? Because there is no need to lie. No reason to be deceitful. I know plenty of men who do it, running around, lying to the ones they love, creating these elaborate schemes so that they can creep on the side. But I don't have to do that. I tell you what I want. What I'm thinking. I've always done that. Those are the rules—the rules you and I agreed to."

"I remember."

"Your friend, Robin? Sorry to say, but she's fucked

up. You? You're going through a really hard time, and I understand you don't trust anyone. But don't stop trusting me. Don't question what we have. Because that's the absolute wrong thing to do. You know me. I'm your husband. I'm Michael. I'm one of the good guys."

Michael stands, letting the soapsuds cascade down his body. Kennedy reaches out for his hand, but he grabs a towel instead, wrapping it around his waist.

"Where are you going?" she asks. "I want to finish this."

"I think we're done," he replies, closing the door quietly behind him.

Chapter 31

The next morning, Joe Goodman is at it bright and early.

His first order of business is to call one of his colleagues, Chandran Nadar.

Chandran answers on the second ring.

"Nadar here."

"Chan the man! It's Joe Goodman from the Fifth District."

"Hey, Joe. Long time no hear."

"I know. Busy and shit, you know how it is."

"Yes, I do. What can I do for you?"

"Chan, I need your expertise. Got this case I'm working on and was wondering if you could spare a little time."

Chandran also works for the Metropolitan Police Department: The Investigative Services Bureau, Office of the Superintendent of Detectives, Operations Section, which handles financial and computer crimes, among other things. Simply put, Chandran is a computer geek, except he doesn't wear a pocket protector, dresses conservatively when not in uniform, and has little to no facial hair.

"What do you have for me, Joe?"

Joe explains. "E-mail sent from unknown sources, incriminating photographs attached, which were accessed from an external drive of a desktop computer. No forced entry to the house. Trying to figure how they did it, and if there are any forensic clues on the computer, hard drives, or wireless network that we can use to catch the bad guy."

"How do you know it's a guy?" Nadar responds.

Joe laughs.

"You got time today if I can arrange a site visit?"

"For you, Joe? Yes," Chandran says.

"Chan, my man!"

"Kennedy, it's Joe."

"Hi, Joe."

"How are you? Anything new?"

Kennedy is at the kitchen table, on her second cup of coffee of the morning. Her laptop is open as she works on something for Jackson Blair and the association. She was readying to check in with Daniel when her cell rang.

"Nothing new. No new e-mail messages or phone calls, if that's what you mean," she says.

"Good. That's good news," Joe says.

"I guess."

"It is. Listen. I've got a guy that I want to bring over to check out your computer and Wi-Fi network. Are you around today?"

"What do you mean, check out?"

"Well, I want to see if there are any clues as to how these photographs were accessed, and to see if there are any indications that either your network or computer has been compromised."

"Is that necessary?" she asks.

"If we want to catch this guy," Joe says, and then

thinks about Chan's comment, "or gal, we need to do a thorough investigation. I know you're not keen on anyone looking at that hard drive, but it can't be helped."

Kennedy sighs. "Joe, can you keep the number of folks who . . . are involved down to a bare minimum? This is embarrassing without having to open myself up *again* to the world."

"I understand, and yes, I will. You have my word."

"Thank you. Yes, I'm available today. Preferably during the day before my son and husband get home." Kennedy immediately regretted the choice of words—she doesn't want Joe to misunderstand what she is saying. Doesn't want to lead him on. "I didn't mean it that way, Joe. What I meant was—"

"I know what you meant. You don't have to explain."

She takes a breath and exhales audibly.

"Thanks."

"One more thing," Joe adds. "I'll begin contacting those . . . individuals on your list that you have provided contact info for. For the others, and as I recall, close to half of the names don't have any contact information listed, I'm going to need you to put together some details—where you or your husband met them, dates, any physical characteristics if you don't have photos of them. A long shot, I know, but we need to pursue all leads. I believe one of the folks on the list is responsible for this—or someone close to them. Okay?"

Kennedy considers his words.

"Yes, I'll get to work on that."

"Good. I'll see you later on today."

The line goes dead as Kennedy shakes her head sullenly.

* * *

"Hi, Momma."

"Michael! Lord, it's so good to hear your voice. Your father and I thought you dropped off the face of the earth!"

"No, Momma, I'm still kicking."

Michael is in his office, door closed, feet up on his desk as he stares out the window. His office looks out onto Constitution Avenue. The Mall lies directly in front of him, the Museum of American History to his left, the Washington Monument to his right. Not a bad view.

"How is my grandson? Oh my goodness, I miss my baby!"

"He's fine, Momma. Growing like a weed. You wouldn't recognize him."

"And Kennedy? How's my daughter-in-law? You ain't driving her crazy, are you?"

Michael smiles.

"No, Momma. I am not driving her crazy. Kennedy's all right. She's had a bit of misfortune lately."

Michael's mother sucks in a breath. "Oh my Lord, is everything all right?"

Michael explains, leaving out the gory details. His mother is suitably concerned. She asks a lot of questions, which Michael expertly deflects.

"I was thinking about coming up, Momma," Michael says, revealing the true purpose for his call.

"Oh my, you know your father and I would just love to have all of you. I miss my baby so much. All of you—I miss all of you."

"I know you do, Momma. We miss you, too. Per-haps," he says, pausing to find the right words, "perhaps Zack and I could pop up for a long weekend."

It takes Michael's mother only seconds to process what her son has just said.

"You mean Kennedy's not coming?"

"I don't know, Momma. Maybe. Maybe not. A lot going on, you know?"

"Oh Lord," she responds. "Let me put your father on. Talk some sense into this boy, would you, Roland?"

Michael rolls his eyes as he waits for his father to come on the line.

Chapter 32

Joe and Kennedy stand behind Chandran Nadar.

He is sitting in front of the desktop computer in the den. Kennedy is a bundle of nerves. She tries without success to squelch the fidgeting that has taken over. Joe notices and puts a hand on her shoulder.

"Mrs. Handley," Chandran says, "what I am attempting to do is see if any traces of remote activity were logged to this computer." He glances back and witnesses the look of incomprehension on Kennedy's face. He smiles. "In other words, we suspect that someone came in via the Internet and then through your wireless network and gained access to the photos here," he says, pointing to the now powered-on external drive.

"And you suspect this because?" she asks.

"Well, according to your statements to Detective Goodman here, the photographs in question have not been shared with anyone. Correct?"

"That's true—as far as we know."

"Okay, fine."

Chandran has a laptop with him. He boots it up and reaches into his bag, pulling out a thick, worn

CD case. He flips it open and finds the CD-ROM he is searching for.

"I have a program that will check your firewall logs and those of your router. We should be able to get an IP address and footprint data that the perp left. At least, that's the plan. . . ."

"Okay," Kennedy answers.

"I need your permission to take the external drive with me. I would like to run some tests on it, and those tests I can only accomplish from my lab," Chandran says.

Kennedy's shoulders sag as she glances over at Joe. He nods reassuringly to her.

"Chan, I've assured Mrs. Handley that the handling and viewing of this drive and its contents will be kept to an absolute minimum. There are revealing photos on that drive," says Joe.

"Of course," Chandran remarks. "Mrs. Handley, you have my personal assurances. No one but myself and Detective Goodman will handle this drive or view its contents."

"Thank you."

Kennedy looks as if she's going to be sick.

"Would you excuse me?" she says.

"Of course. One more thing. What is the password to the drive?"

"It's Celestial."

Joe and Chan watch her go. Chan then returns his attention to the desktop computer. His fingers race across the keyboard, opening an Explorer window. Using the mouse, he double-clicks on the F: drive to display its contents. The front of the drive pulses green. Moments later, Chan is perusing the files and subdirectories. Joe glances toward the den opening, feeling his trepidation spike. This is the moment he's been waiting for, and he feels guilt, knowing that, as an engaged man, he should not be focused on thoughts of his ex with another woman. But he can't help it. Kennedy is a beautiful woman. She is sexy, and it's been a long, long time since he's seen her nude.

Chan's fingers on the keyboard bring him back to the desktop.

Joe's glance goes stealthily to the den opening again before panning back to the computer screen. He is unprepared for what he sees next.

There she is!

Kennedy in the throes of lovemaking with another woman.

Chan clicks on another photo.

Kennedy, her loveliness displayed in full color and resolution.

And another.

And another.

And so on. . . .

Chan silently meets the eyes of the detective behind him.

He closes the Explorer window an instant later.

Continues with his work, gathering evidence.

It is only then that Joe can find his breath again.

Chapter 33

Later on, Joe is at his desk in the Fifth District Station located on Bladensburg Road in Northeast D.C.

He is staring at the list of names, deep in thought.

Sixteen names.

Sixteen liaisons.

Eleven locations.

Six international.

He can't keep the images from the hard drive from peeking into his psyche. He has to force himself to concentrate.

But it's difficult.

He seems to see her and *them* every other moment. And it's not a good thing.

Sixteen liaisons.

Out of sixteen names, six of them have some form of contact info: e-mail, phone, address.

The others—names, vague descriptions—perhaps a photo. That's it. Not much to go on.

Joe concentrates on the names. *Start with the ones you can contact.*

Natalie—Jamaica.

Jayla—Philly.

Makayla—New York.

Chloe—London.

Carrie—Baltimore.

Lacy—Jamaica.

Joe picks up the phone and dials the first one on the list.

"Hello?" Female voice.

"May I speak to Natalie?"

The number he's dialed begins with 858. San Diego, CA.

"This number belongs to someone else. It's no longer Natalie's cell phone."

"My name is Joe Goodman. I'm a detective with the Metropolitan—"

"This ain't her number!"

The line goes dead.

Joe stares at the phone, then hangs up. He makes a notation next to Natalie's name. Picks up the phone again. Dials the second number.

"Hello?" a female voice says after five rings.

"Hi, may I speak to Jayla?" Joe asks.

"Who's calling?" she asks.

Joe's heart rate increases.

"My name is Joe Goodman. Is this Jayla?"

"I'm at work. What is this concerning?" she says.

"Ma'am, I am a detective with the Metropolitan Police Department in Washington, D.C. If at all possible, I'd like to ask you a few questions. Would that be all right?"

Joe figures he'll play this nice and slow. All gentlemanly. No need to get nasty, unless there isn't co-operation.

"I'm at work, I said. Am I in trouble?"

Joe can hear the apprehension rise.

"I understand, ma'am, and no, you're not in trouble. Is there someplace quiet you can talk? I can call you back in a few minutes, but I do need to ask some questions. It won't take long."

"Hold on then. Let me walk to a conference room."

"Sure."

It takes her a minute to come back on the line.

"I'm here."

"Great, thank you. Do you know a couple by the name of Michael and Kennedy Handley?" Joe asks.

There is a long, breathless silence.

"I don't think so? Should I?" she asks hesitantly.

"You met them at a restaurant/lounge called Tangerine on Market Street in downtown Philadelphia several years ago. You were intimate with them."

Prolonged silence.

"What does this have to do with me?"

"Have you had any recent contact with them? Phone, e-mail, in person, what have you?"

"No, I haven't," Jayla says. "I hooked up with them that one time. That was like two and a half years ago."

"Okay. They sent you photographs of your encounter, did they not?" Joe asks.

He swears he can hear her swallow. Hard.

"Yes."

"And do you still have those photos in your possession?"

This time Jayla answers without pause.

"No, I deleted them off my computer the very same night. Didn't trust my—" She stops in mid-sentence before continuing. "You know. I didn't want to leave something like that around on my PC."

"I see," Joe responds. "Ma'am, are you sure that no one other than you ever saw those photographs? Is it possible that perhaps someone you were dating at the time could have gotten hold of them and forwarded them on to someone else?"

Silence.

"Ma'am? Jayla?"

"Yes, I'm here. I'm thinking."

"Were you in a relationship at the time that you met the Handleys?"

Jayla exhales a breath.

"I was in a relationship, yes. But I doubt very strongly anyone found those pictures. If someone had, I would have known about it, trust me."

"Husband?"

"An extremely jealous partner."

"I'm going to need his name, ma'am."

Pause.

"It's a she. And trust me, she didn't see those photos."

Joe asks, "How can you be so sure?"

Jayla's answer is succinct. " 'Cause if she had, I wouldn't be here talking to you now."

Michael walks to the lobby, a look of puzzlement adorning his normally complacent face. He spies his visitor at the security desk, name tag already affixed to his lapel. Michael waves his badge to the guard and comes face-to-face with his wife's ex, Joe the detective.

Joe nods his way, but neither reaches out to shake hands.

"My secretary said you needed to see me?" Michael says without preamble.

"Yeah. I was in the neighborhood and thought we could chat. You got a moment?"

Michael stares at him.

"Concerning?"

"I think you know," Joe responds.

"You signed in already, I see."

"Yeah. Decided to keep it low profile and not flash the shield," Joe says. Then adds, "For your sake."

Michael doesn't know whether to say "Thank you" or "Fuck you." So he says neither.

"We can talk in my office." He leads the way. On the elevator ride up they are silent. Both are considering the other's thoughts. Ironically, they're thinking about the same thing.

The photographs on the hard drive.

The doors open, and Michael leads Joe to his office. Once inside he closes the door and takes a seat behind his desk, gesturing for Joe to sit.

"Nice view," Joe says once he's seated.

"So, this isn't a social call," Michael declares.

"No, it's not. I thought it was time for you and me to speak. About what's going down."

"Okay."

"Tell me, Michael, what's your take on this?" Joe asks, spreading his hands wide.

Michael eyes him.

"Not sure what you mean. It's a fucked-up situation. Kennedy is really affected by what has transpired. I'm sure you know that."

"Yeah. Any idea who or why someone is targeting you guys?"

"None."

Joe's stare burns into Michael's.

"You sure?"

"Yeah, *Detective.* I am."

"Let me ask you this man to man—and you have my word that whatever is said here will be kept between you and me. Any problems at home that I should know about?"

"No. No problems."

"Have you stepped out on your wife? Perhaps a little something or someone on the side?"

"You know what, Joe? I resent these questions. And for the record, it's none of your fucking business."

"Michael, come on, man, I'm asking as a detective. Your wife asked me to investigate this. That's what I'm doing."

Michael glares at him.

"You come in here like we're buddies and shit, but we're not. So watch what you say to me, okay?"

Joe spreads his hands in the air.

"Okay. I apologize for the way I said it. But I'm afraid the question remains. Are you having an affair?"

"No, Joe. I am not."

"You sure?"

"Yeah, Joe, I'm sure."

"Not now, not in the recent past?"

"Joe—for the record, I have never stepped out on my wife. Satisfied?"

Joe switches gears.

"Tell me about these liaisons. How did you meet these women?"

"Nightclubs, bars and restaurants, strip clubs. You name it. Most of the time they were staying at the same resort we were. It wasn't that difficult, especially when you saw the same woman over the course of several days in the pool, at the beach, or in the restaurant."

Joe digests what Michael has told him.

"Okay. Were all of these encounters with women or were there ever men involved?"

"There was another guy one time, but Kennedy wasn't into it," Michael responds.

Joe muses, *How nice for you!*

"Right. Were most of these women single?"

"Yes."

"But not all of them?"

"No, not all."

Joe waits for him to continue.

"Some were with their spouses or partners."

Joe asks, "And these men were okay with their wives or girlfriends going with you?"

"Look. We're not the first people to experience a threesome. Plenty of couples do it. You'd be surprised what people do when they are out of the country on vacation."

"Okay. Let me ask you this. Any jealousy that you saw? Like, some guy is pissed because his woman is getting it on with you guys and he's left out in the cold?"

Michael shakes his head.

"No, we didn't witness any of that. If we did, we stayed clear of the woman. Moved on to someone else." Michael sits back, folding his arms.

Joe nods slowly.

"You make it sound easy," he says.

Michael shrugs.

"It is what it is. My wife is a very sensual woman. And other women pick up on that. It's not that difficult when they're in the presence of unfettered sensuality. It's like a drug."

Michael isn't boasting. He's simply telling it like it is.

Joe merely nods.

And wishes it had been like that when Kennedy was married to him.

Chapter 34

The 727 glides down smoothly onto the glistening tarmac of Hartsfield-Jackson Atlanta International Airport. It's nine thirty-five in the morning as Damian grabs his carry-on and deplanes with the rest of the passengers.

His first order of business is to collect his bags from baggage claim. That is completed without incident. Next he rents a full-size car from Hertz, a Chevy Impala. He uses his business Amex card, and is on the shuttle to the lot with keys in hand in under twenty-five minutes.

Once in his rental vehicle, bags and carry-on sequestered in the trunk, he exits the lot and takes 85 North. Not long thereafter Damian is broaching downtown Atlanta. A few minutes later he steers into a McDonald's and cuts the engine.

He pulls out his Virgin Mobile cell phone that has remained powered off since yesterday, turns it on, and waits patiently for a signal before dialing. It takes five rings before someone answers.

"Yeah?"

"Let me speak to Tyrone. This is Mr. C," Damian says.

"Who?"

Damian sighs.

"Tyrone. This is Mr. C. Met you at the Pink Pony strip club. Remember?"

It takes Tyrone a second to connect the dots. "Mr. C! Yeah, how you doing?"

"I'm well, Tyrone. Remember our business arrangement, Tyrone? Well, today's the day. I'm here now. . . ."

Tyrone takes another second before responding.

"Yeah, okay. Cool. Today?"

"Like now, Tyrone. I need you to get over to the bank. The amount you will be withdrawing is six thousand. Get it in all hundreds. That's sixty hundreds, Tyrone. Make sure you count it and have them put it in an envelope. Keep your cell on. When you exit the bank, I'll be in a car down the street. You'll receive a call from me. As we discussed, please don't do anything stupid, because I'll be watching." Damian is pressed to keep his voice under control. His head is beginning to throb and he wants to scream at the dumb motherfucker, but that would only scare him more than he probably already is. Necessary evil, dealing with dumb shits like Tyrone.

"No problem. Six G's. All in hundreds, right? You'll call me once I'm outside," Tyrone responds, much to Damian's wonderment.

"That's right, Tyrone. Very good. Now, don't forget your license—you'll need ID to make a withdrawal."

"Got it, Mr. C," Tyrone says, much more enthusiastically than when the call began.

"I'll cut you a solid G for today's gig. Not bad for ten minute's worth of work."

He can imagine Tyrone's enormous grin.

"Tyrone, I knew you and I could do business together. That's why I'm gonna throw more work your way. You're gonna make some serious cheddar, working with me."

"That's what I'm talking about," Tyrone exclaims.

Damian shakes his head while ending the call.

He spots him easily thirty minutes later.

Baggy jeans, work boots, a triple-XL dark-colored hoodie, and matching cap. Not exactly the kind of duds he'd pick for the job, but damn, he can't school everyone.

Damian considers calling him on the cell, telling Tyrone he's got him in his sights, just in case he decides to be stupid this morning, but then thinks better of it.

His Impala is parked in a covered garage a block away. Damian is dressed casually, sitting on a bench in a triangular patch of parkland that overlooks the bank. He's wearing a baseball cap and shades, not that he really needs to be incognito here. No one, save for Tyrone and one other person, has seen his face.

Damian met Tyrone a month ago. He had labored over how to pull it off, how to achieve his objective without drawing undue attention to himself. The problem was one of traceability. In this day and age, there is always a trail that can be followed back to you.

Unless you are smart.

Damian knew what he had to do. So he spent a few nights at the Pink Pony in northeast Atlanta. Came there with a fresh roll of bills, ready to befriend someone. And he wasn't referring to the strippers.

It wasn't that hard.

He took a seat close to the dancers' stage—an elevated runway sort of thingy—and proceeded to throw a few bills their way. Thirty minutes later he was buying himself a lap dance. Fifteen minutes after that, Damian was leaning over to the brutha a few seats down, talking about the phat ass on the stripper who worked the pole. They roared with laughter as they gave each other dap. Pretty soon, he was buying a round of lap dances for himself and his newfound friend.

The first two that he befriended, however, weren't right. First guy didn't have a job, therefore a bank account.

That was out.

Second guy just didn't feel right. Would have asked too many questions. Would not have been accessible when Damian came to call.

Not the case with Tyrone.

Tyrone was just right.

By the end of the third night, Tyrone was all his.

Damian had stumbled onto someone who was exactly what he was looking for.

Young, not too swift in the head, with a job delivering furniture for a local store. Most importantly, he had a bank account and a driver's license, and he didn't ask a whole lot of questions, because he was blinded by the prospect of quick, cold cash.

Yeah, Tyrone was perfect.

Damian watches him enter the bank on Peachtree. He checks his watch. Soon he'll be done with this fool and on to the other location.

Same deal, just a different friend.

Seventeen minutes later, Tyrone emerges into

the bright sunlight. He's holding an envelope under his arm as he glances both ways.

Damian places his cell to his ear.

"Tyrone, my man!"

"Mr. C."

"Everything go okay?" he asks.

"Smooth as silk, Mr. C."

"You're the man, Tyrone. Listen, I'm parked in a garage a block away. Head to your right and at the corner hang a right. It's halfway up the street on your right-hand side. I'm heading that way, too. I'm behind you, but don't turn around. I'll meet you at the corner and greet you. Just act natural, and we can walk together to my car."

"Okay, Mr. C."

Damian can detect a bit of apprehension that has crept into Tyrone's voice.

"You okay, Tyrone?" Damian asks.

"Yeah. I got nothing to worry about, right, Mr. C? Like a bullet in the back of the neck or something?"

Nervous laughter, but Damian knows he's serious as prostate cancer.

"Tyrone," he says while crossing the street, taking up position forty yards behind him. "I'm offended you'd think me capable of something like that. You and I are business partners. How would it look if I offed my own partner? Besides, I'm not a violent man. You've been watching too many DVDs."

"Okay, Mr. C. Just checking," Tyrone replies, but there's still an edge to his voice.

"I'll be there in a moment. Just keep walking. You're doing great."

Damian hangs up the phone and pockets it in his jacket. He reaches the corner a moment later, as Tyrone turns right.

"Tyrone!" he exclaims.

Tyrone stops and turns. Grins.

"Mr. C! What up?"

They greet each other quickly, then move on to the garage. Damian is making small talk—how's work? You been back to the Pony lately? Yeah, they got some fine-ass bitches working that spot, don't they?

Tyrone follows Damian as he ignores the elevator and instead takes the stairs. They head up. In the stairwell between the third and fourth level Damian pauses and holds up a hand. Tyrone stops. Together they listen for a sound. Nothing. Damian turns to Tyrone and smiles.

"You done good, Tyrone."

He holds out his outstretched hand. Tyrone turns over the thick envelope. Damian opens it, checks the contents, pulling out the sheaf of bills partway. He runs his thumb over them as if they were a deck of cards. Satisfied, he pushes the bills back down into the envelope, hefting the thing in his hand. He stares at the envelope for a moment, eyeing Tyrone before handing it back to him.

"This is for you."

Tyrone's eyes practically bug out. He produces a toothy smile.

"Are you serious?"

Damian nods.

"You want me to hold this for you?" he asks cautiously.

"Consider this an investment. I'm investing in you, Tyrone. I hope to do more business with you."

Damian lays his hand on Tyrone's shoulder for a moment before glancing upward. "Now, I've got to be going. I've got another appointment that I need to keep, or I'd drop you off—you understand, don't you?"

"No problem, Mr. C."

"Good."

Damian makes a fist and gives Tyrone dap.

"Keep that cell close—you'll be hearing from me soon," he says.

Damian heads up to the fourth level as Tyrone makes his way back down. He stops at the door, waiting until he can no longer hear Tyrone's footfalls before heading to the fifth level. He finds his rental car quickly and climbs inside. Starting the engine, Damian puts the vehicle in gear.

As he steers toward the exit below, Damian considers the job.

It went as planned.

He could have had Tyrone follow him to the rental and exchanged the money inside. But then Tyrone would have seen the car and could have ID'd the plate later.

No good.

This way, all he has is a description of the man and a phone number from a pay-as-you-go cell.

Neither of which will get him very far.

Later on that day, after successfully completing the second job, Damian pulls into a Wendy's parking lot. He heads for the men's room and once inside makes sure he is alone.

Damian reaches for his cell.

Without preamble he drops the phone to the tile floor, stepping on it hard with the heel of his boot.

Twice.

Damian picks up the crushed pieces of plastic and metal and casually tosses them into a trash receptacle by the door.

He washes his hands, checking himself in the mirror before exiting.

A Number Five with a Sprite to go, and then it's back to the Impala for the long drive home.

His head is throbbing, yet he's grinning.

All in a day's work, he muses.

Chapter 35

Kennedy spends the morning with Daniel in Azela Coffee Shop on Eighteenth Street. She had swung by the office to pick him up, but hadn't gone inside for fear that Jackson Blair would be cross with her. They chose Azela because it wasn't overcrowded, as Tryst inevitably would be, even at this time of morning. They chat for a few minutes before getting down to business.

Daniel has nothing new to report. The staff is treating Kennedy as if she is off on vacation. No one mentions the e-mail or the photos. It is almost as if the incident had never occurred.

They drink herbal tea as they work on a number of projects. By two in the afternoon, they pack up their legal pads, laptops, and BlackBerrys, and head to the car. She drops him back off at the association and then drives home.

The message light on her cordless phone is blinking when she arrives. Kennedy drops her keys and BlackBerry on the counter and picks up the receiver to listen to the message. As she's waiting, she opens her laptop and boots it up.

Call received an hour and ten minutes ago from an unknown number.

A feminine voice.

"Hey, you. I know you're tied up in meetings for most of today, but I just wanted to tell you, I've been unable to get out of my mind what you did to me last night. Oh my God, you always know what I need, but last night? Last night you outdid yourself! Seriously, the feeling was amazing! I can't even describe it, other than to say I came so hard I was practically numb afterward. And no, I am not complaining. You are truly wonderful. I love you so much. Tonight, I'm returning the favor. Ciao bella."

Kennedy's breath is arrested.

She replays the message, listening carefully to the words and the way they are enunciated. When it is done, she saves the message then calls up the other saved messages from her phone. She finds the one she is looking for—an unknown voice mail from a female that came in over a week ago. She replays it, noting that the voices are indeed the same.

Same woman.

Unknown number for both.

Kennedy hangs up the phone.

She sighs heavily.

I need to let Joe know about this, she tells herself.

Should I call him now?

Or Michael first?

Instead, she logs in to her computer, while checking her watch.

Call Michael first, and let him know another voice mail came in. Then call Joe.

Okay.

In a minute.

Kennedy brings up e-mail. Quickly scans her in-box. Nothing out of the ordinary. A bunch of spam. Penis enlargements, offers for Viagra. A notification that her Amex bill is now due.

Today is payday.

Shit!

Kennedy almost forgot, seeing how she's not at work. She recalls that she needs to pay some bills by the end of the week.

She opens a fresh browser window and types the URL to her bank. Logs in while contemplating the calls she needs to make. She's procrastinating and knows it.

Over the last few days her heart rate had actually calmed itself down.

No new messages.

Joe has been working the case.

Michael and her—while things were strained, they were still good.

She'd been keeping busy, focusing on work.

But now this.

Kennedy's mind is whirling.

All of a sudden it's back. The threatening e-mails, the incriminating photos, the pain and humiliation.

Now—another voice mail. Someone stalking them—and they are not letting up.

Kennedy suddenly notices something strange.

She directs her attention to the screen in front of her.

She's staring at the online banking page. Down the left side is a column of menus: Account Information, Transfers, Bill Payments, etc. She had clicked, as she does each time she logs in, Account Information to see her total balances—checking and savings.

Her check is directly deposited into this checking account—their joint checking. Kennedy pays the bills from here. A portion of their checks is transferred each month into savings.

She stares now at the balances.

Checking: $5,372.57.

Savings: $622.08.

Suddenly her veins go cold.

That can't be right.

She clicks on checking. Her check had posted last night, as it should. She moves to savings.

A balance of $622.08.

Wire transfer of $12,000 three days ago.

Wire transfer?

Twelve thousand dollars?

Their entire savings transferred?

Kennedy lets out a low moan while reaching for the phone.

Chapter 36

She speaks without preface.

"Please tell me you haven't done something with our savings!"

Kennedy's voice is near frenzy. Michael's response is equally frantic.

"What are you talking about? I haven't touched our savings account."

"Oh God!" she wails.

"Kennedy? What happened?"

"Twelve thousand in savings. Gone. Wired out three days ago. I gotta get to the bank!"

The line goes dead.

"Kennedy? Kennedy, WAIT!"

He stares incredulously at the lifeless phone. He speed-dials his wife, but gets the beep in the midst of ringing that signals she's on a call. He leaves a quick message.

"I'm leaving the office now. Call me!"

Michael grabs his jacket and makes it to the hallway in three steps, calling out to his assistant as he heads the opposite way toward the bank of elevators. "Something's come up. I've got to leave, but

I'll be cellular." She gives him a vacant stare, but Michael isn't focused on her look.

Michael's wondering who snatched their savings.

And how.

The afternoon is a blur.

Kennedy and Michael are at the bank for over an hour, screaming at the befuddled bank manager as tellers and customers look on in muted disbelief.

Joe arrives and takes over, declaring it a crime scene. He ushers Michael and Kennedy outside because their nerves are shot and there is nothing left for them to do here.

The manager, a wiry white woman with bleached hair and an imported accent, has no answers.

Someone with appropriate authorization issued a wire transfer three days ago via the Internet. They possessed the proper ID and password, as that's the only way they could log into the bank's website and initiate the transfer.

Receiving banks: Two separate banks located in Atlanta, Georgia.

Six thousand dollars wired to each account.

Name of the recipient(s): Unknown.

Joe is obtaining a warrant, but it may be several days before they know anything definitive. It's out of his jurisdiction. Since the FBI will be getting involved, getting cooperation may be a problem. He's going to speak to his captain, see what can be done to make sure he stays in the loop. He's thinking of flying down to Atlanta to serve the warrants, assuming the department will allow it.

Michael and Kennedy are like zombies. They want to know one thing: What will be done concerning their money? The bank manager is noncommittal. It's a criminal matter now. It depends on what is found in Atlanta.

Michael directs the bank to take appropriate actions to safeguard what's left in their checking account.

Kennedy goes one step further.

She clears out her checking and savings.

Everything that's left.

Demands the balance in cash.

Then Michael takes his exhausted wife home.

Chapter 37

What Kennedy needs the most right now is rest.

Michael calls in a favor with a Howard University buddy turned physician. He prescribes Kennedy a tranquilizer and sedative.

Michael turns off her BlackBerry (a feat in and of itself, but she's much too exhausted to put up a fight) and leaves her on the couch while he goes to pick up Zack.

When father and son return a half hour later, she's out cold.

Michael makes a few decisions and some phone calls.

He calls his parents, his job, and consults with a close friend. He tells his son over Chinese food that they are all going away for a long weekend, then proceeds to pack for the three of them.

He takes enough clothes for four days.

Sends an e-mail to Zack's teacher to advise her of his impending absence.

Has a brief conversation with Joe to alert him that he's taking his family out of town. He asks that Kennedy not be disturbed, that any new developments be funneled through him.

Then he piles his son, his sedated wife, and their bags into the Range Rover.

At a little after eight PM, Michael steers his family out of the District of Columbia and onto 95 North for the long drive ahead of them.

The trip to Ithaca, a quaint little town in upstate New York where his parents reside, takes a good seven to nine hours. Michael is tired, but he is determined to drive straight through the night, stopping only when his family needs him to.

Michael is taking his family back home.

Where they can relax and be safe from harm.

Kennedy opens her eyes around nine the next morning.

She sits up, disoriented, glancing around frantically for three to four seconds before she recognizes her surroundings.

She finds herself in a good-sized guest room in the midst of a king-sized bed, high off the floor. The down comforter is weighty; the oversized pillows perfect. Directly across from the bed is an old oak chest that sits between two windows. Dark wooden shutters keep out the morning light, but as Kennedy's feet touch the cold wooden floor, she crosses the space quickly to the windows on the balls of her feet, flinging open the shutters and letting in the brightness of a new day. Snow covers the ground. There's a tall red barn off to her right. Behind that is a chest-high fence made of wood that runs parallel to the barn and contains thirty cattle. She watches them for a moment, observing the small brown calves nuzzling against their mothers as their breath is expelled from wet snouts.

Michael is in the kitchen downstairs frying up

bacon and percolating coffee. Kennedy arrives in a terry-cloth bathrobe, with thick pink socks on her feet. Michael kisses her forehead and smiles.

"Where . . . where is Zack?" she asks uncertainly.

Michael grins.

"He's with Nana and Pop Pop. They've taken him to Rochester. They had some errands to run and people to visit. I told them to go ahead without us. Figured you needed your peace and quiet."

Kennedy blinks. Michael pours her a hot cup of coffee. "When did we get here? I don't recall . . ."

"You were out of it last night, thanks to the medication. We drove through the night. Got in around three-thirty AM."

"I slept the entire time?" she asks, eyes wide.

"Yes. To say you were exhausted is an understatement."

Kennedy nods. She sips at her coffee.

"I'm making omelets with ham and cheese. Got some fried onions that I'll throw in as well." He hands her a slice of just-cooked bacon. She bites into it.

"I'm ravenous," she says after swallowing the pork.

"I know, baby. I got you covered."

"Thank you, Michael." Kennedy puts her arms around her husband's neck and kisses him on the mouth. His arms go around her waist as he returns the passion.

"After breakfast I want you to take a hot bath or a shower and then just relax. There's nothing to do for the next few days but chill and enjoy your family. Okay?"

Kennedy nods silently. She sighs, remembering everything that has transpired lately.

"Any word from Joe? The bank?" she asks cautiously.

Michael reaches out to stroke her shoulder.

"Do me a favor and try to give that a rest, at least for a day or two. I know it's hard, but Joe is on the case. There's nothing more we can do. When Joe learns something, he'll call. He knows we're here."

Kennedy nods once.

"Okay."

"I put in a call to a CPA-slash-attorney I know. He's going to check into the bank incident and let me know what our options are. But basically he said not to worry. The law is on our side."

Kennedy stares at Michael for a moment, processing his words.

"Love you," she responds plainly.

"Love you, too, Kennedy. And I will not allow this guy, whoever he is, to destroy our family. I simply won't allow it."

And with that, Michael returns to the task at hand.

Nourishing his woman.

After a scrumptious breakfast, Kennedy takes a long, hot shower. She dresses afterward and joins Michael outside, where he is splitting logs around back. A light snow is coming down, but the temperature feels nice. She is warm, dressed in layers and the L. L. Bean goose-down parka that Michael brought from home. Kennedy helps by stacking the freshly split logs against the back of the house. The work is invigorating, and she finds that she quickly forgets their troubles out here on eleven acres of farmland that has been in the family for generations, where the air is crisp and clear.

They make their way over to the barn next, where

Michael grabs two large bags of chow and slits the opening with a serrated knife, dropping the food into a six-foot-long plastic trough. Then, while Kennedy waits behind a steel fence, Michael trots to the back of the barn over hardened mud and opens the back gates, stepping aside as the cattle rush in, eager for a spot at the trough. They push and shove one another as Michael and Kennedy look on in earnest, feeling sorry for the calves, who are simply too small to maneuver their way around the larger animals to the trough.

Five minutes later, the chow is gone. Michael and Kennedy leave the animals to mill about the barn entrance, their breath misting in the morning air, wondering when the next feeding time will occur.

They make their way back inside, kicking off the packed snow from the bottoms of their boots in the rustic hallway.

Michael prepares a crackling fire in a stone fireplace in the great room. They sit in front of it for a while, silently enjoying the warmth and the way the flames dance, coming alive. They each focus on the light and its movement, deep in the solitude of their own thoughts.

Kennedy is hypnotized by the fire. She doesn't see Michael get up or feel him kneel behind her. Silently, he peels off all her clothes. And she puts up no fight.

She lies on top of the throw rug facing the raised hearth, her nipples distended not because of the air but due to her husband's erotic touch. Michael undresses himself as his wife watches wordlessly. When he is fully nude, he mounts her quietly.

Michael kisses his wife passionately, first on the

mouth, then leaving a trail of kisses that begins at the nape of her neck and follows a line down to her waiting tender breasts.

Kennedy can feel his manhood on her thigh. It is fully hard, and when he shifts his body to reach her other nipple with his tongue, she reaches for him, positioning the head against her moist lips, rubbing herself with him, feeling her clit pulse with pleasure as he drives against her folds, before guiding him inside her.

She is already wet, but Michael takes things slow, pushing himself in unhurriedly, expanding her insides as he goes, taking his time, in no rush, enjoying the feeling, this connection with his wife, the two of them joined together in this sensual way, Kennedy placing her hands on his well-sculpted ass and pulling him into her.

When he is fully inside, entombed like a caterpillar in its cocoon, Michael lifts his chest off hers while kissing her tenderly, staring into her eyes as he slowly, begins to pull out. The feeling is exquisite. The heat ripples over their bodies as Kennedy moans. When he is dangerously close to falling out of her, Michael stops, keeping the head of his cock breached at her opening, rotating his hips as he pushes back in, this time a bit more aggressively. He increases his tempo, placing his hands on the insides of her thighs and pulling her legs up and spreading them apart. He glances down; Kennedy is observing him fucking her, taking her with an urgency that she shares. She encourages him with movement in her hips; she meets his hurried thrusts, watching him slide in and out frantically, his engorged cock filling her up in an instant before pulling out, leaving her desperately wanting more. Michael takes his fingers and intertwines them with hers, pressing his pelvis down upon her body, his forehead against hers as their flesh slaps seductively together.

And then Kennedy is pushing him off, maneuvering onto all fours, glancing back, signaling him without words what she wants and needs next.

And Michael, without a sound, complies.

He positions himself behind her, hands on her ass as he thrusts deeply home.

Kennedy cries out, not from pain, but from intense delight.

The heat is blasting. Her face, neck, and breasts.

The heat between their legs is blinding.

They make love as if this is the last thing they will ever do.

Kennedy is moaning incessantly, her howls increasing to a crescendo as she comes, her entire body shuddering like a tsunami that thunders toward land.

Michael joins her moments later, crying out as if in excruciating pain, washing his seed lovingly into her cavern.

Moments later they are curled up on the throw rug, bodies still connected, Michael spooning Kennedy from behind, a thin blanket covering them as they drift off to sleep.

There they remain, the heat and light from the stone fireplace emanating over them like a surreal fog, for hours.

Chapter 38

"MOM-MEEEEEEEEE!" Zack yells as he enters the front door.

Kennedy jumps up. She had been sitting Indian style on the throw rug, the coffee table between her and her husband as they play Scrabble.

They are fully dressed again. Several more hours have passed since they were laid out naked and spent on the ground like a pair of impatient young lovers, their clothes strewn about them haphazardly as if caught in a jungle cyclone. The fire continues to roar and crackle with a fresh-split log feeding it.

Zack rushes in, his parka hood flapping against his thin neck as he collides with his mother. They hug while she kisses the top of his head.

"How's my big boy? God, I missed you!" she exclaims.

"Missed you too, Mommy," Zack retorts, hugging her tighter as he glances around the room as if searching for something.

"What am I, chopped liver?" Michael muses.

"Hi, Dad!" Zack says before switching gears. "Nana says she's going to play Monopoly with me, and she says you can play, too, Dad, if you promise not to cheat." He giggles, then continues, "Pop Pop told me he's gonna let me drive the tractor, right, Pop Pop?"

Michael's father, Roland Handley, is a good-looking man of seventy-five. He's wearing tan overalls, worn work boots and a John Deere cap. He pulls off his hat and scratches at his salt-and-pepper hair.

"As a matter of fact, I did." He steps to Kennedy and takes her in his arms. "Good to see you, honey. Thank you for bringing my grandson home." He kisses her forehead before stepping back, allowing his wife to swoop in.

Betty Handley is a small woman with a big heart. She gives Kennedy a generous hug.

"You okay, baby? We've been worried sick about you," she says.

"I'm fine, Mama Handley. Thank you for having us in your home on such short notice," Kennedy replies.

Betty waves her hand in the air like she's swatting a fly. "Oh, *hush*. You and our grandson are welcome anytime. It's your husband who needs to make a reservation!" She begins to cackle, and Zack joins her. Michael just shakes his head solemnly.

"Pop Pop, can I drive the tractor *now?*" Zack asks restlessly.

Michael eyes him.

"Zack, let your grandfather rest. Besides, I have some things I need to talk to Pop Pop about. I'm sure he'll take you out later."

"Ahh, man!"

"Boy, you better mind your father or I'll wash your mouth out with soap!" Betty says sternly. But Zack just laughs, holding his stomach with a bony hand.

"Ah, Nana, you are funny. Wash my mouth out with soap? Good one, Nana!"

Kennedy steals a quick glance over at Michael.

"He's *definitely* your son," she exclaims before walking back over to the fire, where Zack joins her to get warm.

"Let me start dinner," Betty says. "You all hungry?"

"Mama Handley, you rest your feet. You just walked in. Besides, your son is perfectly capable of making dinner for this family, isn't that right, baby?" Kennedy asks while standing in front of the hearth, holding Zack to her chest.

Michael glances around the room, counting four sets of eyes staring back at him. He merely rolls his eyes as he sighs heavily.

"I'm fine, Kennedy," Betty says. "Besides, that man you married may be many things, but a good cook ain't one of them! I'll get things started in a minute. Zack, you want Nana to make you some of her famous macaroni and cheese?"

"Yes, ma'am!" Zack squeals, his eyes as wide as quarters.

"Can I talk to you, Pop?"

They are in the cab of Roland Handley's pickup truck, a '94 Chevy, engine running and heat cranking. Roland pulls to a stop on a dirt trail that parallels a shallow, bubbling brook. The water still flows despite the season, meandering through a dense forest.

"What is it, Son?" he asks, turning in his seat to face him.

Michael swallows hard as he glances down at his hands.

"I was hoping to borrow one of the guns."

Roland is silent for a moment.

Michael continues. "Like one of the shotguns."

Roland exhales through his nostrils before speaking.

"Listen, Son. I know you and your family are going through a hard time right now, but this ain't the way to handle things."

Michael turns to face him.

"Pop, you don't understand. This guy, he's out to get Kennedy and me. Maybe even hurt Zack. I can't take that chance. Don't you see that?"

"Yes, I do, but you need to let the police handle this. Don't go taking the law into your own hands," his father says.

"I'm not taking the law into my own hands. I'm trying to protect my family."

"By having a gun in the house? Son, we've been through this before." Roland shakes his head. And Michael has a sudden flashback that causes his insides to ache. He pushes the memory away.

"So what am I supposed to do?" Michael asks, ignoring the remark, hands upturned. "Just sit back and wait for this guy to come and get us?"

"No. Let the police do their job."

Michael sighs. Roland puts a hand on his son's shoulder.

"Apply for a permit. I'm sure you have some connections with folks in law enforcement or the courts down there. Then you can carry *legally*."

Michael eyes his father.

"Pop, I'm not asking for one of the handguns. I'm asking for the shotgun. I can legally keep it in my house, provided it's unloaded."

"Rendering it useless," his father quips.

"Pop, this is my wife and son we're talking about.

I'm trying to be a man and protect them. Don't you get that?"

Roland glances over at Michael. Their eyes meet.

"I don't want anything to happen to you. Lord knows I don't. Not to you. Nor to my grandson or my daughter-in-law."

Michael remains silent, holding his breath.

"Guns are dangerous, Son. Especially around a child."

Michael nods.

"Pop. Let me protect my family. Please?"

Roland glances down. Removes his cap and scratches at his salt-and-pepper hair before replacing the hat, locking eyes with Michael.

"Promise me you won't do anything stupid. What your town doesn't need is a vigilante on the loose."

Michael emits a half grin.

"I hear you. But if this fucker gets within spitting distance of my family, I'm blowing him the hell away. And you can take that to the bank."

Chapter 39

Detective Joe Goodman stands patiently in front of the desk of Captain Renee Watts as he waits for her to finish a call. He's not eavesdropping; rather, Joe's mind is working over the information that he received moments ago.

Captain Watts hangs up the phone and without looking up directs Joe to shut the door.

He does so, returning to the same spot in front of her desk.

"Sit," she commands, glancing up at him for the first time. "You needed to see me?" she asks.

"This case I'm working. We've got a break, and I'd like to pursue it."

"Okay." She waits for him to furnish the details.

Joe knows the drill.

"Couple is being harassed over e-mail and phone messages by unknown person or persons. Several days ago, a wire transfer was initiated from the victims' bank account. Twelve thousand dollars was wired to two separate banks in Atlanta. A warrant was issued, and I just got off the phone with Atlanta PD. They ID'd two men whose bank accounts the money was transferred to. They've got the arrest warrants and are ready to grab them. I would like to question them."

"In Atlanta?" she asks quizzically.

"Yes."

"You are aware that we are having this conversation in the District of Columbia."

"Yes, ma'am."

"And our jurisdiction does not reach to the State of Georgia."

Joe takes a breath and exhales.

"Captain, this is the first and perhaps only break in this case. I need to follow the evidence, wherever it might take me."

Captain Watts glares at Joe for a moment. Neither speaks.

"Bullshit, Goodman. What's so special about this case?"

Joe swallows.

Captain Watts raises an eyebrow. And waits.

Joe sighs heavily.

"The vic is my ex. Wife. And her husband."

Captain Watts grunts.

"I see. This gets better every second. And you want to spend the department's money to chase down this lead?"

"Captain—the two perps will be in custody shortly. They either planned the transfer or know who did. That's our best bet for closing this case. You know how this works. I need to get to these guys now, before they make bail or lawyer up."

Joe knows Captain Watts is considering his words. So he presses on.

"I'd like to fly out immediately. I've asked ATL PD to hold the arrests pending my arrival. I need a day, two tops."

Captain Watts shakes her head.

"No, Detective. You fly in, you arrest, you interrogate, you fly out. No stayovers. I do not have the budget for hotels. Are we clear?"

"Clear as water."

Captain Watts stares at Joe and shakes her head. "Detective, please get out of my office."

"Hey, baby, it's me."

"Hi." Tara is at her desk when her phone rings.

"How is work?" Joe asks.

Tara can detect something in his voice that she can't quite place.

"Fine. What's up? Something wrong?" she asks nonchalantly, trying to quell the anxiety she feels rising.

"I have to go out of town," Joe tells her. He waits a beat and then says, "On business, to Atlanta."

"Atlanta?" Tara's voice rises in pitch automatically. She glances around, knowing that coworkers in cubicles can hear everything. She whispers, "What do you mean, Atlanta?"

"Baby, a case I'm working on? We caught a break. I need to go arrest and interrogate two perps." Joe swallows before continuing. "This is strictly business, Tara. For the case."

"Does this . . . have anything to do with Kennedy?" Tara asks, her voice quivering.

Joe knows that if he lies, things will only get worse. So he tells the truth.

"Yes."

Silence.

"Is she going with you?" Tara asks quietly.

"Who? Kennedy? Of course not! She doesn't even know I'm going down there." Joe states this matter-of-factly, then, as an afterthought, adds, "Besides, she and her husband are out of town." He regrets the last sentence as soon as it's out of his mouth.

"I see you've got her itinerary down pat."

"It's not like that."

Tara is silent. There are things she would love to say, but now is neither the time nor the place to say them. So she quiets her resentment and asks, "When are you leaving?"

"I'm in a cab heading to Reagan."

"And you will be returning when?"

"The captain hasn't authorized me to stay over. So I'll get as much done as I can and catch a flight back. If I can't get out of there later on tonight, I'll find a place to stay. I've got buddies down there from school that I can call on."

I'm sure you do, Tara cogitates. Instead she vocalizes, "Be safe, Joe."

"Love you, baby," he says, relieved.

But Tara has already hung up.

Chapter 40

Detective Joe Goodman sits in the backseat of an unmarked Ford Taurus in the parking lot of the Kings Arms Apartments with two plainclothes detectives from the Atlanta Police Department. It's not even six PM, but it's almost dark, the sky turning a purple-orange haze.

Soon now, the sky will be all black.

Behind the wheel is Frank Cohen, a strapping white guy, ex-marine with short-cropped hair. His partner, DeAndre Jackson, in the passenger seat, is black, also fit. DeAndre passes a photo of Tyrone that he printed from the Georgia Department of Driver Services database. Joe stares at it for a moment, then passes it up front.

"Okay, this should be routine," DeAndre says. "The guy has no priors, no problems with the law. I doubt he'll give us any trouble. And he lives with his moms."

Frank checks the action on his .45 caliber. DeAndre does the same.

"Ready?" Frank asks.

Joe nods, glancing down at his own Glock.

They exit the vehicle and walk to the double-door front entrance. There is a security system, but it's busted. The door swings open easily.

Tyrone lives on the ninth floor. They take the elevator, riding up in silence. When the door opens, the trio cuts right and walks down the hallway until they find apartment 917. DeAndre stands to the left of the door with Joe; Frank is on their left. DeAndre nods once at Frank, and his partner pounds on the door.

"Atlanta PD, open up!"

A few seconds go by. Frank pounds again.

Sounds and movement behind the door.

Then: "Who is it?" An elderly woman's voice.

"Atlanta PD, open up!"

Locks turn and the door opens.

A thin, wiry woman stares out.

"We're looking for Tyrone."

"What has he done?" she asks, but DeAndre has his shield in her face as he pushes the door open, gun drawn. "That isn't necessary, Officer," she stutters.

DeAndre is already moving past the kitchen and into the cramped living room when he shouts, "Freeze! Hands where I can see 'em!"

Frank rushes in behind him. Joe is with the woman, checking her for weapons. He finds none.

More yelling, more commotion from the next room.

Joe enters the living room with the woman in tow. They spy Tyrone already spread-eagled on the floor. Frank is cuffing him while DeAndre reads him his rights.

"What did he do?" the woman exclaims.

She's ignored.

"Anyone else in the apartment, ma'am?" Joe asks.

"No." Her eyes are glassy.

Joe checks anyway. He calls "Clear" from the two bedrooms and a single bathroom.

He returns to the living room. Tyrone has been hauled to a kneeling position. His baggy jeans, work boots, and oversized hoodie make him look like a thug.

Frank cuts to the chase. "Where's the money, Tyrone?"

"What are they talking about, Ty?" the woman asks, near tears.

"What money?" Tyrone answers.

"Oh, it's like that?" DeAndre responds. "Okay, no problem. We'll just get a warrant and tear up this shit hole. Doesn't bother me one bit. Call it in, Frank."

Joe strides into a bedroom—Tyrone's—and immediately begins looking around. It's a small room, unmade twin bed, peeling paint on the ceiling, several posters on the wall of rappers as if the guy were back in high school. A boom box on a bookcase that holds baseball and basketball trophies, a bunch of bootleg CDs and DVDs. An aging nineteen-inch television with rabbit ears in the corner. Joe checks the closet, fans through the gear on hangers and the numerous pairs of sneakers and Timberland boots on the closet floor.

Nothing.

He goes to the bed. Flips the mattress to the floor.

There, on the box spring, approximately two feet in from the wall, a manila envelope. Joe grabs it by the edge, peers inside. Two smaller white envelopes. He inverts the manila envelope, letting the contents fall to the box spring. Cautiously, using the tip of an ink pen, he lifts up the flap of one of the white envelopes.

A thick wad of bills.

Joe clears his throat and bellows into the living room.

"Got it!"

One man down.

One to go.

It takes about an hour to get Tyrone back to the station, processed and fingerprinted, before Joe can interview him. They put Tyrone in a small windowless room with harsh fluorescent lighting, one door, no two-way glass. Joe strides in and Tyrone glances up.

"I'm Detective Joe Goodman from Washington, D.C. You need a drink or something?"

Tyrone shakes his head. Joe nods. He pulls a small digital recorder from his pocket, places it on the table between them, and turns it on. He states his name, date, and location for the record.

"Okay. Let's start with the money. We found six thousand dollars in your bedroom. Fresh new one hundred dollar bills. Where'd you get the money, Tyrone?"

Tyrone looks at Joe. He wears an expression of indifference. Playing the tough boy. *Okay,* Joe muses. *I can play the game, too.*

"Work," Tyrone says. "Payday, dawg. Can I go now?"

Joe smiles.

"Tyrone. You wanna play a game with me, that's cool. But here's the thing. I don't have time to be messing around with you. See, I'm on a mission. And if I don't get what I'm after, I'll just go to D.C. And then your ass will be up on *felony* charges. Yeah, *dawg,* you committed a federal offense." Joe shakes his head morosely. "Your ass won't see the light of day for a minimum of ten years. Damn, son, that's a long time. Long time to be locked up, fucked in the ass every single night. But hey, it's your black ass, not mine."

Joe leans back, watching Tyrone closely. He observes a bead of sweat erupt from Tyrone's forehead. Observes it trickle down the side of his face.

"I don't know nothing, man!" Tyrone exclaims.

"Start with what you do know. Where'd the money come from?"

Tyrone swallows hard.

"The bank."

Joe nods.

"Go on."

"I went to the bank today and pulled out the cash."

Joe gestures for him to continue and says, "Because?"

"I got a call."

"Tyrone, the suspense is fucking killing me. Tell me already!"

Tyrone shakes his head, exhaling loudly.

"Fuck. All right! I got a call from this guy. He says the money's being wired to my account."

"What guy? Where'd you meet him?"

"His name is Mr. C. I don't know his full name. I met him, like, two months ago. The Pink Pony. The strip club?"

"Yeah? Go on."

"Like I said, I met him at this strip joint. We got to talking, drinking, enjoying the ladies, what have you. Anyway, he tells me about this gig he's got going and he needs my help. Needs someone to help him with a cash problem he's having."

Joe raises an eyebrow. "Cash problem?"

"That's what he said. He needed to be able to move cash from one bank to another. Talked about cleaning the money, or some shit like that. Said he'd cut me in if I would let him use my bank account. I was like, as long as I got paid, then hell, yeah. It's not like I got money in the bank that he can rob me of."

"Okay. How many times did you meet with this guy, Mr. C?"

"Only once. That night at the Pink Pony. He called me a few times after that."

"But you only met face-to-face once?" Joe asks.

"Yeah."

"And do you know Michael and Kennedy Handley?"

"Who?"

"Michael and Kennedy Handley."

"Nope."

"You sure?"

"Who the fuck are they?"

"They are a couple in D.C. whose bank account was emptied several days ago."

"Look, man, I've never been to D.C., let alone met Michael and whatever his name is. Mr. C called me today and said the money was in my bank. Told me to go get it. That it was mine to keep."

"Hold up," Joe says. "Run that by me again."

"He told me to go to the bank. The money was in my account, and it was mine to keep."

"That didn't strike you as strange?" Joe asks.

"I didn't ask any stupid questions. He told me he was gonna throw more business my way, and that this was like a down payment for my services. So I did what I was told. I didn't ask where the money came from or how it got there."

"All right." Joe runs what he knows so far around in his head. "What did this guy look like, this Mr. C?"

Tyrone shrugs.

"Dunno. Black dude."

Joe sighs.

"You think you can be a bit more specific?"

Tyrone sucks his teeth, his confidence growing.

"Wha'd'ya want me to say? He's a brutha. He was wearing a Boston Red Sox hat. He had a lot of cash, 'cause he kept buying lap dances for himself and then for me. I was like, that's cool—keep doing that shit all night. I ain't mad."

"All right." Joe stands, clicking off the recorder. "I'll be back." He exits the room and finds Frank and DeAndre at their desks.

"Not much to go on. Can we set him up with a sketch artist? It's a long shot, but maybe he'll remember something specific."

"Yeah, sure," Frank says. "Anything else?"

"Not that I can think of. What about the other dude?" Joe consults his memo pad. "Darryl Johnson, Jr."

"Waiting on you. We can try his residence. Not sure how successful that will be," DeAndre retorts.

"Let's do it. But first let's get Tyrone in front of the sketch artist. Maybe he can recall something useful."

"Worth a shot," Frank agrees, standing. "Let's go catch us another bad guy. . . ."

Chapter 41

There is no sunlight blazing into their family room today.

Today, it's gray skies; a dull, dreary morning that makes Kennedy think of the rain to come, and of sleep.

She's curled up on the love seat that is situated close to the fireplace.

They've been back home two days now. The trip to Ithaca had been just what the doctor ordered. She, in particular, needed to get away. Needed to change her environment, at least for a few days. Refresh the batteries. Not dwell on all of the shit that had put her in a deep, dark funk and held her prisoner there.

Now they're back.

Michael's at work. Zack's back in school. Kennedy's returned to her groove with work. Still not returned to the office yet, but her exile is coming to a close. Soon she'll be back in the saddle, hopefully putting all of this negative stuff behind her.

Kennedy stares at the unlit fireplace. Her thoughts are transported back to the day when she awoke to find herself in upstate New York with just herself and her husband in the quaint farmhouse. She smiles as she recalls the way Michael had stripped off all her clothes, remembers how he took her right there in front of the blazing fire. The heat, the intensity of their lovemaking—yes, she recalls it with vivid clarity.

Michael always knows what she needs.

And she had desperately needed to feel alive again.

She's staring into space now, reliving the moments in her mind, when her BlackBerry rings. Reaching for it, she sees it's her first husband, the detective, calling.

"Hey, Joe."

"Kennedy. How's my favorite ex-wife doing?" he says amusedly.

"Funny. Don't quit your day job and go into comedy."

"I see we're in a good mood. How was your little getaway?"

"It was good, actually. Really nice to separate myself from all of this. Anything new?"

"That's what I called for. I left a message with your husband, too. Wanted to bring him up to date."

"Thanks. So?"

"Well, first your bank situation. We arrested two individuals whose bank accounts received the wire transfers from your bank. Each received six thousand dollars. Here's the thing. Neither of them had any direct involvement with initiating the wire transfer."

"What does that mean?" Kennedy asks, sitting up.

"It means that they had nothing to do with wiring the money out of your account. Someone else did that."

"Who?" Kennedy asks, somewhat forcefully.

"That's what I'm trying to ascertain. We know that this guy, he calls himself Mr. C, befriended these two gentlemen in Atlanta close to two months ago. We have artist sketches of what he looks like. Unfortunately, and here's the bad part, both of these guys described different people to the sketch artist."

"Meaning what?" Kennedy asks. The frustration is evident in her voice.

"Meaning, this guy is slick. He either has an accomplice who assisted in recruiting these guys or he's using some sort of disguise."

"Disguise? Jesus . . ."

"And that's not the weirdest part. This guy didn't keep the money for himself. He left it all for his two little helpers."

Kennedy stands, going to the window. "I don't understand."

"Mr. C arranged the transfer. But he didn't keep any of your twelve grand. He let the two guys whose bank accounts received the funds keep the money. It's like he's playing with you. It's as if he's saying, 'I don't need the money—I just want to fuck with you and your husband.' "

Kennedy is silent.

Joe takes a breath.

"You there?"

"Yeah. Just processing everything you've said. This is unreal."

"I hear you. Listen, I'd like to swing by and show you these sketches. Perhaps you've seen this guy around. Maybe . . . I dunno, maybe you were intimate with him at one point."

"I have *not* been intimate with any men, Joe. I thought I made that clear," Kennedy exclaims, her frustration and anger floating back to the surface, where it's lived for the past few weeks.

"Relax, Kennedy. Your husband mentioned that you had been with a man, that's all. I'm just doing my job—looking at this from all angles."

Kennedy doesn't respond.

"So can I swing by? Won't take but a minute of your time."

"Yeah, Joe," Kennedy says after a lengthy pause, her mind a million miles away. "Swing by."

They sit at the kitchen table, sipping coffee.

Joe takes two folded pages from his inside breast pocket, unfolds them, and pushes them across the table to Kennedy.

She takes the pages and studies them.

The sketches are computer generated. The first depicts a brown-skinned man with a roundish, clean-shaven face, baseball hat, and glasses. The second shows a lighter-skinned man with a thick goatee and no glasses.

Kennedy does not recognize either man.

"You say this is the same man?" she asks, going back over the pages.

"Could be. Or not."

"That's helpful," she retorts.

Joe stares at her.

"I'm doing the best that I can."

"Sorry. I know you are."

She puts the pages down, shaking her head.

"Where do we go from here?" Kennedy asks.

"We traced the cell phone that this Mr. C used to call both of these guys in Atlanta. It's a Virgin Mobile pay-as-you-go phone. And it hasn't been used since they withdrew the six thousand dollars from their respective banks."

"We get the money back, right, Joe?"

"Yeah. Right now it's evidence. But yeah, eventually."

"Thank God."

Joe stands, sipping his coffee as he eyes Kennedy.

"You mentioned that you've received some strange voice mails recently. I'd like to hear them and have your permission to check your phone records—see if those phone calls are related to this Virgin Mobile phone."

"Okay. Yes."

Joe nods, something else on his mind. He puts down the mug and locks stares with Kennedy.

"This case . . . It's taking up a great deal of my time."

"I know. And I appreciate it. We both do," she replies, not sure where this is going.

"Investigating this case has got me reminiscent of the good old days . . . and seeing those photos of you, I have to say, hasn't helped." He emits a short laugh before turning to Kennedy.

"I forgot how incredibly sexy you were. How beautiful you *still* are."

"Thank you, Joe," Kennedy responds dubiously.

"I was thinking back to that time when you came to me because you needed my help. Remember?"

"Joe, please don't go there. That was a long time ago."

"How can I not go there? I mean, I'm staring at pictures of you being intimate with other people. And I'm saying to myself, that could have been me."

"We've been down this road, okay, Joe?" Kennedy gets up from the table and goes to the bay window.

She glances out onto the deck and the alleyway beyond.

"Kennedy, I was hoping you'd provide me with an *incentive,* you know, a little something—I mean, I'm sticking my neck out for you on this one . . . and it's not like you'd be cheating, seeing how this *is* your thing."

Kennedy twirls around, glaring at him.

"Are you for real?"

"Relax. I was just kidding—"

"What? You thought I'd do you because you're working my case?"

Joe laughs. "Why you trippin'? I'm helping you, so what's wrong with you helping me? Isn't that the way it worked before? When your back was really against the wall, Joe came through. Remember that? Besides, it's not like we haven't played this game before. . . ."

"You disgust me, you know that? I thought you were on my side. I thought I could trust you. *Fuck!*"

Kennedy slams her coffee mug onto the table and storms into the family room. She reaches for her BlackBerry and begins to speed-dial a number, then thinks better of it. She glares at Joe, who is watching her silently.

"You need to leave. Now!" Kennedy is boiling.

Joe's hand goes to his cheek, tracing the scar that lines his face.

"I was kidding, baby. Sorry you're so caught up in everything that you can't see that."

Kennedy turns her back on Joe.

"I am *not* your baby, Joe. Go home to your fiancée."

Joe glares at her before letting himself out, the front door slamming behind him.

*   *   *

Two stories up, in the attic/crawl space above the third floor hallway, a small electronic box pulses rapidly. Its front lights blink green as it transmits its data over a Wi-Fi connection to the Internet.

Nine hundred and thirty-two miles away, the data is received and stored on a FireWire hard drive. Later on this evening, the contents will be reviewed and analyzed, as they have each day since the device was concealed there.

Chapter 42

He knocks off early.

It's as if he's a kid on Christmas Eve—he can't wait to open his presents.

Damian's presents await him at his house.

He rushes home, grabs a beer out of the fridge, and gets out of his suit and tie, tossing his clothes haphazardly onto the bed. In his shirt, boxers, and socks, he goes to the office, where his presents await him.

Sitting down in front of the wall of flat-panel displays, he nudges the mouse, bringing the system to life.

On the left screen, still up where he left it last night, is *her*.

Damian sucks in a breath, as he does each time he spies her.

Butterscotch complexion.

Weave halfway down her back.

It's the eyes that kill him the most.

They are sultry, sensuous eyes.

Mystical eyes—they suck you in, and you are powerless to resist.

It was like that with him.

From the very first moment he laid eyes on her, she had sucked him in.

Damian feels the pain overtake the sadness.

Pain, then rage.

A river, its power building, expanding, a turbulent vortex.

He reaches for the Tylenol, spraying his palm with glossy pills.

He swallows a half dozen with his beer.

Middle screen—he logs in and opens a window that displays the root directory of the FireWire drive.

His pulse quickens. He's been thinking about this moment all day. It's why he knocked off early.

Damian glances back to the left screen and to her.

Black widow.

The rage is molten lava.

She did this to him.

They did it to him.

But what goes around comes around.

Then, a funny thing happens—the pain dissipates into thin air.

Like a huge wave that crashes onto the beach, rolling up onto the sand, only to be sucked back out to sea as quickly as it came, the rage simply disappears.

His fingers are on the chattering keyboard as he types commands. Another window opens, and there it is.

Damian smiles.

He has to hand it to himself. He is pretty fucking slick!

They are totally oblivious. Going along like little fucking worker bees, head down, not seeing what there is to truly see.

Damian stares at the recordings. They're voice activated, from mics he's hidden in their house.

Miniature microphones with transmitters the size of a dime. Transmitting to a base station in the crawl space/attic. A base station that uploads the data over their wireless network to his server, right here by his feet.

LOL!

Oh, he is so fucking slick!

He stares at the screen.

The application displays the recordings as a series of analog waveforms that can be manipulated. Fast-forwarded, rewound, copied, or deleted. He can scrub through hours of audio rapidly just like the pros do.

He clicks on today's data.

Hopes there will be some nugget of juicy information there. After all, things have been quiet the last few days. Nothing coming in since last week—they must have been out of town. But today, there's something on the screen. They're back home.

Damian takes a wild swig of his beer and focuses his undivided attention onscreen.

Let's listen in, shall we?

An hour later, after the sun's gone down, Damian sits back abruptly from his desk. His palms are sweating. He can't fucking believe his luck.

Can't fucking believe it!

He rushes downstairs for his fourth beer of the evening.

Runs back upstairs, taking the stairs two at a time, his heart thumping as he slops back down in the chair, staring at the screen.

Damian replays the audio.

And again.

He presses both palms together in prayer as he snickers to the vacant house.

The monitors bathe him with their light.

Damian calls up electronic mail and furiously begins to type.

Chapter 43

Michael gets home a little after nine.

Kennedy is on the couch in the family room. She has a glass of Merlot in hand, glasses on, flipping through a magazine. He goes over to her, kisses her on the lips as he cradles her head.

"Hey, you," she says.

"What's wrong?" he asks, glancing around.

"What?"

"You're not working. No laptop. No BlackBerry in hand. Something must be wrong."

"Ha ha. Very funny . . ."

"Zack asleep?"

"Yep. You hungry? I can heat up some leftovers for you," she says.

"No, I'll do it. Let me check on him first."

Michael takes the stairs to the second floor. Quietly he peeks into his son's room. Zack is asleep on his side. Michael touches his head and kisses him gently.

He comes back down and angles for the den. Bumps the mouse to bring the screen alive. Logs in and calls up AOL.

Michael's tired. He worked late to make up for

the days off. He'll be doing it again tomorrow as
well. Perhaps the day after that.

He's thinking about all that he has to catch up
on when what he sees stops his heart.

Michael's veins grow cold.

A new message.

From egnever620@yahoo.com.

The very same e-mail address of the offending
photos that went to Kennedy's job.

His heart rate spikes.

egnever.

Revenge spelled backward.

Michael opens the message.

Reads it.

In an instant, his world turns upside down.

He shuffles into the room slowly, like some hurt
animal, silently holding a single sheet of paper to
his side. When he is about six feet away and in front
of the coffee table, Kennedy glances up, pulling
off her glasses as she witnesses the look of devasta-
tion on his face.

She's never seen that look before.

"Michael, what is it?" she cries.

He is silent for a moment, his stare boring a
hole into her forehead. It takes everything he has,
every ounce of strength, not to clench up his fists
and attack.

His thumb and forefinger slide against the sheet
of paper separating them.

"Did you . . ." Michael pauses. "Have you ever . . ."

The words falter.

He stares disbelievingly at his wife, incredulity
written all over his face. He is weak; he can barely

stand. The words come as mere puffs, meager whispers.

"What is it, sweetie? What's wrong?"

Kennedy is staring at him, her own heart rate doing double time.

"Joe. You . . . *fucked* him."

It was meant as a question. An accusation.

But it's a statement, plain and simple.

Kennedy's brow furrows.

"What? What are you talking about?"

She puts down the magazine. He has her full attention.

"Simple question. Yes or no. Joe. You had an affair?"

Michael's lips are losing their color. They are mashed together as if he's biting into the flesh of his own lip.

"Baby . . . what's g-going on?" Kennedy stutters.

Michael holds up the paper. And lets it go. It flutters over the coffee table, landing on the carpet by her feet. She stares uncomprehendingly at her husband before picking it up slowly.

She reads the paper and grows cold.

YOUR WIFE IS AN UNFAITHFUL CUNT.
ASK JOE IF YOU DON'T BELIEVE ME.
HOW'S IT FEEL?
WHAT GOES AROUND COMES AROUND . . .

Suddenly, Kennedy's eyes are watery.

She can barely see the form that stands in front of her.

Kennedy opens her mouth to speak, but finds that nothing emerges. Her tongue is dry; she swallows hard, tasting saliva that is like paste.

"Baby, I—"

"Simple yes or no, Kennedy," Michael demands. "This isn't multiple choice or an essay. Answer the question."

Tears are meandering down her face now. She makes no move to wipe them away.

The silence stretches toward infinity.

Michael remains where he is, not moving, a slow, steady breath that is the only sound in the room.

After what seems like an eternity, she responds.

"Yes." Voice quivering above a whisper.

Michael stares at her, his eyes wide. It's as if he's been shot—the pain is sudden. Immediate. His entire body is experiencing death.

No. That doesn't do justice to what he's feeling now.

Michael continues to glare at his wife, his fists clenching and unclenching in anger.

"Baby, I need to explain—" she offers.

"When?" he asks. It's delivered as a croak.

Kennedy blinks and shakes her head.

Teardrops running down her smooth cheeks.

"Seven years ago."

Michael's eyes are unblinking as they bore into her.

"Before . . . Zack?"

She swallows hard, the paste sliding down her throat.

"Yes."

It is the last thing that Michael processes.

At this point he has shut down. He no longer hears or acknowledges her presence.

"My son may not be my own," he whispers, and the words are not lost on Kennedy.

She stands, attempts to reach out to him while silently mouthing the "No." But it's no longer any use. "Baby, you don't understand. Please, Michael, let me explain. Do you remember when you got assaulted by those teenagers? Baby, you were—"

Michael has already shuffled away.

At this point, she no longer exists anymore.

Chapter 44

It's as if she's in a daze.

The last two weeks have been like that. Like she's merely drifting along, being tugged here and there, no longer in control, simply wandering, a leaf in a meandering stream.

A migrant. A nomad.

Kennedy is at her desk. The door is shut. Several legal pads and a few binders litter the surface. Her elbows are on the table with her head in her hands. Fingers massaging her temples.

It's been two weeks.

Two weeks since Michael left.

Left the very night he found out about Joe.

They've spoken only twice since then.

Twice—to make arrangements for him to see Zack.

The situation is unreal.

In two days it will be Thanksgiving. And for the first time in many years, she will be alone for the holiday. Michael has taken Zack back to his parents' home in Ithaca. They will remain there until the middle of next week.

Kennedy could go home to Atlanta, but then she'd have to explain her situation to her family: she and Michael are now separated, the threatening e-mails and phone calls they've received, and the drama at her job. No. Kennedy would rather be alone than go through any of that.

Then there's Robin. She'll be in town this week—alone, of course. Kennedy could spend the holiday with her. But that's a nonstarter as well. Kennedy'd rather slit her own throat than tell Robin that she and Michael have separated. She can just see her friend sitting there over turkey and stuffing, a self-satisfied look on her face as she says not a word.

But the look says everything.

It says, *I told you so.* . . .

So she'll huff it alone. The thought almost brings her to tears. Except she has no more tears left to cry.

She's running on empty.

Kennedy gets up, grabs her coat, and exits her office. She walks quietly past the ten or so staffers on the second floor, sitting at their desks and in their cubicles. Some glance up as she strides by, but they say nothing. They've kept mostly to themselves since she's returned from exile.

Out into the fresh, cold air, Kennedy buttons her coat as she takes the step. She needs air; she needs to breathe. She begins to walk, not really knowing where she's going—she's a nomad now—knowing only that she needs to force her brain to concentrate on something besides her situation.

This fucked-up situation.

She's heard from Joe only scarcely. He's apologized for his behavior, but the damage's been done. He's aware that Michael is gone—aware that he, in some indirect or direct way, depending on how you view it, is responsible for Michael's departure. So he keeps a low profile. Head down, working the case. One case among many. Nothing new to report. It's as if Mr. C has vanished into thin air. And there are no other leads.

Kennedy walks.

Ducks into Azela Coffee Shop to grab some tea. It's quiet in there, very few patrons as most are heading out of town to be with their loved ones. She considers taking a table by the window—there are several open—but decides against it when she hears the music wafting down upon her. A slow R&B song, lamenting lost love.

Kennedy grabs her tea and exits before her eyes grow wet.

Kennedy walks. Away from the bustle and noise of Eighteenth Street. West instead on California and a right onto Nineteenth. Down Wyoming Avenue, where it's peaceful and quiet. Where she can be alone with her thoughts.

Not too long ago she had a family.

Things between her and her husband were good. Hell, better than good. They were damn near perfect.

A husband who doted on her. A beautiful son.

Kennedy remembers with an ache that creeps into her gut just how much she enjoyed herself with Michael in New York. A time that now seems like eons ago. A time when the pressures of everyday life slid off their shoulders like fried eggs off Teflon. When sweet, unadulterated loving took her to heights she never thought she'd achieve.

Those times were sweet. When she seemingly didn't have a care in the world. When everything, she knew, would be all right.

So it's those times that Kennedy conjures up now.

Times that make her smile, if only for a short while.

Chapter 45

My name is Celestial, and I'm your deepest, darkest fantasy come true.

It was Celestial who Michael unleashed from her cage. A vixen, a siren, a dream come true.

Michael had conceived her.

He had allowed her to dream of the possibilities, and he had not chastised her when she spoke of her fantasies. Just the opposite—Michael had nurtured them, allowed them to grow and blossom, until this new being emerged.

Celestial.

Kennedy remembers those times that defied words.

Times that moved in slow motion.

The staccato, hard-hitting, house music had engulfed the underground club in Paris, permeating every square inch of space.

But it was her touch, which was like lightning, igniting fire, but in a slow, steady motion—like midnight rain.

Her breath was on her neck as she stood in the darkened, narrow hallway after an hour of nonstop dancing. Low-voltage strips of neon blue bathed the hard floor. Otherwise it was dark.

She could feel her advancing. Feel her raise her arms as in surrender. Then she was against her, pressing her *weight into hers, pelvis doing a slow grind against her ass.*

Kennedy felt the heat, felt herself powerless to stop.

Hot breath on her neck. A lovely Parisian named Dominique.

Sucking at her earlobes, hands following the contours of hips and torso to her breasts.

Michael was beside her, steadily stroking the insides of her thighs.

Under her short dress, fingers glided under the elastic of her panties, finding the wet spot.

A quick rush of air as he thrust inside her.

Behind her, Dominique grasped Kennedy's head, extending it so she could reach her waiting mouth. Her tongue found Kennedy's. Instantly she began to devour the flesh.

Kissing her. Tasting her. Fingering her.

Almost a dream.

But the experiences were real.

All in slow motion.

There was Isabella from the Dominican Republic.

They met her in Punta Cana among the swaying coconut palm trees and white sand.

She had beautiful dark skin and an engaging smile.

Perfectly upturned breasts with dark cherry nipples.

Kennedy and her newfound lover would lose themselves in their private wood-and-glass cabana that was situated in a lush garden facing the Caribbean Sea. For hours they would make love, just the two of them, only to emerge later with a look of satisfaction painted on their suntanned faces.

Michael's reward for their intimacy?

Isabella would lead him back to the cabana by the hand for some alone time while Kennedy sipped a Cuba Libre and smoked an Arturo Fuente cigar.

Chloe they met in London.

Interior decorator by day, spoken-word artist by night.

*Limitless energy and a wickedly seductive British accent,
she played tour guide to them while they were on vacation—taking them to Plan B, Figit, and Electrowerkz. They
listened to music, ate, and danced, flirting with Chloe until
the passion threatened to wreck them. Then they took the
Tube back to their hotel and fucked until the morning
sun was high in the sky.*

What amazing times they had had. . . .

Jasmine in Aruba during Carnival.

Natalie, Lacy, and Irie in Jamaica.

*A schoolteacher from Baltimore whose name escaped
her.*

Ana from Belize.

*Mercedes, a model residing in South Beach, and an-
other lovely thing whom they met while she was attending
a conference in Miami.*

Jayla and Brooke in Philly.

Brooklyn and Makayla in New York.

They all come flooding back now.

*Their faces, their bodies, the way they felt pressed against
her as they kissed and explored each other.*

*For some she remembers vivid details—the way they
stroked her inner thighs, the way they flicked their tongues
across her clit, driving her insane. For others, the details
are lost—instead, the fond memories are of meeting, conversing, and then loving, either one-on-one or, with Michael
there, as a trio giving each other pleasure until they were
worn out, the scent of spent sensuality hanging in the air
like exhaled cigarette smoke.*

Wonderful memories.

Kennedy holds on to them for as long as she can.

These days, it's all she has.

Chapter 46

It is after nine PM before she gets home.

Lately, there's no reason to arrive at a decent time. Husband and son are not here. And Kennedy hates coming home to an empty house.

It doesn't even feel like home without Michael and Zack.

Her two men.

She brushes the thought away. Doesn't want to cry again.

Tomorrow is Thanksgiving Day. The office will be closed. She hasn't broached the subject yet of how she will occupy her time. Hasn't given herself the time to mentally consider how she will spend her day. For now, it's a nonissue. She'll deal with tomorrow *tomorrow*.

Kennedy pours herself a glass of wine. She folds her feet underneath her body on the couch, reaching for the remote, finding an old-school station on XM that is one of her favorites. Michael McDonald is on, his smooth, sensual voice crooning against a backdrop of a slow, steady high-hat and the distinct sound of a Fender Rhodes electric piano.

She tried calling Michael on the way home from work, but his cell went straight to voice mail. Zack's, too. She hung up, not bothering to leave a message. She was calling to speak to her son, anyway. She'll call again in the morning, dialing his parents' house if she can't get through next time.

Kennedy closes her eyes.

She is tired, both mentally and physically. She should lie down, but fights going to bed. Kennedy knows that sleep will be elusive, and that she'll just lie there, staring up at the ceiling, thinking and worrying.

So she remains on the couch, sipping her wine and enjoying the old-school music—Michael McDonald has segued to Roy Ayers to Kashif—that makes her smile and nod in remembrance.

The cordless phone is on the coffee table.

No blinking light signifying any new messages, thank goodness.

She picks it up now, hefting the plastic and metal thing in her hand.

Reminiscing about happier times has triggered something she hasn't considered before.

Kennedy calls up their saved messages, skipping through them until she finds what she is searching for.

"Hey, you. I just wanted to say that I'm running late, but I'm on my way. I can't wait to see you. To be honest, I've been thinking about you all day. Thinking about the wonderful things you always do to me when we're alone. Well, guess what? I can't wait to be alone with you tonight. I'm wet just thinking about it and of you. See you soon. . . . Ciao bella."

And the next one.

"Hey, you. I know you're tied up in meetings for most of today, but I just wanted to tell you, I've been unable to

get out of my mind what you did to me last night. Oh my God, you always know what I need, but last night? Last night you outdid yourself! Seriously, the feeling was amazing! I can't even describe it, other than to say I came so hard I was practically numb afterward. And no, I am not complaining. You are truly wonderful. I love you so much. Tonight, I'm returning the favor. Ciao bella."

Kennedy replays the first message, then the second. She replays them again. And then again. Something about those messages—she can't quite put her finger on. But there's something about the words and the way the woman says them, almost in a singsong kind of way.

Think, Kennedy commands her brain, but the answers don't come easily.

She puts the cordless phone down.

Picks up her wine and takes a healthy sip.

Listens to Chaka Khan, Lakeside, Change, and Maze.

Something's there.

Right below the surface.

If only she can connect the dots.

If only she can touch what she knows is right *there.* . . .

Chapter 47

That night, Kennedy dreams sweet dreams.

Dreams of her husband, Michael.

Strong hands, razor to his face as he stands nude in front of the vanity, trimming around his mustache and goatee, which have grown thick with flecks of gray, making him sexier than he ever was.

She dreams of pulling him into a half-filled bathtub, shaver in hand as she buzzes his head. They are laughing as she runs the razor around in circles until his dome is smooth as an undisturbed pond. Afterward, she uses the shaver on his chest hairs, trimming around his navel and then, with a wicked grin, going lower, grooming around his cock as he lies back, hands behind his head, eyes closed.

The images are fleeting.

She awakens with a start.

Kennedy sits up, suddenly aware of how quiet the house has become.

That's because she is alone.

She remains there for a moment, covers nuzzled against her hips as her nipples harden from the cold, the wifebeater providing little in terms of comfort. She turns on a lamp on the nightstand, glancing at the time.

Two-fourteen AM.

Kennedy checks her BlackBerry, hoping for a message from her husband. Text message, something.

But the device has nothing for her.

Instead, she stares about the darkened room, considering the dream that was cut short. Thoughts that segue to the sexual liaisons they've shared.

Sixteen partners.

The list that she gave Joe contained the details of their sixteen sexual encounters.

She considers those sixteen individuals and their connection to the threatening e-mails and phone messages.

Kennedy's mind goes to the saved voice mails. Without a second thought she reaches for the cordless phone and presses the button to retrieve them. She replays the message from the unknown woman, listening to her voice.

Hey, you.

And the way she signs off.

Ciao Bella.

She hangs up the phone, those words remaining on her tongue.

Hey, you.

Ciao Bella.

Her mind is racing, attempting to connect the dots.

Her Coach briefcase is leaning against the foot of the nightstand. Kennedy reaches inside for a legal pad, tearing off the top layer of writings until she reaches a clean page. She finds a pen and begins to write.

Sixteen partners.

New York, Jamaica, Baltimore, Atlanta, Philadelphia, Miami, Paris, London, Aruba, the Dominican Republic, Belize.

She works from memory since she didn't make a copy of the list she provided to Joe.

Some names come easily. Others are lost to her. But she jots down what she remembers.

Physical characteristics, accents, anything that she can recall.

She throws the covers off, readying to head downstairs to the computer in the den. The images are on the hard drive. She's in mid-stride, close to the door when she remembers: The police have the external drive in their possession.

Back in bed, legal pad on her lap, she jots down what she can from memory.

Peering at the list of locales, adding names.

She starts with the photos sent in an e-mail to her job.

Think, Kennedy!

Make the assumption that all of this has something to do with one of the women photographed with you and/or Michael. Who were they? How many?

Kennedy glances down her list.

Four, five, six, maybe. She can't recall. Not without the hard drive.

Which names can she cross off?

Makayla from New York.

She's recent.

It's unlikely that she's behind all this.

Who else?

Then back to the voice mails. *Hey, you. Ciao Bella.* Who speaks like that?

Italians.

But she's never been to Italy. Never been with an Italian, as far as she can recall.

Who then?

Who can I rule out?

Did any of these other women say things like *Ciao Bella?*

Not Isabella. Not Ana. She's almost certain of it.

Chloe with the British accent? Kennedy replays their time in London through her mind. No, it wasn't her.

The women they met in Jamaica—Natalie, Lacy, Irie?

Two were American. *No, that isn't right. Natalie was from the States, but Lacy was European,* she thinks. Could she have been from Italy? Did she say *Ciao Bella?* She can't recall.

Irie? She was definitely Jamaican, spoke with a thick patois. It probably wasn't her, but who knows?

There were the two women from Philadelphia, Jayla and Brooke. Both African-Americans, and from what she can recall, neither would have used the phrase *Ciao Bella.*

There were several women whom they met in Miami—the model, Mercedes, who spoke with a thick Puerto Rican/New York accent.

Kennedy doesn't think it was her.

The other woman's name escapes Kennedy. Certain details return—a butterscotch complexion, hair down her back, lovely, sensual.

Hey, you.

Her heart rate begins to increase.

Hey, you.

Ciao Bella.

Something's there.

Just below the surface.

She needs the hard drive to be sure.

Chapter 48

Thanksgiving Day.

Kennedy is in her sweats, hair tied back, hot coffee in front of her as she sits at the kitchen table, laptop open. But it's not getting her attention this morning. Instead she is staring out the window to the deck and alleyway beyond.

Her BlackBerry vibrates.

"HI, MOM-MEEEEEEEE!" Zack yells so loud she's forced to squint in pain. But suddenly she's in ecstasy.

"Hey, Zack, how's my favorite little man?"

"Good, Mommy. Happy Thanksgiving!"

"Happy Thanksgiving to you, Zack. How are you?"

"Fine. Guess what? Pop Pop's taking me hunting for squail today!"

Kennedy frowns.

"Hunting? And I think you mean quail, honey. Not squail."

Zack doesn't hear a word.

"Pop Pop says that squails are sneaky little creatures, but after we shoot one, he's gonna show me how to pluck all the feathers off and give it to Nana so she can throw it in the oven. Do I eat squail, Mommy?"

"It's quail, baby. And I don't think I want you hunting with Pop Pop. You're still too young for that. I'm not comfortable with you being around guns."

"Pop Pop says if I help him feed the cows, he's gonna give me five dollars! FIVE DOLLARS, can you believe that? All for helping him feed a bunch of cows. I don't mind feeding cows, Mommy. It's not like they are nasty or anything. Pop Pop is so great! I asked Nana if she had some chores for me, like setting the table for Thanksgiving, and she said sure, and I said, 'Cool beans, that'll be a dollar and fifty,' and she just laughed at me. Mommy, do you think Nana will pay me for setting the table?"

Kennedy is shaking her head as the tears well up in her eyes. She misses Zack so much she's about to lose it. She wills herself to calm down.

"You shouldn't charge Nana to set the table, Zack. You should do it willingly. After all, she's your grandmother."

She can feel Zack sulking.

"Okay, Mommy."

"I miss you, Zack. Miss you a whole lot!" she exclaims.

"Me, too."

"Zack, I need to speak to your father about this hunting situation. Can you put him on the phone?"

Several seconds go by.

"Daddy doesn't want to come to the phone." Zack drops his voice several decibels. "I think he's mad at you."

Kennedy grits her teeth. She hates the fact that Zack is caught in the middle of this thing between Michael and her.

She sighs and smiles through the momentary angst.

"Okay, Zack. That's all right. Mommy loves you, baby."

"Love you, too, Mommy. 'Bye."

The line goes dead. Kennedy presses END and stares at her phone for a moment before lowering it to the table.

Blinks back the tears as she considers her day alone.

"Joe, it's Kennedy."

He takes several seconds to respond.

"Kennedy. Happy Thanksgiving to you."

"I need my external drive back."

Joe considers the tone of her words.

"O-kay. Can I ask why?"

"I need to check something. I'd appreciate it if you can drop it off today."

"It's Thanksgiving."

"And? You're obviously in town."

Several seconds of silence.

"Can it wait?"

"No," Kennedy responds. "If it's a problem, I can call your commander," she adds rather nastily.

"No need to threaten," Joe replies. "I'll swing by . . . within the hour."

"That would be great."

Kennedy has one of those large easel pads on the kitchen table. Zack uses them when he's in the mood to finger paint. One sheet is affixed to the far wall facing the windows. It lists the sixteen names and locations of their encounters. Using a black marker, she scribbles on the pad, distilling the list down to only those women whose photos were taken by her and Michael.

So far she has five names.

Makayla, Ana, Lacy, Jayla, and the woman they met in Miami whose name she cannot remember.

She needs the drive to confirm any others.

The doorbell rings. She puts down the marker and goes to the door. Checks through the opening that it's Joe. He smiles sheepishly when he sees her.

"Joe."

Joe is holding a plastic bag out to her. Kennedy takes the bag, opens it, and glances inside. The external hard drive, USB cable, and power cord are there.

"Thanks." She remains by the door.

"May I come in?" he asks.

"I don't think that's a good idea."

"Come on, Kennedy. I just want to talk to you. About the case."

She glares at him before stepping back, allowing him to pass. He follows her into the kitchen, staring at the lists on the wall and table.

"Want some coffee?" she asks, deciding to play nice.

"Sure. What's all this?"

Kennedy eyes him. "Trying to narrow the list down."

She pours him a cup of coffee and moves the easel pad out of the way so he can get to the cream and sugar.

Joe nods, stirring in three spoonfuls of sugar.

"Have some coffee with your sugar," she says.

"Funny." He returns his attention to the lists. "How are you narrowing things down?"

"I'm operating under the assumption that who-ever sent those e-mails had something to do with the woman in the photos. Or if not directly related to her, then to a woman who has been photo-graphed with us in the past."

"And that's what these four names are here?" he asks, tapping on the pad.

"Yes."

"Four out of sixteen."

"So far. I need the hard drive to make sure. This is what I remembered."

Joe nods.

Kennedy starts to speak then shuts it down.

"What?" he asks.

"The two voice mails are bothering me," she says.

"What about them?"

"In both, the woman begins by saying *Hey you* and ends with *Ciao Bella*."

"And?"

"I don't know. Something's there. I can feel it," she replies.

"Do you recall any of the women using those words?"

"I don't know. It's been a minute with a bunch of these people. Like years."

Joe glances down at the names.

Makayla, Ana, Lacy, Jayla, and the woman they met in Miami.

"Ana is the woman in the photos that were sent to your job, correct?"

Kennedy nods.

"And if memory serves me, you've had no con-tact with her, right?"

"Right."

"And both Michael and I have spoken with Makayla. It's doubtful she has anything to do with this, especially since your encounter with her was fairly recent. As I recall, the first offending e-mail came in two days after you met her."

"That's true."

"Okay." Joe picks up the marker and draws a line through the names of Makayla and Ana. "I had a conversation with Jayla a few weeks ago. I don't think she had anything to do with this. She said she deleted the photos that were sent almost immediately. Never kept them around to look at."

"Unless she's lying to you," Kennedy says.

Joe shrugs. "Could be, but I doubt it. It didn't sound like she was hiding anything." He draws a line across her name.

"That leaves Lacy and the woman from Miami," Kennedy says.

"Tell me about them," Joe commands, then slurps his coffee.

Lacy was a brown-skinned woman they'd met in Jamaica a number of years ago. They had met at the resort and had a wonderful time over the next three days. Lacy was European, as Kennedy recalls, but she can't place her country of birth now.

Then there is the woman they met in Miami.

Kennedy concentrates on her. Vague details surface. She had been tall, light-skinned. Butterscotch complexion. Yes, it's slowly coming back to her. Long hair, she recalls now. What was her name? A killer body; she remembers that. Hadn't she been attending some convention in Miami when they met?

It had been, what? Four years ago? Perhaps more.

Kennedy closes her eyes. Conjures up images of the woman. Her hair she can see, but the details of her face are beyond her recall. She remembers, though, fleeting images of the three of them intertwined on the bed, their bodies pressed together in the heat of passion.

What was her name?

She wishes Joe would leave so she can fire up the external drive.

And see the woman in all of her splendor and glory.

Her heart begins to beat faster.

Kennedy is pushing her brain to remember details.

Something is there.

Something familiar.

Kennedy tells Joe what she knows.

He considers her words for a minute before responding.

"You need to go back, look through old calendars, e-mails, letters, what have you. See if any of that jump-starts your brain to remember. Look at the photos on the hard drive. It will come to you. Concentrate, and you'll remember."

"I will."

Joe gulps his coffee.

"You ever videotape these vacations? I don't mean the actual encounters. I mean the vacations themselves. If so, you might have these women on tape. If you do, that would be immensely helpful."

Kennedy has a faraway look in her eyes.

"Ken?"

She stares at him for a moment.

"Oh my God, you're right. Why didn't I remember?"

She is up from the table, eyes wide.

"What is it?" he asks.

"We videotaped almost all of our vacations back then. This was before we bought a digital camera. We hardly use it now. Damn, I wonder where it is?"

Joe stands, excitement in his eyes.

"That's great! Let's go find it."

"No, Joe. I need to do this alone." Her mind is racing. So is her heart.

Something there . . . just below the surface.

"Let me find the camera, view the tapes. If there's anything there, I'll let you know."

Joe nods, realizing he's in no position to push further.

"Are you . . . alone for the holiday?" he asks as gingerly as he can.

"Yes. But don't worry about me. I'll be fine. I've got stuff to do. Lots to do."

He follows her to the door.

"Call if you need me," he adds as an afterthought. "Or if you discover anything."

"I will, Joe," Kennedy replies. "You'll be the first to know."

Chapter 49

It takes her thirty minutes to find it.

First the basement, then the garage, then back down to the basement, where she locates the camcorder in a Nike shoebox along with a bunch of 8mm tapes. Her heart is pounding in her chest as she climbs the steps to the main floor.

Back at the kitchen table, Kennedy opens the box and extracts the video camera.

Hefts the thing in her hands before putting it down.

She examines the tapes. Eleven in all.

A few markings and dates written in ink.

Kennedy takes the camcorder into the family room. Plugs it in, powers it on, and flips open the 2.5-inch LCD color screen.

Still works.

She pours herself a glass of Merlot and sits cross-legged on the floor, loading the first tape. She hits rewind and waits patiently for the tape to come to a stop. Then Kennedy hits play.

* * *

Almost four hours later, Kennedy rises from the carpet, stretching her arms and legs as she exhales an explosive yawn. The time has flown by. It's now close to six PM. She's famished. Kennedy goes to the refrigerator, opens it, and peers inside.

Not much stares back at her.

A half-eaten pint of shrimp lo mein, some deli meat, cheese, three eggs, some low-fat yogurt.

Kennedy reaches for the Chinese food, dumps the contents into a bowl and thrusts it into the microwave.

Thanksgiving Day and Kennedy's having leftover Chinese food.

She waits for the food to zap, standing by the bay window, deep in thought. The day is overcast gray. Dreary. There is no color. No leaves, very few evergreens on her back alley, and even those appear washed out. She thinks of Michael and Zack and her heart spikes. She misses them both. Misses them so much she can hardly breathe.

The microwave pings, signaling the food's done.

Kennedy removes the piping-hot bowl, takes it over to the kitchen table and sits down. She embeds her fork in the noodles, readying to eat when she stops herself.

Says a prayer first.

For all the things she's thankful for.

Her son. Her husband. Her health. Her career. For family and friendships.

Kennedy ends with an amen and forks some shrimp into her mouth. Chews slowly, reaching for her BlackBerry. Types out a short text message.

I AM THANKFUL FOR HAVING YOU IN MY LIFE.

Considers saying more. But what else is there to say? She adds:

IM SORRY. MORE THAN YOULL EVER KNOW.

Kennedy hits SND, transmitting the message to her husband approximately three hundred fifty miles away.

Back to the lo mein. She takes several more bites.

Suddenly, Kennedy is no longer hungry.

She gets up from the table, glancing in the direction of the family room and the camcorder on the floor.

Kennedy's found what she was looking for.

It was there, amidst the eleven tapes of her son's early childhood, a family vacation to Disney World, trips to Ithaca and her parents' home in Atlanta, and several getaways with Michael.

It had taken her most of the afternoon to go through the tapes, fast-forwarding through the material but then slowing down to watch the videos, smiling at the memories, some long forgotten.

Some she just couldn't fast-forward through.

Zack learning how to walk, Michael changing his diapers, their son's first bath, their first Christmas with him. Kennedy cried softly when she watched that tape, Zack ripping apart the wrapping paper to get at the Cookie Monster trike that had him blissful for at least half of that Christmas day.

She found what she was seeking late in the afternoon.

They had taken the camcorder on their trip to Miami.

Second week in November. Four years ago.

Stayed at the Tides, Ocean Drive, South Beach.

The video begins with them on their first day outside the hotel. A gorgeous day, sun high in the sky, art deco architecture in the foreground. Michael pans the camera, taking in Kennedy on the curb in a sexy miniskirt and mules. Her hair is freshly washed, and there's a healthy glow to her face. She remembers now—they had just finished making love after checking in.

Their hotel room faced the ocean. Eight stories down were palm trees, white sand, and incredible bodies on rollerblades, clad in little-left-to-the-imagination swimwear. They walked Ocean Drive, taking in the sights and sounds of South Beach: Versace's mansion, the Park Central Hotel, the lively restaurants and colorful sidewalk cafés. Spent time lounging by the pool, being pampered by hotel staff as they drank martinis and took pool-side naps.

On their third day there, a Friday, Michael and Kennedy got dressed for dinner and walked hand in hand along Ocean Drive toward their destination. The concierge at the hotel had recommended B.E.D., an eclectic place two blocks up and two blocks over. B.E.D. was unlike any place they had been to before. No tables, no chairs. Instead, large oversized beds where meals were served on an oval rattan tray. They had ordered drinks—mojitos—and an appetizer—hot passion-fruit caipirinha. Wonderful atmosphere—low lighting, mood music, and waiters that attended to your every need.

Kennedy recalls nibbling on the appetizer and sipping on her mojito, enjoying the conversation that she and her husband were having when a trio of women came in. They must have been early because the maitre d' put them at the bar while their bed was being made.

One woman stood out from the pack.

Tall, butterscotch complexion, long hair done up in a ponytail. Fairly conservative dress—Kennedy remembers the woman wearing a plain dress and shoes (at least for South Beach), as if she were trying to tone down her appearance. But her beauty shone through like bright rays of sunlight breaking through the clouds. Even though her dress did not accentuate her curves, Kennedy remembers thinking that underneath it all there was a very healthy body.

Women know.

Kennedy remembers that night. Remembers seeing her, thinking to herself, *What's her story? Who is she? What is she like?*

She forgot the woman quickly.

Their entrées arrived.

Lamb chops served with chimichurri sauce for her.

Stuffed rigatoni for him.

A wonderful dinner followed by an equally delicious dessert.

The next day Kennedy and Michael were on the sidewalk parallel to the beach, a short walk from the Tides, when they spotted her.

The woman from the previous night at B.E.D.

Alone.

Kennedy went up and spoke to her. Said she had seen her last night. Inquired about her meal.

That's how it began.

A friendly conversation on a delightful Saturday afternoon.

Conversation that moved to an invitation to join them by the hotel pool.

She accepted.

Soon the three of them were lounging by the

pool, sipping on something frozen and something sweet while the conversation flowed freely.

Kennedy calls to mind certain details.

The woman was married four years.

Had flown in from out of town (Kennedy can't recall from where) for a conference.

Nursing? Therapy? Something health-care related.

The conference had ended Friday afternoon, but she was staying the weekend by herself, taking a much-needed minivacation.

They talked for hours, she and Kennedy and Michael.

Afternoon turned to evening.

They invited her to dinner.

She accepted, taking a cab back to her hotel to change into evening attire.

They dined that night at DeVitos, at the southern tip of South Beach.

Great food and even greater conversation.

Libations flowing like a Jamaican waterfall.

Kennedy and the woman got along splendidly. They talked about everything under the sun—their relationships, marriage, men, their careers. The conversation moved to sex, but the woman seemed to be reluctant to share her true feelings.

Kennedy didn't push things. There was no need. She was in no rush.

That night, after they had returned to their hotel alone, Michael and Kennedy discussed the woman while getting undressed.

It was clear Kennedy wanted her.

Michael told his wife she could have her.

The next day the woman met them at the Tides for brunch. The rest of the afternoon was spent by the pool. Kennedy and the woman got facials while

Michael walked the beach, recording the sights with the camcorder.

When he returned, he found his wife and the woman deep in conversation. He knew where things were heading; she knew Michael could sense the change in his wife's demeanor.

Celestial had arrived.

In the woman's space, leaning in close, stroking the woman's forearm as she laughed heartily.

Michael took out the camcorder and videotaped the two of them splashing around the pool.

Shortly thereafter, Kennedy took the woman by the hand. Water dripping from sculpted calves and sensuous thighs. Michael watched them go, the camcorder zooming on their departure.

The woman, acutely aware that she was being filmed, turned on the balls of her bare feet and, still holding Kennedy's hand, smiled for the camera.

She uttered two words before blowing Michael a kiss.

Two words that spike Kennedy's heart even now as she plays the videotape on the floor of her family room.

Ciao Bella.

Chapter 50

She waits until after dinnertime to call him.

Places the call around eight.

Glances at her nails as she listens to the ringing on the other end of the phone.

Starts when a female voice answers.

"I'm trying to reach Joe," Kennedy says, somewhat cautiously.

It's now dark outside. Kennedy has the blinds drawn and the lights on. Still she feels a certain chill from being alone.

"Joe can't come to the phone," the voice says. "It is Thanksgiving, you know."

Kennedy stares in amazement at the phone.

"Excuse me," she begins, the attempt at controlling her rising anger gone, "this isn't a social call. I'm calling about a *case.*"

"Your case, Kennedy. Isn't that right?"

"Whom am I speaking to?" she asks.

"This is Tara, his fiancée," Tara responds acidly.

"Look, Tara, tell Joe I found the information that we were searching for earlier. Do you think you can do that?"

Tara begins a rapid-fire response, but Kennedy, smirk painted on her face, has already hung up.

Joe returns her call about an hour later.

"Gee, thanks for ruining my holiday," he says without preamble.

"Excuse me? You asked me to call you if I found anything," Kennedy exclaims, huffing into her Black-Berry.

"Did you have to get into it with Tara, of all people?" Joe asks.

Kennedy laughs.

"That heifer answers your phone, takes an attitude with me, and you're all up in my face? You've got to be kidding."

"Don't call Tara a heifer. She's my fiancée."

"Joe, I called because of the case, nothing more."

Joe is silent, controlling the storm that is brewing inside him.

Kennedy doesn't wait for a response. She pushes on.

"I found what we were looking for. I found the tape."

"Okay." Joe waits for more.

"The woman who says *Ciao Bella* in the voice mails is the woman Michael and I met in Miami four years ago. It's definitely her. Now that I've seen her on videotape, I'm positive it's her."

That information has Joe's attention.

"That's great. What's her name?" he asks.

Kennedy frowns. "That's the thing, Joe. I don't know her name. I mean, I can't remember, and it's nowhere on the video."

"Okay. Give me what you have. Everything. Don't

leave out any details. We're closing in. This is good work."

For the next ten minutes, Kennedy recounts for Joe everything on the tape and what she recalls from memory. Joe does not interrupt, just lets her talk, taking copious notes. When she's done, Joe stares at what he's written, nodding his head.

"Okay. Would your husband remember this woman's name?"

Kennedy considers the question.

"Not sure. He's not speaking to me right now, so . . ."

Joe, wisely, leaves that one alone.

"Fine. Can you go to the tape and see if there is a date? I want to know exactly when you were down there in Miami."

"I can look. Give me a moment."

"We know she was in Miami at some sort of health conference. Shouldn't be too difficult to backtrack and find out which one. You also said you remember her saying something about her flight. Do you recall where she was from?"

Kennedy thinks.

"I'm almost positive she said she was from Florida. Not sure which city, but I do think she mentioned something about a short flight. So she could be from Orlando or Jacksonville. Those don't ring a bell, but my gut feeling tells me she's from Florida."

Kennedy fast-forwards to the first day of the Miami vacation. There's the date: November 16, 2005. She lets Joe know.

"Great," he replies. "This is good. Let me try and find out which conferences were being held in Miami during the middle of November, 2005. Hopefully, we can get a list of attendees and go from there. If you see her name, perhaps it will jump-start your memory."

"Hope so."

"You didn't keep in contact with her, did you?"

"We exchanged several e-mails, but that was when we were on Verizon. Those e-mails are no longer accessible. She was married and concerned about her husband finding out."

"This could be our guy."

"It's a long shot," Kennedy says.

"Actually, it's not. What's happened to you is a crime of passion. This is coming from someone who's been burnt. It's got to be related to someone you've been intimate with. I'd bet my pension we're closing in."

"I hope you're right, Joe. I really do."

"Trust me. This son of a bitch is in my sights. I can feel it."

Chapter 51

He sits in the cab of his Ford truck, staring out at the shimmering waters. It's early morning, and the sun is still low in the sky. This should be a peaceful, serene time. But it's anything but that.

The hum of nature is strong here—the rattle of a belted kingfisher, sharp cricket songs, resonating frog calls, even reptile sounds of wretched, slimy creatures slithering mere yards from where he's parked.

The noise interferes with his thinking. His ability to reminisce is in serious jeopardy.

His head is pounding. Nothing new there. He can't remember a time when he didn't have the pain.

Actually, that's not true. He knows exactly when it all began.

Lately, the pain has been shifting. Today it's at the base of his skull; he keeps rubbing the protrusion of skin and bone at the top of his neck, wondering if he were to hit it with a sledgehammer would the pain finally dissipate for good? He's already downed a half-dozen Tylenol. That shit's not even effective anymore. He imagines his bloodstream choked with miniature acetaminophen soldiers, marching along his arteries and veins haphazardly, searching (in vain) for a battle, for a demon to slay. Damian wants to scream at their captain and show them the way—incompetent fuckwads.

What is truly needed right now is a couple shots of Evan Williams bourbon. Fuck the fact that it's only seven AM. Only thing that stops him from reaching for the bottle this second is the meeting he's got later in Miami. Can't show up smelling like a distillery. That wouldn't be good for business.

No, siree.

Damian shifts in his seat. Rolls down the passenger window because it's becoming uncomfortable. Now the nature sounds are amplified, like it's Dolby Digital up in this piece. He rubs his neck again, and thinks of her.

Closes his eyes so he can imagine her in all of her glory.

When she was pure. Untainted. Wholesome.

God, Damian has trouble remembering when that was. Seems like a lifetime ago.

In some ways it was just that.

A lifetime ago.

When things were different.

When things were good.

Once upon a time he was married. They loved each other very much. The two of them made up this incredible team: the envy of their friends and family. *Look at those two,* they'd hear, *look at the way she looks at him, the way he dotes on her. They're gonna be together for life, no question about it.*

Yeah, it sure seemed that way, back then.

Before she turned. Before things went bad.

What is it about women? Damian muses.

They say they want a good man. A man who wants to settle down. A monogamous man. A man who desires a family. A big house. A stable career.

Damian wanted all of that and more.

She had that and more.

But it wasn't enough.

Bitches always want what they can't have.

When they've got it good, they want better.

When they reach better, they strive for best.

Bitches.

It don't make no kind of sense.

To have all that—the envy of your friends, and to throw it all away. And for what?

Back then, in his other life, Damian was compassionate. He was zestful, the life of the party. He was everything a woman wanted in a man.

But it wasn't enough.

He even forgave her for her first transgression.

Because he loved her that much.

But when he found out that she was infertile—and had known for *years*, hiding the truth from him—that shit broke him in two. Parading around in front of their close friends and family, telling everyone she couldn't wait to be a proud mommy, going through the motions, trying to get pregnant, saying it would happen in due time, when in fact she had no intention because she couldn't.

That fucked him up.

Made him a changed man.

He saw her then for what she really was.

A whore who used people.

Now he didn't even speak her name out loud.

No longer allowed himself the luxury of uttering her name.

She didn't deserve the good memories they had shared.

Didn't deserve anything but what she got.

What she fucking deserved.

Damian utters a short laugh.

She just about killed him when she said she needed some time apart.

Time to sort shit out.

What the fuck does that mean?

Time to figure out what I want, Damian. What I need out of life.

Damian couldn't believe it when the bitch changed her numbers, changed jobs, even where she banked.

Tried to disappear.

Melt into the woodwork.

Like she could actually get away from him.

Damian laughs out loud.

Bitch wanted to start a new life.

Give herself room to breathe.

To do shit that married people shouldn't do.

You tried to hide from me.

Tried so hard to make it so I wouldn't know where to find you.

Silly bitch, you think I'm not smart enough to connect the dots?

There are tears in his eyes now.

Not from pain.

But from laughter.

You wanted to disappear.

Start a new life?

No problem.

Bitch, watch me work. . . .

Chapter 52

She picks up on the second ring.

"Ken, it's Joe."

It's taken him four days to find what he was looking for.

Four days, using a combination of the Internet and some sweet-talking phone etiquette.

Considering Black Friday and the subsequent weekend, four days isn't that bad.

"Good news. You got a second?"

"Yes. Let me close my door. Hang on."

It is Tuesday morning.

It's been an entire week since Michael and Zack left to go to Ithaca. The time apart from them has been excruciating, like the pain from a gaping wound. Kennedy has spent the days on autopilot, going through the motions, not sure how she makes it through each day.

But she has.

She's back at her desk, raising the BlackBerry to her ear.

"Go ahead," she says.

"I've learned that there was only one health-related conference in Miami the week that you and

Michael were vacationing there. The 2005 Sports Physical Therapy Conference was held at the Miami Beach Convention Center. Six hundred fifty-two attendees. Close to a hundred from the State of Florida alone. About forty of those hundred were female."

"How did you learn all this?" she asks, quite impressed.

"I'm good! Or have you forgotten?" Joe doesn't wait for her to answer. "Finding out information about the conference was easy. Getting them to release the attendee list was something else altogether. But I used my charm, and a little law-enforcement pressure, and, well, here we are. We need to go over the list, Ken. See if any of these names ring a bell."

"Okay."

Kennedy's mind is racing. She desperately wishes she could remember the woman's name. She even texted Michael asking if he knew.

No response.

"You're at work. I can fax over the list or swing by and give it to you in person. The sooner we narrow down these names, the better."

"No, don't fax it. Call me when you're here, and I'll come out. I don't need any more drama here at work."

"Understood. I can be there in about twenty."

"I'll be here," Kennedy replies.

They carry their steaming coffees over to a vacant table.

They are at Jolt 'n Bolt, a coffee and tea house located in a former row house on Eighteenth Street. Joe picks at his cinnamon-raisin bagel while

Kennedy pores over the list. There are five pages, computer generated, and Joe has highlighted the female names with a yellow marker. She runs her finger down the names, looking for those that are familiar.

She flips from page to page, nothing jumping out at her. Frustration lines her face.

"Have you asked Michael about the girl?" Joe asks quietly.

"He's not speaking to me right now."

Kennedy's lips are mashed together, and Joe witnesses her jawline flex.

Joe nods.

"Want me to call?" he offers.

Kennedy shrugs.

"I doubt he'll talk to *you*," she replies.

Kennedy shakes her head.

"None of these names seem familiar, Joe." She drops the pages to the wooden table and reaches for her coffee. "This doesn't make any sense. Why can't I remember her name?"

"Don't worry about it. We have her on video and in several photographs. And you're fairly sure she lived in Florida. I'm betting it's one of these women."

"But none of the names jump out at me."

"It has been four years," Joe says.

Kennedy closes her eyes. Tries to concentrate. Forces herself to drift back to four years ago, South Beach, Miami, the Tides hotel, B.E.D., De-Vitos. Suddenly she looks up.

"Dawn. Her name is Dawn."

Joe suspends his chewing. He swallows hard.

"Dawn? Are you sure?"

Kennedy has picked up the pages and is scanning them quickly.

"Yes. Her name is Dawn. I remember now. Dawn . . . Dawn . . . It's been on the tip of my tongue for days. Just couldn't get it out until now."

She glances up with a grimace.

"No Dawn, Joe. No Dawn on these pages."

Joe's brow furrows.

"Let me take a look."

He goes over the list as Kennedy eyes him impatiently.

"It's not there. I checked."

"Okay. Okay. Let me think. It's possible that Dawn is a middle name or even a nickname. Let me check the other pages back at the station. I'm going to call down to Miami-Dade and see what they can come up with."

Joe sees Kennedy's dissatisfaction. He pats her hand as he smiles.

"Don't give up hope, Ken. This is our best lead yet. We're close. These things take time."

Kennedy nods.

"I've gotta get back to work, Joe. Call me if you learn anything."

She smiles weakly.

"I will," he says as he watches her go.

"Miami-Dade Police Department, Sergeant Costello. How may I help you?"

Joe is at his desk, unlaced boots on the metal top. He runs a hand along his facial scar, feeling the raised flesh.

"Sergeant Costello, my name is Detective Joe Goodman from the Metropolitan Police Department, Washington, D.C."

"How may I help you, Detective?"

"I'm searching for a female who lives in Florida.

She's associated with a crime here in D.C. involving felony stalking, computer fraud, and larceny. I have a photograph and about forty or so names. I need someone down there to go through your DMV database and match the names with the photograph."

"Sounds like something the feebies would be interested in," the sergeant says.

"Yeah, probably, but I'm trying to keep the feds outta this. At least for a while, until we know more."

"I hear you. You say you've got forty names?" the sergeant asks.

"Yeah," Joe responds. "I know that's a lot, but this is as close as we can get it right now. We know the victim and assailant met in Miami several years ago. We've traced her to a physical therapy conference that was held at the Convention Center. We believe she resides in your state. We're starting with those attendees who registered with a Florida address. The vic recalls the name Dawn, but I don't see a Dawn from Florida on the attendee list."

"This is gonna take some time, Detective."

"Understood. Can I fax you what I've got so you can get started? This is a priority for us, as the stalking has escalated."

"Yeah, sure."

"Great. Thanks, Sergeant. I very much appreciate your help. This won't go unnoticed."

"Just don't blow up my phone every hour looking for answers. This ain't the only case I'm working, you know."

"I hear you," Joe responds. "Read you loud and clear."

Chapter 53

She's in their bedroom upstairs when she hears the front door open. Zack's voice slices through the silence.

"MOM-MEEEEEEEEE!"

Kennedy is taking the stairs as fast as she can without tumbling down. Her heart is spiking. Zack looks up, grin a mile wide as he rushes to meet her, backpack bouncing against his bony shoulders. She takes him in her arms, lifting him up into the air.

"Zack, I missed you soooooooooooooo much! My God, look at you. You're getting so big!" Kennedy smothers his face with kisses.

"I missed you, too, Mommy. I'm glad I'm home. That bed at Nana's isn't as comfortable as mine."

Kennedy's eyes brim with tears. She releases her son and stands up, gazing down at Michael. He's looking good in his jeans, sweater, and boots. Relaxed and confident. She resists the urge to rush down the stairs and into his arms. Instead they make eye contact. He does not turn away. She smiles at him and he nods at her.

"Hi, Michael."

"Hey, Kennedy."

The air between them is cool. It is not unexpected, so she doesn't allow his nonchalant reception to get her down. Kennedy moves to the bottom step as Michael places Zack's things to the side of the stairs.

"Can I play my Xbox, Mommy, pretty please? It's been so long. I'm dying here!"

Kennedy glances at her watch and then to her son.

"For a little while. Not too long. We need to get you ready for school in a bit."

Zack heads toward the family room as Michael clears his throat.

"Zack, come here."

Zack stops and turns, then returns to where his father is standing.

Michael reaches out his arms, and Zack embraces him.

"Zack, I had a really wonderful time with you. Pop Pop and Nana had fun, too. Remember what I told you. I'll see you in two days. That's Friday, okay?"

"Okay, Dad."

"Love you, Zack," Michael says, kissing the top of his head.

"Love you, too, Dad." Zack rushes off, leaving Kennedy and Michael alone.

Kennedy stares at Michael. She feels anxiety and anger rising all at once. She glances back nervously into the hallway, then to her husband.

"Can I talk to you?" she asks.

"Sure."

"Let's go outside. I don't want Zack to hear us."

Michael nods as Kennedy turns her head and yells, "Zack, I'll be right back. Your father and I will be out front talking."

"Okay, Mommy," Zack responds from the next room.

Once outside, with the door shut behind them, Kennedy folds her arms across her chest from the deepening cold and her annoyance.

"What's this about Friday, Michael?"

Michael does not blink.

"I no longer live here, Kennedy. I need to see my son on a regular basis, and he needs to see me. I've drafted up a visitation agreement and—"

"Wait a second. Visitation agreement? Isn't that a bit premature?"

"No, Kennedy, it is not. You and I have separated. We no longer live in the same house. We need to spell out our respective visitations with Zack."

"Jesus . . ."

Kennedy shakes her head.

Michael stares at her.

She moves closer to her husband.

"Michael, please. Please come back home. This is not the answer. We need to talk about this. We need to talk about what happened."

Michael backs up.

"No, Kennedy. We're not doing that right now. What we are going to do is come up with a visitation agreement so I can see my son. I'm proposing that every two days I have him overnight. In other words, he'll be with me Wednesday, Friday, and Sunday nights. You can have him the remaining days."

Michael reaches into his back pocket and extracts a folded paper. He unfolds it and hands it to her. Kennedy takes it and reads it.

The draft visitation agreement spells out the

schedule for visitation between Michael and Kennedy.

"I'm also proposing how we can handle Christmas and New Year's. You can get back to me with your comments and we'll take it from there."

Kennedy flips to the second page, slowly shaking her head.

"Michael, this is crazy. Do you hear yourself? Baby, can you just talk to me, please? Just give me a chance to explain myself?"

Michael shakes his head firmly.

"No, Kennedy, not now."

"This is ridiculous! I don't even know where you live, for God's sake!"

"All we need to settle on is visitation." Michael stuffs his hands into the pockets of his jeans. Kennedy watches his breath exhale from his nose and mouth. "What I need to do is take some time to figure everything out. And I'm going to take whatever time I need to accomplish that. In the meantime, you and I have nothing to discuss, except where it concerns the health and welfare of our son."

Kennedy stares at Michael under a deepening sky. The cold air and his harsh words make her shiver. The feeling chills her to the bone. For a moment she says nothing. Then she nods solemnly.

Kennedy sighs heavily.

"All right, Michael."

Michael turns to go.

"One more thing," she says, staring at the back of his head as he pauses on the steps.

"There have been some new developments in our case. Umm, we think we're closer to knowing who is behind all the stuff with the e-mails and our bank account."

Michael ponders her words for a moment and nods his head, exhaling more breath from his nostrils.

"You can tell me all about it in an e-mail," he responds before descending the steps slowly to his waiting SUV.

Chapter 54

Friday evening.

Close to seven PM.

Joe's at his desk, finishing up some paperwork.

It's been a particularly violent week.

The last forty-eight hours have been spent in Washington's brutal southeast quadrant, Anacostia, knee deep in a drive-by shooting of four unarmed teenagers. The prevailing theory has to do with some gang initiation, but with witnesses unwilling to come forward and talk, the work is slow going. Arrests seem as likely as winning the lottery.

A fax machine on the other side of the station comes to life, screaming like a newborn after its first gulp of air. Someone gets up to check it and yells across the room, over the din of phone and chatter of detectives and belligerent suspects, "Goodman, fax!"

Joe stands, stretches his limbs, and meanders over. He gets to the machine and grabs the first page, scanning the cover sheet.

From Costello, Miami-Dade PD.
11 possibilities

See #5. I think she's your girl
—Costello.

Joe notes that this is page one of twelve. He checks page two as it finishes printing. A two-by-two DMV photo. The person staring back at him is named Lucy Alvarez. Driver's license number, name, address, birth date, license expiration date. Sex, height, and weight. Organ donor info. Underneath the info is a phone number written by hand.

Pretty, light-skinned, but definitely not Dawn.

He waits patiently for the next page to print.

Infinity Jackson.

Joe shakes his head. *Why do our people have to name their kids after cars?* If he meets another Porsche or Lexus, he'll pull out his own hair!

Infinity isn't Dawn.

Joe puts the pages down and crosses the office to the other side. He pours himself a cup of four-hour-old coffee, loads it down with sugar to mask the taste. By the time he's returned to the fax, the machine's working on page six. Joe picks up the pages, flipping through.

Delores Childs.

Renee Walker.

Lindsey Rein.

He stops at Lindsey Rein.

The hair is all wrong.

Short, finger-sized curls.

Pretty smile.

Beautiful eyes.

The eyes tell him he's found her.

He's almost positive.

Checks her info.

Age: thirty-four.

Address in Mango, Florida. Joe heads over to his desk without waiting for the other pages to complete. He sits down, fingers to his keyboard, calling up Google.

Mango, Florida.

Clicks on the first search return: Google Maps.

A city/town off Dr. Martin Luther King, Jr. Boulevard and Highway 75.

He zooms out using several clicks of his mouse.

Mango looks like it's less than ten miles west of Tampa.

Joe stares at the number scrawled underneath her photo.

Picks up the phone and dials the 813 number.

Ringing.

He feels the raised flesh of his scar, fingers brushing against his beard as he waits for the phone to connect.

More rings.

Then voice mail.

Automated female voice.

"You have reached 813 . . ."

Joe leaves a message.

"This is Joe Goodman from the Metropolitan Police Department in Washington, D.C. I am looking for a Lindsey Rein. Please call me as soon as you get this message." He leaves his cell number and hangs up.

Goes back over to the fax and grabs the remaining pages. Reads them over as he walks back to his desk.

The other ten women—all light-skinned, some black, others Latino or perhaps Middle Eastern.

Back at his desk, he glances at the photo of Lindsey Rein.

Hair different. But the eyes and smile are the same.

Lindsey Rein.

"Gotcha," Joe mutters to himself. "I think we've found our girl."

Chapter 55

He eases himself inside her and finds heaven.

Joe presses his weight against Tara, kissing her lips softly.

She moans as he hits home.

Finds her chocolate spot and makes his way back home.

It's close to midnight, and Joe's making love to his fiancée.

Feels like he hasn't seen much of her lately, with work being such a bitch.

She's understanding, though. Which is why he made a special effort to clock out before eleven.

Put work on hold so he can spend time with his woman.

Leave work alone, if just for a little while.

He found her in bed when he came in, lights off and television on, watching reruns of *Law & Order*.

Kissed her on her lips, ran a shower before slipping his nude form underneath the freshly laundered flannel sheets, pushing the remote off the bedspread as he slid between her legs and eased inside her.

Where he found heaven.

They found their groove.

Their rhythm. Their rhyme. Her spot.

That's when his cell phone began to ring.

Tara's arms encircle his neck as he moves in and out of her slowly. She is gazing into his eyes when the blaring sound invades the room. The cell is on the nightstand, buzzing around like an insect, causing Joe to miss a beat.

Their beat.

"You better not get that," she says, reaching down to grab his ass, ensuring he continues to thrust. He does.

But the groove is wrong.

The rhythm is off.

"Joe!" she exclaims, marveling as the head of his member brushes against her engorged clit, making her sing. "Please don't stop. . . ."

Joe drives home.

Tries to ignore the incessant ringing.

Finally it ceases.

But the rhyme is wrong.

His mind is back on work.

Just like that.

Tried to leave it alone.

But it wouldn't be left alone.

Joe had made several more phone calls from his desk that evening.

Calls to the Tampa Police Department.

He got the runaround, handed off from one district to the other. Finally, a desk sergeant told him he'd need to contact the Hillsboro County Sheriff's Office for what he was inquiring about.

He made the call, spoke to a deputy who said it was a busy evening (being it was a Friday) and that someone would be in touch.

That was several hours ago.

Now his cell is ringing, buzzing.

It could be work.

Anacostia drive-by.

Two dead teenagers.

Another on life support. Condition grave.

Could be Kennedy.

Another e-mail.

Incriminating photos.

Funds wired out.

Or the sheriff's office.

Or Lindsay Rein herself.

Joe tries to clear his head and focus on this sweet spot where he's burrowed.

Tara pushes him away.

Joe thinks she's pissed.

But she gets on all fours, ass up high, face pressed into the mattress, the folds between her legs glistening like morning dew.

Joe buries himself inside her, flesh slapping against her ass as he pummels her, fucking her hard, the call quickly forgotten.

Tara is fucking him back.

She's meeting his thrusts with parries of her own, palms flat on the bed as she bucks her pelvis hard against his big dick, groans muffled by the pillow, beads of sweat tracing around the small of her back.

Tara moans, "Oh my God."

Her eyes are scrunched tight as her body begins to shiver. A shock wave rockets through her body. Joe feels the tidal wave rolling through as she sings.

They are back to grooving.

Rhythm and rhyming right.

"FUCK!"

He is coming as she hits her high note.

Muscles tight.

Testicles slapping her clit as he offers her a river.

Collapsing then, out of breath, on top of her.

Sweat-sheened, their heartbeats race past the finish line and then begin to slow, lapping around the track, as in victory.

After several minutes of feeling her pulse beat against his own torso, Joe rolls away.

He's on his back, staring up at the ceiling, that post-orgasmic feeling wafting through him when he feels Tara's eyes upon him.

Joe turns, meets her stare with his own.

"Now you can get the phone," she says before easing off the bed and sashaying away slow and sensual, sweaty and naked, a sight to behold.

Chapter 56

Joe walks into his office holding his cell in hand. He can hear the shower running, knows that Tara will be in there for close to a half hour as is customary.

Which is fine with him.

Joe closes the door.

Places the phone to his ear and listens to the voice mail.

Sheriff's office returning his call.

Joe hits redial. A moment later the call goes through.

"Sheriff's Office, Deputy Radcliff."

"Deputy, this is Detective Joe Goodman from the Metropolitan Police Department. Sorry to be calling late, but I'm returning your call."

"Yes, Detective. I just left you a message. You had called here earlier?"

"Yes, I did. Inquiring about a Lindsey Rein of Mango, Florida. Was wondering if you got a jacket on her."

"What's the nature of the inquiry?"

Joe replies, "Running leads on a case I'm working here in D.C. involving felony stalking, computer fraud, and larceny. I was hoping to get some background on her—whatever you've got, any priors, run-ins with the law. You know, the drill."

"Hmm," Radcliff responds. "Felony stalking, you say?"

"Yup." Joe wonders if this guy will be helpful at all. He was hoping for a break tonight.

"Well, we've got nothing on her. No priors. I pulled her up on the computer. Not even a speeding ticket. Your girl's clean."

"Really? Okay. I put a call in to her residence. Haven't heard back as of yet, but I just left the message earlier tonight."

"Let us know when you hear from her," the deputy commands.

"Why is that?" Joe asks.

"Because as of three days ago, your girl's a missing person."

That catches his attention.

"What did you just say?"

The deputy responds, "Missing person. As of three days ago."

"You're shitting me."

Joe can't contain himself.

"Let's back up," he says, reaching for a pen and paper. "Who reported her missing?"

Joe hears papers rustling in the background.

"Let me see," Radcliff says. "Hold on a second." More papers rustling. "Dang, can't hardly read this chicken scratch. Okay. Here we go. Looks like her mother. One Jean Daniels. Said she hadn't heard from her daughter in four days. Usually speaks to her every other day."

Joe is writing feverishly.

"Did you check it out?"

"Not me personally, but yeah, one of the deputies went by the house. No signs of a break-in. Nothing out of the ordinary."

"Significant other?"

"Yup. According to the mother, Lindsey just got out of a marriage. Pretty nasty, the way she tells it. But the ex checks out. Let me see here. Yup, he checked out."

"What's the husband's name?" Joe asks.

"He's an ex, but let's see. Here it is. Damian Rein of Clearwater, Florida."

"Thanks. You got an address and phone number for him? Oh, and can I get the mother's contact info, too?"

"Hold on. Here it is."

Joe scribbles on his pad. "You say the husband checks out. What did you mean?"

"Looks like we went out yesterday or the day before and spoke to him. Says he hasn't seen or heard from Lindsey in close to six months. Doesn't even know where she lives."

"And you believe him?" Joe asks, the feeling in the pit of his stomach rising. There's something here, just below the surface. He can sense it.

"Well, Detective, we may not be a fancy police department like what you got up there in the nation's capital, but we do okay for ourselves. Manage to keep the peace around here. So, yeah, if one of our deputies says he checks out, then he checks out."

Joe counts to three slowly.

"Fair enough. Anything else you can give me?"

"Nope. Now if you'll excuse me, I've got work to

do. Plenty of bad guys to round up, if you know what I mean."

The line goes dead.

Joe grunts.

One step closer.

Chapter 57

It is cold in the trailer at night.

Metal siding rattles from the wind. The mobile home smells of cigarettes and cheap whiskey. Clothes are strewn around haphazardly. On the stove, bacon fat hardens in an old-fashioned cast-iron skillet while day-old coffee languishes in a stained pot.

The phone rings, jarring her from an uneven sleep. A callused hand, one that looks as if it has labored in the sun far too long, sneaks out from beneath the covers and reaches for the corded phone, its base nailed to a square of plywood, which in turn is affixed to the wall.

She grabs the receiver, knocking it from its base. She coughs while following its twisted cord.

"Who's this?" she exclaims, followed by a violent cough.

Joe squints, as if in pain.

"Ms. Jean Daniels? My name is Joe Goodman, and I'm a detective—"

"Oh!" she squeals, suddenly wide awake. "Is this about my Dawn?"

Joe's eyes narrow.

"Ma'am? Is your daughter Lindsey Rein?"

"Yes, yes. Oh my God, have you found her?" Jean Daniels is now sitting up in her twin bed. Her head is covered in a scarf of blue medallions, making her look like some long-lost Egyptian queen.

"No, ma'am, I'm a detective from Washington, D.C. I need to ask you a few questions about your daughter."

Jean Daniels reaches for her cigarettes. She lights one and inhales a quick drag, blowing smoke into the receiver.

"Did you say Washington? What do you all want with my Dawn?"

Her hands are shaking. Eyes dart from left to right swiftly, searching the cramped interior as if she does not belong.

"Yes, ma'am. I'm investigating a case here in D.C. and would like to ask you a few questions."

Joe is sitting in his office, back to the window, staring at the computer screen. In the next room, Tara is fast asleep. The hum emanating from the computer is soft and almost therapeutic. He gazes at the images before him, photos he's copied and hidden from Tara's view, feeling the passion that seems to radiate from the screen. He tries to imagine what it felt to be there, actually being there, immersed in such pleasures of the flesh instead of a voyeur, as he is now.

Dawn.

Thin-framed, killer body. Butterscotch complexion. Weave halfway down her back.

Kennedy.

Sweet like mocha chocolate.

Full inviting breasts, dark erect nipples.

Smile beckoning him like he's the only one she needs.

Bodies pressed against one another as their lips

make contact. Eyes shut and expressions saying it all—this is rapture. He feels himself stiffen.

Dawn astride sexy Kennedy.

Her legs are almost closed. But not quite. He can see her labia peeking out from between her legs.

Jesus.

Then Michael atop Dawn, sinewy brown back muscles shining. The photograph has caught him reaching for her ankles. There on her ankle sits a tattoo, the spot of red ink visible between fingers— the spider, clearly seen.

Black widow.

Dawn is staring up at Michael, and her expression says what Joe feels radiating out at him—the heat—this is rapture.

"Ms. Daniels—"

"Please, call me Jean," she instructs.

"Jean, then. Your daughter is named Lindsey Rein, yet you call her Dawn?"

"Yes, she's the reason I get up every morning. Lindsey is why I'm willing to meet the dawn each day."

Joe processes that.

"Does your daughter have any identifying marks on her, such as any tattoos?"

"A spider. Black-widow spider. On her ankle. Why?" she asks, suddenly feeling vulnerable. "Have you found her? Oh God, you've found my baby!"

"No, ma'am, we haven't. May I ask if she ever mentioned to you a couple by the name of Michael and Kennedy Handley?"

"Who?"

"Michael and Kennedy Handley."

Jean shakes her head although there is no one there to witness it.

"Can't say I've ever heard of them."

"Okay," Joe says. "Can you tell me about her husband? I understand he's been questioned in your daughter's disappearance."

"The divorce was extremely hard on Damian. He didn't take it well. Didn't want the divorce. That was Dawn's idea."

"Why?"

"Because she had outgrown him. They wanted different things. Damian wanted a family. He wanted a traditional wife. In the beginning, when they first were married, she was everything he wanted and more. But time changes people. It changed my Dawn. During the last few years that they were a married couple, she began to spread her wings. I don't think Damian liked who she had become."

"Go on," Joe instructs.

"She moved out about a year ago. Six months later they were divorced. No children, so it wasn't difficult from a legal perspective. She wanted it that way—wanted to get on with her life as quickly as possible. Moved away from Clearwater, took an apartment in Tampa, then moved again so he couldn't find her."

Joe sits up. He tries to ask the next question as delicately as he can.

"Was Dawn afraid of Damian? Did she fear him?"

Jean ponders the question while taking a long drag.

"I don't think it was fear. She *distrusted* him. After they separated, Dawn began to distrust Damian."

"Can you give me specifics?"

"Dawn never shared any details with me. She told me she didn't want me worrying. But I suspected something was going on. I mean, she changed jobs, then a few months later moved to Mango. Told me not to give out her new address or phone number to anyone, especially her ex-husband. I don't know if she was afraid of him, but it was clear she didn't want to be found."

Joe makes some notes.

"What does her ex-husband, Damian, do for a living?" Joe asks.

"He runs a security consulting company out of Tampa."

Joe writes that down.

"And the name of this company?"

Jean Daniels stubs out her cigarette.

"That's easy. Rein Security. Just like their last name."

"One more question, Ms. Daniels, I mean, Jean. Was Dawn involved with anyone that you know of, either while she was married or during her separation and subsequent divorce?"

Jean reaches for another cigarette. The flame from the lighter shivers in the near darkness. She fills her lungs, then exhales slowly, eyes unfocused as she considers the question.

"If she was, sir, she kept it a secret from me. And it would have had to be. Because that is one thing Damian would never have been able to handle. Believe you me. . . ."

Chapter 58

Michael stares at the ceiling, unable to fall asleep. He's thinking about his wife and the e-mail she sent him.

It's been a long time since he's slept alone.

Can't get used to the feeling.

And yet every time he thinks about her and what she did to him, his blood begins to boil.

So he tries not to think about it.

During the day, at work, or on the days when he has Zack, he's fine. He's good.

Work and his son keep his mind active, keep him busy.

They stop Michael from thinking about Kennedy and his situation.

But at night, when there's no work, and Zack's not around, the thoughts come calling.

They invade his psyche without consent.

Fill his head, regardless of how hard he puts up a fight.

So he forces his brain to switch gears.

Replays the e-mail in his mind instead, thinking about those happier times.

The e-mail declared that Dawn, the woman they

met years ago in Miami, may be at the center of everything that's happened to them.

Michael is suddenly whisked away to that time in South Beach.

The Tides hotel.

Kennedy and Dawn lounging by the pool, deep in conversation.

Splashing around in the blue water as Michael records them.

Kennedy taking Dawn by the hand, water dripping from their succulent bodies as they head up to their room, alone.

Dawn pivoting on the balls of her feet, still holding Kennedy's hand, smiling for Michael and the camera.

Blowing him a kiss.

He remembers watching them go.

Knowing what was to come.

He had ordered a drink, sipped at the mojito as the sun beat down, baking his skin a rich golden brown like the oven-roasted chicken his momma makes. And when the hour had passed, Michael had gathered his things and gone to the room.

Opened the door and saw them.

Witnessed Dawn feeding on Kennedy.

His wife opened her eyes when he came in.

He dropped his things quietly where he stood.

Dawn glanced back momentarily before returning her mouth to Kennedy's glistening sex.

Kennedy met the gaze of her husband. Held it for a moment. Then raised Dawn's head in her hands.

Stared into her eyes.

Said her husband wanted to fuck her.

Dawn responded by moving onto her haunches, lifting her ass high.

Her head descended back into Kennedy's lap.

Wordlessly Michael removed his swim trunks. When they fell to the carpet, he was already engorged and hard.

It took him a moment to sheath himself in latex.

Words were not needed.

His heart was pounding in his chest.

His stare zeroed in on that sweet spot between her sugary thighs.

That slice of butterscotch heaven that sang to him.

He rubbed a thumb along its length and was immediately rewarded with wetness and warmth.

Michael slid into her effortlessly, amazed at the way she seized him.

Petite, tight body.

Moving her ass around, meeting his slow, purposeful thrusts with a sensuous drive of her own.

Telling him without words she could handle all of him. Shaking her ass on his pole, taking him all the way inside her to her very core, then back out as fast as it came, the head of his swollen cock tickling her clit in a way that drove them both wild.

Michael recalls that lazy afternoon with a sudden clarity that surprises him.

Recalls how he placed his hands on Dawn's ass and pummeled her into oblivion.

Remembers how good it felt to be inside of Kennedy's lover, watching her watching him.

Experiencing the feeling of losing himself in the velvet folds of a woman who was not his wife.

Remembering what rapture felt like.

Drinking it in until he was intoxicated with its potency.

Rapture.

Wrapping yourself around the warmth of your partner's lover. . . .

Chapter 59

Damian Rein walks confidently into 100 North Tampa Street and waits patiently for the elevator that will take him to the fortieth floor.

He is heading to an office in one of Tampa's tallest skyscrapers, one built on the banks of the Hillsborough River, with unobstructed, panoramic views of Hillsborough Bay, Old Tampa Bay, and Tampa Bay.

He's dressed in a two-piece, three-button dark gray suit, silver tie, obsidian cuff links, shiny black shoes.

Head smoothly shaved.

Wearing the latest cologne from Calvin Klein.

Outwardly he projects power and authority, like someone in charge. He flashes the smile of a winner. But inside he's dying a slow death.

Yeah, they should give him an Academy Award for this performance.

Like when he was in Neiman Marcus last night.

Men's fragrances.

The woman behind the counter was flirting with him big-time as he sampled various colognes, keeping her cleavage in plain view as she showed him her wares.

Thing was, all of those fucking fragrances were making him nauseous.

His headache was already out of control.

And truth be told, when he was leaning in to the woman, returning his dazzling smile to her, gazing down at those fortysomething breasts, all he could think about was tying her sorry ass to a four-poster bed and slapping those middle-aged titties around with a spatula until her entire torso was beet red.

Bitches!

He had no fucking use for them anymore.

He was tired of their shit.

Weary of being the man they desired him to be, only to be pushed aside.

Feeling like last year's model.

Of course he didn't slap the shit out of her.

Not at all.

Instead, he did what he always does. Flashed his straight white teeth, settled on the new Calvin Klein, took the woman's business card that she handed to him with his receipt. Told the biddy he'd call to make arrangements so they could enjoy dinner together one day next week.

Or even better.

Dessert.

Just the two of them.

That got her eyes sparkling with desire. She could barely keep from rubbing her legs together with glee.

Whore.

The elevator door opens.

Damian strolls out and heads to his appointment.

He's been here before.

Pushes his way through the glass doors and greets the receptionist with a grin.

They are expecting him.

He has a seat in the posh waiting area while he's offered coffee.

Damian declines.

He waits about ten minutes before the receptionist stands and asks him to follow her.

Damian walks to the right of the receptionist's desk, where a set of double doors is inlaid. She opens them and stands aside, and Damian is ushered in.

Inside, a large, well-decorated office awaits, the centerpiece being a sleek aluminum and glass desk with a middle-aged white man sitting behind it. On three walls are floor-to-ceiling glass panels, providing an unobstructed view of the water beyond. The man stands, raising his hand to Damian.

"Damian Rein," he says.

"Jason Corcoran, good to see you again."

"Please," Jason gestures. "Have a seat. Can I get you anything?"

"No, I'm good, thanks."

The door closes behind them. Jason returns to his chair and steeples his fingers in front of him.

"So?"

Damian can see that Jason wants to get down to business.

Good.

He's not here to socialize.

Damian begins. "About a month ago you asked me here to discuss your potential run for the governorship of this state. You've been a well-known business leader and philanthropist to many charitable causes here in the Tampa area. No one knows of your serious consideration to run for office, although many local politicians have asked that you enter the race. At this time your desire to run is a closely guarded secret. And you asked me to look into the security aspects of your candidacy for governor. Specifically, what is known or what can be found out about Jason Corcoran that can damage you.

"The issue is a timely one. As you are aware, several high-profile cases have involved politicians whose illegal or unethical dealings came to light— only to serve as their undoing. In the case of the mayor of Detroit, a series of text messages showed that he was indeed carrying on an extramarital affair with his chief of staff and lying about it to the public. In the case of the governor of New York, cell-phone records, text messages, and other electronic data proved that he was frequenting high-priced escort services."

Damian shakes his head.

"Mr. Rein," Jason says, "I know all of this. Tell me what you've uncovered. Just how vulnerable am I?"

Damian nods.

"You are a well-respected businessman. You are known for your charities. But this is what I discovered."

Damian recites what he knows from memory, without the benefit of notes.

"You routinely transfer money to an account in Cuba by way of the Virgin Islands and have done so for the past three years. It appears that you have fathered a child there and are paying a young woman for her silence."

"How did you—"

"May I continue?"

Jason nods solemnly.

"Furthermore, it would seem that you are addicted to porn. Perhaps addicted is the wrong word, but the hard drives of your four computers are littered with gigabytes of movies and pictures. Your fetish is bukkake—the practice of having female subjects ejaculated on by numerous men—in particular the Japanese bukkake variety, not the fake stuff they manufacture in Southern California, and you've spent a good deal of time and money to purchase it."

Jason's face has turned chalky white.

"You have several credit cards that are not in your own name, which are used for these purchases. Those cards have been used to pay for travel to Japan twice—once last year and once the year before that—where you participated in your own bukkake sessions that were videotaped. Those sessions are on your hard drive, but unfortunately, at least several copies are also floating around the Internet."

"Oh my God."

The words come as a whisper.

"Mr. Corcoran, please understand. I am not here to judge you. Your indiscretions are yours alone. I am here to help you. To eradicate any evidence of illegal, improper, or seemingly immoral activity. And that I can do."

Jason Corcoran swallows hard.

Damian continues.

"My fees are one hundred thousand dollars and will buy you absolute discretion and secrecy. It will take approximately two months of work, primarily due to the fact that we have to hack into American Express and All Nippon Airways to delete the records of your transactions. The Cuba situation is much simpler to deal with. Then there is the question of the videotapes. I can't be sure of how many copies exist, so that will take some additional time. In the end, no one can guarantee that all digital copies are destroyed. But I'll do what I can. If the copies exist on a computer, we'll find them and get rid of them."

Damian sits back, quite satisfied with himself. He can see that he's damaged the fuckwad Jason Corcoran to the core. This is the part that he absolutely adores. Knocking down powerful men and their companies with half a minute's worth of information.

Information is true power.

What you know can alter lives.

It can ruin men.

Make them slaves to another.

Damian wants to grin uncontrollably.

LOL!

Instead, he issues a tight smile and says with his hands held open, as if he were Jason's own priest, "Mr. Corcoran, relax, please. Rein Security is here to protect your secrets."

Chapter 60

Happy as a clam.

Isn't that the expression?

That's how Damian feels right now.

Happy as a clam.

Whatever the hell that means.

Heading back to the office, Damian feels great. He's just landed an account that will net him close to a hundred grand for a few months' work. Best thing about it? Damian doesn't even have to get his hands wet.

That's what is so fantastic about this gig.

Damian is not a hacker. Or even a security guru.

But, as with all great businessmen, the key to his success has been surrounding himself with talented people who know how to get the job done.

Rein Security is built on the premise that Damian, as the CEO, goes out and gets the clients. His "employees" are freelance hackers—brilliant yet socially inept computer science graduates or dropouts. These guys will work for cash, and are totally discreet—Damian has made sure of that by having them sign ironclad nondisclosure agreements. Their work can't be traced back, and if it does come back

to them—well, fuck them, they're on their own—
they get paid well enough to protect themselves.

Damian communicates with them over a highly
encrypted link, where the 512-bit symmetrical keys
are changed once a week. Shit, even the Fed doesn't
change their encryption that often.

It's a perfect arrangement.

He gets the jobs, they perform the work. He
pays them cash, pockets 70 to 80 percent of what
each job has been bid out as.

Today he just made easy money.

And his thoughts are transported back to *her.*

Too bad she's not around to share in the wealth.

This is what he means about women.

If she were still around, he'd be making arrangements to pick her up and take her to dinner at the
best restaurant in all of Tampa.

Where do you want to go, baby?

It's on me.

Wanna fly to Miami for dinner?

Or Jacksonville?

*Wherever you wanna go, baby, whatever you wanna
do, we'll do it. My treat!*

I do all of this for you.

He can imagine it right now, and the thought is
sobering.

*Let's take a trip—spur of the moment—to Paris or
Milan. Can't take off that much time from work? No prob-
lem. How about a quick jaunt to the islands? Trinidad,
Tobago, Aruba?*

*Blue-green seas, white sands. Flowing libations and
the tastiest vittles your palate has ever had the pleasure of
experiencing.*

All for you, baby.

I do this all for you.

For a moment, the pain had simply vanished.

Gone.

Like it had never even existed.

He had been thinking about *her*, his ex-wife, about the good old times, and the terrible hurt was no longer there. But then, just like that, Damian's back to the present—to reality—and the ache is a dull throb in his neck and temples.

Fuck *her!*

Damian swats the thought from his mind as if he were whisking away annoying flies.

He reaches his building and takes the elevator to his floor. The office is quiet. His assistant is at lunch.

Good.

He doesn't want to talk to her anyway.

He unlocks his office and shuts the door quickly behind him.

Goes to his desk, fires up his Mac Pro. Checks messages.

Nothing of interest.

So Damian switches gears and thinks about *them.*

Dude and Mocha.

Wondering how life's treating them.

How they are getting by since Damian came into their life and wreaked fucking havoc.

All the pieces are coming together.

He's tying up all the loose ends.

He'll be done soon.

Hopefully, once and for all, the pain will cease to be an issue for him.

Hopefully, soon, he'll silence his pain.

Forever.

Then begin to live again.

* * *

The phone rings.

Damian glares at the screen.

Sees a 202 area code.

Strange.

He lets it ring again.

Then remembers that his assistant is at lunch.

So he reaches for the receiver.

"Rein Security, Damian Rein speaking."

He says it pleasantly enough. And why shouldn't he? He's still feeling good.

Not post-orgasmic great, like a few minutes ago, before his mood was clouded with thoughts of her.

But still good.

"Mr. Rein. This is Detective Joe Goodman of the Metropolitan Police Department. Do you have a few moments?"

All of a sudden his cheerfulness has evaporated.

Just like that, it's gray skies. Cold, unfamiliar terrain.

Storms on the horizon.

The pain assaults him at the base of his neck. He reaches for the Tylenol, grabs a fistful of Gel Tabs and chews them angrily, washing them down with lukewarm bottled water.

"Mr. Rein," Joe says again.

"Yes . . . I'm here."

Control yourself, Damian commands. *Be cool.*

Goodman. The cop from D.C.

Ex-husband of Mocha.

Shit . . .

He had not expected this.

"I'd like to ask you a few questions about your ex-wife, Lindsey Rein," Joe says.

Damian clears his throat.

"I've told the Hillsborough deputies all I know."

"When was the last time you saw your ex?"

"I don't know. It's been at least five, six months. Perhaps longer."

"And when did you last speak to her?"

"We have had very few conversations, Detective. We're no longer married."

"So you can't recall the last time you two spoke?" Joe asks.

"Nope."

"Don't recall what you talked about? Or the nature of the conversation?"

"No idea."

"You don't seem overly concerned about Lindsey. You do know she's missing, right?"

"Should I be concerned?" Damian grunts. "Lindsey's no longer my problem."

"Interesting attitude, Mr. Rein."

"Look, Detective, she left me, not the other way around. She moved away, took a new job, didn't want to be found. So I'm not sure what you expect from me. My sympathy? Nope, you won't get that. Not where she's concerned. That's not against the law."

"Nope, you're absolutely right. Do you know a Michael and Kennedy Handley from Washington, D.C.?"

That stops Damian dead in his tracks.

Careful.

Be extremely careful.

"No. Never heard of them," Damian replies.

"Really? Perhaps your wife might have mentioned them to you. Michael? Kennedy?"

"Ah, no."

"Been to D.C., Mr. Rein?" Joe asks.

"Well, sure. Long time ago."

"Nothing recent, though?"

"Nope."

He realizes the mistake as soon as the words escape him. Nothing he can do about it now.

"Hmm. Okay. You're in the security business, correct?"

"That's right."

"Meaning, you know how to break into people's compu-ters, steal data on hard drives, that sort of thing?" the detective says.

Damian is silent.

"That is your business, right, Mr. Rein?"

"I'm sorry. What exactly is the nature of your investigation, Detective?"

"So you don't deny being a hacker, capable of stealing data from other people's computers?"

"This conversation is over, Detective. If you have further questions for me, I can put you in touch with my attorney."

"You're wrong, Mr. Rein. For what you and I have to discuss, our conversation has just begun."

The line goes silent, and Damian sees nothing but red.

He sits in his chair, very still, the hammer in his skull driving him to near unconsciousness.

Detective Joe Goodman is a dead man.

He just doesn't know it yet.

Chapter 61

It's after eight on a Wednesday night and Kennedy is just getting home.

She drops her bag on the kitchen counter along with the mail that she does not have the energy to examine. Her keys hit the countertop with a metallic thud. Other than that, the house is quiet.

Too quiet.

Zack is spending the evening with his father.

Per the draft visitation agreement.

She can't get used to this . . . this new arrangement.

Her and Michael not together.

Zack not here with her every single day, as it should be.

She's told no one. Not her family. Not her friends. Because she can't even believe it herself.

Denial.

Hoping she'll wake up from this terrible nightmare.

Praying everything will go back to the way it once was.

When they were a family.

A happily married couple.

Not a care in the world.

Kennedy moves to the couch in the family room and sits, unzipping her boots and removing them from her weary feet. She closes her eyes and leans back, taking a moment for herself.

She's been keeping herself so busy that she won't have to think about her situation. But now, with the house dead quiet, she has no choice but to listen to the silence.

Kennedy opens her eyes.

Stares about the quiet room.

Her vision finds the plasma on the wall.

Silver frame, black screen.

Naturally her thoughts go to her son.

A few weeks ago, Zack would have been in this very room, sitting where he always does on the floor in front of the television, playing his Xbox 360. The screen would have been alive with colors and sounds. And as much as those video games drive her crazy, Kennedy realizes she has grown to love the noise, because it means her son is home, and is happy.

She glances around.

Considers pouring a glass of Merlot.

She's been drinking every night.

Lately like clockwork.

It's a way to relax.

Calm her nerves.

Should she tonight?

She doesn't want to become a lush—relying on her drink as a crutch. On the other hand . . .

Kennedy rises from the couch, cutting off the thoughts as quickly as they came.

She moves toward the kitchen, then changes her mind.

Back to the couch, taking a seat again.

Leaning back, head resting on the cushions as she closes her eyes.

The ringing of her BlackBerry brings her out of her reverie.

Zack's cell.

"Hello. Zack?"

Soft crying on the other end of the phone.

"Baby, what's wrong? Zack, are you there?"

Rustling. Then more tiny sobs.

"Zack, are you okay?" she asks while getting to her feet.

She glances down at her phone.

Presses a few keys, enabling the Chaperone feature to locate Zack.

A few moments later an address displays on her screen.

A Northern Virginia address.

She hits the Map button to display his location.

Alexandria, VA.

Less than eleven miles away.

"I miss you, Mommy," Zack says between sobs.

"I miss you, too, honey. What's wrong?"

"I want to sleep with you. But Daddy says I can't. He says I need to go to sleep here."

His voice pulls at her heartstrings.

"I know, sweetheart. I wish you were here. I would let you sleep with me. Guess what? Tomorrow, when you're home, I promise you can sleep in my bed. How does that sound?"

"All right."

Kennedy smiles.

She moves toward the fireplace.

On the mantel above the hearth are four picture frames.

Photographs of her family.

Happier times.

"You're my little man, Zack. Now go to sleep. It's late, and you don't want to be tired for school in the morning."

"Okay. G'night, Mommy."

"Goodnight, Zack. Mommy loves you."

Kennedy ends the call.

And stares at the photographs above the hearth.

She stops nearest the one on the right.

Her and Michael.

On their wedding day.

Michael in his smart tuxedo.

She in her pretty veil and wedding dress.

And the next one.

The three of them—her, Michael, and Zack, taken last year on vacation at Disney World, the spires of the Magic Kingdom rising in the background.

That one makes her smile.

And the next one.

Her favorite.

Zack in first grade.

Dressed in his blue polo shirt, hair cut like his father's.

Smile a mile wide, save for one missing tooth.

Kennedy reaches for the black frame.

Her eyes are beginning to water as she clutches it to her chest.

She wipes at the tears.

Stares down at the photo.

Her little man.

And the skin on her forehead furrows.

Something is . . . off.

The picture frame.

Black frame, narrow edges of wood around the four-by-six photograph.

But on closer inspection it's not wood, but smooth, polished metal.

Kennedy turns the frame over.

Strange.

Doesn't recall this particular frame.

She lowers the latch that secures the back cover.

Flips it open and stares openmouthed at what's inside.

A tiny circuit board with a shiny circular watch battery.

Kennedy almost drops the picture frame.

Instead she stares at it for a good thirty seconds, not moving, until its true purpose is disclosed to her, like fog dissipating, revealing the forest beyond a winding country road.

Chapter 62

The rain has been falling hard for several hours by the time they are ready to wrap up.

Kennedy has divided her time between the couch in the family room and the bay window overlooking the backyard.

Besides Joe, there are two of them.

They are wearing what looks like navy blue flight suits. Kennedy is not sure if they are MPD officers or from some other agency.

Joe isn't saying, and she's too frazzled to ask.

It's late.

Or early, depending on the way you look at it.

Close to two AM.

It had taken a few hours for Joe to mobilize the team after she called him. Then to get over here and get the equipment set up.

The actual sweep of the house took under ninety minutes.

She observed them in stunned silence, hunting with their equipment, sniffing for scents in the ether.

Four items were discovered.

Bug in the picture frame—family room.

Bug in the computer power strip—den.

Bug in a hardcover novel—master bedroom.

Three microtransmitters on tiny circuit boards.

And the pièce de résistance—a small wireless transmitter in the attic.

Communicating with their own wireless router.

Incredible!

Joe motions to the team while they are packing up.

"Looks like we got everything. Your house is now clean."

Kennedy is stunned.

"You okay?" he asks, staring down into her eyes.

"How . . . how did this happen?"

"Someone got into your house and planted those bugs."

She processes that.

"How?"

"I don't know, Kennedy."

"How long?"

Joe shakes his head.

"There's no way to tell, unfortunately. Could have been planted yesterday or three weeks ago."

"My God . . ."

"Yeah. It sucks."

Joe can't think of any other way to put it.

"But . . . why?" she asks.

"Because this . . . *asshole* wants to get under your skin. He enjoys playing God, messing with you, disrupting your life."

"But why? What did I ever do to *him*?" she cries.

Joe looks at her.

"You slept with his wife. He obviously found out about the encounter. Perhaps Dawn told him, but I doubt it. Regardless, he's angry, and it's payback time."

"Are you sure it's him? Dawn's ex?"

"I can't prove it. Not yet. But it's all coming to-gether. The dots are beginning to connect. Damian Rein is Lindsey Rein's ex-husband. He owns his own security company. He has the motive and the wherewithal to do everything that has happened to you—intercept your e-mail, bug your house, ac-cess your bank accounts. It's him. I know it is."

Kennedy shakes her head gravely.

"Then why can't you go arrest him?" she ex-claims.

"Because of what I just said. I can't prove any of it. Not yet, anyway. But I will. I promise you that."

She shakes her head again.

"I feel like I've just been shot. Or like someone's just taken a baseball bat and swung into my stom-ach."

Joe puts his arm around Kennedy.

"I know. You're going to get through this. I'm gonna nail this bastard. I just need to connect the dots."

Kennedy glances up into his face as she blinks away tears.

"Thanks, Joe."

"One more thing. Tomorrow morning I need you to ditch your BlackBerry and buy a new one with a new phone number. Michael needs to do the same. Understand?"

She stares up at him.

"I thought you said they got everything."

"They did. But we can't be sure he's not tapping your phone. I doubt it—he'd need some serious hardware to accomplish that. But I don't trust this fucker as far as I can throw him, so to be safe, get rid of the phones. This way, there is absolutely no way he can tap your cell, unless he discovers your new number."

"Jesus Christ. Is this really happening?"

"Yeah, it is. We live in a technology age. And anything is possible. This evening I went on the Internet and found software that you can install on a PDA like your BlackBerry that listens in to calls. All for less than three hundred bucks per year."

"Are you serious?"

"Yeah, I am." Joe gestures to the door. "I need to get going."

The team has packed up and passes them in the hallway. Joe shakes hands with each of them. Kennedy issues her thanks.

"Lock the door," he says, once the team has gone and it's just the two of them in the house. "Go upstairs and get some sleep. You look like you need it."

"That's an understatement."

"In the morning, do what I told you to do regarding the . . ."

Joe holds his thumb and pinky to his ear, mimicking a phone.

Kennedy nods.

He gives her a hopeful smile before heading out into the steady downpour.

Work still to be done.

Connecting the dots.

Chapter 63

"Denied."

Joe stands immobile in front of Captain Renee Watts's desk.

It's barely nine AM, and yet she's in a foul mood already.

"Captain—"

"Denied."

"May I speak?" Joe asks.

Captain Watts glares at him for a moment, then nods.

"If I'm to catch this perp, then I need to go down to Tampa. The ex-husband is our strongest lead. He's our guy."

"No."

"But Captain—"

"DENIED, Goodman. You are *not* using department funds to question an alleged perpetrator in Tampa, of all places."

"All evidence points to him," Joe exclaims, throwing up his hands.

"Then let Tampa PD deal with it. I won't. Not when we have plenty of unsolved cases right here in our own backyard."

"Ma'am—"

"You must be hard of hearing. I said DENIED! Now, you are excused."

Joe grits his teeth, his jaw muscles pulsing under his cheeks. Renee Watts has returned her attention to the paperwork before her.

Joe scratches at his scar with an index finger.

"Ma'am, I would like permission to take two days' unscheduled leave."

She looks up into Detective Joe Goodman's eyes.

"For personal reasons," he adds, eyes unblinking, "beginning today."

Captain Watts stares for a moment more before shrugging.

"If you've got the vacation time, then I won't stand in your way."

Joe nods once before turning on his heels and walking toward the door.

The captain clears her throat.

"And if you happen to get caught down there meddling in someone else's jurisdiction, you're on your own. Don't call me to bail you out. Understand?"

Joe nods without glancing back. Then he leaves the office.

The captain watches her detective go.

He's packing when she comes in.

Joe wasn't expecting this.

It's not even ten AM, and he's back home, out of uniform, now in jeans, sweatshirt, and sneakers, garment bag sprawled across the bed, placing a change of socks and underwear into the side pockets.

Tara should be at work.

"Going somewhere?" she asks acidly.

Joe ignores the question.

"Shouldn't you be at work?" he says instead.

"I should be asking the same thing."

They stare at each other. Tara's arms are folded across her chest.

Joe blinks first.

"I'm taking a few days off. Going down to Tampa." He adds hastily, "For work."

Tara purses her lips and nods several times.

"I see."

Joe's not sure what else to say.

"Purpose of this trip?"

"The perp is there." Joe continues filling his bag. "I need to question him."

"And yet you're taking a few days off?"

Her head is cocked to the side, an expression of confusion covering her normally peaceful face.

"The captain won't okay the trip."

"Yet you're going anyway and spending our money?"

"My money. I'm using my money, Tara."

"Oh, it's like that now?" Tara nods to herself. "Interesting."

"Tara, please don't start with me, okay?"

"I find it intriguing that I can't get you this motivated where our impending wedding plans are concerned. But you're all into this case, aren't you? Interesting . . ."

He turns to face her, a pair of folded jeans in his hands.

"Just because I don't spend my time picking out invitations and place settings doesn't mean I'm not motivated about our wedding."

"Really? Well, what does it mean, Joe? Because I'll be damned if I can explain how your ex gets your gears cranked so high. I mean, wow, truly amazing. I haven't seen you this enthused in a long, long time."

Joe ignores the comment and throws the jeans into the main compartment. He goes into the bathroom, comes out seconds later with his toiletry bag. This is tossed into the main compartment as well. He zips it up as Tara watches him mutely.

"I've got a flight to catch," Joe says, finally making eye contact with her.

"I'm sure you do," Tara replies.

He grabs the garment bag and leans in to kiss her. Tara's hand comes up, like a karate move, blocking his attempt at intimacy.

Joe pauses, glares at his fiancée for a moment before sidestepping around her, leaving Tara in their bedroom to stew all alone.

Chapter 64

Ronnie Falmouth is at it bright and early.

He loves this time of morning, when the sun is just rising from the marshy grasslands. He steers the airboat slowly through the brackish water, not hurrying, certainly in no rush.

He sits up high in the molded seat, the hum of the Chevy engine behind him, its giant propellers allowing him to travel effortlessly over grass and water.

He's about seventy miles southwest of Miami in the Everglades National Park, cutting through an impressive expanse of water interspersed with swamplands called Midway Keys, heading west toward Shark River Island. There he'll fish until nightfall.

Probably camp overnight at Oyster Bay Chickee or Joe River Chickee.

A perfect day ahead of him.

Ronnie's alone, and that's just the way he likes it. Away from the wife and kids, and his buddies, who could fuck up a wet dream with their incessant bitching and whining.

No, thank you.

It's just Ronnie and the outdoors, this rental Diamondback, and four glorious days away from everything and everyone that gives him a headache.

Open water appears to be about a quarter of a mile away. He'll meander around teeny islands of red and black mangroves, their tentacles reaching deep into the swamp muck, on his way to Shark River Island.

He increases throttle, listens as the 355-hp Chevy begins to whine, startling a heron that is off to his left in a patch of sawgrass. It croaks loudly as it climbs slowly into the morning sky. Around him the water is dotted with floating plants: bladderwort, white water lilies, and spatterdock. The airboat can glide over these easily, yet Ronnie maneuvers around them, enjoying the feel of the steering stick in his left hand and the throttle in his right.

The wind is in Ronnie's face, the scent of brackish water hanging in the air. As he drives close to a copse of sunken mangroves, an alligator, unseen moments earlier, hits the water with a splash. Ronnie is momentarily frightened as the eight-foot beast passes not far from the bow of his boat. He pulls back instinctively on the throttle and angles the craft sharply to starboard, not wanting the reptile to come up right under him.

That's when he sees it.

Something, Ronnie's not sure exactly what, half-floating in the tangle of half-submerged black roots, a whitish slab of what can only be described as *meat*. Ronnie cranks his neck as the airboat slows, and suddenly the stench assaults him, overpowering his senses.

His eyes water.

Involuntarily, he begins to dry retch as the nature of the floating slab becomes clear.

Ronnie has turned as white as the bloated thing in the water.

A leg.

A human leg!

Bitten off above the knee.

Black and dark red tentacles of half-bitten flesh seem to hang in the near-still water.

The thing bobs near the mangrove, its bloated toes scraping noiselessly against the exposed roots.

A blotch of red above the ankle.

Blood?

He doesn't know.

Too much to process.

The leg continues to bob in the water as if it didn't have a care in the world.

He wrestles his stare away, directing his attention toward the interior of dank, dark underbrush.

There he spies another slab of meat.

Ripped upper torso.

Headless.

No limbs.

Just chewed, half-eaten flesh.

Ronnie yells before vomiting onto the side of the airboat.

Wipes his mouth with his sleeve once he's finished heaving up breakfast.

Steers the airboat away into deeper, less putrid waters.

Ronnie cuts the engine.

Regains some form of composure and reaches for the marine VHF radio.

Chapter 65

Joe Goodman rides in the taxi with his garment bag beside him. The window is halfway down, providing a nice breeze. He watches the sights rush past as he's whisked toward his destination. The skyscrapers are what impress him. Not at all like the nation's capital. Down here in Tampa there are real office buildings.

Tall, majestic even.

It's close to one PM.

Joe considers checking in with Tampa PD but decides against it. He mulls over his captain's final words before erasing them from his mind. He's on his own now. No sense involving the local police department until he has something concrete regarding Damian Rein.

He hopes that not involving Tampa's law enforcement will turn out to be the best decision he makes today.

The cab drops him off in front of a tall building in downtown Tampa. The airport lies only a few miles away. He pays the driver a ten and tells him to keep the change.

Joe hefts his garment bag onto his shoulder and

glances up at the partly cloudy sky before heading toward the building's entrance.

He has always known this day would come.

He has anticipated it with a mixture of rising anxiety and giddiness that has added nausea to his normal headache. Earlier today, when he spotted the lead-in for the news, he knew it was finally time.

A body had been pulled from the Everglades.

Details sketchy.

Sex and age of the deceased unknown since the body was decapitated and missing several limbs.

Damian had left the office immediately and driven straight home.

There wasn't much to do.

He had made preparations days ago.

Now it was time to execute them.

Time to get his life back on track.

The pain will soon cease to be an issue.

Damian is about to silence the pain forever.

Then, and only then, can he begin to live again.

"I'm here to see Damian Rein."

Joe pulls his shield from his waist and holds it up so the assistant can see it clearly. He adds "Metropolitan Police Department" so there is no misunderstanding of why he's here.

He stands in the reception area of Rein Security. It's a small waiting room, tastefully decorated. Muted colors, two relatively comfortable-looking chairs.

The woman facing him is not quite thirty, dressed in khakis and a button-down shirt. She peers at the badge as if she's some sort of crossing guard who is going to decide whether to let him pass or not.

Joe shifts his weight and says irritably, "I need to see him . . . now."

The assistant blinks.

"I'm sorry, sir, but Mr. Rein is not in. Did you have an appointment?"

Joe ignores the question.

"Where is he?"

The assistant swallows.

"I'm sorry, sir. He's not expected back in today."

Joe puts down his garment bag and glares at her.

"What is your name?"

"Amanda."

"Okay, Amanda. This is a police matter. I need you to get on the phone and find your boss."

Amanda glances around, looking for help. When she finds none, she nods and murmurs something to herself.

"Oh, all right. If you'll excuse me."

Amanda heads down the hallway, but Joe is on her heels. She turns around, sees him behind her, and winces, but keeps moving. She gets to her desk and sits quietly, reaching for the phone. Joe glances around. There is an office door off to the side. Joe walks over and tries the knob.

It's locked.

Amanda raises her voice. "Sir? Please don't do that. I'm attempting to reach him now."

Joe ignores her.

He glances down the hallway. A few cubicles are empty. The entire suite seems devoid of life save for Amanda. Interesting.

"He's not answering," she says.

"You tried his cell? What about home?"

"I'll call his home."

"Do that," Joe replies.

A minute goes by.

"Sorry, sir, he's not answering there, either." She has replaced the phone and is looking up at him, waiting for further instructions.

"Leave a message. Let him know that Detective Goodman is here to see him."

"Detective Goodman?" she asks.

"Correct."

Amanda picks up the phone again. Joe waits while she leaves the message.

"Thank you. I'll be back very soon," Joe says.

Amanda nods, her eyes darting about the room, full of fear.

Good, Joe thinks.

Time to take it up a notch.

Joe arrives in Clearwater at the address provided courtesy of the Hillsboro County Sheriff's Office.

He pays the taxi driver and asks if he'll wait a few minutes. He doubts if Damian is home, but it's worth a shot.

Joe leaves his bag in the backseat and hops out, admiring the neighborhood. He puts the single-family homes in the seven-hundred-to-eight-hundred-thousand-dollar range, easy. Manicured lawns, clean sidewalks, two- and three-car garages.

Damian Rein lives in a two-story yellow home. The driveway leading up to the attached two-car garage is reddish brick. There are two eighteen-foot palm trees in the front yard. Damian is living large, and that's no joke. The country might be in the midst of a recession, but business isn't hurting at Rein Security.

Joe goes to the door and rings the bell.

Nothing.

He can't peer through the windows because of the treatments covering them.

Rings again.

Still nothing.

Joe contemplates throwing a brick through the window to test the security system.

Undoubtedly Damian's got one.

Joe pulls out his business card and sticks it between the door frame and the door so it won't fall out.

Satisfied, he returns to the waiting taxi.

"Recommend any hotels not far from here?" Joe asks the cabbie.

"Sure," the cabbie responds, putting the taxi into gear and taking off.

Chapter 66

Less than an hour later, Detective Joe Goodman has checked in to his hotel. The Sheraton Tampa Riverwalk Hotel is on the banks of the Hillsborough River and across from the University of Tampa's campus.

Joe is famished, so he decides to grab something to eat. The restaurant has a scenic overlook of the water. Joe takes a table by the window and orders a chicken sandwich and fries. While waiting for his food, he plots his next move.

Some phone calls are in order.

With his memo pad on the table, he reaches for his cell.

His first call is to Tara.

It goes straight to voice mail.

There are so many things he wants to say.

Staring at the slow-moving water, with the university in the distance, Joe's words falter. He keeps it simple. He made it safely. He misses her. And he loves her.

He does.

So why, then, is he down here, on his own dime, way out of his jurisdiction?

Is it for her sake?

Kennedy's?

In a way, yes.

Not because he loves her, although, when Joe is totally honest with himself, as he is right now, he knows that in a way he'll never stop loving Kennedy.

Not completely.

It's as if they were never truly done.

At least he wasn't.

Joe was never really done with Kennedy.

He realizes there is no future with her, knows that he can't go backward, and that's okay. He knows he fucked up. He messed up the best thing that ever happened to him. Joe realizes that now.

He can't go back.

But perhaps he can fix things in some small way. Make Kennedy realize with his efforts here that he's sorry for hurting her.

His thoughts swing back to Tara.

Joe loves his fiancée. She's his life now. He doesn't want to hurt her. Wants this mess to be done with so he can give her his full attention. Show her that he is her man now.

But he's got to finish what he started.

Got to find Damian Rein and shut him down.

Then and only then can he move on.

His next call is to Chandran Nadar.

Chan picks up on the third ring.

"Nadar here."

"Chan the man! It's Joe Goodman. How are you?"

"Joe! Good to hear from you. I'm fine. You?"

"Never better, Chan."

"That's good to hear. How are things going with that case I consulted on? Made any progress?"

"Funny you should mention that, Chan." Joe is ready to tell him he's down in Tampa, but thinks better of it. The word might get back to the captain. "I was wondering if I could draw on your extensive computer expertise again."

"Of course, Joe."

Joe outlines what he needs.

Intel on a Damian Rein of Clearwater, Florida.

Joe can almost see Chan grinning on the other end of the line.

"Piece of cake. Give me a couple of hours?"

"How about an hour? I'm kinda pressed for time."

"All right. I'll do what I can."

"Chan, you are da man!"

Joe's food arrives.

He orders a lemonade even though a beer is what he really needs right now.

Attacks his chicken sandwich and drowns the fries in ketchup. Less than ten minutes later, the plate is empty. An eyebrow on the waitress is raised as she clears his plate and inquires if he was at all hungry.

Joe smiles and asks to see the dessert menu.

His third call is to Deputy Radcliff of the Hillsboro Sheriff's Office.

Radcliff is in the office and takes his call.

"I was calling to follow up on our conversation we had about a week ago regarding Lindsey Rein, a missing persons case. I was wondering if there had been any new developments?"

"Yeah, I remember. Funny you should be calling today, Detective," Radcliff says.

Joe takes a sip of his lemonade and then reaches for his pen.

"Why is that?" he asks.

"Because we received a call from the boys in Metro-Dade no more than three, four hours ago.

Seems some feller out fishing in the Everglades came across a body being chomped on by a gator. He called it in, and Metro-Dade came on out. Body's at the ME's office now. Autopsy not scheduled until tomorrow. Head's missing, so is one arm, so they gonna have to rely on fingerprints and DNA to ID."

"Okay," Joe says, his attention riveted on what the deputy is saying.

"Here's the interesting part. Turns out they recovered one leg, and on the ankle was a small tat. The detectives there are going through the missing persons database, and they come across our missing girl. Lindsey Rein's got a tat on her ankle. Black-widow spider. Not a hundred percent conclusive until they match the DNA, but I'm gonna bet my money it's Lindsey. Looks like they found her."

"Jesus," Joe says. His mind is racing.

This changes things.

This changes *everything*.

"Has the ex-husband been notified?" he asks.

"Hell, no. Not until a positive ID has been made. For now we'll keep things quiet, and that means you not talking to any family members, either."

"I'm not a rookie, Deputy."

"Just saying, Detective."

"Keep me informed, if you would. Thanks."

"Sure thing."

Joe closes his cell and stares at it.

Suddenly he's no longer in the mood for dessert.

Murder has just been added to Damian Rein's résumé.

He can't prove any of it, not yet, but he'd bet his life on it.

Damian Rein is behind all of this.

And what scares Joe the most is the fact that Damian's not finished.

Not at all.

Joe has a feeling he's just getting started. . . .

Chapter 67

Joe's back in his room when his cell rings. He glances at the screen and flips open the phone.

"Goodman."

"It's Nadar."

"Hey, Chan."

Forty-five minutes have passed. Joe has contemplated returning to Clearwater but thinks otherwise. He decides to wait until later on tonight. That way he can surprise Damian, catch him off guard when he least expects it.

"Talk to me," Joe exclaims.

"I've got the information you asked for. You ready?" Chan asks.

Joe sits up, grabbing his memo pad and a hotel pen.

"Shoot."

"Okay. I managed to get Mr. Rein's corporate American Express. He's been busy. Made a trip to Miami a few days ago, and was here in D.C. about three weeks ago—"

"Wait a sec," Joe interrupts. "Damian was in D.C.?"

"Yes, sir. Stayed two nights at the Radisson, Crystal City."

"Son of a bitch! He lied to me." Joe recalls asking Damian if he'd been to D.C. recently. "Sorry, Chan. What else?"

"He purchased a ticket today, Jet Blue, Tampa to D.C. Flight 410. First class. Departed Tampa at eleven fifty-five AM, arrived D.C. three-forty this afternoon."

"Shit! That cocksucker is in D.C. and I'm here? Fuck!"

"Is something wrong, Joe?" Chan asks.

"No, I'm cool. Just thinking out loud," Joe replies.

"Whatever you say, Joe." Chan chuckles. "I've got some other stuff, mostly routine. Address, license, registration. I'm still checking on other credit cards. I pulled his credit report, and he's got a ton of credit cards that he uses for six months or a year and then closes. I have a feeling he's hiding something, but I need more time to be sure."

"Chan, this is great work. Thank you."

"Just doing my job, Joe. But you're welcome."

"Call me if you uncover anything else," Joe says.

"Will do."

Joe ends the call. Speed-dials Kennedy's new cell and waits impatiently for it to connect.

She doesn't answer.

Joe snaps his cell shut.

Opens and hits redial.

No luck getting through.

He contemplates leaving a message. But what should he say?

Damian Rein is now in D.C. I need you to be extremely careful. We need to assume this guy is dangerous.

And one more thing.

A body was found earlier today in the Everglades. The police down here think it might be Dawn, but they won't know for sure until they cross-check DNA.

No.

He can't leave that in a message.

He hangs up.

Joe gets up and goes for his garment bag.

Time to get back to D.C. ASAP!

Call the front desk, see if the concierge can get him a flight straight back home.

NOW.

Before Damian Rein does something stupid.

Chapter 68

Damian Rein's head is about to explode.

There's a dull throb at the base of his skull. It feeds the pain up in his forehead and temples. He's drained the Tylenol bottle that was in his carry-on. But the Tylenol's no longer effective.

Tired, pissed off, he's ready to hurt somebody.

That fucking cop is history.

Amanda's call gave him a huge jolt.

Joe Goodman. Down in Tampa? Looking for him there?

Incredible.

How long before the detective connects the dots?

The body in the swamp. Identity tracked back to him. Which is why he needs to be here now.

Washington, D.C.

To finish things.

He'll deal with the cop as soon as he's done here.

As soon as his work is complete.

It's all been leading up to this.

A path that he had no control over.

One that he did not choose.

It chose him.

All because of *her.*

It's her fault that he's here in the nation's capital, having to deal with this shit instead of being home, in Clearwater, with the woman who used to be his wife.

Damian is sitting in a rental car on Taylor Street. It's dark. The street is quiet. He watches the Handley house like an owl. He knows someone's inside. The lights are on. But who's home?

That bitch, Mocha?

No way to be sure.

And he needs to be sure.

Damian massages his temples with his fingertips. It does nothing to slow the roar inside his head.

He closes his eyes. Sees red behind his eyelids before it passes. Then it's blackness, like molasses, just the way he likes it.

For a moment he feels untroubled and controlled.

And he can actually think.

A story comes to mind.

One of his favorites.

Once upon a time there was a gentle man who loved his woman.

She meant the world to him. So he made her his wife.

He doted on her. Gave her things she'd never imagined.

A wonderful home. Peace and security. A glorious future stretched before them.

For a while, life was grand.

Magnificent.

How he loved her.

And she loved him back.

But then, something changed. She withdrew, grew secretive.

And those lies.

Those fucking lies did her in.

When she left him, the pain commenced.

It was a pain like no other.

Deep, rampant, out of control.

From that point on it grew like a cancer inside him, devastating him with its poison.

It was never far away, as if he were carrying it around like loose change.

The pain was a tumor.

The pain would kill him.

If he didn't excise it.

So he did.

The gentle man became a violent man.

Took care of her.

Took care so that she could never hurt another living soul.

Found her living her new, secretive life.

Located her, even though she didn't want to be found.

Punished her for what she had done to him. To *them* . . .

And that other bitch is next.

Mocha.

Bitches think they own the world.

Think they can waltz in and out of someone's life, wreak havoc and harm, and then tiptoe away as if nothing happened.

Well, the gentle man who became a violent man isn't about to let that shit happen.

Not on his watch.

If he goes down, then so be it.

One way or another, the pain will cease.

He will rip out this throbbing cancer, as God is his witness.

Stomp it to death if he has to.

Then the violent man can once again become a gentle man.

And move on.

The end.

The garage door suddenly opens, bringing Damian out of his reverie.

A sleek black BMW hooks a left into the street and accelerates to the corner.

Damian feels his heat spike.

He spies her behind the wheel as she waits at the light.

Mocha.

Damian takes a slow, steady breath as he eases out from his parking spot.

Eases into the street, taking up position behind her, but not too close.

Heart rate thumping.

Like the pulse in his temples, forehead, and neck.

The light turns green.

Damian steps on the accelerator.

Let the games begin. . . .

Kennedy is at a light on Sixteenth Street.

She glances down at her new BlackBerry on the seat beside her.

Checks her features in the rearview mirror.

Picks up the cell and speed-dials Michael.

The anxiety is there.

In her chest.

She feels like she's back in high school.

The anticipation of what's to come sends her stomach into somersaults.

He picks up on the fourth ring.

"Hey, it's me," she begins, trying to sound anything but nervous.

"Hi," he responds.

"I'm running a few minutes behind. I'm on Sixteenth. Just wanted you to know."

The truth: Kennedy has spent the past hour searching her closet for the right thing to wear.

Didn't want to overdo it.

Was looking for the right mix of sensuality and practicality.

Wanted her husband to *see* her.

See her in a way he hasn't in weeks.

In the end she selected a pair of Michael's favorite jeans that hugged her curves in all the right places.

Knee-high black boots.

Formfitting white turtleneck.

Silver hanging earrings.

A black stone pendant.

Makeup done just right.

Hair flat-ironed down her back, straight out of a Rihanna video.

Yeah. Michael *would* notice her tonight.

She had made sure of that.

"Okay," Michael says. "We're just crossing the bridge now. Should be there shortly."

Kennedy nods.

Considers leaving it at that and ending the call.

But she simply can't.

She misses him too much.

"Thank you, Michael. For doing this."

"No problem."

Actually, it had been Zack's idea.

He'd been missing the three of them together.

So he suggested they go ice-skating.

As a family again.

Michael wasn't going to say no to his son.

And Kennedy was beside herself with glee when he'd called with the proposal.

It was a small thing.

Just an hour together—the three of them—out on Michael's night with Zack.

No dinner, just ice-skating at the outdoor rink not far from his job.

Just the three of them.

Like old times.

Kennedy smiles.

It's a small thing.

But it's a start.

Chapter 69

Kennedy parks on Constitution Avenue and checks herself once again in the mirror.

Satisfied, she grabs her BlackBerry and gets out, locking the door with the remote.

The Sculpture Garden rink is a block and a half away, on the corner, across from the National Gallery of Art. The rink is lit up like a carousel, and she can see crowds of people gliding around the ice.

The weather tonight is cooperating. Not too cold, just right for early December in Washington.

She can't wait to see Zack. Even though she had dropped him off at school only this morning, it feels like a lifetime ago.

For the past few hours she's been running scenarios through her mind.

Michael will be relaxed and in a great mood. He'll be happy to see her. He'll take them out for a late-night snack afterward. Zack will say he wants to sleep in his own bed, and Michael will consent. He'll follow them home in the Range Rover. Help tuck Zack into bed, and then trail Kennedy to their room, where she'll undress him, and lead him to bed.

Kennedy smiles.

The thought is alluring.

What she wouldn't give to put this horrible mess behind her.

Become a family once again.

She'd give anything to have her family back together.

Kennedy angles toward the rink. Couples with their young children are loitering by the entrance, laughing and carrying on, their breath visible in the air.

"MOMMY!"

Kennedy turns and grins.

Zack is stampeding toward her.

Michael stands twenty yards away, smiling as he observes his son. Zack barrels into his mother, who scoops him up in her arms.

"How are you?"

"Good," Zack answers breathlessly. "This is so cool, don't you think, Mommy?"

She's not exactly sure what he's referring to: the fact that they are out as a family again, or this ice-skating rink, or the fact that he'll get to stay up late tonight.

Kennedy grins.

"Absolutely! Are you ready to go skating?"

"Yup!"

"Zack, 'yup' is not a word. Say 'yes.' "

"Yes, Mommy."

Michael comes up and says hello.

He's looking scrumptious in his stonewashed jeans and boots, thin sweater under a sport jacket. She stares for a second longer than she should at the spot where his legs come together.

Spies the bulge, which she knows all too well.

Forces her eyes to creep upward and meet his gaze. Kennedy smiles back.

"Hey. You ready to do this?" she asks innocently.

"Let's do it," Michael says.

"All right!" Zack chimes in.

Inside and to the left is the counter where they can rent skates. They go over; Michael speaks to the attendant and fishes out his wallet to pay for the rentals. Moments later they are sitting on a long, narrow bench, lacing up their skates.

Kennedy attends to Zack, then dons her own skates. By the time she's done, Michael is standing beside her, ready.

They walk carefully toward the ice.

Christmas music is playing.

The trees surrounding the rink are decorated with thousands of tiny white lights.

The moon is rising into a nighttime sky.

"It's beautiful," Kennedy murmurs to Michael, who is alongside her.

"Yes, it is."

Zack gets to the ice first, steps on it unsurely, and once both feet are no longer wobbling, he takes off.

"Zack, wait for us!" Kennedy yells, but her words go unheeded. Michael shakes his head.

"He's your son," he muses.

They begin to skate.

Slowly, not in any rush, following the current of folks gliding around the smooth white ice. Overhead the stars are out, twinkling in the moonlight.

"Haven't done this in a while," Kennedy says to Michael, who nods silently. She almost adds with a smirk, "There are a few other things we haven't done in a while," but holds her tongue.

An African-American couple glides in front of them. They are in their mid-thirties, bundled up, and holding hands.

Kennedy resists the urge to reach out and take Michael by the hand. She's hoping he is focused on them as well.

Thinking about the connection between two people when they are in love.

The bond that is strong as steel.

And as long lasting.

She hopes her husband is contemplating the same thing she is.

Damian Rein is lacing up his skates.

His long overcoat is heavy from what's deep in his right pocket. He's been watching Mocha and Dude for the past twenty minutes.

And their cute little son.

For a moment Damian forgets why he's here. Instead he simply watches them skate together as a family.

And he considers: This could have been me.

If only she hadn't turned deceitful and rotten.

It would be him with his family right now.

Under a cheerful moon.

Holiday music playing.

Lights blinking.

But it is not to be.

Damian shakes away the mental picture.

Stands awkwardly and takes a moment to get his balance. Slowly, he makes his way to the ice.

There's a throng of people out on the ice, and a bunch of youngsters who are showboating, whipping in and out of the crowd like aggressive drivers as they glide on steel.

Plenty of cover.

Plenty of distraction.

Damian steps onto the ice and enters the traffic flow.

He doesn't glance around or do anything to draw attention to himself.

The Handley family is in front, a good fifty yards away.

Perfect.

Arms held behind him, fingers interlocked, looking completely relaxed, Damian hastens toward them.

Chapter 70

After Zack calms down from the initial excitement of being at the skating rink, they fall into a nice groove.

Zack glides between them, holding the hands of his parents.

"This is so cool!" he says to his father.

"Yes, you've mentioned that several times already," Michael responds with a smile.

"I should call Jeremy and ask if his mom can bring him here. He'd have so much fun, don't you think? I bet Jeremy is a good skater. But I don't know if he knows how to skate or not. Mommy, do they have lessons here that Jeremy could take? In case he's never skated before?"

Kennedy is grinning at her son. Her eyes flick up to Michael, and she makes eye contact with her husband. A heartbeat later, Michael looks away. She wonders what he's feeling inside.

Is he happy to be here?

Does he still love her?

She tries not to answer those questions.

Instead she continues smiling at Zack and declares, "I don't know if this place offers lessons, but perhaps they do."

Zack is reaching down into the lower pocket of his cargo pants for his cell phone when Kennedy adds, "Let's not call him right this minute, Zack. Let's instead enjoy our time together as a family. This was your idea, remember?"

"Okay, Mommy."

"You can tell him all about it tomorrow at school, okay, kiddo?" Michael adds.

Christmas carols are emanating into the night-time air.

Kennedy changes the subject by encouraging Zack to sing along, but he just stares up at her like she's insane. At that moment Michael's cell phone rings. He pulls off a glove and fishes the phone from his jacket pocket, holding it to his ear. He begins to speak, but the details are lost on Kennedy. She glances over at him as he puts one gloved finger to his ear, attempting to blot out the ambient noise. He mouths to her "Work," then continues to talk. Michael receiving business calls in the evening is not unheard of, so she nods and catches up with Zack.

A minute later, Michael skates up to Kennedy, phone still attached to his ear. She hears him say "Hold on one second," and then he speaks to her.

"I need to run to the car for a second. Left some paperwork in my briefcase that I need to see. I'll be back in a few. Can you handle Zack until I get back?"

Kennedy's forehead furrows.

"Of course I can handle him."

What did he mean by that? she wonders. For a second she feels herself getting angry, but then discards the emotion. She waves him away.

Michael turns, returning the phone to his ear.

Kennedy and Zack skate away.

About ten yards from them, Damian watches
them go.

Perfect.

He'd been wondering how he was going to accomplish it.

He wants Mocha all to himself.

Having Dude around is a deal breaker.

On the other hand, the kid tagging along is a
problem, but not an insurmountable one.

Damian puts his hands in his pocket as he casually increases his speed. He feels the weight of the
weapon, the coldness of the steel. Moments later
he's ten feet behind the bitch, skating to "Oh Holy
Night." Zack is out in front as they take a curve.
Damian glances back in the direction Dude has
gone.

He's nowhere in sight.

Perfect.

Couldn't ask for more.

His heart is pounding.

The pain is roaring.

Mocha is eight feet from him.

Dude could return any moment now.

Damian may not have another opportunity.

Six feet.

Five.

The pain threatens to render him unconscious.

Months and months of scheming and planning
have come down to this moment.

Four feet.

If he reaches out his hand, he can stroke the
bitch.

The way she did to *her.*

Three.

One final glance back toward the entrance.

The coast is clear.

Two feet.

One.

Damian slides until he is shoulder-to-shoulder with Kennedy. She glances to her right as he enters her personal space, for a split second thinking it's Michael returning but instead seeing a tall, good-looking man with a black wool cap and a long wool coat beside her. He is smiling as he speaks.

"I have a gun in my pocket, and if you so as much as raise your voice I'll shoot your son in the back of the head."

Kennedy's eyes grow wide.

It takes an instant for her to grasp that her worst fears have just been realized.

Everything, every bad thing that has happened to her over the past few months, has been building toward this single horrific moment.

A mother's worst nightmare.

Someone intent on harming her son.

Kennedy's mouth opens as if to scream, but Damian shakes his head slowly.

"Don't yell. Don't you dare scream. If you value the life of your son, then you'll do exactly what I say."

They are coming up on the covered entrance. Using his left hand, Damian reaches for her elbow as he cocks his head to the side.

"Let's go. Call your son over. Do not make a scene. I will not hesitate to shoot him dead without blinking an eye, and then I'll put a bullet in your brain in front of all these people if you fuck with me."

His eyes are unblinking.

"So do not try me."

Kennedy stares at him, trembling. She sees only blackness staring back.

Lifeless.

It's what scares her the most.

"Zack, come here."

"What, Mommy? I'm not done skate—"

"Zack!" She modulates her voice so there is no mistaking her intent. Zack skates over to her at once and comes to a halt.

"Mommy, you said—"

Zack stares up into the eyes of this stranger beside his mother. He pans from the man to his mother and then back again.

"Hello," Damian begins, keeping a tight hold on the gun inside his right pocket with one hand and on Kennedy with the other. "We're going to take a walk, you, me, and your mommy. Tell him, Kennedy."

Zack's forehead creases.

Something does not compute.

He stares up at his mother, who is trembling.

"It's okay, Zack. Do as he says. We need to go now."

"But what about Daddy?" Zack asks, his arms becoming animated.

Damian shakes his head.

"Now."

The way the man utters that one simple word while boring his stare into Zack's eyes makes him shut down any further struggle.

The attendant behind the counter is staring up at the sky while rubbing his earlobe. Damian leads them over and captures the young man's attention. Their skates are exchanged for boots and shoes. Damian, who still has his hand on Kennedy's elbow, leans in and whispers, "Put your boots on quickly and then get your son's on. I don't want any delay. We are going to walk out of here quickly and quietly, before your husband returns. Understand?"

Kennedy nods.

"Good girl. Keep your head on, and you'll live through this. I promise you that. But underestimate me and what I'm capable of doing, and you and your son are as good as dead."

He tightens his grip on Kennedy's arm, digging into her coat.

Tears spring from her eyes.

"Do we understand each other?" Damian asks, his voice nearly a whisper.

"Yes."

Damian grins.

"Excellent. Now, wipe your eyes. We don't want to upset the little one, do we?"

Chapter 71

Less than three minutes later they are on Ninth Street, walking away from Constitution.

Damian walks briskly, keeping Kennedy's elbow in his clutches. Zack struggles to keep up even though he's holding his mother's hand.

"Can we slow down, please?" she asks.

"Shut up," Damian hisses.

More tears spout from her eyes, but Damian wipes them away unsympathetically with the back of his gloved hand.

"Stop crying. You are bringing attention to us, and that's not healthy. Especially for your son."

Kennedy blinks back further tears.

"Good girl."

They meet no passersby.

The street is tree-lined and quiet. Christmas music can still be heard in the distance, but it fades as they walk away from the source.

He smiles to himself when he considers how easy it was to transport a gun to the nation's capital.

Locked gun case in his checked baggage for his most prized possession and the mags.

He didn't break the rules; in fact, he double-checked with TSA prior to planning his trip.

So slick!

A block up is Madison Drive, a street that abuts the Sculpture Garden. Damian forces them to the left and toward a black Chevy Impala. He unlocks the driver-side door, pushes Kennedy into the seat, and opens the rear door, gesturing for Zack to get inside.

He does so, quietly.

Damian goes around to the passenger side, opens the door, and climbs in. Once the door is closed, he turns in his seat, producing a menacing black handgun. He makes sure Zack can see it as he points it at Kennedy's right kidney.

"Just so everyone's on the same page, this is the Heckler & Koch HK45. One of the finest .45-caliber handguns ever produced. It holds ten bullets in the mag and one in the chamber, and I've got another magazine in my pocket. You get hit with one of these—well, your limbs get blown off—"

"Please!" Kennedy pleads. "Not in front of my son. Tell me what you want!"

"Hand me your cell phone. Slow and easy."

Kennedy reaches into her pocket and extracts her phone. She hands it to Damian. He gives her the keys and tells her to drive.

Damian rolls down the window and casually tosses the BlackBerry into the bushes.

Kennedy grits her teeth but says nothing.

Damian, while holding the gun at Kennedy's kidney, turns to face Zack.

"You're doing good so far. Keep it up and nothing will happen, okay? But if you scream or try to jump out of this car, I'll shoot your mother. Do you understand?"

Zack is shaking, but he manages to nod.

"Good boy."

Kennedy steers past the Museum of Natural History. It's closed, but there are people out and about on the Mall. She keeps her head straight ahead, not trying to make eye contact with anyone. She hangs a right onto Twelfth Street and crosses Constitution, passing the Internal Revenue Service and Department of Commerce buildings.

Damian settles into his seat for the short ride to their house.

He's pumped.

He's on fire.

Soon now, the pain will cease to be an issue.

He can already feel its power diminish.

Throttling back, losing steam.

He wants to whistle.

Wants to scream out to *her.*

Show her all that he's accomplished.

Everything that's transpired due to her actions.

He's here, to finish what she started.

Can you hear me?

Can you see everything you've made me do?

Can you, bitch?

But she no longer hears him.

Damian has made sure of that.

They pull up to a vacant space halfway down Taylor Street. Kennedy parks while Damian glances around.

No one on the quiet street.

Perfect.

"We're all going to get out nice and slow like we don't have a care in the world. Then we're going to walk to your front door. One wrong move—"

"We get it," Kennedy says, cutting him off.

Damian's eyes rage for a brief moment, but he says nothing other than "Let's go."

He grabs a roll of silver duct tape from the passenger-side floor.

They exit the vehicle.

Kennedy grabs her son's hand, while Damian keeps his right hand in the deep pocket, his finger coiled around the trigger of the H&K. He nods for her to move.

Moments later they are walking up the stoop to the front door. She fumbles for her keys in the chilling air.

Drops them on the top step.

Damian watches her silently, glancing around only once to see that Taylor Street is devoid of any activity.

Zack clutches her left hand, keeping his body as close to her as humanly possible. He refuses to look at the stranger with the gun, and Damian likes it that way.

Kennedy puts the key to the lock, turns it, and opens the door.

"In we go," Damian says as they move inside.

The warmth assaults them.

"Kill the alarm, and don't even think about pressing the panic button or putting in a panic code. I'm too smart for that. I work in security, and I'm familiar with your alarm system. But I'm sure you've figured that out by now."

Kennedy deactivates the alarm on the wall.

Chapter 72

As soon as the plane touches down at Reagan National, Joe Goodman is on his cell phone.

His first call is to Kennedy.

That goes to voice mail.

He curses, capturing the ire of an elderly white woman who is sitting beside him.

His next call is to Michael.

He gets one of those generic messages stating that the number dialed is no longer in service.

Then he remembers. He directed Kennedy to ditch her BlackBerry and to tell Michael to do the same.

And Joe doesn't have the new numbers.

It takes the pilot several minutes to steer the plane to its gate.

All the while Joe is impatient. It's been like that all afternoon.

Checking out of the hotel.

Fighting with the manager to obtain a refund (he had been there barely two hours).

Racing back to the airport.

At the gate, using his badge to commandeer a seat on the next flight back to D.C.

It worked, finally.

Three hundred bucks lighter, he had swapped tickets with some guy who didn't care that he made it back to his wife a few hours later than scheduled.

Back to the present.

Before the airplane reaches the gate and the engines are shut down, Joe is out of his seat. The flight attendant nearest to him signals for him to sit down.

He holds up his badge and announces to those in front of him, "Metropolitan Police, let me through, please."

Four minutes later he is sprinting up the jetway, cell to his ear as he redials Kennedy's number.

Again it goes to voice mail.

Garment bag swinging from his shoulder, he dials Terrell, one of his partners at the Fifth District.

Another detective, who has backed up Joe numerous times. Body-builder type. When not working the streets, he lives in the gym.

Terrell picks up on the fifth ring.

"What up, Joe?"

"Hey, man, where are you? I need a serious favor," Joe says.

"Me 'n' Tretch are just over the border in P.G. getting something to eat. Wha'd'ya need?"

Tretch is another Fifth District cop. Terrell & Tretch. Known among Metropolitan's finest as TNT, two bad motherfuckers.

"Listen, I'm working this stalking case, and I think my vic may be in trouble. I tried to reach her, but she's not picking up. I'm at the airport heading over, but I need someone to get over there now. The perp is in the area and possibly on his way. Can you check it out for me?" Joe pauses a half second. "It's my ex-wife."

Terrell chews his food and swallows.

"Ex-wife? Okay, yeah, no problem. We're finishing up here. What's the address?"

"Thank you, man. She's on Taylor Street." Joe gives him the address.

"Got it. Let us settle up the check and we'll check it out, let you know."

"I'm gonna hightail it up there."

"All right, cool."

The line goes dead.

Joe can now catch his breath.

He heads out of the terminal to the taxi area. There is a line of people waiting to catch a cab. No official vehicles in sight that he can use. Joe curses under his breath.

He stands impatiently in line for a taxi.

That lasts all of five seconds.

Joe whips out his shield and holds it up, making his way to the front of the line. Most people give him the eye but say nothing.

Getting in the waiting cab, he gives the driver Kennedy's address and tells him to step on it.

He wonders where Damian is right now.

Wonders exactly what he's up to.

Michael ends his call and returns the cell phone to his pocket. He rubs his gloved hands together, staring up at the moon hanging in the December night.

The call had gone on longer than expected. A project he and a colleague are collaborating on.

He walks back to the entrance of the skating rink, thinking not about his call but about the evening.

He had felt apprehension as he got himself and

Zack ready for tonight, knowing he would be seeing Kennedy later.

A family outing.

That's what this is, even though he hasn't felt like he's had a family for some time now.

He contemplates Kennedy and Joe together, and an intense wave of jealousy washes over him.

And when he considers that Zack might not be his, his entire being shuts down.

So he doesn't think about it. Doesn't want that part to be true.

But then he saw her, looking so damn good, and Michael couldn't help but feeling the desire infuse back into his pores.

It had been so long since he had held his wife, and for the first time he acknowledged that he honestly missed her.

The ying and yang of love.

Michael walks into the rink.

Shows the attendant his ticket and grabs his skates. Laces up and heads to the ice.

It's not as teeming as before.

Michael scans the crowd, searching for his wife and son.

"O Come All Ye Faithful" is playing over the sound system, and several families that skate past him are singing along.

His brow furrows.

He doesn't see his clan.

Michael reaches once again for his phone, speed-dials Kennedy's cell.

It rings five times before going to voice mail.

Michael turns. Looks for the restrooms.

Zack probably had to pee. Was afraid to go by himself. He finds the men's room and darts inside.

Empty.

Back out.

Walks across to the ladies' room. He waits patiently for someone to enter or exit. A woman with her tween daughter ambles up, both with their skates still on. He says, "Excuse me, I'm looking for my wife and son. Can you see if they are in there? Her name is Kennedy."

The woman nods while clutching her daughter's shoulder tighter.

Michael waits.

Five minutes go by.

The mother/daughter duo exits with the mother shaking her head.

"No one else in there," she utters.

Michael thanks her.

His brow furrows again.

He speed-dials Kennedy a second time.

Voice mail.

Back to the rink.

Scans the crowd.

Gets on the ice and makes two complete revolutions, just to make sure.

Michael doesn't find them.

Odd.

Perhaps Zack was hungry.

But there's a concession stand here.

He passed it on the way to the restrooms.

He goes back to the rental attendant.

The young man is gone. Replaced by a teenage girl with dark gothic makeup.

"Have you seen a mother and son come by here?" Michael describes Kennedy and Zack to her.

She shakes her head. "Nope."

Michael exchanges his skates for his boots.

His heart is racing now.

His first thought is that something bad has happened to them.

His second thought is something else. Replaced by another emotion.

What if Kennedy took Zack to get back at him?

Preposterous.

Not Kennedy.

But people who are going through marital problems do stupid shit every day.

No, that's not it. It's something else.

Another explanation.

He heads out, hangs a right onto Ninth and walks briskly toward Constitution. His car is a few blocks away.

The temperature is beginning to drop. He shudders under his sport coat.

He glances back, but his wife and child are not there.

Michael walks for several blocks toward his car.

He pulls out his cell again.

Dials Zack's cell number.

"Pick up," he utters to himself.

He passes a black BMW.

Stops, turns, stares.

Kennedy's car.

Empty.

Zack's phone is still ringing as he stares into the darkened interior.

No answer.

So he hits a few keys to enable the Chaperone feature.

It takes but a few moments to locate his son.

He stops dead in his tracks and stares at the map.

Taylor Street, Northeast D.C.

Their home.

If Kennedy's car is here, how did Zack get home?

Michael stares at his phone, trying to connect the dots.

Nothing makes sense.

He hits redial, attempting to reach his son.

The call just rings.

He ends the call.

Swallows his pride.

And calls Joe Goodman, his wife's ex, instead.

Chapter 73

Zack feels the cell phone's vibration in his pocket.

It shudders just below his right thigh.

His hands are bound by duct tape to the Ikea work chair in his room. His ankles are also restrained. His mouth remains uncovered. The bad man felt it wasn't necessary to gag him.

Displaying the Heckler & Koch was incentive enough.

Zack struggles against his restraints. His wrists refuse to budge. He'd need a steak knife to cut through this tape.

There's a clock radio by his bed.

It's on, tuned to an urban-adult station.

Kennedy frowned when the bad man turned it on; she voiced her disdain, only to be told she had more pressing issues to consider.

The door to his bedroom is closed.

The vibration ceases. Then begins again.

It wouldn't be Jeremy—it's way past his bedtime. And he witnessed his mother's phone being tossed out by the bad man.

That meant the call was from his dad.

Zack attempts to reach it. His fingers graze the top of the pocket flap. No way he can reach the phone. He needs about four more inches of fingers.

If only he could lift his leg.

Zack tries, but his ankles are bound to the chair legs. He manages to lift his thigh less than two inches.

The phone remains tucked away in his pocket, silent and unmoving.

He contemplates attempting to rock himself and the chair onto its side. But he figures this is easier said than done. Besides, the sound would surely reverberate throughout the house.

The bad man was adamant about keeping quiet.

Be good and live.

Be bad and die.

The bad man's words resound inside his skull.

Zack desperately wants to live.

So he keeps still.

Thinks of his favorite Xbox 360 game.

His nana's cooking.

That time Pop Pop let him drive the tractor.

He prays his mommy is safe and unharmed.

Prays that his daddy comes busting in, guns blazing, sending the bad man to that place where bad men like him belong.

Straight to hell.

He stands away from the bed, watching her.

She is on the edge, sitting perfectly still, eyeing him back.

Damian goes to the window, peeks out from behind the blinds to the small backyard and alleyway beyond.

It is quiet here, yet the pain inside his head is a roar that will not settle down.

He turns, Heckler & Koch still raised in her direction.

Stares at her, rubbing his temples with his other hand.

For a moment neither speaks.

Then Damian opens his mouth.

"I wonder how many you've fucked in that bed."

"What?" Kennedy says.

Damian grins.

"Don't be coy with me. Your lovers. You know. The ones you bring here to fuck."

"I don't bring anyone here. This is me and my husband's bed."

"Well, we're gonna change that tonight. Take off your clothes."

Kennedy remains immobile.

"I said, take *off* your fucking clothes." He has taken four large strides from the window and is now pressing the barrel of the .45 into her forehead. His eyes are unblinking.

Kennedy begins to undress.

She keeps her eyes trained on him as she removes first her boots, then unzips and slips off her jeans. In her panties, she struggles out of her sweater, placing it on the bed beside her. She sits in bra and panties, eyes lasered into his skull.

"Everything, *bitch*," Damian commands. His voice is barely above a whisper, but the message is received loud and clear.

Kennedy unhooks her bra and removes it, tossing it onto the floor. She stands, pulling down her panties. They go by the bra.

"Please don't hurt my son," she says in a fluttering voice.

Damian retreats until he is standing several feet away, admiring her beauty. He does not respond to her, except to laugh.

"I don't understand. You've come all this way just to rape me?" Kennedy asks. "Is that what this is about?"

"Shut up," Damian growls. "You don't know shit, bitch. You fucked up a good thing, you know that? You fucked up a perfectly good marriage!"

He takes two steps forward and leans in next to Kennedy's face.

"You are nothing but a home-wrecking cunt. So shut the fuck up!" Spittle flies from his mouth as Damian's free hand comes up and slaps her across the face, hard. Instantly Kennedy is knocked over onto the bed. Her hand rushes to her face, eyes wide with fright.

"I'm telling you for the last time to shut the fuck up. Do you hear me? SHUT THE FUCK UP!"

Damian's eyes have grown to the size of silver dollars. They are full of fire, and his hand shakes as he yells.

"CUNT FUCK BITCH! I should shoot you right the fuck here and now!"

"Oh God! I'm sorry . . . Please stop. . . ." Tears stream down her face.

"You ruined what we had. Lie back on the fucking bed and spread your legs. Better yet, bend over like the whore that you are. I'm gonna do you just the way you did her."

Kennedy sobs, holding her face in her hands.

"Please don't hurt me or my son. Just tell me what it is you want."

There is pleading in her eyes.

Damian fumbles with his belt. Unzips his pants.

Pulls out his manhood. Strokes it, glaring at her smooth, mocha-fine skin.

Her nipples are erect, and he is almost hard. God, she is beautiful.

"What I want? I want to violate you for what you did to me. You destroyed my life. So I'm gonna return the favor. Gonna give you a piece of me that can never be ungiven. Something that you'll carry around for the rest of your life."

Kennedy stares back at him. She wipes her tears with her hand. She winces when her fingers graze her swollen cheek.

She moves off the bed.

"Anywhere else but in this bed. Please."

Damian watches her move.

"Fucking whore," he swears, but the volume has been throttled down a notch. "Get back on the bed. I could shoot you dead right now. But that's not my plan. Nope—I want you to live. Want you to wake up every day thinking about how I fucked the shit out of you for what you did to me."

He watches her terror-filled eyes. Fear and dread live there now. He observes the rest of her. His temples throb. He blinks rapidly.

Legs the color of mocha chocolate.

Smooth, like only he can imagine.

Full breasts, dark, erect, inviting nipples.

Damian can't wait to impale her.

Kennedy moves to the left of the bed.

"Your wife was an incredible woman," Kennedy utters softly.

Damian is instantly thrown off guard.

"What the fuck did you say?"

"Your wife. Dawn—"

"Do not speak her name!" he commands.

Kennedy swallows. Blinks.

"I remember meeting her in Miami." She pauses, waiting to see what will come next. A bullet or merely a sigh? She is watching him, this madman with a faraway gaze suddenly painted upon his face. He's remembering her, she can tell. "She was a beautiful woman," she continues. "What a smile. And those eyes. When she stared at you it was like she was looking straight through you."

Damian is silent. The fire is still burning, but for the moment is under control.

"I can see why you fell for her. Anyone would."

"Bitch, you don't know shit about my wife," he hisses.

"I know she loved you."

Damian ceases to stroke himself. He stares hard at Kennedy. He presses the cool steel of the Heckler & Koch against her temple, making her flinch.

"I should blow your stupid brains—" He stops, catching himself. Takes a breath, then grits his teeth. "Keep *fucking* with me."

Kennedy's teeth chatter, and her entire body is shaking. But she presses on anyway. It's her only hope.

"She told me so. We spoke about how conflicted she felt. Loving you and dealing with this way of hers that made her desire other women."

Damian swallows, shaking his head.

"She wanted to tell you," Kennedy says. She nods. "Yeah, she was searching for a way to let you know just how she felt. She didn't want to lose you."

Damian's cock begins to wilt. He is thinking of *her* while rolling Kennedy's words over in his mind. He can see *her,* clear as day, standing in their kitchen, white panties on and nothing else, enjoying a glass of orange juice, a bit of pulp on her lip that he wiped off lovingly with the edge of his hand.

"You lie," he says, voice near a whisper. The pain in his head screams. He winces, shoulders sagging. The gun wavers.

"I have no reason to. It is the truth. She loved you. But she couldn't deny who she was. I understand that. And I understood her. It is why we bonded. I wasn't looking to take her away from you. But I couldn't deny myself the pleasure of her any more than you could. She was intoxicating. You of all people know that."

Kennedy places one knee on the bed, one hand on the headboard, leaning over. She reveals the fullness of herself to him.

Damian is enthralled. The sight of her coupled with her words takes his breath away. Blood is returning to his member.

And for a moment, he sails off.

Drifting, if you can call it that, thinking about *her*, here and now as he marvels over Mocha's exquisite form. Readying to devastate her, this goddess bitch before him. How many hours did he dream of this sweet revenge, this very moment when vengeance would be his, spilling his river as he imagined hurting her for what she's done? Countless hours. So much spilled seed. Yet he thinks of her.

Dawn.

There.

He allows himself this one micro-moment to speak her name.

He says it again.

Dawn.

What a lovely thing she was.

He remembers her as he desires things to be.

Back when they were together. As one. A unit. A family.

A family with a future.

Damian remembers her smile. The smile that could cure any ailment.

Any disease.

She told him it was he who refreshed her.

Rejuvenated her.

Just one look, and the smile would return.

How that used to warm his heart.

He couldn't wait to get through his day and get home to her.

Everything, every single thing he did was in direct response to her.

He was always trying to get back to her.

For a time it was like this. Just the two of them.

Their love bound them together.

Two against the world.

Then something changed.

He remembered how she looked when she came home from Miami.

Something had changed.

He'd have to have been blind to miss it.

She didn't look at him the same way anymore.

Oh, she tried, tried to pretend things were the same after South Beach, but he saw right through that bullshit charade.

That's when things began to unravel.

That's when things fell apart.

It took him a week.

One week of reading her e-mail.

The account she thought he knew nothing about.

The one she hid from him.

But he found out.

One look at the photos changed *everything*.

Mocha. Dude. Butterscotch.

Together. In ways that stopped his heart cold.

Dude buried to the hilt. Entombed. And her expression said it all.

This is rapture.

His Dawn.

What he saw stabbed him deep and vicious. Raped him of all that was to be.

He almost killed her then with his bare hands.

Thought about it. Considered it so long and hard his brain began to hurt from the inside out. Like a nail was being hammered into his skull. The pain spread like cancer. Enveloped where it could. Took up residence in his bones, veins, muscles, flesh.

One look at the photos, and he was an invalid for life.

Damian blinks.

Shakes his head, and Dawn abandons his psyche.

She is as she was before.

Kennedy.

Left side of the bed.

One knee up. One hand on the headboard.

Legs the color of mocha chocolate.

Her sweet spot speaks to him. Beckons him near.

Like a tasty piece of candy. She is a delectable morsel of delicacies, spread before him in all of her glory.

Damian moves, going to the other side of the bed to retrieve the duct tape. He returns momentarily.

"Hands in front of you, wrists together."

Kennedy's face begins to wilt.

"Hurry up, bitch, we don't have all night."

She places her hands together and in front of her breasts, raising them up to him. He pulls an eighteen-inch strip of tape away from the roll and advances on her.

"Make one wrong move as I bind you, and I swear to God you'll be rewarded with a bullet to the forehead. Do *not* fuck with me!"

Kennedy nods.

He wraps the tape around her wrists. Loops the roll around her hands, once, twice, three times. He considers tearing the tape from the roll, but decides otherwise. He leaves it dangling from her wrists.

"Turn around. Knee up on the mattress, as before."

Kennedy swallows, turns her head to meet his gaze.

"Do whatever you want to me, I will not resist. Just do not hurt my son, I beg you."

Her eyes seem to sparkle. He's unsure if it's from her tears. But the effect is magical. Damian doesn't move. For a moment he is locked where he stands.

Unable to proceed further.

He drinks in her features, and her sexuality, which shines like a beacon.

He can understand how *she* was drawn to her.

He understands the power she commands now.

For the first time in as long as he can remember, Damian is afraid.

And that gives him pause.

Chapter 74

"Goodman," he barks, answering on the first ring.

Michael swallows hard.

"Joe, it's Michael. Something's wrong. Kennedy and Zack have disappeared."

Phone to his ear, Michael is sprinting to his car a block away from Kennedy's BMW.

Joe is in the backseat of a taxi, heading north on Seventh. They're in Chinatown, just passing the Verizon Center on the right.

"Zack's cell phone shows he's at home. But Kennedy's car is on Constitution. I just saw it. They were with me less than thirty minutes ago."

"Michael, I'm on my way. Let me call it in. I'll get some uniforms to your house as well. But stay away from there. Let us handle things."

The call goes dead. Michael reaches his Range Rover huffing, his breath vaporizing in front of his face. He gets in, cranks the engine, and takes off with a screech of tires.

Meanwhile, Joe is yelling at the cab driver to run the red light at Massachusetts Avenue. The cabbie, a wiry man from Pakistan, is telling him he won't

break the law, regardless of the potential tip he
may receive.

Joe dials his district station. Gets a sergeant on
the line.

"Davidson, this is Goodman. Connect me with
dispatch, please."

A few seconds later, a female voice gets on the
line.

"Dispatch."

"This is Detective Goodman from the Fifth. Code
eight, backup for a possible kidnapping. Suspect is
armed and considered dangerous."

"Code eight, possible kidnapping. Officer needs
assistance," she repeats.

"I'm en route but need all available squad cars
in the area to respond." He gives the Taylor Street
address.

The light turns green, and the cabbie punches
the gas. They whiz by Mt. Vernon Square. In the
distance, Joe can see Howard University, its steeple
standing tall. He's still a good ten to fifteen minutes out.

The dispatcher reads back the address.

"Affirmative. Goodman out."

Joe bangs his fist on the door frame as he yells
to the cabbie, "Jesus, can't this piece of shit go any
faster?"

Tretch is behind the wheel of the blue Crown
Vic when the call comes over the radio.

"Code eight, officer needs assistance. Possible
kidnapping. Suspect considered armed and dangerous. 1365 Taylor Street, N.E. All units in the area
respond." Terrell, in the passenger seat, takes notice. He reaches for the radio.

"One fifty-nine, copy. We're code three, en route."

Tretch hits the lights and sirens, stepping on the gas.

"Shit, that's Joe's call," Terrell says, staring at Tretch. His partner nods.

"ETA four minutes away."

They are speeding down Bladensburg Road, heading westbound. They are no more than a mile and a half away.

"Make it three," Terrell says. "The vic is Goodman's ex—old lady."

Tretch stares at Terrell.

One of their own.

He nods.

Punches the pedal again as his face tightens.

Kennedy lays her bound wrists on the bed. She leans in, taking a breath and exhaling, her entire frame shuddering as she places her knee up, arching her back and ass to the ceiling. The fullness of her speaks to him. In Damian's world, it's a song. It's a symphony.

Damian blinks. Indecision is etched into his forehead. But what he sees takes his breath away. He wants to drink her in so bad he can taste it. Consume her in one bite. He wants her that bad. But the pain is threatening to debilitate him. He can feel his heart in his throat. Working overtime. Primed to explode.

Kennedy presses her face to the comforter.

The act forces her mocha-colored ass higher.

Her sweet spot is spread before him, and he finds he can barely breathe.

In an instant, Damian rushes over, grabs her ass as he drops to one knee, opening her wide. He licks her repeatedly like it's his last meal, long swathes with his tongue before pulling back.

Kennedy shivers in disgust.

The gun wavers.

Fingers to his temple, digging at the flesh, hoping for a respite.

And then he's rushing toward the bathroom door.

She watches him go. He stops at the door. Takes one step inside, feet straddling both rooms. Opens his mouth.

"Do not fucking *move*."

Kennedy refuses to blink.

Damian swallows hard and steps inside.

He disappears momentarily from view.

Kennedy waits only a second.

Then she makes her move.

Chapter 75

Face to the mirror.

Damian gapes at the person staring back.

He no longer recognizes himself.

Gone is the man he used to be.

Replaced with this thing standing before him—he can't even say what he's become.

The H&K goes on the sink with a loud clatter. He turns the water on and scoops a handful into his palms. Splashes some on his face and chin. Damian is grateful for the cool, the momentary reprieve. He raises his eyes to the mirror again. Checks his reflection as he reaches for a towel.

He focuses on the worry lines that have etched themselves deep into his skin.

It's come down to this.

Standing before him is a man he does not know.

A man with deep, unbridled pain.

A pain that is unrelenting.

All because of her.

The bitch in the next room.

Damian turns off the water.

He's conflicted. So many emotions running rampant inside. No time for this shit now. He brushes them away.

Collects his weapon. Weighs the H&K in his hand.

Finish this thing, he tells himself. *Finish what you've come to do. What you've dreamed of doing.*

Only then will the pain cease.

Do what you must do, Damian muses.

That is the only remedy left.

It's where Michael put it.

The Mossberg 12-gauge shotgun.

Six-shot. Blued finish. Eighteen-and-one-half-inch barrel. The one Pop Pop gave him last time they were in Ithaca. Hanging from two large hooks that he drilled into the wall behind the headboard.

Kennedy had put up a major fight.

A loaded gun in their home? With Zack around?

They had fought hard about that issue.

But now, as she grasps the barrel with her bound hands, feeling the weight of it against her chest, she whispers a short, silent prayer.

She has mere seconds.

Seconds before Damian returns.

She is out of time.

No time to consider the realm of possibilities. No time to ponder the various courses of action. She has to act. Without thinking. Move. Act. Survive. All without conscious thought.

Kennedy backs up to the bedroom door situated to the left of the bed. She crosses it in three paces, the sound masked by the thick carpet beneath bare feet. The door is slightly ajar. She uses her ankle to force it the rest of the way open. Positions herself halfway out into the hallway. Puts herself down on both knees. Wrestles with the gun until it is resting in her lap. She can hear him fumbling in the bathroom. Kennedy moves her hands up underneath the smooth, cold barrel until her hands are by the molded grip. Thumbs the safety off. Inches her fingers forward until she reaches the trigger. Curls her index finger around it. Her other hand twists as much as the duct tape will allow so her palm is pressed against the left side of the barrel.

All of this—from grabbing the shotgun to stepping over to the door, getting down on her knees, and fingering the trigger—has taken six seconds.

Six seconds.

But to Kennedy it has stretched out to eternity.

She can still hear him in the bathroom. Suddenly he's on the move. Footfalls loud on the tile before he reenters the bedroom.

Damian strides into the room, hard dick thrusting out from his pants at an obscene angle. The gun arcs up from the ground and over to the bed.

"Where are you, bitch?"

His captive's no longer there.

"Fuck!"

Kennedy sucks in a breath. Her heart is pounding. Temples throbbing. All she can think about is Zack, bound in the next room, and her husband, whom she may never see again.

God, please let me see my son and husband again.

She snaps her eyes shut once she's confident the gun is trained on Damian.

Squeezes the trigger at the exact moment his face pans left and finds her down on both knees.

He's contemplating the sweet fucking she's about to receive, when the explosion nullifies all conscious thought.

A defeaning boom. The recoil jams against Kennedy's gut as the gun goes airborne, somersaulting, flinging itself backward into the hallway.

Damian drops instantly, as if his legs were pulled out from under him. A blood-curdling scream escapes from his mouth. It's a wail that rises up, enveloping the buckshot-charged air. It takes Kennedy a split second to crab walk backward into the hallway, but before she does, her ears ringing and abdomen throbbing, she spies her captor on the ground, the left side of his face, shoulder, and arm a bloody mess.

His face is pressed to the carpet.

One eye appears to be missing.

He is struggling painfully slowly, gritting his teeth as blood flows from his open mouth. The pain is instant and complete. What he felt before was NOTHING compared to what he's experiencing now.

Left arm pinned underneath his broken body.

His right arm is barely moving.

Attempting to locate the H&K.

Kennedy's knees are stinging, but that no longer matters. The adrenaline coursing through her veins wills her to go on. She moves with surprising speed, locating the shotgun, which she picks up with her still-bound hands. Up on her haunches, she places the shotgun end up on the floor, pistol grip into the carpet.

She is wheezing. Struggling to fill her lungs with air. In an instant Damian may materialize in front of her like an apparition, searing hot lead from a .45-caliber slug in her brain, killing her at once.

Kennedy brushes the image away.

Her hands grasp the barrel and pump it once,

ejecting the spent shell and loading another into the chamber.

She doubts Damian is getting up any time soon. But she can't be sure. Better to be safe than sorry, her mama always says.

Kennedy rises, shotgun in both hands. One, two, three steps and she's in Zack's bathroom, down the hall from his room.

She's panting like a runner, sweat dripping into her eyes. Her ears still ring from the deafening roar of the shotgun blast.

The tile is cool on her feet. She steps over porcelain and into the bathtub, down on both knees, hard. Blood streaks the white surface.

Ignoring the pain and her nudity, Kennedy places the barrel of the shotgun on the edge of the tub facing outward, toward the door and hallway.

Finger shaking against the trigger.

Heart thumping into overdrive.

Let that motherfucker get up.

Go on, get up and walk past me.

I dare you.

Should Damian find the strength to come after her, Kennedy will blow him away. This as sure as there is a God.

Over the din in her ears, she imagines she is hearing someone shout "POLICE, OPEN UP!"

It's like a dream.

One in which she's floating outside herself, observing from above as this woman she's never met battles to protect her family and her own life.

There's another sound. Like breaking wood. Then multiple footsteps. Glass shattering. Screams and moans. It's all happening so incredibly fast.

She tries to discern fact from fiction. But it's close to impossible with everything going on.

Kennedy wipes the sweat from her face with her forearm.

Sinks lower into the tub.

Wills her finger to stop its tremble.

And waits for someone to cross her path.

Chapter 76

Terrell is taking the steps to the front door two at a time when he hears the blast.

Tretch is right behind him, on the shoulder mike. "Shots fired, shots fired, 1365 Taylor Street. Officers need assistance!"

"POLICE, OPEN UP!" Terrell yells.

He draws his Glock 22, nods firmly to his partner, who rushes up the stairs past him and barrels his large frame into the door. The frame buckles and splinters on the second try, and they rush in. Gun drawn, Terrell takes the first level. Tretch makes his way up the stairs, his Glock leading the way.

"Police, Police!" His Glock is swinging from left to right and back again, covering one hundred and eighty degrees as he creeps up the steps. He hears Terrell announce "Clear!" as he makes it to the second floor. Tretch pauses, glancing down the empty hallway. Two open doors, one closed. He places his foot on the landing, steps toward the closed door. Terrell joins up behind him. Tretch glances back, taking his position by the closed door. He nods to Terrell, who nods back. Tretch's hand goes to the knob and turns it, his body out of the line of fire. He pushes the door open forcefully.

Waits a beat before popping his head in quickly. He spies Zack by his desk, bound by duct tape.

He rushes in, gun trained on the closet.

Terrell goes to the boy.

"Clear!" Tretch announces and rushes out into the hallway. Terrell approaches Zack.

"We're the police. You all right?"

Zack gulps, shivering and unable to speak.

Tretch is inching his way to the first open door—a bathroom—when he hears glass shattering. It comes from the room at the other end of the hallway.

"Police!" he yells.

"In here," Kennedy announces a beat later.

"Terrell!" he calls to his partner. "Ma'am? Come on out."

"I'm in the tub. I . . . have a shotgun."

Tretch backs up. "Ma'am, I need you to put the gun down and come out with your hands where I can see them."

"He . . . he's in the bedroom," she cries. "He tried to rape me."

Tretch eases his head around the doorframe. Spies her splayed naked inside the tub, hands bound, the shotgun pointing up. He rushes in, Glock trained at her.

"Easy, miss. I've got you." Terrell is behind him an instant later.

"Jesus," he whispers.

Tretch reaches for the shotgun, ejects the remaining shells. He leans the weapon behind him by the door. Pulls out a folded knife and cuts the duct tape from her wrists. He pulls Kennedy to a standing position, trying to ignore her nude form.

It's damn near impossible.

"You all right? Here, let me put this towel around you."

"My son. Is he all right?" Kennedy rubs her wrist as she allows the towel to be wrapped around her shoulders. She begins to push past Tretch, but he holds up a hand.

"Hold on. He's fine. Wait here until we secure the other rooms."

Terrell has advanced to the bedroom door. Cautiously he peeks around the door and into the bedroom. He spies splotches of wet blood oozing onto the carpet. The window several feet from the dark spot is blown open. The metal bar holding the curtain is dangling from one end, and half of the curtain is pushed outside. Shards of glass are everywhere.

He checks the bathroom. Empty.

Goes back to the window, glances down where glass, wood, and plaster adorn the deck. He can see a man in dark clothes scaling a wooden fence that surrounds the backyard. He yells out, "Police, hold it!" just as Tretch approaches the window. The man clears the top and lumbers over, landing on his feet. He ducks down, out of sight.

"Tretch, he's escaping out back."

He gets on his radio.

"Suspect fleeting the scene. Scaled a fence and is heading west on the alley behind Taylor Street. All units be advised."

"Copy. Suspect heading west, alley behind Taylor Street."

"Roger that."

Terrell retreats to the hallway. He walks past the bathroom and into the little boy's room. By the time he has cut him loose, Kennedy has swooped Zack into her arms.

"Oh, baby, are you all right?"

"Yes, Mommy. I'm scared." Zack stares at her wrapped in a towel. "What happened to your clothes?"

Kennedy straightens up and adjusts the towel tighter around her frame.

"Mommy's fine. I need to get my clothes on. Can you stay with him for a second?"

Terrell nods.

Kennedy goes to retrieve her clothes. Tretch is at the window of her bedroom, on the radio. He turns when she enters.

"Can I have some privacy for a moment? Just want to get dressed."

"Of course."

Tretch leaves after eyeing her for a moment longer than necessary, closing the door behind him.

Chapter 77

The cab screeches to a halt in front of two squad cars blocking traffic on Taylor. Joe Goodman's money is already out. A twenty is tossed at the driver. He's out the door before the cabbie has fully depressed the brake. The driver swears in Punjabi, but the detective is already gone.

Garment bag and shield in hand, he runs past the two black-and-whites, their red and blue lights flashing. Sprinting around a young uniformed officer setting up crime-scene tape, he dashes up the stairs and into the townhouse. There is another uniform right inside the front door. He nods to the detective.

"Where is she?"

The uniform gestures upward.

Joe drops his bag and takes the stairs.

Hits the landing and finds Terrell in the second-floor hallway holding a black shotgun.

Joe looks at him.

"Get him?"

Terrell shakes his head slowly.

"Jumped out the window and onto the deck.

Scaled the back fence. He's wounded, Joe, but he's running."

Joe sighs. Terrell nods in agreement.

"Tretch called in air support. We'll locate him."

"Where's Kennedy?"

Terrell thumbs in the direction of Zack's room.

"Joe?"

"Yeah?"

"Your ex shot him. Twelve-gauge." Terrell hefts the shotgun into the air. "Definitely slowed him down. We also found an H&K semiautomatic handgun in the back bedroom. Think it's the perps. Thought you should know."

Joe nods, putting his hand on Terrell's shoulder. "Thanks, man. Tretch, too."

"Wish I had caught the son of a bitch," Terrell says through gritted teeth.

Joe walks into Zack's room. Kennedy looks up. She is dressed in the clothes she'd been wearing before the ordeal began, sitting on the bed with Zack and trying to bring some sense of normalcy to this crazed situation. She stands when Joe enters.

"Hey," she utters.

Joe crosses the floor.

"You okay? I was worried sick."

"Yeah, I'm fine," she replies.

Joe eyes Zack on the bed. He moves in, taking Kennedy in his arms before stepping back. He puts his hand on Zack's head. Rubs his short hair.

"How you doing, fella?"

"Good," Zack responds, glancing up.

Kennedy stares into Joe's eyes.

"He's . . . gone?" she asks gingerly, afraid of what the answer might be.

Joe bobs his head.

"Yeah, but we'll catch him. He can't get very far. Not with Metropolitan's finest on his you know what." He glances down at Zack and grins.

Joe takes Kennedy by the arm and leads her over to the door.

"You shot him," Joe says, his voice low.

"Yes."

Joe stares at her for a moment. Then he smiles for the first time this evening.

"That's my girl," he says with a wicked grin.

He crouches on the other side of the wooden fence, a few houses down from hers, blood streaking down his face and shirt.

He's in shock, and there's blood in his mouth. He feels a hurt he's never experienced before.

The pain he feels now has eclipsed the pain of before. That aching wasn't shit compared to what he's dealing with now.

His face and shoulder are on fire.

The last few minutes have been a whirlwind.

Did the bitch actually shoot him? How is that even possible? Where did the gun come from?

Nothing makes sense.

He's gone from being in complete control to . . . this.

Readying to impale her, the sweetness, like nectar, so fucking inviting.

But then the blinding, searing pain came at him. Struck him down in an instant.

And now, nothing makes sense.

The pain is intense. His cheek, his nose, his lips. He can barely fucking see.

His eye.

Damian reaches gingerly to touch it and practically passes out.

It's no longer there. How can that be?

He can't even begin to process that. Nothing makes sense anymore. So he stops trying to connect the dots. Instead, it's now about survival mode. Get away from this crazed bitch, escape from the police that have suddenly showed up like on *Cops*. He can hear the sirens wailing, see the red and blue lights strobing.

He gets to his feet, keeps his head low. His entire left side is on fire. The H&K is no longer in his hand or his pocket.

Fuck!

Keep moving. Get away. Survive. Regroup. Leave this place that makes him dizzy. Find somewhere to rest. Close his eye and sleep. For a minute or two.

Regroup and then figure things out.

His head throbs. He can no longer think. Just move.

Move, move, and keep moving.

That's the only thing left to do.

Chapter 78

Michael screeches to a rolling stop, pans both directions rapidly before punching the accelerator. He races past the stop sign, up Thirteenth, just a few precious blocks away from home. Passes Ritchie Place, then Shepherd Street. The next road is Michigan Avenue. Thank goodness he has the light. He flies through the intersection and cuts an immediate left onto Taylor, doing close to forty.

Three cop cars assault his view. They are blocking the street a hundred yards away, directly in front of his house.

Michael makes a quick right, jumping the sidewalk as he steers the Range Rover into an alley. Flooring the accelerator, his mind is on one thing. Getting to his family.

As soon as possible.

All negative thoughts have erased themselves from his mind. Over the past few minutes, from the moment he dialed Joe until now, all he's thought about is finding his wife and child safe from harm. His heart is beating in his chest. He's unsure of what he'll find. He prays it isn't too late.

Please, *please* don't let it be too late.

The alley ends at a narrow intersection. Forks left and right. Michael jams the steering wheel left, hearing the screech of tires as he practically careens into a Dumpster. He overcorrects, sending the SUV lurching to the right and into a bunch of garbage cans. He hits them head on, sending trash flying over his hood.

Michael curses loudly but doesn't slow. Accelerates down the narrow tree-lined alleyway as if his life depends on it.

Fifty yards away is the back of their house. He can see lights on in every room. He spies his deck, just above the wooden fence that adjoins the alleyway. Someone, it appears to be a uniform cop, is at their bedroom window.

Please God, don't let him be too late.

Please let Zack and Kennedy be okay.

His adrenaline is spiking. He can barely breathe. His chest is about to burst.

Damian finally realizes what it is he truly wants.

To rest from this madness.

He's been running for so long.

Running away from *her* . . . and from himself.

He's grown so incredibly tired.

And for what?

Nothing is ever going to be the way it was.

The way it was back then, when things were sweet and simple.

He can barely remember the details of life before. The images are fleeting. Soon they'll be gone forever from his grasp.

But he knows this: It was a time without pain. Without aching.

Life was sweet back then.

Everything throbs now. Inside and out.

And it will never stop. The pain will never dissipate. Not until he rests.

He thinks of her once again.

Dawn.

He's shuffling, stumbling alone in some dark, narrow alleyway, cold, bleeding, unseeing, and afraid.

Trying to remember her as she was.

Before she became polluted.

Before she turned foul.

Butterscotch complexion.

A smile so dazzling and bright.

A smile to die for.

He focuses on her smile now.

And follows it into the blinding light.

A disturbance off to the left captures his attention. It's a blur that Michael barely picks up in his peripheral vision. Before he has time to react, before he can even consciously consider what the disturbance actually is, the left bumper connects with a sickening thud, and instantly the blur becomes a solid object, smashing headlong into his windshield.

Michael screams and jams on the brake, instinctively cutting the wheel hard to the right. A hundred-year-old oak tree appears in front of him. It is almost surreal in the whiteness of his xenon headlights. He watches it all in a kind of slow motion, the ghostly face staring back at him through the cracked and splintered windshield, one eye cold and unblinking, the other just a mass of blackened, bloody gore, before the Range Rover crashes violently into the tree that has stood for three generations, sending the body flying brutally forward. Whiteness assaults

Michael. It is instantaneous, shutting out all sight within his vision.

What Michael doesn't see, thanks to the air bag that obstructs his view, is the body, which hits the unmoving mass of roots and bark, branches and leaves with a revolting thump a split second before the unmistakable sound of cracking bones, twisting metal, and breaking glass pierces the nighttime air. The old tree shudders as if exorcising a moan. Then it grows still once again.

Then everything around him fades to black.

Chapter 79

It's after three in the morning when he hobbles inside. Drops his keys on the countertop and makes his way slowly upstairs.

She is waiting for him.

On the bed, wearing a bathrobe. She mutes the television as he drops his garment bag on the floor.

Removes his shield, cell, and Glock. Places them on the nightstand.

Tara goes to him.

Kisses him gingerly on his lips.

"You okay?" she asks softly.

"Exhausted," Joe responds.

She nods.

"We got him."

Tara nods again, leading him to the bed.

"I know. It's been all over the news."

The WRC-TV and Fox 5 choppers had lit up the sky, and it was like daylight bathing the crime scene. Surreal.

Joe slowly undresses. Leaves his clothes in a heap on the floor.

Tara pulls him under covers.

Holds him against her warm body.

Feels him shudder, respite elusive.

Sleep is a game that Joe is losing.

For several minutes they are silent, holding one another, each reveling in the comfort the other brings.

"Is this thing done?" she asks finally.

It takes Joe a moment to respond.

"Yes."

He knows what Tara is asking.

Kennedy. Is this thing with Kennedy done?

And it is. He means it.

It's done.

"You're a good man, Joe Goodman," she says, kissing his face. "And I love you."

In the darkness, Joe smiles.

"I love you, too, Tara. Can't wait for you to be my wife."

Then sleep finds him. It wins the game.

Chapter 80

He opens his eyes slowly, adjusting them to the harsh fluorescent light.

His stare is unfocused, but as he pans left he can make out a selection of tubes running in and out of him. Machines, blinking, a steady metronome of soft sound. To the right, the face of an angel comes into view. He stares at her features, mesmerized, holding on to them like he would a child's hand, lest he let them slip and this goddess disappear from his sight forever. She is beautiful. She is incredible. A voice inside his head sweetly whispers in a voice faintly erotic, "I am Celestial, and I'm your deepest, darkest fantasy come true."

He attempts a smile, but his jaw aches. He endeavors to sit up, but the pain is sharp and abrupt, so he eases back down with a suffering moan.

"Welcome back to the land of the living," the angel says, beaming.

Overhead, a television, suspended from the ceiling, is tuned to the Disney Channel. Directly underneath the TV sits Zack, head down, absorbed in his PSP. He glances up, eyes suddenly as big as silver dollars. He rushes around the bed and is hoisted up by the angel.

"DADDY!"

Michael coughs. Stares at the angel before recognition fuses into his brain.

"Kennedy."

He coughs again.

"Drink some water, baby," she says softly. She brings a glass up to his lips, holding it for him. Michael takes a sip, savoring the liquid as it meets his parched tongue.

He drinks some more. This time swallows long and hard.

Kennedy takes the glass away as Zack touches his hand.

"Hey, buddy," Michael says.

"Hi, Daddy. Missed you!"

The door opens, and his parents, Betty and Roland, enter. His mother has her hands to her face. There are tears in her eyes.

"Lord, my baby is awake," Betty says, making her way to the right side of the hospital bed. She kisses his cheek and squeezes his hand.

"Hi, Mama." His father comes up behind her, nodding in that paternal way of his, looking slightly older and a lot more tired than the last time Michael saw him.

"Very proud of you, Son," his father says. "Very proud indeed."

Michael looks over at Kennedy.

"What time is it? How long have I been . . . here?"

Kennedy checks her watch and smiles. "It's close to dinnertime. You're at Georgetown University Hospital. You were brought here last night after your accident."

Michael tries to sit up again. The pain spikes in his gut, and he winces.

Serious pain.

"Easy, baby," Kennedy says, her hand to his shoulder. "You fractured a rib, and you've got lacerations over your face."

The events of the previous evening start trickling back into his psyche.

"My car?" he says.

"Let's just say we'll be shopping for a new vehicle really soon!" Kennedy exclaims.

Michael blinks.

"You don't remember anything?" his father asks.

Michael stares around at the room at the faces glancing back at him. He blinks again, trying to conjure up the details.

"You got him, Daddy," Zack says, face animated. "You kilt the bad man!"

Nana hushes her grandson.

"What?" Michael asks, his face showing bewilderment. He turns to Kennedy for answers.

It takes her a moment to respond.

"Damian. The one who's been terrorizing us. He's dead, Michael."

"You kilt him, Daddy. You the man!"

"Zack, hush," his mother says.

"Well, he did!" Zack returns to the chair and his PSP, instantly taken with the game in front of him.

"It's over," Kennedy says.

Michael's forehead wrinkles. "I . . . killed him?"

"I shot him," Kennedy says, glancing quickly over to Pop Pop before returning her stare to her husband, "but you finished him off with the Range Rover. It's done, baby. Over."

He stares at her, and she bends in to kiss his lips gingerly.

"Can I have a moment alone with my husband?" she asks.

"Come on, Zack," Nana says. "Let's go find the cafeteria. Your Pop Pop owes us some dinner anyway."

Zack jumps up.

"Pop Pop, do you think the cafeteria has pizza? You know I love pizza. But not that kind with the cheese in the crust. That's just gross. My mommy says that stuffed crust isn't good for you. She says it makes people fat. How can pizza make a person fat, Pop Pop? It's *pizza!* That makes no sense to me. Right?"

Michael's father raises his eyebrows at his grandson as they walk out with Nana. The door closes, and Michael and Kennedy are finally alone.

Chapter 81

"Quite an ordeal," she says.

Michael nods.

"How are you feeling?" she asks.

"Sore as hell. My side is killing me, and my face feels like someone took a razor to it."

"I'll call the nurse in a minute, get them to up the Demerol."

Michael looks at his wife for a full minute before speaking.

"Are you okay?"

Kennedy nods.

"Yeah, I'm fine. We made it through. It was gray skies for a while, but now the sun is shining through the clouds once again. I can see the sun, thank goodness. I'm just glad we're done with him."

Michael processes what's been said and what has not.

"Did he . . . Did he hurt you?"

"No. When I shot him, the gun hit me in the stomach, but that's about it. I am so glad you insisted on the shotgun in the bedroom. Without it, I might not be standing here now."

"You shot him." It's not a question, but a statement.

Kennedy smiles. "Yeah, I did. Pop Pop said he's proud of me."

"I am, too. You did what you had to do. Protected yourself and your family. You protected our son. Thank you for that."

Kennedy swallows.

She takes a seat on the side of the bed.

"I have something else to say. Can you listen to me and not interrupt?"

"Where am I gonna go?" he asks with a grin.

Her expression grows serious.

"I need to explain to you what happened." She pauses for a second, then continues. "Between Joe and me."

Michael swallows but says nothing.

Kennedy carries on.

"Do you remember seven years ago when you were mugged?"

Michael instantly frowns.

Suddenly, a million images rush to the surface, like a tidal wave. It crashes into his chest, making him heave in pain.

Seven years ago, late one Friday night, he'd been in the Adams Morgan section of the District, having beers with some college buddies who were in town for a conference.

Afterward, heading to his car on a darkened street, three young black males, angry at the clean-shaven, sharply dressed black man who seemingly had everything they did not, had attacked him.

He had been savagely beaten when his wallet revealed only thirty-five dollars.

They beat him because of their intense anger and hatred for anything not like them.

He spent two weeks in the hospital.

Concussion, dislocated jaw, multiple lacerations about the face and body.

When he got discharged, the fury burning inside him propelled him to one of the roughest sections of Washington, D.C.

Where a twenty-year-old crack addict who looked fifty sold him a handgun for a hundred dollars. Offered to suck his dick for another five.

Michael took his weapon and went on the hunt.

Searching for the thugs who had maimed him.

Ready to maim them back, with 9mm heat.

But he got caught in a routine traffic stop late one night on Eighteenth Street, blocks from where he had been savagely beaten.

They found the loaded gun beneath his seat.

A loaded handgun in D.C. meant five years.

Mandatory.

No questions asked.

"Remember the night you got stopped?" Kennedy asks. "The night they found the gun?"

Michael exhales.

That night was the worst of his life. He saw every single thing he had worked so hard for spilling down the drain. His wife. His career. Everything dear to him. A conviction meant jail time. Sixty months. Michael knew he couldn't do five years. No way he could last inside that long.

"You were arrested on a Friday night. Couldn't make bail until Monday morning. Those were the longest sixty hours of my entire life."

"Mine, too." Michael *remembers*. His voice is close to a whisper.

"You spent the entire weekend behind bars. I spent the entire time trying to get you released. I called your boss at your law firm. . . ."

Michael's eyes grow wide.

"I didn't tell you because I knew you didn't want them to know. But I had very few options. And we had precious little time."

"Frank, he *knew*?"

"Yes. I brought him in to help. It turned out there wasn't much he could do, but he promised to make some calls—to judges he knew, and a few prosecutors, to see if some sort of plea deal could be reached."

Michael sighs audibly.

"Wow. He never said a word to me."

"I told him not to. He couldn't guarantee results, so I had to do something else. I couldn't let you go to jail. Couldn't stand the thought of being without you. It would have killed me."

Michael stares at his wife. He's no longer breathing. The air is caught in his throat.

"I reached out to Joe. I had no choice, Michael. I had run out of options. I figured Joe could fix this. Would fix it . . . for me.

"You need to understand, Michael. I was desperate. I can't even explain to you how I felt. It was as if I were standing on the edge of a towering cliff with a herd of stampeding buffalo on my tail, and my only option in order to survive was to jump. We had our glorious life in front of us, and suddenly this *thing* threatened to shut it down cold. I couldn't let that happen. I wouldn't let it ruin us."

"Joe fixed it," Michael utters.

For three seconds she is silent. Then, with an audible exhale of breath, she responds.

"Yes. He made it go away. Talked to the arresting officer. Went down to the station and did something with the gun and the paperwork. I don't know the details. Didn't want to know. All I cared about is, come Monday morning, you walked out a free man. A man without a gun-possession charge hanging over his head."

Michael processes her words.

"You traded—"

"Michael—I didn't sleep with him. But, yeah, I was intimate with him. I did what I had to do to get my husband back."

Kennedy sits forward.

"And to tell you the truth, the way I feel about you, the love that I have for you as my husband, I'd do it again. If that's what I have to do in order to keep something from happening to you again, then, yeah, I'd do it again. Think what you like, but you mean the world to me. I can't ever imagine living my life without you by my side."

Michael swallows. For a moment he says nothing. It is just the silence between them.

"So, Zack. He's—"

"Michael Handley, if you ever, ever, EVER hint that the little boy out there is not one hundred and fifty percent your son, so help me God!"

The tears sprout and meander down her cheeks. Michael reaches out and gingerly wipes them away.

"I am sorry, baby," he says. "Very sorry for doubting you."

Kennedy nods, blinking and wiping at the corner of her eyes.

"Just say you'll love me for all of eternity."

"I will love you for all of eternity," Michael repeats.

"And mean it."

"I mean it. I've missed you."

"Yeah? Care to show me just how much?" There is a dazzle to her eyes that Michael finds irresistible.

Kennedy and Michael embrace.

At that exact moment, the door opens and Zack rushes in.

He jumps up onto the bed, almost crushing Michael with his weight. Michael yelps like a hurt puppy.

"Sorry, Daddy. Mommy, look what Nana bought me! It's a superhero."

He holds a molded plastic doll proudly out to his parents.

"See, he carries two guns in a holster just in case one jams, and a shotgun in a pouch on his shoulder."

Michael eyes his mother, who has just entered with Pop Pop, with disdain.

"This is so cool. And if you move him like this"— Zack illustrates, twisting the molded plastic limbs— "he can stand on his own. You have to raise his arms up like this so he doesn't lose his balance. See, he's totally the bestest! Can I take him to school and show my friends? Please?"

"We'll see."

"Mrs. Knopfson always says we can bring in stuff for show-and-tell. Hey, I have a great idea. You and Mommy should come to show-and-tell with me. I could tell my class about Mommy shooting the bad man and Daddy running him over with the car! How's that for real superheroes?" Zack starts laughing. "Man, Jeremy will be so jealous when he hears what you did, Dad. His mom and dad *never* do cool stuff like that!"

Michael stares in amazement at his son. At this moment he feels an intense rush of emotion— love—toward each person in the room. He wishes he could walk over to each one right this second, hold them tight, show them just how much they mean to him, and never let them go.

Instead he grins, gritting his teeth as he attempts to sit up in the bed.

Kennedy shakes her head and leans forward. Michael winces as her cheek brushes against his.

The tears begin to flow, winding down Michael's nose and cheek.

And he considers that there is no place he'd rather be than right here, even if it means in this uncomfortable hospital bed with tubes and God knows what else inserted inside his veins, with his lovely wife, his precious son, and his incredible parents, those whom Michael loves the most in this crazy, messed-up world, all safely by his fractured side.

Epilogue

One Year Later . . .

The azure waters off Providenciales of the Turks and Caicos Islands contrasts sharply with its white, pristine sands. It is half past nine, and the sun is climbing high into an already breathtaking sky.

They sit with their feet in the warming sands not twenty yards from the water's edge, finishing up breakfast.

Eggs Benedict, Belgian waffles, blueberry-filled pancakes, fried sausage, well-cooked, hickory-smoked bacon.

Their plates removed by a cute, attentive waitress, they drink strong Mediterranean coffee while Zack, scuba mask and snorkel already donned, his feet stuffed into oversized fins, stomps impatiently around their table.

"For the hundredth time, Zackary Christopher Handley, you cannot go in the water unsupervised." Kennedy is wearing a turquoise bikini, halter top and low-rise bottoms courtesy of Victoria's Secret. Her hair is cut short in the style of Halle Berry in *Die Another Day*. Michael is sporting a pair of printed

oversized boardshorts with dark Ray-Bans and a
khaki surf hat. He chuckles at his son as he observes him tossing a mock tantrum.

"Why don't you go play over there in the sand?"
Michael suggests. "Mommy will take you snorkeling as soon as we're finished."

Zack huffs and puffs, his eyes rolling into the
back of his head. "You guys take *way* too long!"

"We are in no rush, young man," Kennedy says.
"We're on vacation, remember?"

"You promised me a massage before lunch,"
Zack retorts. "*Hello?*"

Michael busts out laughing.

Kennedy simply shakes her head.

"He is *so* your son," she says.

"Whatever."

Zack plods off, the scuba fins making forward
movement across the sand extremely difficult, especially for an eight-year-old. But he is determined
to get as far away from his parents as possible.
When he's gone about twenty yards down the beach,
Kennedy calls out to him.

"That's enough, honey."

"Aww, Mommy!"

They sip their coffee, enjoying the momentary
peace and serenity.

"I could get used to this," Kennedy says.

"Amen."

A few moments pass between them. They stare
out at the water. The back-and-forth rhythm of the
rushing tide is hypnotic.

Michael breaks the silence.

"I'm horny."

Kennedy exhales sharply.

"You know just how to—"

"I know—fuck up a wet dream!"

"Basically."

"I'm just saying . . ."

Kennedy cocks her head to one side. Lowers her voice.

"Didn't I take care of you last night?" she asks demurely.

"Yep. But that was *last* night. Today is a brand-new day, baby!"

Kennedy shakes her head.

"I'll see what I can do. In between snorkeling and your son's massage."

"See that you do," Michael says. "I have needs, you know."

They both laugh.

Several more moments of uninterrupted silence pass between them.

"Question," Michael says.

"Shoot."

Michael takes a few seconds to frame what's on his mind. "Do you think our lifestyle will change as a result of what happened?"

Kennedy stares at him.

"You mean, do I think we'll continue to sleep with other people after what went down with that madman?"

"That's what I'm asking."

Kennedy looks away. She relaxes her stare, and it drifts far away, out to the horizon and beyond. She knows that beyond her vision lies Haiti and the Dominican Republic.

"I don't know," she finally replies. "It's not something I've made a decision about."

"Okay."

"You're mad." Statement, not question.

"Not mad."

"Disappointed."

Michael turns to her.

"I wouldn't even say I'm disappointed. I loved what we had—the freedom to express who we are. To define ourselves as sexually free beings. Yeah, I'd miss that if we couldn't go back, but your safety and that of our son is my first priority. Nothing else even comes close."

Kennedy smiles.

"I'm glad to hear you say that."

Michael nods.

"Not saying no," Kennedy says. "Just saying we need to give it some serious thought before jumping back into the frying pan."

"Agreed," Michael says.

"I'll tell you one thing," she says, draining the last of her coffee, "if we do decide to play, I'm instituting new rules."

Michael's eyebrow rises.

"Oh, really?"

"Yeah. Rule number one—no married folks. And nobody in a committed relationship. Only singles allowed."

"Okay." Michael pretends to be taking notes.

"Rule number two—ID and background check for everyone before we do *anything*. You hear me?"

Michael grins.

"Go take your son snorkeling."

Kennedy rises, kisses her husband long and hard on the mouth before raising her voice.

"Zack, you ready?" she asks.

"YESSS!" he exclaims, bringing his fist into his waist.

Michael watches the two of them go.

His woman.

His little man.

He signals the cute waitress for a refill.

The Mediterranean coffee is good. Smells of coca, cinnamon, and a pinch of orange peel assault his nostrils as she pours the hot brew.

The waitress leaves, and Michael is alone with his thoughts.

They are good thoughts.

Peaceful and serene.

"Excuse me."

Michael looks up into the brilliant sunshine.

A gorgeous dark-skinned woman in a stunning white off-the-shoulder one-piece is standing beside him. Michael holds his hand to his forehead in order to keep from squinting.

"Hello," she begins.

Her accent he can't place. British, Australian—he isn't sure.

"Hi," he responds.

"May I join you?" she asks, displaying a wonderful set of straight white teeth and full, sensual lips.

"Sure, I guess."

The woman sits, folding her well-oiled legs. They go on for days, and Michael has to concentrate hard not to stare.

"You have a lovely family," she says.

Michael smiles.

"I observed the three of you earlier during breakfast."

"Ahhh."

"Your wife is beautiful. Quite striking."

The woman is grinning, and Michael begins to laugh.

"What's so funny?" she asks.

He shrugs.

"I was just thinking. Never mind." He waves a hand away.

"No, go ahead. Tell me, please."

She pats his arm playfully. And that accent. Lord.

Michael licks his lips.

"You said my wife is beautiful. I was about to say, 'You should see her naked.'"

Their eyes lock for a brief moment, and then Michael chuckles, enjoying his private joke.

"I'd like that," the beautiful dark-skinned woman retorts with a straight face.

Michael considers this creature before him.

Breathtaking. Sensual.

He sips his coffee, contemplating a suitable response.

Finally he sets his mug down.

"You here . . . alone?"

"Yes."

"Too bad we're not. Our son is with us," he says, gesturing with his thumb toward the waves.

"I see," she says.

"But if we were alone, we'd need to see some ID," he retorts playfully.

"We?" she asks innocently.

"My wife and I. We're a package deal."

She doesn't miss a beat.

"Sure. It's back in my room."

Michael stares unblinkingly, his breath for a moment arrested, his lips curling into a radiant and consenting smile.

Don't miss Devon Scott's

UNFAITHFUL

Available now wherever books are sold

Chapter 1

Olivia—

I've tried for days to tell you what, for me, is an absolute new feeling. I've been asking myself if what I dare to express is real and worth fighting for, given our circumstances and the fact that we've been friends for so long. But I've come to the point where I can no longer NOT let you know how I'm feeling.

I know a letter is not the best way to communicate affairs of the heart, but in the interest of so many things, I feel this is the only way to start.

So, here goes . . .

Something changed within me that night at the party. Two weeks ago, almost to this day, my life was indelibly altered. I can't tell you exactly why it began, but all I know is I don't look at things the way I did before. I find myself dreaming about new things—whole new realms of possibilities, and each one includes you.

Olivia, what happened between you and me that night cannot be ignored. It was profound. It was deep. And I pray that it happens again and again and again. Yes, Olivia, for me it was so

*much more than just physical . . . it affected me
that much. . . .*

Ryan doesn't hear the door open until the footfalls are inside his cage. He glances up to find his
boss, the president of the company, standing before
him. He swivels away from his laptop and quickly
closes the clamshell, ensuring no one will witness
this spilling of emotions.

"Ryan."

"Rodney. Have a seat."

"No, thanks. This won't take but a second." He
glances back toward the door as if expecting company.

Ryan witnesses Olivia's dark locs rise into view.
Before he can breathe, she is moving through the
door. Russet-colored skin and toned calf muscles,
sculpted flesh that curves upward to the hemline of
her short, yet fashionable, skirt. The crisp white
button-down top is fitting, following her curves the
way a sports car does a winding road. Eyes drift upward to her full breasts pressed against cotton—no,
that is not right. They are straining against the fabric—yes, straining.

"Ahhh, perfect timing, Olivia," Rodney says.

She grins at Rodney before flashing her alluring
smile in Ryan's direction.

Rodney begins without preamble. "I need the two
of you in New York, tonight. Sorry for the late notice,
but, Olivia, your guy is having second thoughts—
something he's hearing on the street about a man-
ufacturing defect with the optics. Pure bullshit, of
course, but we need to squelch this thing before it
gets out of hand."

Olivia is nodding, as if she expected this. Ryan is
turning a sour face, as if he has no idea what they

are talking about. He opens his mouth to speak, but Olivia beats him to the punch.

"Rod, Ryan and I met earlier today regarding this issue, and I've already had my staff prepare a briefing just in case. So Ryan and I can finalize it on the shuttle going up. We'll be ready, no problem. Just tell us when and where."

Ryan remains silent. He is observing her, cool under fire. Her stare is unwavering, her smile captivating. He feels himself stirring, readying the switch that turns the windows opaque so fast it would make her head spin. He longs to push Rodney out of his office, then rush to her the way a cheetah attacks its prey.

"Outstanding. Jackie has all the details." He turns to leave, swatting Ryan on the shoulder. He winks at Olivia as he says, "As usual, the two of you make quite a pair." Then he is gone, leaving Olivia alone with Ryan, a smirk painted on her sensuously full lips.

Six hours later, he sits across from her, forty-seven floors up from Broadway, enjoying the tastiest broiled salmon of his life. She is dressed casually: tight jeans, dark boots, and off-white sweater showing off her curves. As she excuses herself to go to the restroom, he stares silently at her perfectly shaped ass, thanking God for answering his prayers.

When she returns, looking more refreshed than before, he focuses on the gap between her thighs, that sweet spot, attempting to make out the cleft that forms her core. He knows what it feels like. He has committed its form to memory . . . has touched it . . . even slipped a finger inside.

God, what a night that was.

He hopes tonight he will finish what they began.

The biz trip to New York was a godsend.

He is drinking rum and Coke. The buzz he is feeling helps his thinking along. He stares at her, pondering just how alluring she can be. They talk casually about stuff, already exhausting the technical problems that sent them there. Once again, he is barely listening. Instead, he remembers a scene very similar to this one.

Months ago, the two of them were out on a client call . . . another late night, one of many. For some reason, he was feeling depressed that night. Can't recall why—but it was one of those times when self-esteem was at an all-time low. Perhaps he was just going through a midlife crisis—or reexamining his life from a different angle. We all need to do that from time to time. Right?

Regardless, he was feeling down, and needed to believe in something else for a change.

Warmth.

"Do you find me attractive?"

He recalls blurting out the question over dinner. She had glanced up, incomprehension etched in her usually smooth brow.

She was thinking.

"What do you mean?" she asked cautiously while setting down her wineglass stem and giving him her full attention.

"Just what I said. Do you find me attractive?"

He was thinking about her husband, Miles. How could he not? They had been talking about him earlier. And Ryan found that he was comparing himself to the man. Ryan was thin and lanky, like a ball player, whereas Miles was muscled, stocky. Ryan was light-skinned; Miles, on the other hand, richly brown. Ryan wore his hair short, tapered, professional, almost boring to a fault, whereas Miles wore his to fit his personality—wild, free, unencumbered. His locks were thick, dark, and long. Women loved his hair.

He received stares and comments from women everywhere he went. Sometimes it made Ryan sick.

Olivia stared at him for a moment, pondering the question, and in the ensuing silence, he wondered, Could I have gotten her? Could I have been her man?

Her brow furrowed. She smiled and then said something simple that blew him away.

"I think you're beautiful."

Ryan considered her words for a moment. Head tilted down, he pondered their meaning.

He didn't see her get up, didn't notice her move to his side of the table until she was bending down. He glanced up, meeting her stare as her mouth opened. Before he had time to consider further action, her mouth was upon his, kissing him, loving him with her mouth, those luscious lips pressing against his with a passion that ignited something so deep and primal he hadn't felt in decades.

When she was done—he wasn't sure if it took mere seconds or minutes—Olivia finally pulled back, wiped the locs from her eyes, and sat down. She then picked up her wine and took a sip. No words were needed. He knew now how she felt. . . .

"Penny for your thoughts?" she asks, bringing him back to reality.

He smiles in remembrance. "Just thinking."

"About?"

"You. Me. The party a few weeks ago."

Olivia grins. "Fucked me up."

His breath catches in his throat. Then, he smiles. "Yeah. Almost."

Olivia stares at him unknowingly. "What do you mean?" she asks.

He ignores the question. Instead, he drains his drink and places the glass down, staring into the kaleidoscope of ice patterns for a split second before sucking in a breath, then exhaling loudly.

"Let me ask you a question."

"Shoot . . ."

"That night, did you want things to go all the way?"

Again, that look. Furrowing brow.

"Pardon?"

"You . . . me . . . the party. Hel-lo?"

She laughs. For a moment, the tension had risen to the point where one could cut it with an axe. Seconds later, thanks to her mirth, it had dissipated. So, he laughs with her before turning serious.

"Something funny?"

Olivia responds. "Yeah. As I recall, we were all pretty fired up. You, me, Carly—oh, my god—"

"This isn't about Carly," Ryan states, interrupting her, willing her to stay on track. To not talk about his wife.

She pauses. Stares at him hard.

"Okay."

"I've known you a long time, Olivia. We go way back, right?"

"Right."

"So, no sense in pussy-footing around." He chuckles at his own joke. "I mean, it's something we need to discuss."

She opens her mouth to speak, then thinks better of it and nods instead.

"That night at the party, something happened between us. Something that can't be denied. Two weeks later, we've yet to fully acknowledge it. I don't know about you, but I can't just waltz around here like nothing happened, 'cause that's not the case."

"Ryan—look, I know—"

The annoying clamor from her cell phone cuts the conversation short. Olivia reaches for her hip, mouthing her regret as she answers it. Her face changes—a glow emerging in place of a frown.

Miles . . .

He stands, slaps some bills on the table, and is walking away before she stops him with a brush to his elbow.

"Miles wants me to remind you about Friday. He's made reservations at Bluespace for noon," she says, gesturing to her phone. "Don't be late, he says."

Olivia smiles in an attempt to cut through the apprehension that has risen again between them. He smiles in return, but their conversation is done. Dejected, he heads for his room.

Chapter 2

He was standing by the refrigerator, the door open and shielding his lower body from view. To someone standing across the room, one might assume he was naked. Fact is, he was wearing boxers—the Scooby-Doo ones Carly gave him for his birthday as a goof.

He was just standing there, head pounding from a night of crabs, Coronas, apple martinis, and cigar smoking. Just the last two were more than enough to make his head spin.

One-thirty in the morning, standing in the kitchen of his best friends' home, Olivia and Miles asleep upstairs, Carly crashed on the futon in the basement below—and Ryan, his cotton mouth and tongue begging for moisture as he rummaged through the fridge searching for something to drink. He found a liter of Sprite and, not having the strength to search for a cup, tipped the bottle to his lips and thirstily drank.

As he dropped it back into the slot in the refrigerator, he stepped back to close the door.

That's when he saw her.

She was standing motionless, observing him silently. He was caught off guard. What he saw took his breath away.

Olivia was clad in a button-down shirt—little else. The shirt hung open and he could see the dark patch of pubic hair that spread over her mound—and a large purplish nipple peeked out from the side of the shirt. Her hair hung free, locs surrounding her beautiful darkened face. Between her lips hung a burnt-out cigar. She moved forward on her toes, like a dancer; she seemed to glide toward him effortlessly. He glanced quickly toward the closed doorway that led to the basement stairs. Behind her, the back of the family room couch was sprinkled in shadows; the rest of the room was indigo.

He couldn't wrestle his gaze from her body, which seemed to writhe as she moved near—the illusion of a serpent— and the fullness of her spoke to him. Not like Carly's slender form, certainly not overweight. Just curvy hips, meat on the bones like his mama. Legs and thighs that spoke of substance and full breasts that hung invitingly. When she was within touching distance, her eyes never leaving his, the cigar now inches from his face, his cock swelling in his boxers with the certainty of a raging flood, he reached for her. Her legs parted; her eyes were unblinking. His fingers traced a line down the cotton fabric of the man's shirt, past buttons, parting the halves, and resting a hand lightly on her breast. Gently, he circled the hard nipple before dipping down farther past her navel, which he traced gently with his fingernail before meandering through her dark patch of hair. Finally, after a splendid minute, he felt the rise of moistened flesh that met his touch.

She reached out and expertly slipped her hand inside his shorts. His cock came alive as she palmed the bulbous head, stroking the shaft, raking her fingers lightly over his balls. He found her opening effortlessly, slipping a finger inside.

His cock stretched out in front of him, gently bobbing beside her waist. She stroked it with her palm, then, just as she found her groove stroking him, she ceased and moved to the back of the couch that was dappled in darkness. Her hands spread lengthwise along the edge of the furniture as she bent forward and down, lifting up the shirt in the process—Miles' shirt, the same one he had been wearing earlier that evening—and spread her legs wide, exhibiting in all of its splendor her heart-shaped, chocolate-colored ass.

He groaned contentedly, marveling at the exquisiteness on display before him. He could clearly see the lips to her sex, which glistened even in the half-darkness. He thought of the kiss they had shared months before, her intoxicating scent that night in the elevator, the way her skin felt when he massaged her shoulders in his office, the electricity that coursed between them. He gripped himself decisively, readying to impale his hardness into the wetness of her sweet cavern. Suddenly, unable to contain his hunger, he lunged forward with a purpose that surprised even him.

In that same moment, they clearly heard the rustling coming from upstairs, the weighty, uncoordinated footfalls, and Miles' unmistakable deep voice calling out, "Olivia, baby, is that you I hear?"

Chapter 3

The hallway is silent. He stands in front of the door to her room, glancing down at his feet, listening for sounds, willing his breathing to slow. It is after one A.M.; the hotel and most of its occupants are fast asleep.

He has been standing there for the better part of five minutes, not moving, fingering the letter he holds in his hand. He's ready to slip it under her door, but each time he musters up the strength to bend down and release it, an ache appears out of nowhere, righting him.

He knocks on the door. Hears rustling. Knocks again. More noise, then footsteps. Locks and bolts undone. The door opens, and he finds himself facing her.

"Know what time it is?" she inquires, wiping at the corner of one eye. She is clad in a wrinkly, man's button-down white shirt, way too big for her frame. He looks her over, musing about what, if anything, she wears underneath. Immediately, his thoughts return to the party two weeks ago, and the night that made him a man obsessed. Even at the lateness of this hour, her sensuality reaches out and tickles his skin, caressing him in the lonely hallway. He smells her, takes in the smoothness of her skin, the roundness of her cheekbones, the surety of her stare. Her graceful curves cannot be concealed by another man's shirt.

All of this conspires to confuse him, tear him down, and make him weak, a slave to the physical. Yet, it is his stare that is unyielding now. He can hear the pulse in his ears. He is growing hard, can feel it tighten his jeans, and is certain she can sense his awakening, too.

"Anything wrong?" she asks, her gaze washing over him hastily, hand on her hip, making no move to let him pass.

"Need to talk—didn't get to finish what we started earlier."

"This can't wait?" she inquires, somewhat exasperated. The hour is late.

"Obviously not."

They stare each other down for a moment before he hears her sigh. She retreats, and he enters the room.

The bed is unmade, oversize pillows and thick comforter haphazardly situated. She climbs onto the bed, exposing thighs. A hint of white emerges—and he conjures up images of silk panties, erotic g-strings, and other sexual things. She witnesses his stare. Asks him what it is exactly that he wants.

Silently, he hands her the letter, which has occupied his time for several evenings.

"What is this?"

"How I feel." With nothing more to say, he sits on the edge of the bed, facing away from her.

She repositions the comforter over her legs, ensures she is buttoned up top, unfolds the letter, and glances over at him. Then she begins to read.

It takes her a minute to complete. He is silent watching her. Her expression doesn't change, as if she has been expecting this. When she is done, she refolds the letter slowly and glances up.

"Ryan."

"Yes." He is waiting, breathless.

She is cautious with her words.

"This is my fault," she says. "I've led you on. Things happened after that party which cannot be undone. I would be lying if I said I regretted them all, but the truth is"—and here she pauses for a moment to search the ceiling, as if she can find comfort there—"they shouldn't have happened."

He is silent. She takes his silence as an approval to continue.

"For several reasons, Ryan. One, I am married. We both are. We love our spouses, and are not about to jeopardize what we have."

A statement, not a question.

"Two, you and I are friends—been that way for as long as I can recall. Don't want to mess that up—right? I mean, what good can come of this? Lose a friendship for twenty minutes of pleasure?" She stares at him, yet he looks away. "Ryan, is it really worth it?"

She barrels forward, finding the strength—the energy to go on, regardless of the effect it has on him.

"Three, we work together. We're on the same team. You and I built this company together. I love what I do, and I know you do, too. Don't want to do anything else; don't want to work anywhere else. I know you feel the same."

She spreads her hands wide, palms upturned. "So you see, Ryan, what happened that night was a mistake. All of it a serious error—I realize that now. I was being selfish—enjoying the attention, the stares, and the energy you threw my way."

Olivia smiles weakly.

He has been sitting patiently, rubbing his palms together. He stands now, goes to the window, and parts the curtain to glance down at the street life below. He turns toward her to speak, his voice a whisper.

"You said I was beautiful." Mustering up the strength to continue, he barrels forward. "I know things aren't simple. I wish to God they were. I wish there weren't these obstacles in our way. I wish we could just finish what we started. I'm not disagreeing with what you've said, nor am I implying that your reaction doesn't make any sense—'cause it does. But affairs of the heart never make sense. They defy logic, Olivia.

"I know what I feel—what I felt that night, when you took me in your sweet mouth. I know what you felt, too—know it as sure as I'm standing here."

Her expression has changed. It has suddenly soured and forces him to pause. She is staring at him as if he is not of this world. Instinctively, he waits.

"What are you talking about?"

"Kind of late in the game for coyness. You know what we shared."

He moves forward, a wave of elation surging through him as he remembers the sweet details of their last encounter.

Reaching the foot of the bed, he climbs on. Olivia retreats to the headboard, back pressed into the veneer wood, hearing it groan.

"I think you should leave," she says with sudden finality.

He strokes the lump where her thigh is positioned under the cover. She recoils like a caged animal.

"Stop it. This isn't going to happen. Not tonight. Not again."

He pauses, hand in mid-stretch. His gaze is galvanized with hers; her locs seem to tremble along with the rest of her body. In that moment, he feels extreme pity . . . and intense pain.

"Do you deny how you felt? How good it felt when we were together?"

Silence.

He reaches for her again. She lets his hand rest on the comforter. His lips are upturned.

"You said I was beautiful. . . ."

Her head thrashes, but in slow motion. She opens her mouth to speak, and is interrupted by the high-pitched scream of the smoke alarm.

Hands immediately rise to their ears; both are shaken by the intensity.

It is close to 1:30 A.M., and the fucking fire alarm is wailing.

Unbelievable!

The next thirty minutes pass in rapid-fire succession—into the hallway, down countless flights of stairs, out into the pouring rain, away from the hotel complex that has been maddeningly roped off by the NYFD. Sirens, fire engines, police vehicles, hoses, hotel staff, and guests are everywhere. The guests scatter; already clogged streets become choked to near bursting with equipment and panicky, half-dressed out-of-towners. By the time he leads Olivia hesitantly to an all-night diner four blocks away, Miles' shirt is soaked to the bone. Her nipples shine like beacons. Either she hasn't noticed or no longer cares. She is freezing, dead tired, and drained of all emotion. At 2:18 A.M., they have only each other for comfort.

That thought alone is sobering.

They sit across from each other now, Olivia and Ryan, in a cramped, dingy booth, sipping lukewarm coffee. The silence and wobbly table are the only things separating them, as she tries unsuccessfully to forget this night, this man, this situation.

She is thinking, *How on earth did things get to this point?*

Look For These Other
Dafina Novels

Available Wherever Books Are Sold!

Check out our website at www.kensingtonbooks.com.